Copper Hollow

A Novel By

F T Moore

Pergados Press
Gainesville, Virginia

For bulk sales and distribution, contact:
Pergados Press

www.FTMoore.com

ISBN-13: 978-0-9725368-1-3
ISBN-10: 0-9725368-1-7

This book is a work of fiction. Any similarity between real people, real places, or real events is entirely coincidental, or are used fictitiously, and are a product of the author's imagination.

You may think you see yourself, your friends, or your town in these pages. But it is not real.

Library of Congress Control Number: 2013942409

1. Espionage thriller – Fiction   2. Homeland Security – Fiction   3.
Afghanistan – Fiction   4. Blue Ridge Mountains – Fiction
I. TITLE

Dedication

With gratitude, this book is dedicated to Dr. Christine Chung, Dr. Susannah Ellsworth, Dr. Christine Gourin, the Infinity radiation team, Nurse Pierse Byrnes and Nurse Rachel Fornwalt, of the Johns Hopkins University Hospital Oncology department. While they were dedicating their lives to curing cancer, this book was written in their waiting room.

Prologue
Present Day
Copper Hollow, USA, and Paris, France

Jeanine Sherwood found Will Pruitt's body, on a Monday morning, when she arrived to pick up her blackmail check. There was no answer at his front door. She knew Will would never risk stiffing her on a monthly payment, so she went around to his home office in the back. The office was an enclosed porch, weatherized for four seasons, right off the kitchen. Carefully, Jeanine negotiated her way through the weedy grass to the back door, cautiously avoiding the horse droppings as she rounded the house. Will's horse barn was entirely too close to his house, in Jeanine's opinion.

The office was dark. Closed blinds covered the windows all around, but she could peer in the side window on the door. All she saw was the blood on the floor and Will's legs lying in it. She would have used her cell phone to call 9-1-1, but cell phone towers didn't cover the rural mountain area where Will lived. Jeanine drove back toward town, until the cell signal improved. All she could think about while she drove was how much she and her young son were going to miss that blackmail payment. She'd been collecting it from Will Pruitt for a long time. She tossed her long, red hair

1

back as she maneuvered her Subaru hatchback along the dusty, unpaved mountain road. The tears welled up; her sobs caught in her throat. *Will Pruitt was a good man*, she thought, and she pulled her car off the narrow road, into the shielded forest, so she could cry.

The ambulance arrived at Will's house in seventeen minutes, which was reasonably fast for that particular twelve-mile mountain drive. Officer Darrell Monk was already on the scene. He broke the window on the back door to let the medics inside. The body lay on the floor, with the head and shoulders propped up against the desk. The hunting rifle had fallen off to the right side, its butt now soaked in blood from the gaping wound that had once been Will's face. Monk turned away; he couldn't look. *Not Will, he thought. It shouldn't have been Will.* The copper smell of the still-oozing blood overwhelmed him, and he rushed outside to catch his breath. The horses whinnied, and Monk heard the confusion in their jittery movements inside the barn. The death smell made its way to them, Monk thought. The horses, he assumed, objected to this declaration of Will's death. It would mean changes to their lives, and Monk suspected that they knew that. He headed to the barn, so the horses could comfort him.

From all first appearances, Will had inserted the end of the rifle into his mouth, and propped himself up so that he could reach the trigger. The two paramedics dropped their stretcher on the grass outside. "Nothing we can do," one of them told Monk. "We'll wait here for the medical examiner." They went off to sit in their ambulance and prepare their paperwork. Monk went back into the house to call the sheriff and the medical examiner on the landline. Mountains, even the low mountains of the Blue Ridge, greatly interfered with radio communications, so Monk needed to use the house phone.

It took an hour and thirty-five minutes for Sheriff Freel to arrive with the coroner. The sheriff's responsibility covered a wider territory than just Copper Hollow, and Will's house was deeply remote. Doc Marshall, however, lived in Copper Hollow. He was both the coroner and the general practitioner. He handled his patients dead and alive. "It looks like a suicide, Doc," the sheriff said.

The old country doctor took some time, on his knees, on the left side of the body, away from the blood. He got up, steadying himself by leaning against the desk. "It only looks that way from a distance," Doc Marshall answered. 'I don't see how you can shoot yourself twice." He pointed to the second wound in Pruitt's back.

Sheriff Freel narrowed his eyes, stepped around the blood, and looked where the doctor pointed. Without a word, he made a call to his contact in Washington, D.C. He turned back to Doc Marshall. "Headquarters says this is an attack on an active operative. They want to handle it. They said to report it as a suicide."

The doctor, the sheriff, and their Headquarters' bosses marked the coroner's official report "Classified." They called the local newspaper, the *Copper Hollow Mercury,* and offered them the information about Will Pruitt's suicide. But when the ambulance drivers loaded the body onto the stretcher to carry it to the morgue, the medics saw the second wound. Sammy Ellingham held his finger to his lips

3

to warn the other paramedic, George Merkel, not to let the sheriff know they knew.

Officer Monk pulled the assignment to notify Will's wife of his suicide. Monk and Pruitt had worked closely together over the last twenty years, and Monk knew Margaret Pruitt well. She and Will had been separated for a while, but they hadn't divorced. Monk rummaged in Will's desk drawer, looking for her phone number. There he found the yellow envelope with the cash payment for Jeanine Sherwood. He slipped it into his inside shirt pocket. He would deliver the money to Jeanine himself. He hoped she would understand that he could not personally accept the responsibility to make payments in the future. To ensure that Jeanine would continue to remain silent, Monk decided to tell her about the second bullet wound. Jeanine Sherwood had lived in Copper Hollow all her life. She would get the hint.

Andrew Meyers, reporter for the *Copper Hollow Mercury*, only moved to Copper Hollow one year ago. He did not know for a fact that Will Pruitt had two bullet wounds, and he did not understand life as the people of the "Holler" knew it. He heard that Will had two bullet wounds, in the ether of town gossip. When he wrote his front page story, all he could print was the official version, given to him by the sheriff. All he could say in his story was that the sheriff and the coroner reported a suicide. The Copper Hollow grapevine, however, said it was murder. The people of Copper Hollow talked about the murder of Will Pruitt at the coffee shop, Jo-Beans. They told the story over kitchen tables, and at church suppers, and around campfires. Will Pruitt was murdered, and they covered it up, the gossip said. It was already a quickly spreading Copper Hollow le-

4

gend, added to the many Copper Hollow legends. It was another story like the extinct mountain lion, whose cubs were sighted repeatedly in the forest.

Sammy Ellingham, one of the nearly 300 great-great-grandchildren of the old mountain man, Billie Ellingham, was the likely source of this rumor about Will Pruitt, Andrew guessed. Andrew knew Ellingham was one of the paramedics on the scene. When people had very large families all living nearby, rumors could travel faster than viral YouTube videos. Folk tales and mythology erupted from these hills regularly. "Do not follow these rumors as news stories," the *Copper Hollow Mercury* editor told Andrew. "There are rumors and whispers of rumors in this Holler. They are all bunk," his boss said.

Andrew's future career in journalism depended on developing a solid investigative piece that would be picked up by the press beyond the borders of Copper Hollow. Now, he thought, he had done it. There was a cover-up of something going on, and he could uncover it. He knew his boss at the *Mercury* would not pursue this lead, so he sent the article's link to his journalism career mentor, Olivier Beauchemin, in Paris.

Early the next morning, in his tiny office in the Marais district of Paris, which happened to also be his own apartment, Olivier Beauchemin savored his first espresso of the day. The dark, rich coffee invigorated him and made him feel sharp, ready to concentrate. He wore his usual work clothes: gray sweatpants, a black tee, bare feet. His ashtray was clean; he tapped his cigarette on the red formica tabletop before lighting up his first smoke. His bare feet felt the cold through the unpolished wood floor. This morning, as he smoked, he watched the sun come up, through his kitch-en window, where his table pressed against the drafty glass. He had a sixth-floor view of a city alleyway. The sun peeked hesitantly through the crevice between his building and the row of retail stores across the alley. He liked the colorful ac-tivity in the street scene below.

Six feet tall, one-hundred-sixty-five pounds, with a re-ceding hairline and a square clean-shaven jaw, thirty-five-year-old Beauchemin was an experienced, award-winning, free-lance investigative journalist. He contributed regularly to the French publications, *Le Figaro* and *Les Observateurs*. His blog about freedom and democracy boasted thousands of daily visitors. He submitted articles to Truth Digs, Al Ja-zeera, Mother Jones, and Russia Today. Occasionally, he uncovered some evidence which he uploaded to WikiLeaks, the site for whistleblowers to submit evidence of govern-ment and corporate corruption. He was making himself a name in journalism. That was more important than money, for now.

In his early career, Beauchemin worked for MNM, Main-stream News Media, out of the Paris office. He found writ-ing for mainstream media withering. Beauchemin wanted to write stories with meaning and substance. For that, he be-lieved he needed independence. Corporate sponsorship pol-luted the work of a serious journalist, he contended. Too many issues of profit caused important stories to be muf-fled, in his opinion. So Olivier gladly surrendered a steady income in favor of his journalistic integrity. Luckily, he lived with his *petite amie*, his girlfriend Madeleine Fontaine.

Madeleine slinked into the kitchen from the shower, her long dark hair wrapped in a towel turban. Her sleek body displayed her red lace lingerie; she looked like a fashion-shop mannequin. She had a dancer's body, with her ribs peeking out from under her sheer bra. She had applied her makeup before getting dressed, of course. Why get mascara on a silk blouse? Her jasmine scent arrived at Olivier's work area before he could get his hands around her, so he contented himself with admiring her from a distance. She opened the refrigerator and pulled out the orange juice, took a swig from the bottle, and replaced the bottle in the refrigerator. She smiled at him, and his thinning blonde hair barely covered the blush.

Olivier always blushed when he wanted her. It was his "tell." He shook his head, to clear it. She was busy, getting ready for work, at the only paying job they had between them. She held a steady job at the Bourse, the French stock market. Madeleine was a stock broker.

Street sounds signaled the beginning of a work day. Garbage collectors banged their dumpsters into trucks. Police car sirens wailed. The open window allowed voices from the street to be heard from Olivier's sixth-floor apartment. Cars growled to life from their overnight hibernation, speeding by on the narrow side street, skillfully missing pedestrians and moped riders by the legally-required three inches. It was another cloudy day. The clouds captured the texture of Paris, and smothered Parisians with the fog of their own sensuality.

Olivier yawned and stretched. Hopefully, he would finish his work before noon, so he could join Madeleine for lunch at the café on the boulevard. He worked while sitting at the kitchen table, typing on his MacBook. He opened his web browser. Ready to begin, he clicked the link that pulled up *The Copper Hollow Mercury* online.

COPPER HOLLOW

Prominent defense attorney found dead in his home office, the headline read. *Will Pruitt of Copper Hollow shot with a rifle. The Copper Hollow police have ruled it a suicide.* The byline on the article read *Andrew Meyers, Copper Hollow.* Olivier had been corresponding with Andrew online for more than a year. They were introduced through Madeleine's college friend, Ann Kiernan. Ann worried that there was something very big and very wrong going on in Copper Hollow. She asked Olivier to look into it. Since then, Olivier had taken a sharp interest in the information Andrew Meyers sent him about this American town and its unusual events. It was a curious situation; it piqued Olivier's long-term interest in the state of democracy in the world. Beauchemin tabbed back to his open email. The email to him from Andrew, which linked to the online article, read: "Suicide? With two bullet wounds? *Vraiment?* Really?"

Madeleine set two plates on the table between them. Their breakfast would be cheese, a soft-boiled egg, and fresh bread. She worked around his computer, treating it as a fixture that never moved from its spot on the kitchen table. She had put on a thick white cotton robe, over her crimson lingerie. There was a chill in the apartment.

"I've been thinking about that thing you told me last night. About the drones and the timing. There are some times when I think you are *not* nuts, you know," she said, taking a fork and tapping her egg to open it onto the bread. Everything about her was delicate. Her fingers, her hands, the way she tilted her head and tossed her hair. She was aware of her sensuality and used it as a tool. Communication between two people lives in a place far deeper than spoken words, she understood.

8

"It's facts," Olivier answered. It was clear to Madeleine that he had to work to keep his mind focused now. "Not conspiracies. Mali is becoming what Afghanistan was in 1996. The new Al Qaeda training camps will be in northern Africa. It doesn't matter what France or NATO or America did in Afghanistan. It will start all over in Africa." He ate with one hand, and continued running the cursor on his computer with the other. "Now, I just have to follow the money, to see who funds it, and where this originates."

Under the table, Madeleine ran her bare foot along his leg. She liked to goad him in the morning, to see if she could distract him from his passion for work. He pulled his leg back, as if he needed to distance himself from her in order to continue his quest. "You see," he said, licking his lips to erase the dryness that arose in his mouth when he spoke to her, "France is looking at this as an Islamist insurgency. As if it were a small matter. I say it is about the oil fields. Just as Afghanistan was."

She knew she'd disturbed him, but she enjoyed the tease. "But there is no oil in Afghanistan, Olivier," she said, hoping to frustrate him to the point that he would stop working. Then, her plan was, she would jump up and say she was late for her own work, and hurry out the door. This would ensure that he would be waiting for her at lunchtime.

He didn't answer at first. He was busy eating and searching. Mornings were his most productive work time, and he chose to make the best of them. After an intense minute, his face reflected his "ahah" moment, and he closed the lid on his laptop. He looked up at Madeleine, who was still eating.

"In 1996," Olivier said, "an American oil company, Unocal, got the United States state department and CIA to

9

help them out. They wanted to build a gas pipeline from Turkmenistan through Afghanistan. This would allow the natural gas to be funneled from the Caspian Sea area, without having to go through Russia or Iran. But Afghanistan was too dangerous. The mountain areas were easily attacked, and the nation was in a constant state of civil war. A group of Afghan refugees, living in Pakistan, promised to go back to Afghanistan and keep the peace, so the pipeline could be built. The CIA began giving this group money and weapons. The oil company invited the Afghan refugee leaders to Texas, to discuss how things would progress."

"Hmmm," Madeleine nodded. "I'm picturing the beards and the turbans boarding that plane right now. I am glad I was not flying on that trip." She dropped her eyes, and gave him that provocative slight smile.

No snide little sarcastic pokes could divert Olivier from his passions, so he continued talking. "The American oil company thought they had a deal with this group, who called themselves the Taliban. But then Pakistan, under Benazir Bhutto, made a different deal, with an oil company from Argentina. Now both oil companies were paying the Taliban. The Taliban didn't care. They took everybody's money."

"So Bhutto had to be removed," Madeleine guessed.

"Of course," Olivier confirmed. "She was accused of corruption, and run out of the country. General Musharraf took her place, but Prince Turki, of Saudi Arabia, continued to push for a contract with the Argentinian oil company. The Taliban continued to take money from both sides. Eventually, the Argentinian company ran out of money to pay, and sold themselves to another American company, Amoco. Now it was two American oil companies paying the

Taliban. With all of this money and weapons coming in, the Taliban were able to take control of the government of Afghanistan."

He was boring Madeleine. She really didn't care about politics. *The American oil companies paid the Taliban so they could get into power, he says. So what? Who cares? What's the difference? How would one know if it were true?* She took their empty plates into the kitchen. Maybe someday Olivier would sell a story to some newspaper that would actually pay him. Maybe he should pay more attention to that murder story Andrew sent him. That story had more potential to sell, she thought. "What do you think about this Will Pruitt murder?" she called over her shoulder, as she washed the dishes in the sink.

His laptop was open again, and he was typing furiously. "I think, *ma cheré*, that if this man had not been killed by a shotgun, he may possibly have been targeted by a drone."

Madeleine turned off the water and turned to face Olivier. Her friend lived in that small town, Copper Hollow, where this Will Pruitt was murdered. Her friend, Ann Kiernan, was married to a man who worked with Will Pruitt and knew him well. "A drone?" Madeleine questioned. "Why a drone, Olivier?"

Madeleine's friend was deeply upset, because her friend's husband worked for the Terrorism Defense Unit of the United States' government. He travelled frequently to parts unknown all around the world. "Are you saying that this attorney was murdered by the U.S. government, Olivier?"

Beauchemin, ever the friend of anarchy, carrier of the flame against tyranny, and dedicated defender of the right for liberty, opened his electronic file code-named SENS, in-

11

serting his password. He wrote the last paragraph of his article, wrapping up the work to which he had devoted most of this last year. He looked up from his computer screen. Madeleine waited for an answer. "If that were all I was saying, *ma cheré*, you and I would be safe and happy here," he said. With a deep sigh and a regret for what was about to happen, he clicked **Submit.**

And thus it began.

BOOK ONE:

THE CULTURE

Chapter 1

Present Day
Copper Hollow, USA

From the time he wrote his first article for the local community paper in sixth grade, Andrew Meyers dreamed of becoming a reporter. Yes, he understood that the publishing industry was changing; he knew that the Internet and blogging were alternative paths, and that TV was more important than print these days. But he pictured himself as an investigative journalist. He wanted to make his contribution by uncovering truth. *Revealing the hidden motives. Exposing the secret agendas.* He believed this was the vehicle through which people could make free choices. Open discussion stimulated intellectual debate, and lead to fairness in the world, in Andrew's view. Throughout high school, he edited the school paper, turning it into a real leadership vehicle, he believed. Under his editing, the high school paper took on controversy, rather than becoming the usual mouthpiece for the school administration. In Andrew's mind, he saw his future and the light was blinding. At state college, he majored in journalism, where his teachers told him he would have to pay his dues on a small-town paper. His path was to build a portfolio of groundbreaking articles, get noticed regionally for his reporting, and then move to the big time. That's what he was doing in Copper Hollow, working for the small-town paper, *The Copper Hollow Mercury*. He was initializing his career.

Sadly, his dream was proving to be a nightmare. He had moved from the cosmopolitan Philadelphia suburb of Bala Cynwyd to the tiny mountain region of Copper Hollow. It was more of a culture shock than Andrew expected. His pay was substandard. He could barely afford his efficiency apartment, which was already subsidized for the poverty-stricken. There was no Starbucks in the Hollow. No Whole Foods grocery. No selection of French wines. No night life. No entertainment for young people. Nothing but a neighborhood bar, filled with smoke and homeboys. There were a few other twenty-somethings in the town, but they were not Andrew's "type." For now, Andrew resigned himself to being friendless. He told himself he could get out of this place within the next year, if he just got on the stick and made his mark quickly. Until then, he would confine his social life to the virtual world, and communicate with others purely online. In the end, he decided he just needed to get out of Copper Hollow as quickly as possible, and get on with his real life. This piece about Will Pruitt's murder, and its cover-up as a suicide, could be his ticket out.

After Andrew sent the *Copper Hollow Mercury* article about Will Pruitt's supposed suicide, Olivier Beauchemin said it was no longer safe to email their conversations. They had been discussing the situation in Copper Hollow for months. The murder of Will Pruitt meant the cover-up was in process. Beauchemin believed Andrew was in danger.

"Danger?" Andrew asked. "What kind of danger could I be in?"

"Someone is covering up a murder," Olivier said, 'and that someone includes the local sheriff, the coroner, and the police who found the body. Doesn't that make bells ring?"

"Well, I think there must be an explanation, that's all. The sheriff wouldn't do that unless it was a matter of national security, would he? I want to ask questions."

"In these days, questions can be dangerous. If the cover of national security is being invoked, that danger extends to journalists who reveal the truth. Erase your hard drive, Andrew," Olivier told him on the phone. "Pack your bags close your bank account. You can stay with us until you get re-established."

"Hello? Bank account?" Andrew protested. He was twenty-three years old, barely out of college, paying off loans. "With my salary? Where would I get a bank account?"

"Put your plane ticket on a credit card," Olivier countered. "Just pack up and leave, and do it now. If I could explain over the phone, I would. I'll tell you when you get here. Don't worry about the expense. It will all be a moot point soon. Don't argue with me about this. I know what I'm saying."

Andrew hesitated. *How could he just pack up and leave?* After a moment of silence, Olivier said, "Andrew, you are not the first young reporter in Copper Hollow. In 2008, Mitchell Davis held your job, and looked into the events which have now ultimately led to the murder of Will Pruitt. Mitchell disappeared, and I feel responsible for allowing him to get caught up in these events. Do not look up the records of Mitchell Davis while you are still in Copper Hollow, Andrew. Leave town now, tonight, and I will explain everything after you arrive here."

Andrew did delete his hard drive, but not before he uploaded his data to his cloud service. After all, those accounts are private, so he believed there was no worry. Losing his data? Out of the question, he thought. He could not delete the work he'd done for the last year. He grabbed his laptop, leaving his desktop computer behind in his apartment. He packed his back pack, and drove to the airport. He expected he would not return. If Copper Hollow was the center of a cover-up, as Olivier suspected, he needed to be gone before the exposé hit the blogs.

Partly, he was excited about this adventure. He loved the idea of an exposé. National exposure was his goal, for his career. Luckily, his passport was up-to-date, and he had a place to go. He had to drive to the nearest big city airport, of course. The Copper Hollow airport didn't take passengers. But as he waited in line for his evening flight to Paris on United Airlines, he thought, "If I told my mother what I've done, she would tell me I've lost my mind." And he wondered if his mother would turn out to be right. He'd never met Olivier Beauchemin in person. Was he insane to walk out on his job and depend on a person he'd only met on the Internet? He supposed he would soon find out, because whether it was a crazy move or not, he was going to do it. He had the ticket to Paris in his hand.

Olivier picked up Andrew at Charles de Gaulle airport at six o'clock the next morning. They took the metro to Olivier's apartment. "You'll need protection for a while," Olivier told Andrew, "but I suspect it will die down in a few months. You can relocate after that. I'd suggest California or New England." Andrew could sleep on the sofa. The apartment had two rooms. The ceilings were high, the windows drafty. Olivier shared the bedroom with Madeleine. The combined living room-kitchen area was about 20 feet by 15 feet. The 8 foot tall windows overlooked a city side street, narrow and dark. The bathroom had a shower stall, a sink, and a toilet, all in a closet-sized area. The kitchen table was Olivier's office. Andrew would have to use his laptop on his lap, sitting on the sofa.

The flight had taken all night., and Andrew was tired. Before Andrew slept, however, they went out to the *Rue Rambuteau*, Rambuteau Street, to the brasserie *Le Bouledogue*, The Bulldog. They took seats outside, ordering coffee and pastries. Chocolate bread and espresso. Olivier lit his cigarette. "I know you are anxious to hear about the mysterious disappearance of the young reporter who held your job before you. However, Andrew, I need to start the story from the beginning. History cannot be understood in the two-minute sound bytes of a television headline. It requires the viewpoint of generations.

"The story of Copper Hollow began in the U.S. Depression, before World War II. The families of Copper Hollow were forcibly evicted from their homes in the mountains. It was the beginning of the reign of Wild Bill Donovan," Olivier began. "Wild Bill was one of the upper class elites, a lawyer and also a military man. Franklin Roosevelt selected him to be the first U.S. Coordinator of Information. In effect, that means he was the first American spy. And now, it appears that spying has come full circle."

"Spies in Copper Hollow? But the spies are restricted to international venues," Andrew said. "Outside the United States."

"Vous souhaitez," said Olivier. *You wish.* He flicked his cigarette onto the sidewalk and crushed it with his shoe. "People," he said, "have flaws. Anointing flawed people with authority only magnifies their flaws. In Copper Hollow, there was a strange relationship between those in authority and the regular people. There was a shared secret between them. Spying is about secrets, and when something is secret, then how will you know? When secrets are carried on through generations, they become ingrained within the culture. The society accepts them as a form of truth. They change reality, for the people of that place, through all time."

Chapter 2
1927
Somewhere in the Blue Ridge Mountains

"Silent Cal" Coolidge was President of the United States. Prohibition, outlawing alcohol, was the law of the land. The economy roared. Americans flapped their way through excesses of material success. But in the Blue Ridge mountains, many children did not know they were Americans. They never heard of Calvin Coolidge. They didn't go to school. They only knew their family and their clan, on their mountain.

"The worm is what keeps the smoke from comin' out and drawin' eyes to the place when yer runnin'." The young mountaineer paid close attention to his grandfather's teachings; the older, wizened man felt proud to welcome this fine and fit teenager as his apprentice. Joey Anhalt stood at attention in his new work boots, exhilarated to be included in the family business. His grandfather, Dean Anhalt, ran this moonshine still for as long as Joey could remember. They were out in the back, by the still, in the afternoon sun. The stills always had to be hidden, in the woods, behind some rocks and brush. It was Springtime. Everything was turning green, smelling fresh and new. The robins, sparrows, and bluejays sang in harmony now. At dusk, the whippoorwill would call. Spring was always a time of new hope.

When Joey turned eighteen next Fall, he'd be marrying Susie Shoal, who would be fifteen by then. It was good for him to get started on making a living. He had his eyes on a piece of land on the other side of the hilltop, close enough to keep company with family, and far enough to have some private time with Susie. Family would help him build a small cabin.

Joey knew there was a time when old Dean sold his apple brandy and corn whiskey at the general store in the town, but those days were gone. Some time ago, they set the law against the mountain man. About the only good thing that came of that law: the price of a jug was up considerable. Prohibition made moonshine a profitable farm product. Of course, Joey was learning to be a business man, so he knew you had to find the right customers for those jugs. His father never did take much to running whiskey, preferring to ride into town to get a job in the grain mill instead. That left Joey to inherit the family moonshine business. As the oldest son, and the oldest grandson of old Dean, Joey intended to make his mark.

Joey didn't have much schooling. He couldn't read books or write letters, but he knew some things about how money works. He knew there were people who had a lot of money, and they lived in a place called The City. They came here to visit. He knew those people would pay $5 for a jug, and that $5 would buy supplies for a whole family for a month. Joey figured it would be better to sell some jugs of whiskey to those people. Then he could spend the rest of his time hunting and fishing in the woods. His only other choice would be to ride a horse ten miles into town. Then he would be locked up in a stuffy, closed building all day. His pa did that, and that's why Pa didn't have any quality of life. As Joey saw it, that explained how Pa had gone wrong. Living in the woods was real living; working in a mill was for slaves, Joey believed. He would never go to work in town. He wasn't like his pa at all. Pa had been fairly worthless, Joey had to admit. One day Pa stopped coming home from his trips to town to work. Ma said she didn't care, and nobody went to look for him. So it was just grandpa, and ma, and the kids. Plenty of uncles and cousins lived nearby.

Selling moonshine was the career path that would get him to his dream of a good lifestyle. Yes, indeed, Joey Anhalt was proud to be his grandfather's heir, and proud to be taken into his grandfather's confidence. He would do his absolute best to earn the family respect, and make up for his father's failure.

Joey was a good-looking young man, with sandy hair, tousled a little but not too long. Six feet two inches tall, and fit as a cougar. He moved like a cougar, too, they said. Slinky, stealthy, and quick to pounce. Not an ounce of fat on his body, like you would expect from a boy who spent his life running wild in the forests, cutting trees, hauling logs, hunting squirrels, 'coons, 'possums, and rabbits. Joey knew these mountains. He'd combed these hollows, and he'd followed these clear streams since he first could walk. There were people living all over these mountains. A good number were Joey's kin: first cousins and second cousins and some just cousins by law from marrying. Some people had apple orchards. Some had corn fields. Some knew where to buy sugar. Some took trips to get things for trade. These people would be Joey's suppliers. He knew who they were, and for the most part, he figured he could pay them in jugs. It would be how he kept his costs low.

Then, Joey figured, he'd have to offer the best product around. High quality. Not that rot-gut the Ellingham brothers put out. Joey knew his competition. He'd beat them out by paying close attention to old Dean, and learning the craft as a fine art. He'd use the best supplies, and run a clean still. That would be his leg up on the neighbor's operations. His plan was to get known as the best hootch in the hills.

So Joey had his business plan all laid out in his mind. He had his suppliers lined up. He had his equipment in place, with old Dean's still. He had his costs under control. It would be just him and his little brothers, once old Dean slowed down. He had his competition analyzed and his strategy mapped. His last little piece of his business plan was the customers. That was his key success factor, as Joey saw it. And that, in his own mind, would be his biggest strength. Ever since he was twelve years old, Joey had been helping out up at the resort on the top of the hill. There were plenty of customers up there, he believed. He was pretty sure he'd be able to take advance orders.

The vacation resort at La Terre, on the top of the mountain, served rich people who came from the East Coast cities. As Joey saw it, they came there to build silly little-girly bonfires. They'd sit around in a circle, sing songs, eat too much, and get drunk. He and his sisters would go up there and hang around. He'd haul firewood, and clean up the horses. His sisters would pick flowers and try to sell bark baskets. In return, the visitors, and sometimes the owner, would give them tips. The rich ladies sometimes gave his sisters their old clothes and hats, but after the girls got tired of playing dress-up, Ma would throw them fancy dresses in the basket to use for cleaning rags. They were useless clothes, because the girls couldn't run in them. Joey's mind flashed back to the last time he was up at the resort, and he wondered if he should tell his grandpa what happened. Standing there in the clear mountain air, with the sweet smell of Spring wildflowers wafting past his nose, and the random gnat buzzing his eyes, it was easy to get lost in his own thinking head. He pulled himself out of it when old Dean started to talk again.

"Yo' gotta be wary, son, of the people who don't have enough business of their own to mind. You'll run into a man, one day, who will act friendly, buy your product, and then turn you in to the sheriff. To stay in business, you have to know who it is y'er sellin' to." Old Dean walked while he talked, putting away tools, picking up clothes, fiddling with his chawing tobacco. He never sat still and looked Joey in the eye.

The old man's hair was all white, and too long, hanging over his ears. The plug of tobacco he kept in his left cheek seemed to have left a dark stain on one side. That, and the missing teeth on his bottom front row, made his words sound slushy. There was no real telling how old he was, but old enough to walk with a slight stoop, and weathered enough for the skin on his face to seem leathery. Through Joey's eyes, old Dean looked fine. He was his grandpa, and he still looked like the straight-backed man he was ten years ago, as the little boy remembered him. Joey loved old Dean, and when he saw him, he saw the years of following him around the yard, trying to be a boy growing up, loving his primary caretaker. But, to the casual city visitor, such as the social worker who came by once a year to nag about how the children should be going to school, old Dean was a scary sight. That social worker didn't see old Dean's tattered jeans as a responsible choice for a man doing hard labor. Who would sensibly choose to ruin a new pair of pants by wearing them to butcher a hog? More than likely, the social worker who came by, seeing old Dean toting a rifle around the yard, in his tattered jeans, with his callused hands and tobacco- stained fingernails, would find his appearance spine-chillingly scary. Joey didn't know that, though, even with all his imagined business savvy. Joey saw his grandpa through the eyes of loving respect, and to Joey, old Dean looked like a Super-Hero.

Old Dean got down on his knees, peering into the metal firebox of the still. He carefully covered it with brush, hiding it from prying eyes and meddling do-gooders. For thirty years, that moonshine still had meant the difference between a winter of plenty, or a winter of growling bellies, for their family. While he'd lived a long life of farming and hunting, there had never been quite enough. Not enough to both eat and also get his teeth fixed, for example. Not enough to both build a cabin and also fix up beds and bedrooms for each baby that was born in it. Many a year, the moonshine still provided their income to buy household supplies. Joey would soon begin to step in now, and help Old Dean keep it going. There was a lot to learn, and not much of the learning was about the skills of farming. Mostly, what had to be learned was about life and the people living it. Just then, old Dean looked up at Joey and called out, "What's eatin' at ya, boy?"

Joey'd been thinking about that thing up at the resort. He'd gotten a haunt in his eyes, and Old Dean recognized it. Joey loved Old Dean for always knowing these things. 'Pap, some men up on top wanted to know about chicken fightin'. They said they'd pay to take 'em to one."

Joey knew the old man knew some things he couldn't quite put his finger on to tell about. Sometimes he knew things, he didn't know what he knew or why he knew it. It was just a knowing, without a reason. Joey saw in his eyes that Old Dean had that knowing right now. "Tell 'em you don't know nothin' 'bout it, boy. They ain't the right people fer gawn' thar."

Later that week, up at the Top, on the LaTerre Resort, five horses got saddled, with provisions for a Sunday's journey. The women clucked about the men missing Sunday church service. The men strutted in their "cowboy" clothes, telling the women the fresh mountain air was closer to God, and the ride would be good for their souls. They promised to stop by a stream at lunchtime, to read the Bible and say a prayer. They assured their true loves they would come back the better for their time spent "close to nature." Mrs. Perry was secretly glad they were going, as she had hoped to get the women together for a séance at some time during their vacation. Séances always worked better when the men were absent. She envisioned this time to be an opportunity to gather a group for some communication with the dead. Mrs. Perry was well aware that the mountaintop carried special auras, which allowed spirits to break through. As the men loaded their packs on the horses, she noticed each one take his flask. By the looks on their faces, she could see they seemed a little too excited, almost giddy, about their day trip.

Mrs. Perry noticed that mountain boy, Joey Anhalt, collecting firewood. In her eyes, he looked particularly manly today. That boy had always struck a chord with her. She suspected he knew more than he let on about things. He had such a haunted look in his eyes. Once, when she had gone "under" in her séances, she had seen an Indian guide, and the guide warned her to look out for a mountain boy who would teach her some ancient ways. Perhaps this was that boy. She would try to contact her guide again today. She needed to know if she should approach this boy to help her in her quest for enlightenment. She'd been feeling faint lately, and she was sure it had to do with something in her soul. Too bad they would be leaving the camp tomorrow, for their trip back to the city. She felt she needed more time to be here right now, to contact the spirit world and gain direction. Maybe she would stay longer, on her own. The city and Mr. Perry could get by without her on this trip. Perhaps Mrs. Roberts would stay here with her. They would have the other men who were still here, and the staff, for protection.

Joey was mounting his own horse now, looking like he was going to follow the same way the men had gone. That wouldn't do for her plans. He had to be here, when she spoke to her spirit guide. Thinking quickly, she screamed and pretended to fall. As she expected he would do, Joey Anhalt turned his horse around and came back to help her.

Before he saw Mrs. Perry faint, Joey was gathering firewood. When he heard the commotion from the group of men, he saw his arch-rival and fellow moonshine competitor, Billie Ellingham, ride up to the city men. The men mounted and rode off back east with Billie. Joey understood what they were doing. He figured they'd gotten Billie to agree to take them to the chicken fights. Old Dean wouldn't like it. But what could be wrong with it? *Too bad old Dean hadn't let Joey take their money to be the guide. Now Billie would sell them his whiskey, too, and Joey would lose business to his competitor.* He mounted his horse, thinking maybe old Dean didn't know everything. Joey would have to be thoughtful about this subject. He would have to consider whether his business could be run on old Dean's terms. For now, he'd have to put off thinking about this issue, because he had to help Mrs. Perry, who had fallen.

One would have to really know chickens to fully understand what went on that day in the hills. Mr. Perry and his little sporting party had little clue of what they were walking into. In their own minds, they were attending a gentlemen's sporting event. They expected it would be something with a little spice, and a touch of naughtiness to it, made ever so much more seductive by the disapproval which their wives and Bishop Hardy would dispense, should they learn the truth. They had enticed young Billie Ellingham to be their guide, and so they set out in search of adventure, by means of a gamecock tournament. Certainly, only two of them had ever attended such an event before, and that incident had occurred during a visit to England. The two who believed they were experienced in such things assured the three novices that this afternoon would be an exciting treat. It was one of those "for men only, wink wink" things. As they turned on the winding trail, the distant wow-growl of the mountain lion foretold the danger of their day ahead. As

29

their horses hesitated, testing the wind for the smell of puma, the men felt the tingling chill of stepping into an unknown world.

Back to Present Day
Paris

"So this murder of Will Pruitt had something to do with a moonshine business in the 1920's?" Andrew asked, eager to get to the meat of the story.

"Yes, it did," Olivier responded. "A moonshine business, a war of economics, and a culture that centered on farming. Along with a clash of cultures coming from those who thought they knew what was best for the people of the mountains, and the people of the United States of America."

"Will Pruitt was that important?" Andrew asked.

"As important as a canary in a coal mine," Olivier answered. "When Will Pruitt died, it was clear that there was no longer enough air in the system for the rest of us."

Chapter 3
1927
At the LaTerre Resort

His grand camp had come a long way since its beginnings in Henry Carver Perry's imagination. He'd first come to the Blue Ridge as a teenager, to survey his father's land, look for investment opportunities, and find a way to make his mark in the family. He'd been paid by the Smithsonian Institution to search for artifacts here, in the Blue Ridge; there was a wealth of historic Indian lore in these mountains. He'd also been considering some type of copper mining; it was said there was copper to be found on his father's land. But since he first spent time here, he'd been smitten by the land itself. The land drew you into it. It struck something deep in the core. Try as he might, young Henry found himself unable to get around to the task at hand, when he was settled into the seductive womb of the Mountain Mother. So Henry dabbled in investments, piddled around with archaeology, and went through the motions of being a business man. In truth, despite his feigned interests, Henry just wanted to stay in the mountains.

However, Henry's father was a member of the elite. That made it unacceptable for Henry to shuck his pedigree and move to a log cabin, rifle slung over his shoulder, hunting for food. The life of the mountain man seemed compellingly attractive to the young socialite. Henry felt conflicted. Part of him craved the life of a mountain man. Part of him believed it was his obligation, as a member of the class of elites, to make fun of the mountaineers. After all, they didn't have fancy clothes, and they talked funny. They said "ar" for "air", and "nestiz" for "nests". Most interestingly to young Perry, they didn't travel far from the mountain. They grew up here, and they stayed here. They had dozens of relatives living nearby, all with the same last name. When you talked to the young children, they didn't bother to say their last names, because all their last names were the same. They said, "I'm Sarah's Willy," or "I'm Nellie's Sam." It was their mothers who differentiated them.

Their family relationships were close and meaningful. This fascinated Henry, for he didn't know closeness in a family. His family life built on expectation. Approval, in his family, was conditional. Here he was, trying to prove himself, living in a world where love was conditioned on achievement, and he comes across a place where the people can just "be", without needing to "be something." Curious, it seemed to Henry. Curious, but also compelling. He'd lived all his life with an expectation that he had to make something of himself. What if there were a world where people could just "be"? It comforted him. He wanted to stay.

That, of course, and the land itself. The land, owned by his father, was breathtakingly, bone-shakingly, soul-shiveringly, beautiful. This was land that could reach right into Henry's chest and grip his heart. It could wrench his stomach, squeeze his throat, release his soul. He was here in this mountain, and he felt unable to leave. His legs collapsed under him if he even thought it. But Henry had no money of his own. All the family money belonged to his father, who wanted Henry to come home and get a job. So he married Eva. She had already inherited her family money. To support his desire to live in the mountains, Henry came up with a plan.

There were so many rushed, hurried, and stressed socialites in Henry's circle, back in the cities of the East Coast. What if they could come here to take a break? What if there were a luxury resort here for them? Then Henry could stay, and share with his friends the beauty of the lifestyle he'd found. It would be the best of all worlds. He could live here in the mountains, and he would still be a business man and a rogue. He used Eva's money to build a resort.

The La Terre Resort opened in 1922, and Henry's father's friends began to visit. As they visited, Henry talked to them about investing. There was copper in these hills, Henry told them. Not only can you be part of this beautiful resort, where your family can come for vacations, but your investment will grow as the copper is mined. One by one, Henry's father's friends bought mountain land. He invited them to vacation at La Terre, and promised them the delights of learning to fish and ride horses in the fresh mountain air. It was a place of summer breaks, good food, parties, target shooting, and illicit alcohol. It developed a reputation among the elite, and they planned their trips eagerly.

Nettie and Lorene Ellingham, aged thirteen and sixteen respectively, dressed in the fancy waitress uniforms given to them by Mrs. Perry up at the "Top." The Top was the name the local mountain folk gave to the La Terre Resort, because they had to climb up to the top of the mountain to get there. Their mama warned them not to get the dresses dirty on their way back up the hill. "What's goin' on up thar?" Mama asked Nettie.

Nettie, her auburn brown long hair pulled back into a braid, generally did all the talking for both sisters. Although Lorene was older, Lorene had always shied away from talking. She never spoke much, ever since she was a baby. "Mrs. Perry hired us, Ma," Nettie said. "She's always hiring Billie to do work, and now she hired us, too. We're going to serve food at her party." Nettie, like all the mountain people, spoke a unique dialect seldom understandable to outsiders. "Muz-purry-harred-us-Ma-shuz-alluz-harrin-Bullie-ta-do-wurrk" It was this dialect that Nettie knew as English. She thought Mrs. Perry and her friends talked funny.

Billie Ellingham, their older brother, held a regular job at the resort. He brought firewood for the nightly campfires and the indoor stoves. He groomed the horses and did odd jobs as required. He also sold the family's moonshine to the guests, although his product didn't sell as well as Joey Anhalt's moonshine did. This created hostility between the Anhalt and Ellingham families. The concept of competition was not well-developed in the mountain culture. With resources scarce, it was thought among the families that it was best to cooperate, not to compete. If one family served a customer, or bid on work, it was considered bad form for another family to offer a competing bid. Competitive actions, in a resource-constrained world, were outright rude. But the guests at the resort encouraged Joey and Billie to try to best each other. It was a sore point that festered.

"Mrs. Perry said she'd pay you if you'd bake pies, Ma," Nettie continued. "She said just bake 'em and whenever you do, she'll buy what you got. She said we should just bring 'em up. You could get a dollar fer each one. "

"I'll think about it," Ma said. "But I don't have enough sugar right now."

Nettie was going to offer to get some sugar from Mrs. Perry, but she got the feeling mama didn't really want to bake pies for the resort. Mama didn't like Mrs. Perry and the ladies at the Top. Maybe it was because she went up there to work once and she came home looking really sad. Or maybe it was their dresses. Mama made all the dresses for herself and her daughters, out of the lining from the feedbags they bought in town. The ladies at the top gave their dresses to Billie to bring home for mama sometimes, and they were fancy, with zippers and shiny cloth. But mama never wore them. She'd look at them hanging in her closet a while, then she'd throw them in the rag bag.

Nettie didn't know why Mama had a problem with working at the resort. She felt excited about her first real job there. Last week, she and Lorene picked wildflowers, and they stood by the road up there and tried to sell the bouquets to the ladies when they passed by. Some of the ladies paid for the flowers, but then she saw them whispering to each other and pointing at her feet. She had her shoes on, so she didn't know why they did that. The ladies went inside the resort building, and a little bit later Mrs. Perry came out and asked Nettie if she needed a job. She asked if they was Billie's sisters, and Nettie said yep. So she told them they could work at the party tonight and gave them their big break. She gave them the uniforms and told them if they did good, they could work more times when

35

she had parties. Nettie was going to use the money to buy some lipstick the next time they went to town, so she was proper excited.

Only a few mountain families got to work at the resort. You had to already have a kin working there, so you could get recommended. Nettie knew the Anhalts worked there, and the Wenzels, the Willetts, the Krugers, and the Merkels. But it wasn't a job where you go to it every day. You just go there when they tell you they need you. Only Billie and Joey worked there every day all the time, and Mrs. Kruger and Mr. Willett. Some families came a long way to get there. You had to walk, or if you had your own horse, you could barn it there while you worked. Although, Mr. Perry sent a horse and carriage to pick up Mrs. Kruger, because she ran the kitchen, and that was an important job.

When the girls arrived that evening it was still light out. Earlier, when she gave them the uniforms, Mrs. Perry told them to tell their parents they would be back after dark, and Billie would bring them home. The girls were sent right to the dining room to see Mrs. Kruger. She showed them what to do and how to serve the food properly. No reaching across people's plates to get things, and don't put your fingers on the food part of the plates. It sounded easy enough. Nettie could do it.

As the guests arrived, Nettie gaped at the women's sparkly dresses. They had feathers and beads and shiny things sewed all over them. And their breasts were almost falling over the top of their teeny shirts! The ladies held these little bright-colored masks over their eyes. The masks were on sticks, and they'd hold them up and smile and then put them back down again. The dresses were shiny material, and bright colors like Nettie'd never seen in a dress before. These were much fancier than the dresses the ladies wore when she saw them on the road last week, or than the dresses they'd given to Billie. "It's a costume party, girls," Mrs. Kruger whispered when she saw the girls' mouths hanging open, gaping at the women's dresses.

"What are they dressed up as?" Nettie asked, with the innocent incredulity of her thirteen years. She wasn't sure if they were princesses or fairies.

"They're saloon girls, Nettie," Mrs. Kruger told her quietly. "It's a Wild West costume party. The women are saloon girls, and the men are coming to the saloon."

"Why?" Lorene snapped out of her usual silent coma to express a sudden interest in what was going on.

"Never mind, girls," Mrs. Kruger said. "It's just what they do for fun."

The table was set with mismatched china. In the forest setting, surrounded by fires and logs and log cabins, it looked elegant. Like picnicking with bone china, and the mismatch of it made it seem more enticing. The food set out was pork roast, from the pigs that ran wild in the forest. A family would catch a pig, and make a mark on its ear. Each family had its own mark. Then the family would put food out, and that pig would settle into a territory. The pigs didn't roam far from their food source, so everybody would know who had the right to butcher that hog. Mrs. Kruger brought the pig from her own family's claim, and Mrs. Perry paid her for it. The steaming pork, sweet potatoes, and roasted cabbage filled the room with delectable promise. Freshly baked apple pies waited their turn on the back-board. Nettie noted that the city people ate mostly the same food she ate. Ma and Mrs. Kruger knew the same recipes.

Fancy ladies in their pastels, feathers, sequins and bo-som-revealing dresses, milled about the room, occasionally peeling off an elbow-length white glove to nibble on a cheese canapé. Then horses' hooves clattered, and shortly thereafter the men arrived. Each man wore a cowboy hat, cowboy boots, a vest, and a holster with a pistol. Each carried a knife in their holsters with a four inch blade.

They charged into the dining room, rowdy, like men who had spent their hunting afternoon drinking instead of shooting bucks. They strutted around the room, cussing and shouting, and each man selected his woman for the evening, patting her bottom and pulling her back to kiss her in a backbend. "Don't be concerned, girls. They are each selecting their own wives," Mrs. Kruger assured them. "It's just a game." The girls could not pull their eyes away, as the men pawed and kissed the women.

"It's weird," Nettie said out loud.

"Just do your work and mind your own business," Mrs. Kruger told her. She screwed up her nose in a wrinkle. "But let's keep what we think about it to our own selves," she winked.

The cowboys and their saloon girls ate and drank, while the women sat on the men's laps. Now and again, a few wives switched briefly to husbands whose names did not match the names on their marriage certificates. The food kept coming, and Joey Anhalt and Billie Ellingham both had the opportunity to sell plenty of jugs of 'shine. Nettie heard Billie say a jug of 'shine went for $5. She knew if he sold it to other mountain families, he'd get less than a dollar. Pa told her $5 was all their whole family needed to live for a month. Now Nettie knew why Billie had gotten so much reverence and credibility in the family lately.

Finally, the food was nearly gone. Mrs. Kruger told Nettie and Lorene they could pack up some leftovers and take them home. She said Mrs. Perry always let the staff take the leftovers home, and if they came to work, they could always get that. Lorene said she didn't think Mama would eat stinky stuff like this cheese and fish, when she had perfectly good cabbage and potato soup on the stove, but Nettie thought Lorene was being rude. So they packed the food up, while the Perrys led their guests outside to sit around the campfire and listen to Mrs. Kruger's son, Ray, play the guitar.

Outdoors, torches lighted the circle around the fire, and chairs carved out of logs, with the bark still on them, offered the guests comfortable places to sit. Mrs. Perry handed blankets to the ladies, so they could keep their dresses from getting dirty on the log chairs. The women took their places on the south side of the fire. The men mostly stood to the right, continuing their drinking, and lighting up cigars.

A little while later, Nettie and Lorene finished cleaning up and came outside. They had to wait for Billie to take them home, as it was well after dark. Nettie didn't really think it was necessary, but Mrs. Kruger said Mrs. Perry would keep paying them as long as they stayed there, and Mrs. Perry wanted them to wait for Billie. As Nettie settled in to wait for Billie, whom she hadn't seen around for a while, she heard drumbeats in the distance. Suddenly, Mr. Perry stood up from his position around the fire. "Hark," he yelled.

Hark? Nettie said. What's "hark" mean?

"Hark," Mr. Perry yelled again, and the crowd quieted. "Drumbeats! The Redskins!"

"Geronimo," yelled one of the cowboys, jumping up and pushing the saloon girl out of his lap onto the dirt in front of the fire. She laughed and pushed him back, and he fell over like any drunk would, and then the whole crowd was laughing.

Then one of the cowboys lifted the pistol from his holster and fired into the air. "Indians!" yelled the group. "Let's get the savages!"

"Let's go get 'em, boys!" another yelled, jumping from his seat. The men shoved the women out of the way to run off into the dark shooting guns into the air.

Nettie was horrified. Pa always told the boys that they don't waste bullets. Bullets were used to shoot food, not to fly around in the air where they could land in trouble. He said wasting bullets was like a sin and you could go to hell for it. Everybody knew you don't shoot guns while you're drinkin' 'shine. Nettie knew the men still did it, but they at least knew they weren't supposed to do it. This caused them to control themselves, to keep their wives and mothers from finding out. Hunting and drinking happened, regularly, but it was not supposed to happen, and the men hid it, or were real careful about it. They did it just a little bit, and knew to stop before they were falling-down drunk. All the families knew about the story of Matt Willett. Matt was a sixteen-year-old boy who accidentally shot his friend, Earl Kruger, when the two of them were out hunting. It was an accident, but it was an accident that happened because they were both drunk while they hunted. Well, accident or not, the Kruger family lost their boy.

In the mountains, losing a boy is something you don't forget. The families needed to settle the debt. The Willett family offered to pay the Kruger family, and the Kruger's took a piece of land and some goats that were offered. But you can't pay for a boy with property, so the Kruger's wanted something else. They wanted Matt Willett, to hang him. The Krugers said the feud would never be over until they got Matt. A son for a son. It was what the Bible said. Well, the Krugers and the Willetts lived close by each other, and some Krugers were married to Willetts, so it was a big problem. There were fights, and there was one night when the Krugers took a shot into the window of the house where Matt lived.

After that, the grandpa of the Willett family made a decision. He said Matt had to leave. They collected up all the money they could get from all the members of the Willett family, and Matt's cousin Jimmy Willett was picked to go with him. Jimmy was eighteen at the time. They gave Jimmy and Matt all the money they had, and Grandpa Willett took them to town and put them on a train west. He said get far away and don't come back. It was the only way. Then the Willetts told the Krugers they had lost two boys now, so it was all even and the feud could stop. Nobody ever heard from Jimmy or Matt again, and that was the way it had to be.

Now that Nettie thought about it, she wasn't really sure if that was a true story, but everybody she knew had heard it and believed it. The mountain families told stories a lot, and the stories were to teach you what was right. What Nettie knew was that these crazy city people were shooting guns while they were drunk, and that was just plain dangerous.

And then, something Nettie never could have imagined in all her young life, played out in front of her. "Kill the savages," she heard one of the cowboy-men yell. The drum-beats got closer, and there was Billie, Joey, and some other boys from the mountain families. They came running along, wearing leather-skin outfits and big feather headdresses. They had bows and arrows on their backs. They were heading toward the campfire, beating a drum. And the troop of wayward cowboys ran toward them, yelling, "Kill the savages." A bullet rang out, and it wasn't pointing up in the air.

Nettie screamed, dropped her packages of food on the ground, and ran straight toward the group of women around the fire. "It's only Billie! It's only Billie," she screamed. Mrs. Perry seemed to pull herself out of a mental fog. She looked at the men hooting and whooping in the dark, and she looked at Nettie screaming and crying. She quickly ran to the large bell they used in the camp to call everyone in for dinner. She started clanging the bell, over and over. The men, conditioned to responding to the dinner bell, looked back toward the fire and saw their women waving and jumping in the air, calling them back. At least a few of them sobered up, and Mr. Perry led them back to their senses. Everyone settled back down for a quiet discussion around the fire, and the Indians were told they could go home. Later that night, when Nettie and Lorene were safe in bed, Nettie told her sister, "Sumpin's wrong up thar. They's los' ther senses. Tha's why Mama don't like 'em." Lorene agreed.

The next day, she told Mama what happened, and Mama told Papa, and Billie didn't go work there anymore. Papa delivered the moonshine himself, and he raised the price to $6, and he talked to Mr. Anhalt, and they both agreed to raise the price of moonshine for the guests at the top, and he told Billie to stay away. "Those people ain't got sense in ther' heads," Papa said. "The'r a'acciden' waitin' ta happen."

Nettie could never have known that Mr. and Mrs. Perry were not told why Billie stopped coming to work. Soon, other mountain families heard about the cowboys and Indians night, and other sons stopped showing up for their shifts at work at the resort. Now and then, some family would need money bad enough to let a young man do a little work, but mostly, the boys were told to stay away. The attitude was: work if you absolutely must do it, but only until you have enough to live. Then leave there and stay away. So the work force for the Perrys dwindled, and the workers steadily became more unreliable. The heritage of mountain stories had a new tale to tell, in its portfolio of life's lessons, and mountain folk steered their children away from the Top. But the Perrys never heard the story, as the mountain folk told it, and they took their dwindling workforce as a further sign of the lazy shiftlessness of mountain families. Nettie could never have understood that the Perrys would tell their guests, and the government investigators, that the people in the families she loved were shiftless, lazy, shirkers who did not want to work.

Henry Perry's guests had invested money in the mountain land. They wanted to know when the copper mines would yield a profit. They began pressing Henry to give them a date for payment of their dividends. The more his guests pressed for a return on their investment, the more Henry felt humiliated. He gave them the right to vacation at La Terre, at a discount rate, in return for their investment money. Did they think that was not a value? He'd built this resort from his father's land, and ran it on money from his wife's inheritance. It lost money every year. Many failed attempts at making something of himself made him feel inadequate in the eyes of his family.

Much of the land around the resort had been sold to his father's friends in New York, Baltimore, Philadelphia, Raleigh, Atlanta, and Washington D.C. The marketing he'd done had been on the strength of one concept: that there were copper mines in these hills. The investors had bought this land expecting a solid return from mining, but time passed, and no significant copper mines were found. Now the investors were pressuring his father for a way to get out of their land holdings. But, frankly, without copper mines, there were no buyers for this land. Henry had invited ten of the most vocal investors to La Terre Resort for a vacation combined with a business meeting. They would discuss how to get their money back. It was Henry's hope they would agree to sell the land to him. Sadly, Henry had no money to buy it. He hoped to convince them that the resort itself could be a money-maker, with a little more investment for marketing. If his guests could see the value in this resort camp, perhaps they would allow him to pay them from the profits over time. There never had been any profits in the past, but to Henry, that seemed to be an unimportant detail. Henry had never been good with money. When General Weber showed up that morning in his military fatigues, Henry's plan unraveled.

The group assembled in the conference room in the late afternoon, before dinner. Their ladies were diverted by preparations for a costume party Mrs. Perry had planned for that evening, to be held around the outdoor firepit. Henry purchased sufficient pints of the local whiskey, and he'd bought venison from the mountain people for their dinner.

Weber started in right away, "I have some possibly very good news regarding our investments, gentlemen," Weber boomed. Carson Trent paused from topping off his glass. He and Lowell Lincoln took their seats across from the general. "Do tell," Carson coughed.

"It seems," the general drawled, pulling pleasure out of the delivery of his message, "there is a movement afoot to set aside some land for a system of national parks. The Coolidge administration wants land all along the Blue Ridge. We should set forth a good lobbying effort, to help to ensure that the federal government can be the purchaser of our holdings."

In no time the group agreed to do what had to be done. They would contact every person they knew in the administration to promote this area for one of the new national parks. They set to work determining who should be contacted, and what pressure needed to be applied.

Henry became worried. Selling to the federal government for a park could mean he lost his right to operate the La Terre Resort. He also had mounting bills, while his wife's fortune dwindled. How would he survive this plan? Could it be stopped? "Wait," he interrupted. "What about the people who live here? If you sell the land for a park, where will the mountain people go?"

"What are you talking about, Henry?" Carson asked. "How can people live on land they don't own?"

Henry looked confused. Then he realized that Carson and the others had never met people like these before. "They're mountain people," Henry explained. "They've lived here for generations. They can't read, so they don't know they don't own the land. They were born here, and their daddy was born here, and their grand-daddy was born here. Some of them have deeds, which they may have made up and passed around among themselves. Of course, they don't file the deeds at the courthouse. They seldom leave the mountains, so it's possible nobody ever told them they don't own the land. Most of them don't even know land can be owned!"

"What do they think?" James Pritchard added, setting his whiskey glass on the table. "You just call out that you got here first so it's yours?"

"Basically," Henry told him. "They mark the trees, like the Indians did. Their grandfathers came here. It's a theory that some of them might have deserted from the army, to hide in the woods during the Revolution. There are many caves in the forest, and they would have provided shelter. They staked out a spot, maybe even drew up their own ownership papers, and they've been selling the ownerships among themselves. Mostly just the same family keeps living in the same places, expanding as they grow. So one family lives on one mountain, another family lives on another mountain."

"And they interbreed?" asked Pritchard. "They marry among themselves?"

"As far as I can tell, yes," Henry swallowed a big gulp, his Adams apple bobbing. "There are only a few last names among them. I've seen some signs of interbreeding in their work habits, certainly. Some of them can read, but not most, and they have no churches or schools. Eva and I do what we can to help them, but they breed quickly and marry at age fifteen."

A shocking situation, all the men agreed.

"All the more reason to get the government in here to take care of the problem, then," Carson scoffed.

The group agreed to move quickly to sell the land to Coolidge's men. General Weber took the lead to push the project. "Aggressively, under the circumstances," the general added, as he lifted his cashmere jacket from the armchair and set his Russian muff hat on his graying head. Henry Perry swallowed hard. What would become of his resort, if the government bought the land from his father, and turned it into a national park?

The land seemed to know something was afoot. The mountains had their own mystic connection with the residents within them. Before long, the mountain sent out warnings, and Mrs. Kruger's grandmother, Old IdaMay, heard them.

Old IdaMay had been born in this cabin and lived in the mountains her entire 82 years. For a little while, she'd married Clem Anhalt, but he was worthless and lazy. Everybody knew it, except for IdaMay. Anyway, Clem went and got himself shot on a hunting trip. Accidentally. Nobody to blame for it. A guy like Clem, you'd almost expect it. Sam and Bluford, Mary's cousins, witnessed it, and the Caldwell brothers came running to help carry the body home for burial. Bluford said they needed four men, because they had considerable luck killing a deer, and they had to bring home both carcuses, Clem's and the deer's. The townspeople said thar warn't deer in these woods, and maybe thar warn't too many, but thar was some. Anyway, this day, Sam and Blu had a deer, and they warn't leaving it for the buzzards. It was good IdaMay already had four young'uns with Clem, and she also had a bun in the oven, so she'd have five children to take care of her, and she wouldn't be alone. She moved the family back in with her folks, and that's how she came to be dyin' here in the place she was born. It warn't too far away, her folk's place. Her folks moved their two oldest boys out, and the boys took over Clem's old place, so IdaMay and the kids could have their bed. It warn't much hardship, and her Poppy thought it would be good to have the young kids around after his own kids grew up and moved away. IdaMay grew up thar, and she moved back in, and she raised her kids thar, and it looked like soon she'd be dyin' thar.

At least to me, her granddaughter, Alice Kruger, it seemed IdaMay was dyin'. Mommom, as we called her, was starting to see things, and hear things, that the rest of us agreed jest warn't thar. It warn't the haunts, she was seein'. Mommom knew the haunts, alright, but this was different. She was seein' real things. Wall, I should say, she was seein' real things that was gwan to happen later. But we din't know it yet, so we believed old Mommom was "tetched". Crazy, they say it. I remembers we all went along with what MomMom said so as not to get her riled. She'd holler that the lights was gittin' in her eyes at night, and the windows had to have some blankets pulled over 'em. This was all long before thar was any talk about the road. Long before the conservation corps boys came. We jest thought she was crazy.

Turned out later, they built that parkway right by the cabin. The lights from the cars came by, with the big roaring noises from the engines, and all the lights shined right in through the window where MomMom lay on her deathbed.

The mountain sent out its messages like this, but the people on the mountain could not understand what the mountain was telling them. They never knew what was going on. Until it happened. The Blue Ridge Parkway was built right there. Right by old MomMom's grave. They say at night, you can hear her turnin' over in it, and the mountain lion prowls and growls to mark the spot.

Present Day
Paris

Andrew shifted in his chair. "I've been living in Copper Hollow for almost a year," he said. "I don't see how a mountain can get into a person. All I see is poor people, living in slum conditions. They live in shacks; some of them don't have indoor plumbing."

'You're living in the town, Andrew," Olivier smiled. "The people in the town are the ones who have lost their places in the mountains. Have you gone into the mountains, to see what it's like in there? No, of course you haven't, because there's no Internet service in the mountains, so you wouldn't go."

Andrew looked around at the bustling city street. "You don't have any trees or nature here," he said.

"But I regret it," Olivier answered. "And I know it's missing."

Andrew considered what his mentor said. He did stay out of the mountains, driving only on the paved roads. *What was in there? he though., Why does Olivier care?* He looked around at the bustling, living, exciting city of Paris.

This was real life, he thought. The mountains of Copper Hollow seemed more like the Emerald City of Oz.

"The people thought there was copper in the mountains of the Blue Ridge, but there were some mountains that were made of emeralds, real emeralds, and there were back woods people living in those mountains, too," said Olivier.

Chapter 4

1997

Somewhere in Northern Afghanistan, in the Hindu Kush Mountains

The wizened and sun-wrinkled old man lovingly tended the young lettuce-like leaves of his poppy crop. He appeared much older than his sixty-some years, his skin leathered from exposure to the sun. Pride in teaching this farming skill to his teenage grandson beamed from the old man's expressive and sparkling eyes. The harvest of poppies fed their family. When his sons went to war, and the old man was left to care for the women and children, the poppy harvest kept them all from starvation.

"Soon, Farzam," the old man slurred through a mouth with five missing teeth, "the flowers appear. These are white; over there," the old man pointed to a field farther to the west, by the setting sun, "those others are red. The petals of the flowers die, and underneath is a hard capsule.' The old man beckoned to his grandson, entreating him to look more closely, to be sure he understood and learned. His thick bun of white hair, covered with a brightly embroidered skullcap, leaned away to allow the boy to see the plant. He lifted his chin, pointing his dyed-red beard toward the stem.

The tall, lanky boy leaned closer, eager to prove he would be a worthy apprentice. His loose-fitting long-sleeved shirt draped all the way to his knees, covering half-way down his baggy, sand-colored trousers. A cloth sash, embroidered along the edges, girdled the shirt. Man-pajamas, the American soldiers would call his clothes. He wore a closed, moccasin-like shoe, made of leather, which he could easily push off with his toes when it was time to pray. He prayed five times a day. He loved God.

The old man continued to talk about poppy. "You must carefully squeeze this capsule until the milky cream oozes onto the stalk. Every day, you come back to collect the *tor*, which is the milk after it turns brown and hardens. You squeeze a little more, until the capsule no longer yields. The tor goes into these bags, slapped into cakes. Keep the bag moist until the traders come through to collect it."

Farzam straightened his back. He stood to his full height and stared up at the mountain road leading into their village. Like everyone in his rural village, he had fair skin and green eyes, with a hint of Asian ancestry in their slant. The Hindu Kush mountains pirhouetted behind, beside, and before him. Their rocky blue and white peaks sparkled and danced as the sun flashed off crystalline rocks, splaying shadows over the dots of scraggly vegetation.

"Only a few years ago, robbers prowled that mountain path, Farzam," the old man told him, getting up to stand behind him, placing a hand on his shoulder. "The robbers attacked the traders, as they left here with the tor. The traders would not risk visiting our village then. The poppies still produced tor, but I could not get it to market. Our family suffered, and your mother cried. Now the road is safe; the robbers are gone."

Farzam nodded. "Allah made the robbers go away, Bo-ba," the boy stated. Allah ruled everything, he had learned.

"We could say that, Farzam," the old man answered him quietly. Farzam could hear his grandfather's sadness. "Allah sent the Taliban. The Taliban cleared the road, in the name of Allah. This was a good thing for us." Farzam heard the tone in his grandfather's voice. He recognized that his Boba was not sure of his own words. Farzam turned to look at his grandfather's face, to see if he could find the truth written there. To fill the silence, his Boba kept talking.

"Yes, the Taliban stopped the robbers, but there is still danger from the warriors of the tribe of the Lion of Panjshir, Ahmed Shah Massoud. We are the same tribe as the Lion, and we revere him, but his soldiers are not all as trustworthy as he. When they come here, they make us pay them. They take our sons, and force them into their army. This is what happened to your father, Farzam," his voice broke. His eyes filled up with the water that would become a tear. "Your father was killed fighting in Massoud's army, against the Soviets."

Farzam knew that Massoud was the famous and powerful warlord of their tribe. He held his grandfather's arm as the old man struggled to sit down on the rocky ground. His grandfather could not stand and work for long periods of time. Farzam barely remembered his father, who was taken away to fight when Farzam was five years old.

"Our people are called Tajiks, Farzam," the old man continued, patting the ground to invite the boy to sit beside him. "Tajiks descend from the people of Tajikistan, to the north. In our village, we speak Dari. It is a language different from Pashto, the language that Afghanis in Kabul speak. I don't know why we are part of Afghanistan, instead of be-

53

ing part of the tribe of our ancestors. Our cousins who live on the other side of the mountain are called a different nation, with a different government and different laws. This was a foolishness decided by invaders outside our tribe."

It pleased Farzam when his grandfather taught him things. He wanted to learn the history of his people and their place in the world. Of course, he learned, there had also been times when nobody protected their mountain trail. Then bandits came, demanding food, payment, and even sometimes the village daughters to be taken as wives. Of the three choices, Farzam knew that his grandfather preferred the Taliban. He had lost too many sons to Massoud's fighting cause. It didn't matter to their family if the Taliban wanted the women to stay home. They lived in the mountains. The women already stayed home. Where would the women go? It was a nit-picking detail. The women did not complain.

The people of Farzam's village hardly knew whether the outside world considered them Afghans, or Tajiks, or anything else. They seldom left the village, and they had no regular communication with cities. Everything they knew about the outside world came from the traders who navigated through the steep, winding mountain routes, on their way to somewhere else, carrying supplies and buying their village's harvest. This dusty village hugged the mountain path, clinging to the same rutted and rocky road that carried silk in the time of Genghis Khan. The flat-roofed mud-brick houses ringed a modest sand and mud mosque, in which the people prayed.

Their work completed, the old man and the boy walked back down the sloped path to their village. That night, there was a festival for Navruz, the new year, celebrating the return of life in the spring. Farzam excitedly washed up from his work in the field, and put on his best clothes for the party. He hoped he would see Darya there. She was his cousin, who was eleven years old. Farzam was fourteen. In four years, he expected to marry her.

As he entered the outdoor area where everyone would sing and dance, he saw the men gathered together to the east of the dining area. They had built a fire and gathered around it to dance. To the west of the area, another fire marked the place where the women gathered. They, too, would dance, around their own fire. The children, who usually counted Darya among their rank, ran freely between the two groups. Tonight, Darya was not among the children. Where was she? He couldn't get his mind off her. Darya was Farzam's best friend.

His mind was helped in its distraction, however, by the wafting smells of halwa and fragrant tea. He loved the smells that promised the satisfying flavors of lamb stews. Smells foretold the soothing and healing comfort of *kabuli pulao*, the rice dish simmered with roasted carrots, turnips, goat and olive oil. How could any joy of life be more fulfilling than having a full belly and a loving family? What more did Allah offer, in a happy life? The music started, and the men danced and laughed around their fire. The women danced and laughed around their fire, also. The children danced and laughed everywhere. But Farzam did not see Darya.

His grandfather told him they had once lived in a true garden paradise, with orchards of pomegranate and mulberries. They grew wheat. Then the droughts came. The orchards dwindled. The wheat failed. Their only good crop, in the dry, unirrigated fields, came from the poppies.

That night, Farzam listened as the men talked spiritedly, far into the night, over the wafting smells of seemingly unlimited healing foods. They spoke of philosophy, politics, God, and duty. Farzam wanted nothing more than to join their ranks, when he was older. He wanted to participate in the self-governance of their village. He heard the men recite poetry, as they shared food and tea on mats laid on the ground before the fire. The poetry painted a future for him, and inspired his soul. He wanted to be part of that learning society of men, sitting together over succulent and sensual meals of fragrant lamb and cardamom tea, solving the problems of the world.

As the evening grew late, the men spoke of poppy. Some worried that poppy traders were dangerous men. Cotton also grew in their fields, but its sale produced less than one tenth the income of poppy. The village elders agreed. They could not live on the cotton harvest. The poppies could withstand the drought, and so they voted. These men who self-governed their village, in the tribal Jirga, chose to plant more poppy. They knew that there was danger, from the traders, the robbers, and the government that existed a world away. But it was the best way to feed their families, whom they dearly loved.

Spring progressed, and Farzam felt the burden of winter lift from his chest. The scent of fresh new life infused the warming air, as the whistling cackle of a mountain snowcock marked his memory, sending the message that this was home. Afghanistan is the harmonic that turns poetry into lyrics, Farzam believed. The land winds its soul inside you, haunting your inner being, until you cannot separate your Self from the land and the culture. This, Farzam knew. Your soul becomes entwined with the mountains. Your mind believes you would not breathe, outside of Afghanistan. This, he understood. This village decided, by tribal council, to survive, through whatever means necessary. Its devoted and faithful sons would learn the trade to protect their families. The young Islamic boy, Farzam, understood this. He would grow and sell poppy, to feed his family. Superpowers, from Soviet Russia to NATO to the great United States of America would eventually go away. They would retreat, as thousands of years of conquerors who passed through these mountains always retreated. These invaders were like the mountains, large and imposing. They would loom and intimidate, but in the end, they would crack and yield to the fresh green will of Spring.

When Spring came, blades of green burst in random tufts, erupting from cracks in the dry mountain stone, refusing to yield their right to survive. Miles of dusty rocks on the narrow paths surrendered to these sturdy green precursors of summer bushes. Rock yielded and split, defeated by the seeds of an unending will to survive. Farzam Parvanda embodied that fresh green will. He was the living hope of Afghanistan. All Farzam wanted was the peace to enjoy living in his paradise home. He went to sleep that night, dreaming of Darya.

It was earlier that morning, while Farzam helped their grandfather, Wakil, on the day of the festival of Navruz, that Darya's mother helped Haji Abdullah Khan lift her onto his camel. He would take her away to Helmand Province, where she would become his second wife. Darya's father stood by, his head hanging in shame. She was dressed in her pink tee shirt, with the flowers on it, and her knee socks, that she got from Boba Wakil when he went to Balkh last summer. Little girl clothes. Darya was a little girl. She was eleven. Abdullah was thirty-five.

Over her clothes, her mother placed a light blue burka. Its embroidered silk covered her completely, so that she had only a slit to see through. Her mother had embroidered a special design on the headband. "So that I will know you when I see you again," her mother said. Darya did not know why she had to go with this man. Her mother told her she was going to be married, and they would see her again someday, but not for a while. Her mother promised she was going to have a wedding, with dancing and fruits and many guests. Like all little girls everywhere, Darya played at getting married. She wanted to be like her mother. She played with her dolls, and put them to bed at night, and got them up in the morning, and fed them. To be a wife was what she wanted, so she wasn't completely miserable about this. All the little girls talked about how their weddings were going to be, and who would be coming to the wedding, and what they would wear, and what food they would serve their guests. It wasn't a bad thing, in Darya's mind, to be getting married. But her father was crying.

Darya's father sobbed uncontrollably, in shame. His big heaves and flowing tears poured relentlessly. Mother tried to comfort him, and Mother said things were not so bad. But Father could not stop crying, even to hug her and say good-bye. He was inconsolable. Behind those tears, Darya knew, there would be a deep and explosive anger. Part of her was glad she would not be home when the tears stopped and the rage began.

Last year, when there was trouble on the mountain pass, Father had tried to take their *tor* to market himself. He was beaten, and the tor for the entire village was stolen. But the smugglers had already paid for it. The money for tor is advanced, so that it does not travel with the drugs. The smugglers said Father owed them the money. The village tried to raise it, but they could not pay the debt. Darya's father agreed to allow Haji Abdullah Khan to marry Darya, in payment. Abdullah had arrived on this day to collect his property.

"This is your fate, Darya," her mother told her. "Behave as a good wife and you will be fine."

Darya had not gotten her period yet. She clutched the handmade doll her mother gave her, and waved good-bye. This is what it was, to be a woman, and Darya was anxious, but she was not afraid.

Chapter 5
Return in Time to 1930 - 1934
The Blue Ridge Mountains

Herbert Hoover was President of the United States. The Great Depression began. City people jumped out the windows of the stock market building. But in the Blue Ridge Mountains, cabbage and potatoes still grew, pigs still produced litters of piglets, boys still married girls. The mountain folk did not use much money, so there was no Depression, in their world.

Henry Perry agonized over how all this was playing out. This was all completely wrong, he thought. This business of the Chestnut Grove National Park was out of control. He never meant for the park to take over La Terre. He tried to make a deal to keep La Terre, as part of the park. Why wouldn't President Hoover want the park to have a luxurious resort inside it? Years had passed since Calvin Coolidge first introduced the concept of the park, and his friends had endorsed it. Coolidge was no longer president, and Herbert Hoover took office. Hoover had been preoccupied with the Depression, so no progress had been made on the park. The park was coming, but when? This uncertainty was bad for Henry's business.

Henry wanted the government authorities to under-stand the mountain families. Sure, they were shiftless and worthless and lazy, he believed. But the mountains were their home. This is what they knew. He had made friends with some of the mountain people, and it was from them that he learned to love these mountains and to really enjoy his life. During the Coolidge administration, the wheels of bureaucracy began to roll. Lobbyists successfully pushed for the national park to be located here, right on the land surrounding La Terre Resort. He had tried, unsuccessfully, to get the resort exempted from the plan. Now, he was ne-gotiating with the park authorities to let him keep it run-ning. He wanted to live there and manage it, even though it would be part of the park.

That morning, Henry had taken his horse and carriage into the nearest town. There he borrowed a Model A Ford, a black coupe, from his friend. The model A was square-bodied, with red wheel spokes. Mrs. Perry insisted that he be accompanied by her friend, Swami Kirtisiva, on the trip. For good luck.

Swami Kirtisiva lived at the resort. He gave psychic readings for the guests, and advised Eva Perry on her life decisions. Henry didn't have much use for the swami, but he did think it would be wise to have company on such a long journey. He was going to drive to Washington D.C. He would meet with the head of the parks department. The deal for the park was still in flux, and he needed to do every-thing possible to influence its outcome.

The Swami got into the passenger seat of the Model A. He'd chosen his blood red turban today, worn with a stan-dard American business suit. Henry suspected that turban colors had some deep meaning, but he hesitated to open up the conversation. A long car ride would not mix well with an educational lecture about Sikhs versus Hindus. The swami was a nice guy and all, but Henry didn't buy into it. He left the spiritualism up to Eva.

By late afternoon, they arrived at the government offices of the Department of the Interior, where the activity for the parks occurred. They would be meeting with an assistant to the Assistant Undersecretary, Peter Benton. It took them some time to figure out how to park the car and find their way into the right hallway, but they were finally seated in the waiting room of Mr. Benton's office. Mr. Benton's secretary, Mr. James Gale, announced their arrival.

"There are two gentlemen here, Sir," Mr. Gale whispered to the assistant to the Assistant Undersecretary. "One is wearing a turban."

Peter Benton's reading glasses drooped down the bridge of his nose. He set down his pen and pushed his glasses back. He expected Henry Perry this afternoon. General Weber had warned him that Perry would be eccentric. But travelling with a man in a turban? That was quite unusual, in Mr. Benton's experience. He stood, and walked around his desk, to greet his guests.

They sat on the sofa in Benton's office, side by side, Henry Perry and the red-turbaned Swami. The Swami's dark skin and black hair contrasted to Henry Perry's winter-white pallor, thick glasses, mousey brown hair, and bobbing Adam's apple. Benton gave them his full attention, sitting in the straight-backed chair on the other side of the coffee table. His chair was just a little higher than the sofa, to make it clear to his visitors that he had the power. The conversation passed through its superficial phase quickly, and Henry got to his point. The park should not go forward quickly. People lived there.

"To throw them off the land and force them to live in towns would be like putting wild animals in a cage," Henry pleaded with the government official. "They need to be cared for," he entreated. "When I see them, I always help them. They are like the feral kittens, showing up at my kitchen door, begging for food."

Out of concern, Henry tried to explain to Mr. Benton the nature of these primitives. These are innocents, Henry told him. Practically mentally disabled, he said. In his own mind, Henry was pleading, 'don't hurt them.' But, as often happens in the life of bureaucrats, what Henry meant was different from what Henry said, and even different still from what Mr. Benton heard.

Henry said 'these people are illiterate'.

Mr. Benton heard that they had fallen outside the government education system. They needed to be brought back in. And that could mean taking their children away. Children had to go to school. Primitives could not be trusted to keep them.

"How many of these mountain people are there, living on the park land?" Mr. Benton asked, picking up a pen and a pad, leaning forward, addressing Mr. Perry. He appeared deeply concerned about this new information. Nothing in the proposals for the park had mentioned that there were any significant numbers of residents on this land. The owners were primarily absentee owners, who had agreed to modest payment. The government plans had not expected to deal with squatters.

"How many?" Henry repeated, looking confused. "I don't think they've ever been counted. But there are a lot."

It was clear to Peter Benton that some critical information was missing from the proposals he had evaluated for the park. He knew Henry Perry's father, of course. A fine man. But something odd seemed to have happened to Henry, or he wouldn't be sitting here next to this silent man in the turban. This was all too unusual. There would have to be some further investigation into this situation. Benton made an immediate executive decision.

"We're going to send some social workers out to see you, Mr. Perry," Benton said. "We'll commission a study, to examine what needs to be done for the people of the mountains." Benton stood and extended his hand, to indicate that the meeting was over. "If we need to pay them for their land, build houses for them, whatever it takes, we will take care of their needs. But first we will need to send a team out for a study."

Perry looked confused. They hadn't discussed his resort yet. He took Benton's hand anyway. It would be unthinkable to leave it out there, unshaken. As he shook Peter Benton's hand, he said, "And you understand that the LaTerre Resort is a fine contribution to the national park, don't you, Mr. Benton? I can be assured that it will continue to operate?"

Benton vaguely remembered some mention of Perry's little camp, in his reports. "Yes, of course, Perry," he answered. "We'll consider it."

Back in the mountains, Jessie Willett took her sick baby into the town to go to the hospital. "The baby is malnourished," the doctors said. "He needs to be better cared for." The doctors placed the baby with a family who would feed and nourish him. Jessie walked the mountain trail home without him. They sold him, Jessie said. And they never gave her the money. She'd have bought him back, but nobody would tell her where he was. The mountain grapevine quickly picked up on this example of what happened when mountain people allowed the government authorities into their business. The family went back into town with Jessie, to get the boy back, but it took them a month to get everybody together. They had to wait until the whole clan could make it. By that time, the child had been adopted. He was judged by the court to have been abandoned, and too sick to be returned to the mother who allowed him to become so ill without seeing a doctor.

Mountain people heard these lessons, and incorporated them into their book of right and wrong. Soon, the children were being told to hide from strangers, keep their mouths shut, and stay in the bushes when government people came by. When Peter Benton sent the social workers, they found children hiding in bushes, frowning at strangers, and refusing to speak. Dutifully, they wrote these "symptoms" in their notebooks. Before long, they were filing reports. These people hibernate in the wintertime, the social workers said. They have evolved to accommodate their harsh living conditions. Their women do not feel pain in childbirth. They have no schools and they have no churches. We must help them, help them, help them. Save them from themselves, and put them on the reservation.

In the nearby town, people knew there was a Depression. The grain mill was hit hard. Some of the tradespeople who sold their wares reported hard times. The good news was that this national park would be built here. It had been decided that money would have to be raised from the citizens to buy the park land from its owners. The park authorities had determined that they would have to pay both the actual landowners and also the squatters. The squatters would get less money, but they would also get the opportunity to live in subsidized housing in the town, for which they would pay rent. The park would increase jobs in the town, because tourists would visit. Tourists would eat at the restaurants, buy products from the town's stores, and stay at the local hotels. If there were a local hotel, of course. Maybe they could build one.

However, the deed situation on the land was less clean and clear than the government would like it to be. After Peter Benton's investigations, they realized that some of the squatters actually had legal deeds. There were multiple deeds filed in the courthouse, all on the same property. More money would be needed than they had originally planned.

Money had to be raised, to get this project rolling. Henry Perry's friends arranged a campaign. Buy an acre for a dollar. They set up a campaign headquarters on Chestnut Grove's Main Street. They made yard signs, and posters, and buttons. "I bought an acre." The *Chestnut Grove News* ran pictures of the storefront, decorated with signs and banners. They printed up flyers to explain to people that it would be a good thing for the town. A national park! Right here in Chestnut Grove! Hip-hip-hooray!

When Jessie Willett's family came to town, looking for their baby boy, they found the storefront and the flyers. They asked the people what was going on. It didn't make any sense, and they couldn't understand what people were talking about. But it sounded so stupid, they thought it couldn't be about them or their mountain. They took some flyers back to show to others. But they couldn't read, so it didn't matter.

The social workers wrote that the people were illiterate (which was true), and that they lived in harmony with nature (which was true) and that their children were starving (which was most definitely not true) and that they were lazy, dishonorable, and unreliable (which is what they heard in Henry's stories.) They commissioned a government grant to study how this evolution occurred, which allowed the people to hibernate in winter. They wrote that, horror of horrors, these people did not go to church. Mostly, a neighbor would self-appoint himself as a preacher and make the rounds to spout the Bible. Based on these first-person studies, the government workers found reason to justify forcibly removing the families from the land. For their own good. The park authorities looked for a place to build some "welfare housing" for the displaced mountain people.

Present Day

Paris

Andrew nodded. "It was like the Indians," he said. "They made them a reservation."

"Surprisingly," Olivier said, "there were hundreds of mountain families all along the Blue Ridge, from Pennsylvania to Georgia. The government may have had in mind to place them on a reservation, but when the armed troops moved in, the mountain men proved that they would not be passive spectators."

There wasn't going to be anyone clicking the heels of their magic red shoes in this Emerald City, Andrew thought.

"Then who killed Will Pruitt?" Andrew asked. He stopped walking. He did not want to shut the conversation down just yet.

"In a town like this," Olivier told him, "you can never be sure what part of the myth actually happened and what part was legend. Everybody said Will was open to taking suitcases full of cash. But nobody was willing to testify that it happened. So it isn't known whether it happened or not."

Olivier looked at his watch. He wanted to get Andrew home so he could meet Madeleine, alone, for lunch. "Years have passed since the events that led to Will Pruitt's murder, Andrew. In a way, the murder actually was a suicide. It was Will's own actions that caused him to be marked. He could have avoided it. We cannot understand how Will Pruitt came to be a target for murder until we know the real role of Chance Kiernan in Copper Hollow."

"Chance Kiernan?" Andrew asked. "Isn't he the guy who works for the telephone company?"

"Only to the extent that the telephone company is a cover for the intelligence units of the United States government," Olivier answered.

This is getting too weird, Andrew thought. *What have I gotten myself into?*

Chapter 6
1934
The Blue Ridge Mountains

Franklin D. Roosevelt was President. The Depression raged. The New Deal was implemented. The Civilian Conservation Corps offered jobs to young men, to build roads and repair bridges.

Shortly after Franklin D Roosevelt took office, agreements were made. In the town, town residents busily collected money to "buy" the Chestnut Grove National Park. They were excited because they expected that a national park would bring tourists and jobs to their town. Papers were signed. Perry was to be allowed to continue to operate the resort, and to live there. The resort could be part of the park. Those who lived in the mountains were to be allowed to live out their lives there, as long as the houses were never sold outside the family. Henry Perry had finally succeeded in convincing the park authorities that the mountain people would add a curious tourist attraction, which would increase visitor traffic to the park. The investors received payment for their land from the pennies collected by the townspeople. It looked like there would be a deal all around. Rational decisions had been made, and life appeared good.

The Civilian Conservation Corps was set up to build the parkway, providing jobs for men during the Depression. Barracks were built for the workers, and arrangements made to send their paychecks home to their families. Plenty of work was available. The Depression would be solved, because of all the work that was being made. President Franklin D. Roosevelt was going to open the park. Hands had been shaken all around, in agreement.

And then the deal changed.

In February, 1934, the Secretary of the Interior announced that the park would not go forward until all the mountain residents were removed from the land. Now, they all had to get out. All of them. The land had to be emptied. The Park would not open until the land was completely cleared of all human residents. In Washington, D.C., the head of the Department of the Interior called the head of the parks department into his office. There was too much noise and too many complaints about this park removal effort. What was going on?

"The people are resisting, Sir," the park supervisor told him. "They say the payments aren't enough, and they don't want to live in the houses we've offered. Some of them have hired lawyers."

"I don't understand," said the President's Cabinet level official. "How else are their children going to go to school? We've been more than generous. We've even paid the ones that don't own the land!"

"Many of them don't see the value in sending their children to school, Sir. They say the deal was that they could stay on the land, as long as they and their children lived there. They'd be a tourist attraction for the park, Sir. Frankly, I thought it was settled that they would be able to stay there."

"Remove them, however you need to," the Secretary said. "It's an executive decision."

Jolene Kruger had just passed her seventh birthday when she first heard the rumors. Her father, Earl Kruger, told her not to worry. She thought he was tricking her. A thing like that seemed to be worth worrying about. Her mother, Lorene Ellingham Kruger, aged twenty-three, looked worried, and Jolene knew that was a bad sign for the baby her mama was carrying. The year was 1934. The Kruger family had their own house. Her mama and daddy were second cousins, twice removed, and the family was real close. The house was made of logs, with a wood floor. It had a kitchen, a living room, a dining room, and three bedrooms. It wasn't a mansion, but it didn't have a mortgage. Plenty of people in America have found a six room house to be a fine-enough residence for raising a family, and Jolene's family was no exception. They were normal Americans, but maybe not typical Americans. The depression had been going on for years, but it didn't make any difference in their lives. When you live off the land, it doesn't much matter what is going on in the world outside the mountains.

The two Kruger boys shared a bedroom, the two Kruger girls shared a bedroom, and there was a bedroom for the parents. Jolene knew her father would get the boys, and maybe her grandfather, to help out adding a room when the new baby came.

Jolene's father spent a lot of time with his boys. Earl's boys put a light in his eyes, every time he thought about them. He'd taught them everything he knew about farming the land. They put the furrows in along the hillsides, to keep the rain from eroding the soil. Farming wasn't easy in the hills, but it could be done, if you put your heart and your back into it. That's what Earl taught his sons, and what Earl's father taught him. It was how he took care of his family. It was the same as the way his own father had done it, and his wife's family, too. Each family staked out their plot of land, made a deal to buy it from its perceived owner, and built a house for their family. They plowed the fields, planted what they needed, and what was leftover, they would sell. They got themselves some cattle, a few pigs, some chickens. They lived in the mountains. In the mountains, there were rabbits to shoot, fish to catch, and now and then, venison. Wood was available for building. Stone was free for the lifting. Raw materials were provided by nature. The real value was in knowledge of how to use wood and stone, and a willingness to work hard.

The neighbors, many of whom were blood relatives, helped out when there were big jobs to do. Lorene's parents, John and Mary Ellingham, lived just over the hill. John was a minister, and ran a church for their little part of the universe. Not too many people could read, but John could read the Bible, and he taught its ideas to everyone who would listen. Lorene had gone to elementary school one year. She could read, but there wasn't that much need for it, where they were living. She had her hands full, raising a family. Four growing children, living on a farm, made a lot of work for their mama. She had birthed each child right there in the house, with her friends and family helping, and nobody'd ever been real sick. Thank the Lord! They lived in a place that was truly the Lord's house. It had a fresh water mountain spring and lots of different trees all around. *Say what you will about fancy houses, I'd take the crisp air of a Fall day in the mountains, walking the fields and noticing the round furrows, any day over a painted closed room with brocade curtains, just about anywhere.* At least, that's what Jolene would have said. She loved the mountain, the land. They were poor, but when everybody around you is poor, you don't notice it. You don't miss what you don't know exists. You don't need money if you can't think of what you might want to buy. They had food, shelter, clothes, plenty of work to do, and the close company of family and friends. When you come right down to it, what else is worth having?

In Jolene's family, they didn't use money for much, but about twice a year, they took a wagon into town and took their trade into the store. They needed kerosene, and feed for the animals. They would trade eggs and produce for it. Lorene collected the feedbags. Inside of them, there was a cotton lining, decorated with a colorful small print. She could sew attractive and cheerful clothes for the family with it, just like her mother used to do for her and her sister, Nettie. She taught her daughters how to cook and store food, how to sew and knit, how to crochet. It's true none of them went to school, because there wasn't any school nearby at the time. Lorene always thought she'd made a mistake not keeping up with her ability to read. She'd had it a little bit, but she didn't pursue it, to get better at it. With all they had to do to keep the farm going, it seemed unnecessary, at the time.

Still, Jolene thought, if Mama or any of the children had learned more reading, maybe one of them would have seen the notices and the flyers when they went adventuring into town. Maybe one of them would have gotten a copy of the *Chestnut Grove News*, and read the Letters to the Editor. Maybe her father would have known what was going on in time to get some of the others together to put a stop to it. But, probably not. Probably it wouldn't have made any difference.

At least, that's what Jolene believed. Jolene wished she had learned to read. She thought maybe if she had read what was going on, she could have gotten in there herself and put a stop to it. If she'd known how to read, she might have noticed the signs on that building in town, where they were collecting the money to help raise the funds to buy the land for the park. But, maybe not. Maybe taking on the entire United States government would have all been too much to handle for a seven-year-old girl. All the same, if Jolene had known what was going on, or how it was all going to turn out, she always thought she would have done something to stop it.

By the time the Kruger family saw the road being put in along the top of the mountain, and the camps started being built for the boys from the Civilian Conservation Corps, it was pretty much all determined. The money'd been raised, the laws had been passed, and the wheels of progress were in motion. Soon, the Chestnut Grove Sheriff was going to be knocking on their door with papers. The papers were going to tell Earl and Lorene Kruger, and hundreds of other families very much like them, to get off their own land, and leave their home, by order of the state. They were going to be paid one dollar an acre, a sum so ridiculous it would do nothing to find them a comparable place to live. There was no recourse. There was no person, nor agency, nor committee, to whom they could protest. There was no process to follow to get relief. They were just told to pack up and leave. Jolene's family packed their bags and left. They'd heard, through the mountain grapevine, what happened to Rufus.

Rufus Trout told the story.

The time had come for the Revenuers to move us off the mountain. Sheriff Plotsky and the state troopers joined up with the men sent from the Park service. Young Mary was set to marry one of them Civilian Conservation Corps boys, but Uncle Rufus didn't want the family moved out. He said he didn't care what they promised, 'cause they was all liars. Promises don't mean nothin', when they pour out o' the mouths o' liars. Anyway, the sun came up that day, same as any other, and it was jest early Spring, so it was a beautiful day with the smell of lilac and honeysuckle in the air.

Sheriff Plotzky had his own version.

The order came from the state that we had to move Rufus and his family off the mountain. It was something about how the feds wouldn't take the land until all the people were gone. Two months ago, they were telling us they could stay if they wanted to. I'd been up there twice talking sense to Rufus, but he was as stubborn as those chickens he was raising. About as dumb, too, if you ask me. Rufus had a way of looking at things, and I can't say as I don't see it partly his way. As Rufus sees it, his land is worth more to him than they was will-

ing to pay for it. You might look at his scraggly acres and see rocks and brush, but to Rufus, he saw the work that went into getting it as scraggly as it was. His granddaddy passed that land and two cabins on to him, and they was enough of a field that they grew corn, potatoes, and cabbage for the winter. They was also near Clem Pritcher's apple orchards, and the boys made some extra money pickin'. His old lady had a garden planted, and she put in a wisteria by the cellar door. Rufus hollered it would be years to grow back those dogwoods and magnolias she planted, and you had to admit, she had her yard laid out pretty.

Anyway, it warn't nothin' could be done about it. Rufus' grandpappy never did have a deed on that land, even though Rufus says he paid for it. He mighta' done, but nothin' was on file. The Park people was being nice, offering him something for it when he didn't have no papers. I s'pose I didn't have to go with the state troopers that day, but I went to see if I could help Rufus and his family.

Unfortunately, Mr. Rufus Trout was of the opinion that if he refused to accept the money offered for his "squatter's rights," then there would be no transfer of land, and he would not have to move. He firmly believed that his use of a rifle would prevent us from carrying through with our promise to remove him forcibly. I offered to go with the officers that day, simply for the sake of the children. I expected there may be an ill-advised scuffle, from which the children would need to be comforted. Goodness knows those children had been through enough. The Park was offering Rufus a chance to get his children and his grandchildren to a place where they could be educated, and they could get medical treatment. Not one of those children had ever been to a doctor, not even at their own birth.

The social worker had something to say, too.

We made arrangements for them to get a house in the settlement in town. They would have electricity and running water there, and they would be able to attend school regularly. One would expect that they would be grateful, to be able to raise their standard of living by so much. I fear, though, that Mr. Trout has given them stories about what will happen to them when they leave these mountains, and they seem fearful to go. I expect that he and his sons would rather live in squalor here in the mountains, than be forced to get a job and earn a living. I was just glad the ordeal would be over soon.

Even the landowners from the city chimed in.

We were considerably pleased to hear that the last of the squatters had been removed from our land. It was a relief to get the nasty business behind us. Our original investment in the copper mine was recouped, with a reasonable profit. This lifted a burden from our shoulders, as we realized we would not need to concern ourselves with the disposition of the squatters. The park service did for us what we could certainly never have done for ourselves. The mountain dwellers were removed from our lands.

There had never been a proper way to get the copper out of those mountains, so I fear we were sold a bill of goods when we made our first investment. However, with the sale to the park service, we were more than made whole on the modest price we originally paid for what was essentially worthless land. We heard it took six state troopers and three from the local mayor's department to remove the squatters. We were greatly relieved of a burden when this deal was concluded.

And on that fateful day, this is how it happened.

Sheriff Plotsky led the group of nine officers, two park officials, and a social worker on horseback through the mountain trails to the Trout's place. The land was four miles from a passable road. Rufus Trout was the patriarch, and his family had built four cabins, two barns, three chicken houses, and a cabbage patch in these hills. Rufus had five sons, and between them they had three wives and seven children. The family, altogether, was made up of seventeen people, living in what you could call a compound.

Three married sons, each with their own house, built close by the father, on the father's land. People in the cities maybe didn't do it that way, but it made sense in the mountains, where every hand could help with the work.

Rufus Trout's family had a lot of sense, and that's why each grown son had his own cabin, his own garden, and his own plans for his family's future. Life in the mountains might look bleak if you were on the outside, living an outsiders' life, where things and money matter. But on the inside, family members had something money couldn't buy. They had each other. In their world, that meant something. Some rich people, living in the cities, searched their whole lives for what was right here. On this particular day, Ray Plotsky could only hope nobody was going to get hurt. The group plodded forward on their trek. It was a beautiful day in the mountains. The scent of lilac and forsythia enlivened the air.

As they approached the Trout homestead, the offic-ers each unconsciously reached for their guns. There could be trouble, as they were too aware. Mountain men could cause a scene. They were well-armed. They had an army of sons and sons-in-law who would help them out. More importantly, they were defending their homes and believed they were right. Mountain men be-lieved the United States of America was a free country. They couldn't imagine that the U.S. government was ac-tually taking their homes. It was inconceivable, com-pletely outside the values they'd been taught. Ray Plotsky was well aware that the mountain men would consider defense of their homes to be the act of pa-triots.

Whether or not the state troopers had a similar aware-ness, Ray didn't know. That's why he was here. To make sure the troopers didn't freak out when they encountered the patriotism of the mountain men. He could see how this all could have an unhappy ending. Years later, we would call this a Ruby Ridge. But in 1934, it was just a stubborn, il-literate mountain man facing off against the guv'mint.

Mrs. Trout stood on the porch as the group approached. She slipped into the house to get Rufus. He came out with his 12 gauge Winchester. Mrs. Rufus scurried the children inside the house.

"You know we gotta do this," Ray called. It was his job to get Rufus to cooperate. Ray figured he had to convince Ru-fus not to fight, because there was no doubt in his mind Ru-fus would lose that battle, and that would be mightily dis-turbing to the women and children inside.

"Put your weapon down, Rufus." Ray hollered. Before Ray even saw it coming, the troopers had Rufus on the ground, and they were pulling his hands behind his back, and handcuffing him. The little faces of the children pressed up against the screen door saw this happening, and they started to cry.

"Ray," Rufus was calling. "Ray!" and Ray knew it was up to him to keep the troopers calm, keep them from over-reacting. "Don't fight, Rufus," was all Ray could say before he saw the little ones push the screen door open and wriggle away from their mothers. He saw one of the troopers lift little nine year old Mary Alice into the air, and she scratched his face and drew blood, while she squealed. Then Ray thought maybe his best bet was to just pray. And he started counting the children and women as the troopers pushed them along to the wagon. Then he heard a roar, and a scream, and he felt the flames coming from the house as the troopers torched it and burned it down. He couldn't get the screams of those children out of his mind, as they sat there in the wagon, with armed guards all around them, watching their house burn down. Jolene Kruger had the events of that day seared into her mind. It changed how she thought of herself and the country she lived in.

Hundreds of families along the Blue Ridge of the Appalachian mountains, all the way from Pennsylvania into Georgia, lived this experience. Mountain families. In the height of the Depression, they were thrown off their family land, ripped forcibly and violently from a place where they had been able to feed their families, work together, and make their own way. They were told to go find jobs at a time

when there were no jobs to be had. Up until that day, Jolene had never gone hungry.

After the mountain families moved into town, the men
got on the buses to go to orchards far away to pick apples.
They were gone for weeks at a time, when the harvest was
in. Some of them snuck back into the hollows, to keep their
moonshine stills running. But life in Chestnut Grove was
never the same as it was when the families lived on the
mountain. Food that had been plentifully provided by the
mountain mother, now needed to come from grocery stores,
where it would cost money. That was money the mountain
people never had. Jolene Kruger felt the purple bruise in her
gizzard every day for the rest of her life.

It was Joey Anhalt who first noticed the construction and
the tunnels being built within the forest. He saw the men
dressed in business suits and fancy shoes coming out of nowhere near the caves. Joey didn't understand what was happening, but he told the others. There were government men
in the forest. Not park people. Men who looked like Big
Shots, and other men who looked like soldiers. Men who
carried briefcases and men who wore uniforms and carried
guns. They were building fences, and housing German
Shepherd dogs behind them. They built barracks, for the
men who would build the roads and the tunnels. The mountains were infested with men in the caves, building tunnels.

Five years later, the United States of America would join
the war in Europe. Fortunately, there were no people living
near the tunnels built within the caves, under the Blue
Ridge Mountains. Within the tunnels, deep inside the
mountains, the Office of Strategic Services of the United

States of America, would operate their communications infrastructure. Fortunately, Franklin Roosevelt had the foresight to remove the mountain people, so that he could build the tunnels to hide and protect the communications network infrastructure inside the mountain. Fortunately, the nation had prepared this critical asset of defense far in advance. Fortunately, Franklin D. Roosevelt was prepared for war. As it always had, the mountain pulsed with ever more magnetic secrets.

Chapter 7
Present Day
Back in Paris, France

Olivier and Andrew continued their conversation at the Bulldog café. "Now, Wild Bill Donovan, Roosevelt's first spy, lived near the Blue Ridge," Olivier said.

"But the OSS was not set up until five or six years later, after the war started," Andrew objected. He had researched the Office of Strategic Services, which Roosevelt began as the precursor to the CIA.

"True," said Olivier, puffing and blowing out the smoke, as he leaned back in his delicate bistro chair. The day was sunny and cold, and Parisians continued their rotation through the chairs and tables all around Andrew. "The information about the war existed, and FDR was on top of the information about Europe. He could never have waited for the war to start in the U.S., and *then* looked for a place to hide the infrastructure. After the war was in progress, it would have been too late to build it," Olivier pointed out. "So he prepared in advance. FDR liked to say he never let his left hand know what his right hand was doing. He believed that keeping secrets was a strategy for winning the war. So in the end, this Office of Strategic Services had a significant presence, hiding in the tunnels under the Blue Ridge."

Andrew felt a fluttering in his stomach. *I never learned about this in school,* he thought. *High school, college, history classes. Nobody ever mentioned that Roosevelt prepared for war before Pearl Harbor.* "So this is why all the people had to be removed," he said, rolling his tongue over his lips, which had suddenly gotten dry. "They couldn't risk having people finding these tunnels and talking about them before the war." He reached for his glass of water.

"Yes, and as a result, they developed a little contingent of Central Intelligence Agency staff that worked and lived in a place nearby the tunnels," Olivier continued. He leaned forward and lowered his voice, looking straight into Andrew's eyes. "That should not have been a problem. Government employees live and work in many places. Normally, it means nothing. But this particular place was uniquely different from any of the surrounding towns or counties. It held a special secret."

"What secret?" Andrew said. What other secret, he meant. He looked around at the city buildings on the Paris street. He realized the buildings surrounding him were hundreds of years older than the United States government. *Paris is a city with a long, tumultuous history. It has seen empires come and empires go.* His eyes flitted nervously up and down from the rooftops of the buildings to the cigarette butts thrown on the street and the graffiti smeared along the stone basements. Olivier saw his nervous movements.

"There was a time, Andrew," Olivier said, "when the government of France beheaded people in the square. The square is not far from here, if you would like to see the spot."

Andrew dropped his eyes. His chin fell.

"While it was important and terrible that the government did that, what was even more important was the people's response to it." Olivier waited for Andrew to look up.

"The people gathered to watch. Like a bunch of zombie ghouls. They cheered when the blade sliced the neck, and the bloody head dropped into the bucket of blood that caught it." He timed his sentences, puffing on his cigarette in between thoughts.

"And after the blood scent filled the air, prostitutes worked the crowd, looking for a man whose libido was so aroused by the violence that he would empty his wallet for some sort of medical release of the sexual tension. They would pull their victims into the tunnels under the city, and allow them to release their tension in return for money. Violence intensifies and creates that hormonal drive. The brain spots that control sex are close to those that control violence and religion. They make a power triad in the physical brain: sex, violence, spirituality. All so close they share brainwaves. Many times, in many men, these three legs of power get confused. Madeleine calls this testosterone poisoning." Olivier smiled, leaned back in his chair, waited for Andrew to process what he had heard.

"The mountain families that came off that mountain had a set of beliefs about life, and a way of looking at things that was different from the value systems of the elites who ran the government. The mountain society was communal. They believed in helping each other, because they were a society without money, and with strong maternal leadership. Competition was a foreign concept. They didn't compete with each other, and this, too, became a data point that the social workers used against them. Failure to compete looks like lack of ambition, to American capitalists. It lacks testosterone."

The waiter came by, and Olivier motioned for another espresso. The café was getting crowded, and they pushed their seats farther to the right, so their conversation could not be so easily overheard. Many Parisians speak English, and sometimes one cannot be careful enough with privacy. Olivier wanted Andrew to fully understand.

"Testosterone poisoning is apparently a culturally learned phenomenon. In some types of societies, it is suppressed. The mountain families, while appearing outwardly to be run by mountain men, were matriarchal clans. They understood that Mama had to be happy, if anybody in the family were going to be happy. Their way of life used all the testosterone, hunting for food. It was spent, and had no need to turn inward, where it would poison the lives of the families.

"When the families were removed from the mountains, a certain set of them refused the offer of subsidized housing in the town of Chestnut Grove. Some took the offer, but many did not. Among the families who refused, a few of them found a new mountain hollow where they could move. It was outside the boundaries of town and the Chestnut Grove National Park, but it was still in the nearby mountains. It was a small and isolated mountain hollow, difficult to reach by automobile. It was even more rough and isolated than the area that had been chosen for the park. And its appeal? Well, Joey Anhalt and Billie Ellingham were smart young men at that time. The way they figured, if there had been talk about copper in those hills, there probably was, somewhere, copper in those hills."

"Joey and Billie found the copper?" Andrew guessed.

"They did. They were sharp and attentive. They knew the hills inside and out. They joined forces and sniffed it out. When they found the copper in one of the many hillside caves, they understood that it had to remain a secret among the families."

"How could they keep a secret like that?"

"They picked eight families, staked out the land around the copper mine, and started a new town. The town was ruled by the eight patriarchs of the founding families. They laid out some rules for how their society was going to be governed.

"First, they had to protect the secret of the copper mine. Joey and Billie figured they would find a way to mine that copper and share the money among the eight families, to get them all set back up. They all needed new houses, new animals, barns, fences, and gardens. If they could get the men to work together to mine the copper, and sell it, everybody could get an equal share in their new town.

"Second, they had the problem that they had to buy this land, and they didn't know who owned it. Billie thought they could get the copper out first, while everything was still in flux. While the park service was still settling on buying the land, there was still confusion about the ownership. They figured they would rush in and get the copper out. When everything settled down, they would buy the land with money from selling the copper. They'd have to do it quietly, though, before anybody knew there was a mine. That was the biggest reason for keeping it secret."

The story was exciting to Andrew. He pictured Billie Ellingham and Joey Anhalt, cooking up their scheme together. "It would be like moonshining," he suggested. "They knew plenty about operating under the radar."

"Exactly," Olivier responded. "The two young men had to build a society sworn to secrecy, and they had to enforce the bonds of that secret. Nobody could know what was going on inside Copper Hollow. Nobody from the outside could come in. Nobody from the inside could go out, at least until the copper was mined and sold, and the land was purchased."

"And they succeeded?" Andrew asked. He raised his eyebrows, expecting that the answer would be yes.

"They succeeded at getting the copper out," Olivier said. "The eight men of the families parked their women and children in the subsidized housing at first. They told the families they would have to go away to work for awhile. The patriarchs took their able-bodied men – sons and brothers. They all got together and worked those mines, until the copper was removed and sold. In the end, it wasn't much copper. It would never have been enough for the original investors to recoup their money. But what is not much to one person, can be a treasure to another, in different circumstances. They got enough money from selling the copper to find the owner of the land, and buy it. They still had enough to get each family started out with a new spread, and recoup their farms. But the secret could never be revealed, and only the eight patriarchs ever knew the full story. The new society was built on a principle to keep outsiders away from their business, and to reject anyone new from coming into their sacred space."

Andrew thought for a moment. "But Copper Hollow is a real town now. It even has a newspaper."

"Eight large families, in four generations, can produce a lot of people," Olivier said. "The tradespeople in the new Copper Hollow, the Holler, they called it, wouldn't give competing bids for their work. They developed a shared society, because they're all kin, Andrew," Olivier answered. "They didn't want to step on their cousins' toes. When the families of Copper Hollow were evicted from the mountain, they were suddenly living in a new world. They valued family, and they believed in working the land. Their new society evolved to have the markings of a town, as the families produced more citizens. Copper Hollow grew to have one restaurant, one hardware and farm supplies store, a school, and its own mayor. It had a couple of churches, and over time, it grew as the families grew. Boys learned trades and set themselves up in business. There would be one plumber, one electrician, one team of carpenters for building houses, one blacksmith, one veterinarian. They tried to pass on their values to their children and grandchildren. It was a grand experiment in communal living. But times changed, and the experiment fell apart. As children grew up and married, new families came into the Holler. The original eight families couldn't say no to distant cousins who needed a place, and they started breaking the land up into small lots.

"By the fourth generation, the original eight families had over ten thousand members, most of whom were residents of Copper Hollow. Jobs never came to Copper Hollow. Why would they? The roads were winding and steep, and the valley was surrounded by land owned by the park. Serving such a small community, the businesses quickly realized they did not have enough customers. Trucks couldn't get to Copper Hollow, because trucks couldn't handle the mountain roads, and the speed limits, driving through the park. Factories depend on truck transportation, so there was never any significant work. The families didn't want their children to leave. The children had no means to explore options outside the family. They didn't want to move from their valley paradise to a city. So they stayed. Within eighty years, the families were exceeding the space they had for their community."

Andrew got excited. He was catching on to where this was going. "When the families lived on the land, it did not matter that they had no money. Poverty was meaningless, because they had food, shelter, and family. Lack of money only became important when food was no longer provided by working the land."

"Exactly," Olivier agreed. "Without jobs, life became too hard. Even with only a few families setting up in the Holler, the population grew explosively. The land was limited, because of the restrictions of the park property surrounding the mountain hollow. Some of the children had to move away to get jobs, but those who stayed found that they could not make it on the land that was left. Rather than the hardness of surviving on a mountain plot, it became the hardness of surviving on welfare. In the Holler, a welfare culture developed, sometimes with attendant drug use. When the park police prevented them from hunting on park land, the families lost access to a major food source. Cycles of poverty appeared, trapping some of the future generations. The kids had no one to show them how to get out, how to survive in the big city. They often didn't even speak clear English, just their own dialect. You had an entire town of poor people, with big hearts and happy families, who were deteriorating because of lack of employment. In the days when they could live off the land, lack of employment did not mean starvation. The land provided for them, the way it provides for the forest animals. When the land was limited, and they could not expand to new land as their families grew, they became resource constrained, and poor. When land was no longer theirs to cultivate, this situation caused increasing domestic violence, and a spreading drug use."

"Like many small, remote towns in Appalachian mountain areas," Andrew added. "Tiny towns like this dot Appalachia."

Olivier agreed. He continued, "The kids grow up too poor to know what else is out there. The search for food switches from hunting for game to being hired for coal mining or construction work. By the time the kids are old enough to go exploring in the outside world, they might have kids of their own. They're trapped by their own thinking, unwilling and unable to leave the family. Psychologists give this a name: learned helplessness. It's what happens when people believe they cannot overcome their environment. They begin having their own children while they are still teenagers, so they have only a short window to make the break and move away."

"I've heard of that," said Andrew. "In the circus, the elephants stay in place, with only a light rope tied to one leg. They could easily pull the rope out of its stake in the ground and run away. But the rope was placed there when they were very young, and they couldn't escape it then. Now that they are older, they simply believe that they cannot escape, so they stop trying. They don't continue to test the premise."

"Exactly," Olivier acknowledged. "This happens to people, too. They believe they cannot escape, so they stop trying."

Olivier got up and walked over to a newsstand kiosk, halfway down the block. Bringing back the paper, he pointed out that today's news discussed many issues around the world. "If you live in remote, rural areas, and you do not read, how would you know world events? There are many places in the world where the population is poor, isolated, and primarily illiterate. They become attractive bait for exploitation."

"Like Afghanistan?" Andrew asked.

"Yes, Andrew," Olivier confirmed. "Appalachia in the 1920's had a lot in common with the rural areas of Afghanistan. And in many ways, the Chance Kiernan's of this time and of that time, played a parallel role."

"What do you mean, 'the Chance Kiernan's?" Andrew asked.

"Ah, Andrew," Madeleine interjected, pulling up a chair for herself as she joined them at the café, "When there are matters of power and dominance, there is always a Chance Kiernan. These are the alpha males of every society."

Chapter 8

2006

In the Hindu Kush mountains, northern Afghanistan

The U.S. Marines who called themselves Puma Platoon had spent the previous evening painting a mountain lion logo on their Humvees. Captain Jagger rolled with them, and Sergeant HamHock Hartman, as always, actually led the group. Everybody respected HamHock Hartman. If you had to go into a battle, that's who you would want to have your back. This morning, they headed out early, on another of their routine meet-and-greets in the mountain villages. The idea was to roll into a village, meet the elders, and clean out any Taliban that might be lurking nearby. On these missions, their key personnel included their own 'terp. Their interpreter was Juma. Unfortunately for the Marines, they were also saddled with the burden of dragging a unit of the Afghan National Army along with them. Babysitting the ANA was always a chore.

The bad thing about mountain villages was, they were in the mountains. The Hindu Kush mountains were not those sissy hills of the Blue Ridge, like Marine Corporal Luke Trout was used to, where he grew up in Copper Hollow,

USA. These were MOUNTAINS in capital letters. To get to these villages, you pushed your ride slowly up the incline. The roads were narrow, barely wide enough for one vehicle. If you happened to meet another one going the opposite direction, one of you would have to back up until you found a pull-off place wide enough to let the other pass. To fall off the side would send you tumbling to a certain death. God help you if you didn't get back to base before dark. That's why everywhere they went had to be a few hours ride from a base. They set up forward operating bases, FOBs, to solve this problem. Their FOB on this mission was called Fort Puma. They named it after themselves. It was a community of plywood shacks and tents, protected by some bags filled with sand-cement and a roll of barbed wire.

It was still early, and cold, as they turned at an angle to continue their climb, when suddenly the convoy stopped. In the lead, the ANA had four trucks. For some unknown reason, the first truck stalled. Luke looked out the plastic window on his right side, and saw HamHock getting out of his Humvee to investigate. HamHock was pulling Juma by the arm. Juma would help him talk to the ANA. Juma was jabbering something about this being a bad place to get out of the car. He noticed they were wedged between a steep, straight cliff on the right, and a steep, straight drop on the left. There was a wadi at the bottom of the drop, a riverbed that, at the moment, was mostly dry.

It took only a few seconds for the weapons fire to begin. Luke saw the flashes around HamHock and Juma first, then he heard the big explosion behind him. The last car in their convoy was hit by a rocket. Now they could not go forward, because the ANA trucks blocked them. They could not back up, because the exploded and burning final car blocked them. Luke saw the Afghan Army soldiers jump out of their trucks and run, climbing the cliffs to their right. Why weren't they driving away? Damn ragheads.

The rocket fire continued, and Luke realized they were stuck in exactly the wrong place. Their machine guns could not fire back, because the shooters were well-protected in their positions above. The curve of the cliff along the road would deflect the bullets if the big guns went after them. By hitting their last car, they could not back up. They couldn't move their weapons into the right position. Even worse, the mountains on both sides blocked their radio reception. They couldn't call for air cover, and they couldn't talk to each other. Luke realized the obstacle presented by the ANA trucks could not be a coincidence. Those trucks had stopped strategically, to trap them.

The ANA trucks were not well-protected and well-armored, like Puma Platoon's Humvees were. All Luke could conclude was that the ANA knew this was going down, and at least one of them, the driver of the first truck, was part of the ambush. It only took one. The rest of the ANA, when they realized they were about to be ambushed, would run away. That's what they always did, in Luke's experience. When a fight was about to start, the ANA ran away. He remembered Juma telling him they weren't cowards. They just didn't see the point in fighting. They were here for the paycheck, not the principle. You can't train somebody to believe in a principle, no matter how many decades you camp in their midst.

Luke saw other Marines jumping out of their Humvees and following HamHock, running low on the right side between the mountain and the trucks. They were going to go up there and move those ANA trucks, he understood. It was the only way out. He could only pray they got there be-fore the enemy blew them up. It was good that the first truck was around the bend, so that rockets from the direc-tion they were coming could not reach them.

He heard the trucks' engines start, and saw the convoy move. They had just enough Marines to drive each truck and each Humvee, minus the one in the rear that had been hit by a rocket. As soon as they got the convoy out of the vulnerable area, they regrouped, and the machine guns started looking for targets.

HamHock had set up an operations point, where they were pulling everybody who was injured into one of the ANA trucks, and the medic was in there. It didn't look too bad. No missing limbs or cracked heads. The last car in the convoy held two Marines, "Crater" Johnson and Bill Charles. That car was exploded, and their bodies were gone. Nothing to bring back. Luke tried to keep his mind off that. The path was forward. Attend to the wounded. Later, mourn the dead, after everyone else is home safely. Captain Jagger called for air cover. Within fifteen minutes, the top of that mountain, where the insurgents hid, was being strafed. The mountaintop would soon be unfit for habitation, because of the amount of power that landed on it. Luke scanned the mountaintop, with the firepower smashing into it, and hoped there had been no innocent civilians living there.

When the last of the firing stopped, Captain Jaggers de-cided now was the right time to go get those bastards, while everybody was mad enough to kill them with their bare hands. He sent the truck with the wounded back to base, along with a squad to protect them. The rest of the platoon re-loaded and directed their rage at finding the ragheads ---no, the *"insurgents,"* -- who did this. Sadly, to Puma Platoon, pretty much all ragheads, or insurgents, look alike, which makes the task infinitely difficult. How can you pick out the civilians from the insurgents? Pretty much, Ham-Hock told them, if they were males between the ages of eighteen and thirty, they were insurgents. *But don't say I told you that,* HamHock warned.

Near the top of the mountain, they found the supply caves. Ammunition, weapons, food, and water, stored in multiple caves along the ridge. The elders of the village denied all knowledge of who had put these supplies in the caves. The village elder, an old man identified as the leader by his dyed-red beard, was named Wakil, grandfather of Farzam and Darya. He pointed to the East. "That trail," he told the interpreter Juma, speaking in the Dari language, "leads to Pakistan. Look for your aggressors there. They do not live in our village." Despite the culture within their society of offering hospitality and food to strangers, the village elders held no kindness within their hearts to offer the U.S. Marines.

Corporal Luke Trout, great-great-grandson of Rufus Trout, on his father's side, and Billie Ellingham, on his mother's side, felt the chill of the old mountain man's venom toward the Americans. All his life, his family had told the children their story of the uniformed troops who threw their ancestors off the mountain. *Then he heard a roar, and a scream, and he felt the flames coming from the house as the troopers torched it and burned it down.* Stories from his childhood welled up into his consciousness, as he smelled the burning trees from the strafed mountaintop. Deep inside, so deep he would never admit it, he wasn't so sure this was a worthy mission to help the Afghans. It felt like a deep, inexplicable, purple bruise on his inside. He'd rather be home, in Copper Hollow.

Back in Copper Hollow, USA, near the Blue Ridge Mountains

At The Sportsmens Club, Founded 1813

The long line of cars parked on the grassy field sported mostly out-of-state license plates. At the gated entrance, two armed men dressed in jeans and hunting jackets had to personally know you by name. If they didn't, you needed a special ticket, pre-printed with the name of the person who invited you. From the road, you couldn't see the place. Thick yews and firs surrounded it, in a double planting, so that there was no space for someone to peek through. Inside the evergreens, a privacy fence, 8 feet tall, shielded the stadium. Inside the fence, two rows of bleachers flanked a cement-block concession stand. It wasn't fancy, but it was extremely private. This was the gamecock tournament that Joey Anhalt and Billie Ellingham visited with their elite guests in the 1930's. Now, however, the old stadium had been rebuilt, to add capacity for four hundred fans. The air was crisp, and brightly sunny. A few clouds floated lazily across the brilliant blue sky. Once in a while, a light breeze cooled the spectators.

Left to themselves, roosters fight. It's what they do. Gamecock tournaments, known in Copper Hollow as chicken fights, have a long history. Some say the wild gamecock was domesticated by the Chinese in 1400 BC. In ancient Pompeii, a mosaic was found depicting two cocks in battle. In England, Henry VIII built a cockpit in his palace. Andrew Jackson had his own pit at the White House. The University of South Carolina has a gamecock as its mascot, in honor of General Sumter, known as the "Gamecock of the Revolution" because of his courage. George Washington once said he had gone to a cockfight, which he hurried to attend immediately after church. And "Honest" Abe Lincoln? Gamecock enthusiasts say his "honest" title was inferred upon him because of his fairness as a judge in a cockfight. In Copper Hollow, chicken fights were a heritage sport. They'd been around long before Joey Anhalt and Billie Ellingham started taking guests from the Top in to see them.

Roosters have a spur on their legs, and rooster-fighting human beings, called "cockfighters," breed the roosters to have bigger and better spurs. The spurs are used to injure opponents in a fight. Technically, it wasn't the rooster fighting that caused the problem with the law. It was the knives the cockfighters fit onto their gamecocks' legs. The Sportsmen's Club of Copper Hollow, in business for nearly two hundred years, would have been in much less trouble, if it had not allowed that vendor in the concession stand to sell gaffs, a knife-like attachment for the roosters' spurs. Of course, the gaff meant there would be more blood, and more blood meant the audience would be more excited. A more excited audience meant more betting. And betting? Well, to the owner of the cockpit, betting was the point, wasn't it? What does the "sport" in "sportsmen" mean, if it doesn't mean gambling?

That night, Josh Bockenheim, a visiting businessman, sat in the box seats. He was an honored guest of the local Business Association. Copper Hollow wanted to put its best foot forward when such a successful businessman as Josh Bockenheim came to town. The entire group settled into their seats, beer all around, when the first gamecocks entered the pit.

Cletus Willett was a fifth-generation resident of Copper Hollow. A "born-here" from the mountains. He spoke with the mountain dialect. Cletus eyed Bockenheim suspiciously. He didn't know this man, and he didn't like his looks. He looked like a crook, to Cletus. A crook, in Cletus' world, was a person who makes his living using his mouth instead of his hands. "That thar's a Allen Roundhead," Cletus told the group around him, but kept his eyes keen on Josh Bockenheim. One of Cletus' perfected skills was that he could talk and stare at the same time. Unlike most people, his mouth didn't have to speak where his eyes were looking. "That 'un with the blue neck. He ain't got no comb. The chickens all get their combs shaved off, else a other chicken'll get ahold o' that. Now t'other one's a Lord Derby. Mos'ly these chickens get fed dog food, apples, and potatoes. They need a lot o' protein. They get cared for, tha's assure."

The pit beneath them was about fifteen feet in diameter, round, surrounded by a wire fence so the chickens didn't fly into the open bleachers on the left and the right. The birds entered the ring, carried by their handlers. The referee wore a red jacket and stood off to the side of the ring. Cletus kept up a steady stream of explanation, for his honored guests. "Now, these two is both stags, which means they's each about one year old. Later on, we'll get to the cocks, which is the older birds. They put the gaff on each bird afore it goes in ta fight."

As each handler entered the pit, they weighed the birds in front of the audience, to prove they were evenly matched. The referee checked the gaffs, to make sure they were fitted right and wouldn't fall off during the fight. Then the referee said, "Bill your birds."

Each handler held his stag near its opponent. The birds started pecking at each other. "Ther' gettin' em mad now," Cletus explained. "Rilin' 'em up, so they'll be ready to fight." The handlers held the birds tightly, but thrust them at each other, then pulled them back. Finally, the referee announced, "Toe the line."

At the referee's announcement, each handler set his bird on the ground, facing the other, with its toes on its pitting line. Holding their tails, the handlers held the birds back until the referee declared, "Pit your birds." At that, each handler released his grip on their birds' tails, and the stags flew at each other, meeting in mid-air at the center of the pit.

They shuffled in mid-air and then fell to the ground in a flurry of feathers, slashing at each other with their gaffs. Blood spurted into the air. The birds wrestled, blood drizzling and spurting for another ten minutes. At times, the referee called in the handlers, and the birds were separated, pulled back to their pitting lines, and freed again. The audience milled about the ring, drinking beer, eating hot dogs from the concession stand, and cheering as their favorite bird pulled ahead. It was a real family affair. Men, women, and children all watched excitedly. Like a Sunday afternoon baseball game, right after the family dinner. Blood, even chicken blood, rushes the adrenaline. Spurting and splattering blood stimulates the primitive desires. The men and boys peered closer, eager to see every dripping detail of the bloody carnage. The women and girls covered their eyes with their hands, peeking through open fingers to check for the finale.

One woman, however, did not cover her eyes. She was young and arguably beautiful, though she wore no makeup and dressed modestly. Her long dark brown hair was pulled back off her porcelain face in a tight pony tail. She threaded the pony tail through the back of her blue suede baseball cap. Her tight jeans fit way too perfectly, and her sweatshirt hung loosely. This was a good thing, as she needed the loose sweatshirt to cover the badge in her pocket. FBI Agent Juliette March was on the job. It was her first big assignment operating on her own. Unlike most other women in the audience, she kept her eyes open. She was accompanied by her partner, FBI agent Ron Goodman, going by the name of "Grady Pell." Grady was hamming up the girlfriend-boyfriend angle, and she pushed him away as he snuggled too close for her comfort. She wanted to see the fight.

Lunge after lunge, the birds attacked, slashing and spurting. Finally, one bird lay dead, and the match was called for the winner. It was the visiting businessman, Josh Bockenheim, who first asked Cletus Willett whether the police harassed the patrons here at the cockfighting ring. And there it was. Cletus knew all along this guy was a ringer. Stupid question deserves a stupid answer, he supposed, so he fed Josh Bockenheim his very best party line.

"I reckon the poe-lees here is the same as the poe-lees anywhar," Cletus told him, in a practiced sing-song pace. He'd said this before, and he'd say it again. "If th'ar ain't nobody complainin', they fin' th'ar selves somethin' more important to do."

Chance Kiernan, retired agent of the Defense Intelligence Agency, and contractor to the newly-formed Terrorism Defense Unit, United States Government, was not a member of the Copper Hollow police force. He was, however, at that very moment, meeting in the regional office of Joe Freel, the sheriff whose authority included Copper Hollow. Chance Kiernan missed the rooster show because he was discussing "retired" TDU business with a fellow "retired" TDU colleague, Joe Freel. Homeland Security was on the job, keeping America safe. In a world where the war had come home, agents needed to stay alert, always aware and well-dispersed throughout the population. The TDU boasted of many fine agents, retired from the military, but receiving contracts for work they did now. After all, the war had come to American soil, hadn't it? Dispersing TDU agents around America was prudent military strategy, for an enemy who lived among us.

The next morning, after an evening with his family, Chance would leave on a trip to another place where cockfighting is common Friday night entertainment. There, it is called murgh jangi. It takes place in the open air in the Babur Garden, in downtown Kabul.

Chapter 9
2006
Kabul, Afghanistan

They said the road through the mountain pass could be travelled by Land Rover, and Chance Kiernan was glad of that. In the past, he visited villages for which the only access was a caravan of mules, or sometimes, camels. Land Rovers felt like limousines, when compared to a camel convoy. As he bundled his long legs into the open car, he reviewed the mission goals in his mind. He wore an American business suit, dark gray with a blue and gray striped tie, under a cashmere overcoat. On his feet he wore business-meeting wingtip shoes which were completely impractical and inappropriate for this harsh and dusty environment. But, his porter-guide-interpreter told him their destination was a mere three-hour ride. His American-style clothes, non-military and moneyed-looking, would be a key part of the Kabuki theater that marked his upcoming negotiation. His red hair and freckles sometimes distracted potential partners when he talked. Somehow, his Irish-American appearance made him seem too likable for serious business dealings.

In this negotiation, Chance played the part of the lender to the Pakistani buyer of the agricultural produce from this Afghan village. Distribution of the product was a problem faced by the rural mountain farmers. With the American occupation, and the subsequent installation of the Karzai government, rural poppy farmers hid their activity. Complex arrangements had to be made to get their products to the market towns in Helmand province, near the Iranian border. They had to pass through hard-to-navigate, rough mountain trails. All along the way, officials had to be paid off, and the transport mafia had to be appeased. Business skills not formerly required by farmers in an agricultural province had to be developed. Playing into this drama, Chance hoped to secure a deal, at the behest of his employer.

During this time in Afghan history, the Karzai government, with pressure from the Americans, sent armed troops to the countryside to burn the poppy fields at the time of harvest. Of course, to do this at the time of harvest meant the farmers had already invested all the work into the production of poppy. Burning the fields at harvest burned the income for the families for that year. It ensured hardship and starvation for the poorest citizens of the nation. The poppy eradication teams continued to be sent from the Afghan government. Sadly, the troops decided to burn some, and accept bribes not to burn others. This resulted in reports of burned fields that were not burned, and charts submitted to governments and aid organizations that overstated the numbers of acres eradicated. More and more, the citizens complained that the Karzai government was corrupt. Karzai's election in 2005 boasted more votes from rural areas than there were citizens in residence, but that was not the corruption the citizens found outrageous.

The citizens objected to the corruption which allowed thugs in police uniforms to extort poppy farmers, by taking payment to prevent the burning of poppy. All along the way, from growers, to traders, to smugglers, to processors, to distributors, to dealers of drugs in the population, the money from poppy found its way to the pockets of the continuing insurgent fighters. In turn, the insurgents recruited teenage boys from the countryside, indignant and angry when their poppy fields burned. The burning of poppy fields ensured the insurgents a constant, fresh supply of new young recruits.

Chance Kiernan's employer was the Terrorism Defense Unit of the United States government. He was a contractor to this arm of Homeland Security. His assignment was to get inside this system of drug distribution, and figure out what to do to stop it. To do that, he was posing as a financier for poppy. Bringing along a Pakistani face to pose as his purchasing agent seemed to be a reasonable chess move for the circumstance. The Pakistani face was Chance's colleague, CIA agent Hanif Maluod.

Their team would arrive at the destination for negotiation in the early evening. Long into the night, they would sit on intricately woven wool carpets on the floor, drinking tea and debating. Kiernan had a rudimentary knowledge of Farsi, a Persian dialect only slightly different from Dari, the language of this rural village. This would allow him to understand some small bit of the conversation, but he would hide his skill, deferring always to the interpreter on his team. The lead negotiator would be his colleague, Hanif.

Chance could never remember Hanif's last name, but he figured both the first and the last name were aliases, so he forgave himself the transgression of forgetting it. Hanif was a Pakistani-American; tonight, however, he would play the role of a resident Pakistani. Agents of Pakistan regularly protected drug smugglers, the U.S. government believed. Over all the years of war, Pakistan continually played both sides. Before the attacks of September, 2001, the U.S. government sent aid for the insurgency to Pakistan. In those days, the insurgency were considered the good guys. They were fighting against the Taliban, who had taken control of the government. Pakistan was to pass the money through to warlords, called *mujahedeen*. But the government in Pakistan split into factions within it. Some of the government agents backed the mujahedeen; some backed the Taliban. U.S. money ended up in the hands of both sides. To the Afghans, this appeared to have the purpose of equipping and fueling the war, from both ends. Afghans did not believe it was intended to be an aid for the citizens. Why would they? There was no evidence of citizen aid that the citizens could see.

In Chance's mission today, Hanif's presence would calm the poppy sellers and lend credibility to the deal. Their team would stay as overnight guests at their host's home, returning to Kabul the next day. Unlike the practices at Chance's headquarters base of Washington D.C, business here was done inside private homes. There would be no business discussion in expensive restaurants, or in office conference rooms, where prying ears could catch a phrase. No cadres of secretaries would type up the contracts. The issue would be settled with an approving nod, a handwritten note, and an armed escort, Chance knew. In the hills of Afghanistan, privacy and safety existed only while surrounded by one's personal army of blood relatives. Even then, blood and tribe may be corruptible. Constant vigilance and paranoid surveillance characterized security.

Endless debate, bottomless cups of tea, and the vulnerability of being an overnight guest in your potential partner's home were all mission-critical elements of a successful contract. Chance tossed his overnight duffel bag to the porter-guide. Hanif took the shotgun position in the front seat, leaving Chance to sit next to the translator and the porter in the back. They would make the trip from Kabul with only one car; perhaps a risk, but necessary for discretion. Their hosts would be cautious, and wary of visitors. Trust would come slowly.

The sand-colored Land Rover was outfitted with military-level arms, including the Heckler and Koch 9 mm MP5s. They started their journey from the relatively luxurious, and extremely expensive, Kabul Serena Hotel. This is where Hanif and Chance stayed whenever they were in Kabul. Chance told his wife it was like a Courtyard Mariott, at four times the price. They left the city without incident, pulling out from the Serena's horseshoe drive and heading northwest, onto Ebn-e-Sina Road, until they could get onto the Asia Highway.

Their driver was Pakistani; from their interactions, Chance suspected he must be a blood relation to Hanif. Chance half-dozed in the car; he let his mind drift toward the other times he had been in situations like this. Many days, months, and years of his life began in similar adventures. He had been part of the Army's Delta Force. His missions had been in Somalia, Sudan, and Iraq. Through many field operations, he had advanced from the frontlines to the backlines of the intelligence service, and retired at an early age after twenty years of service. By the time he retired, he had become an active agent in the Defense Intelligence Agency.

After retirement, Chance took a one-time contract with his former employer. It paid enough for him to buy a ranch in Malibu Canyon, California. He lived there with his sheep, his puppy, and a gaggle of aggressive geese; the geese served to effectively guard the driveway. But, Chance soon realized the quiet life was not for him. Times are always changing, and after Homeland Security became a concern, some of Chance's colleagues from the Defense Intelligence Agency went to work for a new agency, the Terrorism Defense Unit. When his former colleagues called on him, Chance accepted the new opportunity. He moved to Copper Hollow, a small town in the Blue Ridge mountains. Along with his new wife, Ann, Chance quickly learned that this quiet small town was a hub of retired CIA and TDU agents. They were retired like himself: in name only. Among his neighbors, he met Hanif, an American citizen, born in Missouri, and an active CIA asset. In the small town of Copper Hollow, Hanif owned and ran the town's private airport. Private, meaning it ran on a CIA contract that was written for Hanif's shell company. The local citizens couldn't hop a ride to The City from there, although a few private planes shared access. Mostly, Hanif's wife and adult sons ran the airport, while Hanif travelled for his real job. Chance had worked with CIA before, and while he considered the bureaucracy of the CIA to be a nuisance, he found no trouble working with Hanif.

The Central Intelligence Agency of the United States government had a long, and in Chance's mind, sordid, history within Afghanistan. For many years, he had heard they had set up a counter-terrorist task force in the suburbs of Northern Virginia – probably Manassas or Herndon, Chance figured – which was nicknamed The Manson Family. The Manson Family had one mission, to which they were committed with a cult-like fervor: getting Bin Laden. They developed a reputation that they would do anything, to anyone, anywhere, to fulfill their purpose.

The Manson Family, like the crazy cult of killers that attacked and stabbed people in California! Ha, ha, very funny nickname, Chance thought. But personally, he disapproved of making light of the mission of the United States Government. The U.S. government did serious things, with serious consequences, resulting in world-changing events. It was no laughing matter, in his life view. This was his primary objection to the practices and policies of the Central Intelligence Agency. The CIA brought back information, as Chance saw it. They wrote analysis. Admittedly, they got such information by being sneaky and snooping around, and that part was okay with Chance. But when it came down to rubber hitting the road, where actionable tasks were undertaken, he believed the real impact came from the Defense Department. The military, as Chance saw it, did the work. The spooks of the CIA were ghosts and nowhere men. Writers of theories. Analyzers of data points. Presenters of hypotheses. When something needed to be done, who are you going to call? Not the ghosts. Chance saw himself as a military man, even though he was technically a contractor to the Terrorism Defense Unit, not an employee of it. He felt pride in keeping his body fit and action-ready, even as he approached his mid-forties. Although he was no longer tasked with any military-style action, he liked to think he could rise to the occasion if necessary.

The Land Rover jostled along the mountain paths, and Chance allowed himself to appreciate the majesty and power of the scenery. After leaving the bustle and rotting garbage smell of Kabul behind, they headed north on the rutted and potholed road toward the Salang Pass. At times, the road appeared to have asphalt covering it, but the asphalt cracked and crumbled in the dry weather. The road climbed up; ravines along the sides revealed the skeletal remains of Land Rovers which had come this way before, and did not survive to tell their tales. They were riding in a car that was like a terrier, attacking a mountain road that was like an elephant. How dare this rat of a vehicle expect to conquer the behemoth that was the Hindu Kush?

Power is always perceived to be beauty, Chance thought. He believed that people respond to power and run from weakness. This is what his life experience taught him, and he believed it like a religion. He had observed it in every culture and every geographical area, and he was sure it would always hold true. It was important to him to pay attention to every nuance of body language, every wrinkle of a face, and every intonation in a sentence. Noticing and paying attention to these nuances had served him well. The skill of paying attention caused luck in everything he did; he intended to keep doing it every minute of his life. His military-cut red hair and freckles made others think of him as a lucky Irishman. Chance attributed his powers of observation to years of careful preparation, not luck.

The rough and daring ride continued. At times, the road was so narrow that they could not have opened their car doors without hitting the mountainside. They could not have gotten out of the cars without sliding down the cliffs. Chance and Hanif each settled into their own thoughts. Neither man was a casual talker. After a trip twice as long as originally estimated, they reached their destination. The house of the Tajik village leader, Wakil, was typical of other houses in the village. A mud-brick structure with a flat roof, hidden behind a similar mud-brick wall. The porter and driver left for accommodations in a different house, while Wakil's lieutenant, his grandson Farzam, led Chance, Hanif, and their interpreter to the main house. They sat on deep red woven wool carpets in an inner courtyard. Around them, the mud-brick walls of the house enclosed a fragrant garden complete with persimmon trees. The cardamom tea wafted its cinnamon-like scent through the air, and pastries of mulberry and pomegranate exuded enticing, mouth-watering smells. In the background, low music played on a CD player, infusing the room with the oriental chords of lutes over an underlying beat of the drum. A generator hummed in the backyard.

As expected, the talks stretched far into the night, ending with a handwritten "chit," giving their permissions for passage of the cargo through the mountains. In accordance with their agreement, the next morning, Hanif arranged for trucks to leave Kabul for the village, loaded with AK-47s --- Bulgarian Kalishnikovs. The arms would be payment for the drugs; Afghan insurgents considered them superior to the AMD-65s, which the Afghan police used.

As they prepared to leave, the young man who served as Wakil's lieutenant, Farzam, tossed his representative sample of *tor* into the back of the Land Rover. He squeezed as a fourth person into the back seat and headed with their party to Kabul.

When they returned to Kabul, back in his hotel, Chance changed into casual jeans and an army green tee shirt. His room had the standard layout of an American chain hotel. With its red-orange paint in the hallways, and the arched structures over the windows, he could have convinced himself he was in Texas. Regardless of the blistering heat of the sun and the brown dust settling into a haze around him, he had a meeting to take and a place to go, so he would not have time to take the nap he needed after the long trip. Walking across the marbled lobby floor, past the polished mahogany reception desk, he set out from the Serena. He walked up the steep incline of Zargona Road, past the sizzling smells of the kabob vendors on Chicken Street, to his designated meeting place.

It was the one German beer garden in Kabul. High adobe-style walls covered by vines surrounded the entrance. Inside, hidden down the basement stairs, behind a pass-keyed door, Chance entered the private club, built specifically for NATO intelligence. The bartender acknowledged him, and he took his glass of Hefe Weisen to the dark paneled booth in the corner. A dark-complexioned man in his early thirties, with a Spanish look about him, dressed in a dark blue business suit, with a white shirt and red-patterned tie, waited. Chance sat down across the table from him.

"Everything is in place, I assume," Josh Bockenheim stated matter-of-factly. He had already ordered. A mouth-watering smell of chicken korma with vegetables and rice arrived first, before the light-green jacket of the waiter appeared. Chance waited for the waiter to set the food down and move away from the table before he spoke. When they were alone, he said, "Your supply and distribution channel are in place. It appears as secure as it is going to get, under the circumstances." He watched as Bockenheim dispassionately focused on his food, staring into his plate, and picking selectively at the colorful vegetables. "I'll watch it through the initial logistics, and finalize the security when I've seen it fully operational," Chance concluded, getting up to leave.

As he stood, Chance narrowed his eyes. His attention zeroed in on Josh's posture. He was trained to watch words, sentences, intonation, and body expression. It took all of those to communicate intent and send a message. Meanwhile, Chance took care to monitor his own body movements and facial expressions. He practiced his poker face.

Josh nodded, lifting his shoulders to indicate that he had taken on a burden. Before speaking, he picked up his glass, finishing off the last few gulps of his beer. Chance noted the perpetual smirk on Josh's face, which he felt a compelling urge to obliterate. "I believe our mutual employer will be fully satisfied," Josh said, using a napkin to wipe the beer foam from his mouth.

Chance saw more than the outer façade of a young, clean-shaven face and manicured nails. He held no respect for Josh Bockenheim. Josh Bockenheim ran a band of private mercenaries. It saddened Chance that the U.S. government believed it was forced to hire outside security. He saw the mercenaries as clowns. Politics, and an increasing need for secrecy of movement, accelerated this trend toward private contracts for military action. Too much of the reduction of the budget for the military shifted to an increased budget for commercial security services, Chance believed. It was a political environment that he dismissed as a passing fad. He expected that the pendulum would swing back, and the contractors' money would dry up, in due time. Carefully, he erased the contempt from his subconscious facial muscles. He nodded once and left. This is what it meant, to play ball. You had to work with the team the coach picked. Ever the good soldier, Chance Kiernan, ex-Delta Force, current TDU contractor, played his position exactly as ordered. When his task was completed, he left the game and went home. Home, to Copper Hollow.

Back in Copper Hollow

The gentle, rolling Blue Ridge mountains cradled this lush, green valley in every direction around. These are soothing mountains. Hills, really, compared to the Hindu Kush. Gentle country, with roads, some of which are paved, to take you from one place to the other. The mountains here are a few miles high. Maybe as high as the Salang Pass, but not as high as the villages beyond the tunnel that marks it. Here people have electricity 24 hours a day, running water, and indoor plumbing. Mostly. Most of the people have indoor plumbing.

Here, families drive cars, and live in houses that have refrigerators. Here, women walk the streets without male relatives to escort them. Here, the children all attend school. Here, parents bring their children to a community ball game. After Chance parked his Subaru pickup in the ballfield parking lot, his nine-year-old twin sons, Jeff and Timmy, hopped out, baseball gloves and caps in hand. His wife,

Ann, stepped out of the passenger seat in the front. Chance married Ann last year, two years after the boys' mother died. Although he felt he needed a stepmother for them, it seemed to have been too soon for the boys. They were not adjusting to Ann as well as Chance had hoped. He and Ann both worked on blending her into the bond he had with his boys, but his absences seemed to make the boys more resentful of her. It was not her fault, but the boys associated her presence with Chance's absences. Part of the reason he married her included the ability to leave home extensively for his work. Perhaps that was not a pure and honest motive to begin a lifelong marriage. The boys seemed to be smarter than their father, he noted. They knew he'd made an expedient, but perhaps not well-considered, choice. When he was home, Chance knew he needed to focus on the family relationships.

He thought that Copper Hollow would be a good place for his so-called "retirement." After leaving Malibu Canyon, California, Chance worried that he'd be stuck living in the suburbs of Northern Virginia. To him, Northern Virginia meant heavy traffic, crowds, lines, and shopping malls. His personal living arrangements had been a major obstacle to returning to the TDU as a consultant. "I live in paradise," he'd told Joe Bridgewell, the Army colonel who was his direct contract supervisor at the TDU. "I can't go from this garden of Eden to the suburbs of Washington, D.C."

"We understand that," Joe answered, sitting in Chance's cabin on his land in Malibu, when he came to make the proposal. Joe Bridgewell had once been Chance Kiernan's best friend. When Chance was deployed, they had worked together, drank together, and faced death together. "Everybody objects to their living arrangements after they come back from retirement. We've got a fix in for the problem. We have a town. Our own town. Hundreds of acres of forest. Few people. No traffic whatsoever. Rural. Agricultural. You don't come into the office; we bring the office to you. We'll meet you out there, in the town where you live. On the rare occasion when we need you back in D.C., we'll send a Blackhawk. You'll never have to drive; it's too far to commute. Your colleagues are already set up there. Your family can live in an old farmhouse. We've got you covered with a fake executive job at the telephone company. The place is perfect. Your wife will love it. Get her involved in the local community theater."

"Yeah," Chance answered, "Ann is not a joiner She won't be interested." The suggestion made him think about his wife, Ann. He married her because she was good-looking, even-tempered, cooperative, obliging, and a good fit for the job description of wife and mother. He met her less than a year before their wedding day. She was cheerful. He needed cheering up. Was she a "joiner?" Chance realized that maybe he did not really know. It was Kate, his first wife, the boys' mother, who was not a joiner. He needed to remember that Ann was not Kate.

It took Chance a few hours to reflect thoughtfully on Joe's comment about the town. "We have a town," Joe had said. He let the comment pass that day, but later he looked into it. He realized that Joe meant that phrase literally. Over time, the town of Copper Hollow had essentially become a TDU-CIA asset. So many retired agents lived in this town, it became hard to tell which of the town's events and activities were actually occurring. Some of the events turned out to be a spook-military exercise. However it happened, this town seemed to have become a part of the military-scenario playbook. A spook exercise could easily be carried out here. No one would know it wasn't real. For example, there was a five-star restaurant right inside the airport. It was always empty. The locals couldn't afford to patronize it. Its entire clientele consisted of visiting dignitaries, hosted by the CIA.

The town, or as the locals called it, "the Holler," had a unique population. There were the remnants of the "born-heres," who were descendants of the original eight families who had founded the town in 1934. Most of the town's residents were born-heres. There were the also the CIA-TDU agents, who rotated through, depending on their active assignments. They were known as the "come-heres." During their time in Copper Hollow, the "come-heres" generally held most positions of authority in the town, except for the town mayor, who was elected by the population. The mayor, of course, was always a Plotzky. Ray Plotzky had been the sheriff when the founding families were removed from their mountain homes. Ever since, his descendants had been elected as the town's mayors. Mayor of Copper Hollow was not a fulltime, well-paying job. The Plotzky family also ran a working farm. Outside of Copper Hollow, it would be called "organic," but the Plotzky's never called any government agency to certify it. They just farmed the old-fashioned way.

Sheriff Freel, for example, was a "come-here," but all his police officers were "born-heres." Copper Hollow was not big enough to have a full contingent of state officers. They just had their mayor. The sheriff, the judges, prosecutors, and other officials rotated through from surrounding "official" jurisdictions. Copper Hollow seemed to be a place in time separate from the norm. Not every "come-here" in town was a CIA-TDU agent. The veterinarian, for example, and the doctor-coroner. They were come-heres who just happened to move here to retire.

In general, the Born-Heres did not like the Come-Heres. They didn't socialize with them, they didn't invite them to their homes, and they mostly didn't participate in events that mixed with them. The founding patriarchs had taught their families: keep outsiders away. Although they no longer knew why this was important, since the secret of the copper mines had long died off with the last patriarch, it was a value that had been written into their hearts. The Come-Heres were relegated to their own, separate society, like a group of expatriates in a foreign land.

All things considered, Chance saw the town as a great place to live. He'd lived that military-playbook scenario for almost thirty years of his life, and it fit him. He moved his family into an old farmhouse fronting the river, and signed his kids up for public school. Living in Copper Hollow was like living on an upscale military base. In his world view, this was a very good thing.

Back at the ballpark, the cement-block concession stand, painted gray, may not have been much to look at, but its siren song of sizzling burgers and fries called seductively to the crowds of eager children. The hot and clear summer day beckoned. Its promise of an adrenaline-boosting competition among rival elementary schools loomed.

Chance noticed the local elites, parents or grandparents all, clustered together by the chain link fence, to the right of the building. Tommy Sherwood leaned against the chain-link fence in his white shoes. When he saw Chance, he raised a hand to acknowledge him, and headed his way.

"Rotary tonight?" Tommy asked.

"'fraid I'll have to pass," Chance answered. "Ann has a Board meeting; I'll be home with the boys." Any or every excuse, the way Chance saw it. He could not stand that hail-fellow-well-met crap. Besides, Tommy would know Chance's wife served on the Board of Elisa House, the organization that ran the shelter for domestic abuse cases. There really was a Board meeting tonight. Chance turned away and entered the ball park. He didn't mind letting Tommy fume over the insult.

Chance's phone rang. He pulled it out of his pocket and turned his head so no passersby could overhear. "The plane will be in tonight," the deep voice said through the receiver; then the line went dead. Chance flicked his phone shut. He needed to find Ann, to explain that he was leaving and to give her the car keys. She would take the boys home. She would be with the boys tonight, missing her Board meeting at Elisa House, on just his third night home after a month away. Chance's employer would see that a ride came by to pick him up at the ball park very soon.

Late that night, the runway lights on the small town airport guided a corporate jet to a landing. One balding man, whom everyone knew as Milton Fork, met the plane. Fork was at least sixty years old, short, with a growing beer belly. His sweater stretched around his bulging stomach. That night, Milton Fork had the sniffles. He kept sniffing and wiping his nose. He jumped at every noise, while he waited on the tarmac, turning his head nervously at every snorting buck that came out of the surrounding forest. He wore a dark green suede jacket, with brown elbow patches, over his sweater, though the night was not cold.

120

When the plane landed, Hanif Maluod, Chance's colleague on the recent trip and a CIA agent, descended the stairs, carrying one suitcase. Milton Fork ran to help him, then walked with him back to his car. He opened the door to his Audi and offered Hanif the back seat. Already sitting in the back was Josh Bockenheim. Fork got into the front seat alone, like a chauffeur. It was a short drive to the downtown main street of Copper Hollow. Fork took them to his own restaurant on Main Street, called "The Spoon 'n' Fork.' It served hamburgers, French fries, and Creasy Greens, a local favorite made from a type of garden green that also grew as a backyard weed. There was a private room in the back of the restaurant, with a door that closed. In the farthest back corner of that private room, away from the tightly closed, curtained windows, Chance Kiernan nursed a beer. That night, the balding restaurant owner, the Pakistani airport owner, the visiting businessman, and the telephone company executive, a.k.a. TDU agent, mapped out their strategies through the night.

Chapter 10
Present Day
Paris

Madeleine came home from work that night to find a sleeping Andrew on her couch. Olivier was eager to talk privately, so they went out to dinner at a nearby restaurant, La Noces de Marie. They called ahead for reservations, of course, and were fortunate to get an early spot at 7 p.m, just when the restaurant opened. All the later spots were booked, they were told. They took the metro to the restaurant from their apartment, walking in the cool night air. The streets bustled with people, coming home from work, stopping at the cafes for a Happy Hour drink after their work day. The wide boulevards were well-lighted and the metro stops crowded. Nearly as many city-style motorcycles travelled the streets as cars, as Parisians overcame the traffic and parking problems by zipping around on customized mopeds. Thirty years ago, those would have been bicycles, but technology advances.

As they arrived at the restaurant, an American couple was leaving. Olivier and Madeleine overheard their conversation. The woman said, "That whole restaurant is empty, and they refused to seat us. I can't believe how rude these French people are."

"They must not care about getting any business," the man added. "It seems like the whole city is that way. This is the third restaurant we've tried."

"And on top of that, they're snooty about it," the woman complained.

The couple passed by, continuing to whine about the rudeness of the French. Madeleine and Olivier stepped inside the restaurant, gave their names for their reservation, and were shown courteously and graciously to their seats.

After they were seated, Olivier said, "This is what I want Andrew to understand. The American couple assumed that they could walk into a fine restaurant and have dinner. They saw empty seats, and they took that to mean there was room for them. But they did not think about the cultural difference between France and America."

"Of course," Madeleine added. "In France, dinner is elegant and important. It takes a long time to have dinner with a friend, no less than two or three hours. The restaurant prides itself in its service. If they had seated the Americans now, the French assume that the seat would still be taken an hour from now, when the parties who had made reservations arrived. So the waiters will hold the table, and allow no one to take it, in order to provide good service to the customers who reserve the space. The American couple, meanwhile, complains about the waiter who is being conscientious and responsible. They see the empty table as an indication of laziness. An empty table is a loss of profit, in their eyes."

"And they do all this complaining in English," Olivier added. "Expecting the waiter to adjust to a foreign language. Then they call the waiter rude."

"You wish to show Andrew that profit is not everything, Olivier?" she asked, as she placed her hand over his, with a sparkle in her eyes.

"I hope to show Andrew that profit is almost nothing, *ma cheré*. I do not want him to rush to the answer, and fall into the trap that will inevitably present itself to him." Olivier smiled. He stroked Madeleine's face with his free hand. "After all," he said, "economics and profit are the weapons that killed Will Pruitt, and Andrew may have some adjustment in his thinking when he learns this."

"It certainly hit Ann Kiernan hard when she learned it in her job at ENRON Corporation," Madeleine agreed.

Back to a scene from 2006
Copper Hollow

On the day after her husband left for Kabul, Ann Kiernan was not at all sure she could make a life for herself in Copper Hollow. She woke to the alarm, alone in bed again, at 6:30 a.m. The queen bed filled the modest-sized bedroom in their hundred-year-old farmhouse. The house was old and charming, if you were taking magazine pictures of it. If you were living in it, however, the floorboards creaked. The radiators heated unevenly. The windows were drafty. The closets were too small and too few. The plumbing needed work. The electricity flicked in and out every week or two. And, most importantly, her husband was not home. When

Chance Kiernan was not home, all was not right with her world. The skies were darker, the stars more isolating, the bears in the forest more threatening, and the locks on the doors could not protect her. Life when she was alone in Copper Hollow loomed. Days, she could handle. But nights on this isolated country dirt road, with neighbors nowhere nearby and a wild, teeming forest, scared her to her core.

This morning, she showered and dressed quickly. Then she woke the boys. Timmy and Jeff were good boys, but they missed their mother, who had died. Since moving to Copper Hollow, they also missed their father, who travelled too frequently after taking this job with the TDU. Ann slipped two pieces of bread in the toaster and scrambled eggs for the boys while they dressed. She was a stepmother, and stepmothers had to try harder. Real mothers could throw a box of cereal on the kitchen table, or reach for a frozen waffle, but stepmothers had to cook breakfast.

"Good morning, Timmy. Good morning, Jeff," she chirped, as if she believed it. But inside, she didn't feel chirpy and happy. She turned away from them and slathered mayonnaise on Timmy's turkey sandwich, for his lunch box. Jeff would get peanut butter and jelly. He announced last night that he was a vegetarian now, because he'd met a chicken in his friend's back yard yesterday.

"Is Dad coming home this weekend?" Timmy said, with that hopeful tone, between bites of his egg.

"He said he would," Ann answered. She could only hope, just as Timmy did. Before he could ask her for a percentage of certainty on that prediction, she said, "Please eat your apple and carrot sticks today, boys. Don't bring your lunch bags home with them still inside."

Timmy gave her a look. "In the cafeteria," he said, "you can't even give those away. Do we have cupcakes?"

A real mother would put cupcakes in those lunch bags, Ann thought. Only a stepmother has to justify herself, and prove she's doing a responsible parenting job. "I'll have cookies for you when you come home from school," she told him. She reached to give him a good-bye hug before he left for the school bus, but he slipped out of her reach. Jeff was already walking out the door, not even saying good-bye. Ann felt the stab of rejection. They're only boys, she told herself, and they miss their mother. A real mother would have called after them, hollered, "Come back here and hug me." But Ann wasn't a real mother, and she didn't know that's what real mothers do.

Ann was 32 years old. She had been born and raised in Thousand Oaks, California, on Westbrook Drive. A dyed blonde, with an athletic figure, great posture, green-tinted contact lenses, and orthodontist-straightened white teeth, Ann always wore brand-label mix-and-match skirts and blouses. The sweater arms were always tied around her shoulders, indicating her membership in the tennis players' society of America. She was the magazine-perfect soccer mom. She had been introduced to her husband at a party in the Malibu beach house of her father's business partner. She was clean-cut, attractive, and gave the appearance of an idle socialite. Chance Kiernan, still grieving the loss of his wife, reached out for a stereotype of the suburban teacher-turned wife-and-mother. He had a job opening to fill, and Ann fit his job description.

Sadly, he misjudged her. Ann was not what she seemed. Ann Baxter Kiernan had earned an MBA from Pepperdine University. Right out of graduate school, she went to work for an obscure company named Enron. She was a financial analyst. Her youth and inexperience made her the perfect foil to become the spokesperson for the accounting department. Her mentors taught her the job. Taught her what was right and what was wrong. Taught her to fudge numbers and obscure balance sheets. Told her to forget her book-learning. This was how it was done in the real world, where boots were on the ground, they told her. She knew the assets were not real. She knew the rolling blackouts in California were staged. But her bosses were big shots, who had dinner dates with the President of the United States and sat in on Cabinet level meetings with Dick Cheney. They asked her to prepare talking points for those meetings, with facts and figures pulled from her notes they had given her. So who was Ann Baxter to tell them their job? She was twenty-six years old at that time, and her paycheck was in six figures. Her mom and dad were proud.

When the proverbial crap hit the wind turbine, and Enron bankrupted amidst a global scandal, Ann felt betrayed and vulnerable. For a time, there was some considerable probability that she would be charged with a crime. She had been naïve, taking orders without question, and following directions that led down nefarious paths. Her job had been to cover the tracks, and she had done it well. Until the bottom fell out. Investors lost their investment. Employees lost their retirement funds. Luckily, Ann only lost her job and her savings account.

She moved back into her parents' house to lick her wounds. Her father paid for her attorney's fees, and she escaped the scandal unscathed. Her self-confidence, however, was gone. She no longer wanted to be part of a corporate hierarchy. After a mourning period, she took some education credits and switched careers. When Chance met her, she was teaching high school math. Over time, she told him all these things, but he never seemed to grasp how really compelling this experience had been for her. He never seemed to fully understand that his wife had worked passionately, eighty hours a week, cooking the books for some dirty scoundrels. He never realized his wife had lost her dream, her illusion, and her vision of herself in her future career. It just did not appear to click in his mind. As a result, he never really noticed how vigilantly Ann remained "on the lookout" for fraud, corruption, and injustices to the little people. This was her insecurity. She worried that the world was not as it seemed, and that she could not trust her own judgment, or put her faith in the authority figures around her.

To fill her time, and give herself some purpose and meaning, Ann joined the Board of Directors at Elisa House, the domestic violence shelter in Copper Hollow. Visiting there one day, Ann Kiernan wept when she saw the bruises on the back and legs of the seven-year-old little boy, Johnny Ellingham. She sat on the gray sofa, in the middle of the common room, with Johnny in her arms, wiping her tears with the tissues from one of the many boxes of tissues placed around the room. Mavis Ellingham, Johnny's mother, stood in the kitchen, nearby, protesting, where Ann could hear her.

"I tol' 'im 'e shoulda' lissened," she whined, her voice coarse and low, as if her throat was damaged. She had thinning black hair, visibly falling out, as patches of it laid on the kitchen dish towel she'd used to wipe the blood from her split lip. Her sallow complexion and dark-circled eyes suggested this was a methamphetamine user.

"Anyhow," she said, "I'm jes' leavin' 'im here tonight, and I'll pick 'im up in the mornin'."

Roberta Bertram, the staff person in charge for the evening, spoke kindly and softly. "Mavis, you know you can't leave Johnny here unless you stay with him. We have a nice bed for you. We'll get you some ice for your lip. And there are leftovers in the refrigerator. We can heat up some meat loaf for dinner for both of you." Roberta gently stroked Mavis' upper arm, letting her know she was safe here. They'd been through this before. Mavis was a regular.

"Wull, wull, I cain't stay. Ralph said to come back home. An' I fergot ma cigarettes." Mavis' hands shook. She jumped up and down as she talked. Ralph was her boyfriend, Ralph Merkel. He was not Johnny's father.

The shelter had no sign on its front door, in a feeble attempt to hide its location from the husbands and boyfriends who were, without exception, the perpetrators of this violence. The center relied on word of mouth among the women, to lead the women to find it. Steel doors, double deadbolt locks, cement construction, and a complete absence of windows on the first floor, illustrated how serious the shelter perceived the threat to be. Backwoods boys had guns, plenty of guns, and hiding their women from them was no trivial matter.

Charlotte Trout came into the kitchen from the nurses' station, bringing some Neosporin and a bandaid for the cut over Mavis' eye. "Mavis, you're goin' to stay here tonight, with us. Ralph needs some time to hisself. We'll call up your brothers to go talk to Ralph. And there's cigarettes in the kitchen drawer." Ann Kiernan knew that Charlotte was a temporary resident here. Charlotte had been living here for more than a month. The center was helping her find a

129

job and get her own apartment, with the two grandchildren she was raising. Other "come-here" women, like Ann herself, filled the center's closets with "interview suits," which the women could wear for job hunting in towns across the mountain, an hour's drive away. The local hospital nurses, on their own time, came over to check them and treat them. The women sat with them and talked to them, comforting them, teaching them, and encouraging them, to help them find their own way. Ninety percent of the time, the women who used the services of the shelter, went back home. Ninety percent of the women who went back home, returned to the shelter for another round, wearing fresh bruises. Ann worried that the ones who didn't return might be dead. In the hollows, Ann was learning, a person could die and no one would know. Late that night, she brought up her concern to Charlotte, as they shared a glass of wine in the center's living room, after everyone else was safely in bed.

Charlotte poured a glass of chardonnay for each of them, from the two-liter bottle of what Ann would consider cooking wine, stashed under the sink. Charlotte added an ice cube to hers. Her salt-and-pepper hair was well-kept, with hair spray holding it tightly in place. She wore a tailored, light-green polyester suit and a string of imitation pearls, as if she had gone to a PTA meeting earlier, instead of spending her day in a shelter. She sat on the frayed, stuffed green chair, across the coffee table from Ann, who was looking pale and disturbed. "Dead?" Charlotte repeated, her eyebrows furrowing. "Oh, no, I doubt it," she said sincerely, leaning forward to express her concern. "Family would come looking for them if they didn't show up in a while."

"But I don't' understand why the women stay in danger-ous homes," Ann continued. "What could they be thinking?" It was outside of any behavior in Ann's experience. She came from a suburban middle-class neighborhood in Thou-sand Oaks, California. She did not know any women who would need a shelter from their home life.

"They're thinking there is no place else to go, I imagine," Charlotte answered, matter-of-factly. This was a common experience of life, in her world. "That's why we have Elisa House."

Charlotte Ellingham Trout was a woman of fifty years. She was Copper Hollow born and raised. Rufus Trout was her husband's great grandfather. Billie Ellingham was her great grandfather. The Trout family still told the story of the day the troopers burned their house down. Charlotte had three children, all grown, and all moved away, and the two grandchildren who were legally in her custody. "Their mom is in rehab," she confided. "My oldest didn't make some wise choices," she added in explanation. Proudly, she pulled pic-tures out of her wallet. They were pictures of her youngest son in his Marine Corps uniform. "He's in Afghanistan, peace-keeping," she said. Her pride beamed from ear to ear. Her face lit up with it.

Sporadically, over twenty-eight years, Charlotte's hus-band beat her. Now, she was going to leave him. Charlotte hoped to get a job working at Fine Lines department store. She was interested in "fashion." There was no Fine Lines in Copper Hollow. Copper Hollow's only clothing store was the Thrift Shop, where Charlotte bought her clothes. Char-lotte had never held a job before.

Roberta Bertram joined the women, having seen to it that each of their guests was tucked in for the night. "I've been telling Charlotte she might want to work at BoxMart first, to get the idea of a job and have some experience on her resume," Roberta said, slipping into the kitchen to pull out the bottle of cooking wine. She poured some into a water glass, and took a seat in the straight-backed chair next to Charlotte. "It can be hard to go to work every day if you've never done it."

"I don't want to be here in the same town as Jimmy," Charlotte whispered, her lips tightening to emphasize her determination. Jimmy was her husband, whom she intended to leave, but not to divorce, she told the group. "I'm going to move to Reichtersville, where my second daughter lives. But she don't have room for the kids, so I have to get my own place. They have a Fine Lines near there."

Ann felt pretty sure Charlotte's dreams would be dashed when she found out she couldn't afford her own apartment and raise two children on a part-time salary in retail. Roberta had told Ann to be very careful about bringing up any disappointing information to the women who were guests at the shelter. "If there is even a hint of information that says they won't succeed, they will dwell on that as a reason to give up and not try to overcome the obstacle," Roberta had said to her. So Ann kept quiet, and let Roberta lead the conversation.

"Charlotte, we're going to have to do something for Johnny Ellingham. He can't go back home with Mavis," Roberta said. "Do you know his Ellingham relatives?"

"He ain't no relation to me, I don't think," Charlotte answered. With that, Charlotte drank down the rest of her wine in one gulp. Her speech, which earlier had sounded nearly like American English, quickly reverted to the local dialect. "Ah'm tarred. I'll be seein' ya in the mornin'." She got up to go to bed.

"It was nice talking to you, Charlotte," Ann said, a little confused at the abrupt departure. When Charlotte was safely out of earshot, Ann turned to Roberta. "What was that about?" she asked.

"I suspect," Roberta answered, "that little Johnny is a child of incest. When that happens, the families react by declaring that branch of the family to be cut off. Suddenly, you'll find two branches of the Ellingham family, one saying it is not related to the other. Mavis' son is probably also her half-brother, or her nephew. The family would have divided over it."

"Divided, as in some of them supported the man who did it?" Ann said.

Roberta nodded.

"And the families leave the woman to deal with it alone?" Ann said that last part way too loud, and Roberta quickly raised a finger to her lips. *Shhhh.*

Ann felt a deep churning in her stomach. She could not understand this. It was beyond her context of the world, and it made her feel nauseous.

"To varying degrees," Roberta answered. "They send brothers out to deal with brothers, but if it's fathers and un-cles, they let it alone. They say 'what's in the family stays in the family,' and they tell the women not to talk."

Roberta saw the look of horror on Ann's face, and reached over to touch her arm. It was a gesture Roberta had developed as a reflex, to calm the women and offer solace with a gentle touch. "It wasn't always like this," she said quietly. "The families weakened over time. Most of the children move away after high school now, to search for jobs. The ones that stay try farming for a while, or they get involved in drugs, and have no place to go. Not all of them. I'm not saying the whole town is like this. For the most part, this town is full of wonderful, generous, and charitable people with loving families. But it's an imperfect world, and there is a significant problem. The lack of jobs encourages increased methamphetamine use. The children grow up in families that can't hold it together. They no longer resemble what we used to see in strong farming families. Some parts of the family are still strong, but branches break off and lose the land. It creates that cycle of poverty that you read about in studies."

"What can be done?" Ann asked.

"We are doing what can be done," Roberta said. "Here. We offer the women a safe place to go, where they can get help and pull their children out of the cycle. Some of our success stories come back to work here and be part of our staff. But the problem is so deeply rooted, it gets into the heads of the children. Many of the children live in violent families, where no one has a model of how to resolve conflict without hitting. They come to school, expecting to hit their classmates, like they hit their siblings at home. They don't know how to have an argument without calling names, swearing, and getting revenge. Those are the only communication tools they know."

Ann sat stunned, unable to think of the next question.

Roberta continued talking. "The Mayor helped us get a grant to send specialized teachers into the elementary schools. They bring videos of how conflict is resolved in normal families. Non-violent families. They show children playing without fighting, resolving conflicts through words. They show how fathers and mothers teach discipline without hitting. We have to start in the elementary schools, or the children don't know how to ask for help. When every person around you lives in a state of fear from a bullying parent, you, as a child, do not know this is abnormal."

Ann still sat silent. Her mind boggled.

She felt badly shaken when she left Elisa House that night. She didn't like what she was hearing. Ann shook her head, to pull out of the fog she felt after what she had seen. *Where was she? She looked around at the breathtaking mountain scenery, saw the forest teeming with life, the flowing, healing river, heard the singing birds, and smelled the fragrant wildflowers and the pine trees. She felt the crunch of the dirt road under her feet, and the wetness of morning dew. A chill traveled down her spine. How could this beauty allow such ugliness to live within it? She wondered. What happened to those families from the mountains? What force triggered this change in the family bonds? Roberta told her there were many happy families here, but an undercurrent of trouble was brewing, and Ann felt the hot water filling with potential for its boil.*

Chapter 11
Present Day
Paris

It was the next day and Andrew had caught up on his time-zone adjusted sleep. They were talking in the apartment. Madeleine had explained to Andrew the situation in which Ann Kiernan found herself, living in Copper Hollow. *Why was Will Pruitt paying Jeanine? What did Jeanine know? Who did Will Pruitt cross, which resulted in his murder?* Andrew had so many questions, and they would all be revealed. But he could not understand the answer yet.

Madeleine tried to explain. "Will Pruitt had been a Navy officer in the JAG unit before his early retirement on disability. He had been on a ship, working a case, when a kitchen fire erupted on board. In his excited heroism, he pulled a fellow seaman out of the fire, and badly burned his right arm. The arm hangs limp now, and his disfigured hand cannot hold a pen. This made his work as an attorney difficult, as he had to speak everything into a tape recorder and became highly dependent on his secretary. Ultimately, the injury and its recurrent pain forced him into early retirement.

"But after his retirement, Will received an unexpected offer. He could move to Copper Hollow and work under contract to the TDU of Homeland Security. It was easy enough to get clients as a defense attorney in Copper Hollow. There were plenty of neighborly disputes and Saturday night knife fights to defend. But for the most part, Will's clients didn't have the money to pay him. He depended on his monthly retainer from the TDU for his primary income. Will wasn't sure why the TDU paid him for defending clients in Copper Hollow, but he was a military man at heart. So he didn't ask why. He had a good deal, he liked living in the rural setting, and he could raise his family there. It didn't feel important to question the motives of his employer.

"He set himself up in an office downtown, with nice wood paneling and a lovely secretary, Jeanine Sherwood. His office was right next door to the Spoon 'n' Fork restaurant. He had plenty of clients and began enjoying his life. After a few years, when he was fully ensconced in the life, and had bought himself a nice house and a few horses, his employer told him he would be taking on a new client, Mr. Josh Bockenheim. His duties would be preventive. Make sure his client did not run afoul of the local law. Keep him from stepping on the toes of local police officers, visiting judges, or rotating prosecutors. Keep his head down, look out for his client's interest, and make sure his client's activities did not break any local laws. Operate as the attorney of record, and intervene when called. Standard stuff.

"But shortly after meeting Josh Bockenheim, Will Pruitt could smell that there was a problem. He didn't know exactly what it was, and he didn't have a security clearance to look into Bockenheim's defense contracts. But he knew there was something bad going down. As Bockenheim's defense attorney, he decided he did not want to know. He understood that it was his job to be an ostrich, and keep his head in the sand. This was a government operation, right? Will Pruitt strongly believed he did not have a need to know."

"At least, that's what happened for the first year or two," Olivier added. "Until everything collapsed."

"Will Pruitt tripped on the wire that sets up the booby trap," Madeleine continued. "Over a drink in a bar, Will threatened the security of the people in power. Like a machine, that system set about to eliminate him. Until you understand how the system works, the answer of who killed Will Pruitt will not make sense to you." Madeleine crossed her legs, sitting on the chair across from Andrew and Olivier, on the sofa. She was wearing a short red skirt, with no stockings or shoes. Her toenails were painted red. Madeleine was a woman who wore bright red colors regularly.

"The real question," Olivier inserted, "is not who killed Will Pruitt. The real question is: what was Josh Bockenheim doing in Copper Hollow? How did this small town, starting out from eight patriarchs, turn into a place overrun by government agents and defense contractors? How did many of the families' descendants lose their land and their sense of culture? Will Pruitt spent most of his time defending the local citizens for their various arrests. Pruitt knew that Chance Kiernan was running an operation there, because Pruitt was in on most of what was happening. He didn't know the details, because he didn't need to know them. Pruitt knew that Chance Kiernan's orders came from JSOC, the Joint Special Operations Command. He knew that meant he should not ask questions. Pruitt also knew that

Josh Bockenheim had some type of shady deal going on, and was also working for JSOC. He didn't know everything about it, but he knew he should look the other way if he wanted his quiet lifestyle to remain quiet."

"And that's what happened to Mitchell Davis?" Andrew asked. "Mitchell Davis, the reporter from the *Copper Hollow Mercury* who held my job five years ago. The one who disappeared. He didn't look the other way, did he?"

"No, Andrew, I'm afraid Mitchell was a nosy guy who didn't know when to keep his mouth shut. He was intent on blowing the whistle," Olivier said. "At the time, Mitchell believed he would be seen as a hero when he reported these activities of Josh Bockenheim to the mainstream news. He had a lot of faith in the system. He saw himself as an investigative reporter, like you and me. Unfortunately, Mitchell did not know what system he had stumbled onto. It was not the one he learned about in eighth grade civics class."

"The system Mitchell stumbled onto was the economic system," Madeleine added. "It is a very different animal than most people understand. Once our government turned over the ability to operate under the 'classified' shield, many business activities found themselves protected from prying eyes and regulation. This happened because the military started contracting out its activities. If Mitchell had been successful in blowing his whistle, it would have made international news. If his whistle had been heard and understood, it could have averted a serious crisis. But Mitchell's whistle was heard no farther than the corridors of power in Washington, D.C."

"And then," Olivier stated with a grim set to his jaw, "before he could set the wheels in motion that would lead to the revelation of what he found, Mitchell was gone."

"I don't understand," Andrew protested, sipping water from the glass Olivier set in front of him. "Why would it be dangerous to tell the truth? And how can a person just disappear? Isn't finding the truth and telling it the job of a journalist?"

"It was," Olivier answered. "Back in the days when information did not travel virally and reach millions of people in an instant. Fifty years ago, journalists could tell the truth, and it was not dangerous. Maybe because few people heard. Now, thanks to technology, truth can ring out and cause the Middle East to boil in anguish. It can incite riots. It can overthrow governments. It can recruit insurgents. It can influence votes. Both truth and falsehood can do this, if it is believable by the culture of people who hear it. Governments and banking systems both operate from an environment of trust, Andrew. Either truth or believable myth can interfere with that environment, and change the balance of power. This became the reason that governments began to crack down on knowledge and information."

"It was 2008 onward," Madeleine said. "Whistleblowers began to be perceived as spies, rather than as patriots. Things began to unravel in the American system of freedom. Revealing what was happening became a crime."

Andrew interrupted. "2008? When Obama was elected?"

Olivier put his glass down on the table and opened his laptop. "More like 2008, when the financial system collapsed. The crackdown on whistleblowers coincided with the realization that trust in authority is a key component of stability in the banking system. And quite honestly, Mitchell, it doesn't matter who is President of the United States, if the economic underpinnings are threatened. Money seems to have its own survival response. If it is threatened, it doesn't matter who it is that gets in its way."

"Our entire system of economics depends on the trust of all the people who pick up the hammer to pound the nail," Madeleine continued. "If they decide they will not do it, the house will not be built. Power is at the bottom of the pyramid, Andrew, not the top." She leaned in, to look directly into Andrew's eyes.

"This is what makes it critically important to keep the people at the bottom from knowing they have this power," Olivier inserted. "The man who picks up the hammer to pound the nail has the final say of whether or not the house will be built. If that man on the bottom refuses, the exploiters have no power. This refusal cannot be tolerated, and the system will rise up to remove the threat. Often, the man who refuses pays a painful price for his victory, because it becomes essential to keep the masses from knowing what they can do."

"And in Copper Hollow, who was the man on the bottom who refused?" Andrew asked.

"That would have been the Mayor, Ray Plotzky IV," Olivier explained. "He was helped by your predecessor, Mitchell Davis, the young reporter on the *Copper Hollow Mercury* who disappeared in 2008 and has never been found. And a local hardware-store owner named Joey Anhalt. Joey was the great-grandson of Joey Anhalt, the old moonshiner.

Back to a scene from 2006
Copper Hollow

Mayor Ray Plotzky IV had big plans to make life better in Copper Hollow. Ray took after his great grandfather. Pap was the sheriff in this town, back in the 1930's. Back in the beginning, when old Billie Ellingham and Joey Anhalt got this town started, folks decided the Plotzky family should be one of the eight founding families. They'd been happy about the role old Pap had played as sheriff, because he tried really hard to stand in the way of progress, when that park thing went down. So they invited him to be mayor of the new town. Ever since, Plotzky's had been mayors of Copper Hollow. It was the tradition. Ray's great grandfather had been mayor, and his father and grandfather also became mayor.

The mayor tried to see the big picture, to make things happy for all the people. All the same, for all its good points, Copper Hollow had a large population of unemployed men, and that always meant trouble, wherever it happened. In Copper Hollow, there was plenty of "heritage" type crime. Moonshine, poaching, gambling. Those were the heritage sports of a gun-totin' town. As mayor, he didn't pay much attention to those things. There were plenty of domestic violence and bar brawls to keep the local police busy. It was a town of knife fights and hunting accidents, child-support shirkers, and petty theft. But beyond that, the worst was stuff like what happened last night. Somebody shot Pete Fink's prize bull. Shot him dead in the fields. What was the point of that? Just nastiness and unneighborly.

Tradition was a big thing here. A very big thing. There was a way you do things, when everybody is kin. It ain't exactly the same as it says in the book. Unless you're talking about the Big Book, that is. The Bible was the only law the mountain men would agree to follow, they said. And the only quote they remembered from it was "an eye for an eye." In the mountains, an eye for an eye was Gospel.

What did Ray want to leave as his legacy? That was easy. He wanted to get the drugs out of here. He tried to do it, but it was like a game of Whack-a-mole. Every time he turned his head, another dealer popped up. He needed to find the leaders, not just the monkeys who took the drugs. The monkeys who took the drugs were the men, women, and children who were kin to the families of Copper Hollow. The way Ray saw it, drugs in the town were the business of the mayor, not just the police force. He knew the history here and he figured it was outsiders causing this trouble. In his experience, for every Plotzky who made good in life, there was another unfortunate Plotzky who was behind bars. Drugs. It was drugs that did that to Copper Hollow, and locking up the losers didn't stop the war. It could only be outsiders who brought those drugs in. Ray knew every single person who belonged in Copper Hollow, every kinfolk of all the eight families. It couldn't be any of them; he'd know if it were. It had to be an outsider. If Mayor Ray Plotzky was going to improve life in the Holler, he figured, he was going to fight drugs, and keep out the outsiders. He was a man who took things on in a big way.

While Mayor Ray Plotzky had no trouble excusing the local boys for most of their transgressions, he had a big problem with outsiders coming into this town. Outsiders, who didn't grow up here, didn't graduate from the local high school, and didn't take part in this community – well, they were the real threat. When outsiders brought drugs in here, where local teenagers would buy it – that was where Ray Plotzky drew the line. Bringing drugs into Copper Hollow, selling it to the teenagers? That was a travesty Mayor Plotzky would pounce on, and he wasn't shy about calling in the law.

Plotzky was ambitious. He'd done a good job of getting state and federal grants in to the town, and to get solid training for everybody on his team. He had his eye on bigger things, in the future, and part of that goal included getting to know his Congressmen. He hoped to build a career beyond the borders of this town someday, maybe as a consultant or in politics beyond Copper Hollow. His experience told him having friends in the Republican party was his ticket to that dream. He'd already proven his worth in that area by the big grants he got for Copper Hollow. Ray hadn't married yet, so he had plenty of time to work for the good of the people. Mayor was an elected office, and Ray always won the popular vote with more than eighty percent. The reason was simple. Everybody in town knew Ray Plotzky cared. Cared about them like family, which many of them were, and cared about the town.

When Ann Kiernan called to tell Ray Plotzky about her experience at Elisa House with Mavis Ellingham, Mayor Plotzky was outraged. Of course he would intervene to help Johnny. Absolutely he would talk to the sheriff and see that Ralph was arrested. Mrs. Kiernan could rest assured that Mayor Plotzky was on the task. He would stick to this task like stink on shit, and he would solve it. Yes, sirree, that was Ray Plotzky's way. When he set his mind on something, he followed through. Mrs. Kiernan could leave it in his hands, and set her mind at ease.

Mayor Plotzky knew Mavis Ellingham and her family real well. It broke his heart to see her and Johnny that way. He took a trip out to talk to Ralph, but he knew Mavis would refuse to press charges, and he knew the rest of the family would show up at his office hollering if the state took Johnny away. So he talked to the rest of the family and they promised to move Johnny into a cousin's house for a while. Mavis and Ralph would work it out. All he could do, he told Ann Kiernan, is keep pressing on this methamphetamine problem. He had to find out who was selling it to the people of Copper Hollow. "It's the drugs that are messing up the families," Mayor Ray told Mrs. Kiernan. "Families are real strong here."

Following through on his promise, Ray thought he was onto a lead, about this meth selling in Copper Hollow. He'd discussed it with Tommy Sherwood, the local Republican Party chair. Whenever there was a business problem, Ray asked Tommy's opinion. There was a new guy in town, Josh Bockenheim. Bockenheim had been hanging out with Hanif, the airport owner, and Milton Fork, the owner of the Spoon 'n' Fork restaurant. A lot of planes flying in and out. Ray planned to stake out the airport and start watching what was going on over there. He sure would like to catch somebody in the act of bringing in these drugs. He told Tommy about his plan, and what he was looking for. Tommy didn't think Josh Bockenheim had anything to do with drugs. "He has a corporate jet," Tommy said, "and he parks it at the airport."

Ray thanked Tommy for his opinion. Ray thought Tommy was not the sharpest knife in the drawer, but it didn't hurt to ask his opinion. The more you asked people's opinions, the better they liked you, Ray believed. Besides, to hear Tommy tell it, Tommy was well connected up the line in politics. Ray expected that politics might be his own future some day, so he thought he should stay on the good side of Tommy Sherwood.

Ray Plotzky really wanted to get some help with this drug problem. He set up a web page showing what happens to a person who takes methamphetamine or heroin. He showed the women with their sallow complexions, their bad teeth, and their thinning hair. He posted videos showing a healthy young woman, deteriorating year by year until she became an ugly hag, sick from meth. He submitted grant proposals, trying to get state and federal help for Copper Hollow, to fight drugs. He made appointments with his state congressional representatives. He wrote to his state senators. He invited the Drug Enforcement Agency to give talks at the city hall, so people could recognize drug users and drug activity. He raised so much fuss, that he started getting a high profile in political circles. "That Ray Plotzky. Good fellow. Maybe he's destined for higher office," people said. "Oh," they mentioned at cocktail parties. "Copper Hollow. Isn't that where Ray Plotzky's from? Isn't that the place that has the drug problem?" He was building a name for himself, that's for sure. Trouble was, the way people are, Ray was building a name for Copper Hollow, too. Ray tried to explain all his efforts to get drugs out of Copper Hollow, and all it did was leave an impression in people's minds: Copper Hollow is where drugs come from. True or not, it was becoming a "brand."

146

Wherever he could pop up in state politics, Ray tried to get involved. Being a local boy who made good, Ray thought it would be a good thing if he brought down this drug ring. He thought it would give him a good name in politics, in addition to being the right thing to do. Ray thought everybody wanted to solve this problem, and he'd be well on his way to success if he could get a handle on it. So he brought the Deputy Sheriff, Charlie Wenzel, to the spot on the hill behind the county airport where the planes could be seen but the patrol car could not. He showed the officer where to point the binoculars. "It looks weird to me, Charlie."

Charlie agreed. "It's been suspicious out here a long time," he said. "Since that federal grant came through to expand the airport, I've wondered what was going on."

Plotzky got out of the car and looked out over the land. "First, the airport gets a grant for the money to expand it. Then they get another grant to put an eight-foot chain link fence around it. Then they come up with money to put two dozen closed hangars all around. What' they need that for? We ain't got nine people in this Holler who have airplanes."

Charlie handed the binoculars back to the mayor. "Milton Fork is down there loading boxes onto a twin engine plane. Somebody need an emergency shipment of the delightful dining at The Spoon 'n' Fork? Is this a Takeout Emergency? Maybe Fork got hisself listed on Takeout Airplane Taxi," Charlie joked.

"I've been making a note of who goes in and out from this place," Ray told him. "I want you and Darrell to take shifts to keep the log. Somethin's weird here, and we ought to know what." As he continued nosing around into the business of Josh Bockenheim, Ray Plotzky didn't know that rumblings in the halls of Congress were bringing his little campaign to many ears. Ray assumed that all government officials wanted to rid the world of drugs. Naturally. Who wouldn't assume that? So as he railed and churned and beat on drums about his desire to rid his little piece of the world of the demon drug lord, Ray Plotzky never figured out that he needed to be watching his six.

Three weeks later, Ann Kiernan stood at her mailbox at the end of her quarter-mile driveway and read the formal letter she received from Elisa House. The Board asked her to resign. They cited "breaking confidentiality." In a letter. Without a phone call to explain. Her first thought was to talk about this with her husband, but Chance wasn't home. He was in Afghanistan again. Chance was never home, and she was here, raising his two boys, in a place so weird and freaky, she didn't know what to do with herself. This was certainly not California.

Ann had skills, training, and intelligence. Her stepsons were in fifth grade. They didn't need much mothering. She wanted to do something good in Copper Hollow, and she thought Elisa House would be her mission. Being thrown off the Board unbalanced her. She felt strongly that she had to correct the misunderstanding. She thought she was making friends with the women on the Board at Elisa House. *Why would they do this to her? What did she do that was so wrong? Yes, she knew they did not want her to call Mayor Plotzky. But, good grief! He was the person who cared enough to take an action. Didn't they all have a responsibility to little Johnny?* With Chance away so often, and all her friends back in California, Ann was having a very hard time adjusting to her life in Copper Hollow. She felt isolated.

She'd met Jeanine Sherwood, who worked in Will Pruitt's office. Jeanine confided that finding a man to take care of her was her life's goal. This was not Ann's concept of womanhood. She couldn't relate to Jeanine.

She'd met Charlotte Trout, at Elisa House, desperately deluding herself that she'd be able to support her grand-children when she'd never worked before. She had tolerated years of abuse by her husband. Ann couldn't understand why a woman would do that.

She'd met Mavis Ellingham, of course. Wow. A total meth head. Users of crystal meth become agitated, break out in rashes, lose their teeth, lose weight, and get deeply hollow eyes. Ann wanted to help Mavis and her little boy, but she surely didn't want to be friends with Mavis.

She'd met Sherry Sherwood, of the low-cut dresses and the jingly jewelry, and the "girl-talk." Jeanine's mother. Charlotte's sister. Tommy's wife. Sherry, too, was a woman who defined herself by the status of her man. This upset Ann, and made her turn away.

Ann was looking for a woman like herself to be her friend, someone who set her own standards and defined her own value system. Ann didn't mind that Chance was gone all the time. Not really. That was his life. She had her own life. She didn't need to cling to his life, and she had no in-tention of defining herself by what he did or who he was. But she really wanted to have a friend, at least one friend, here in Copper Hollow, so she wouldn't feel so alone.

She'd met Roberta Bertram, who ran Elisa House. Of her choices, Roberta was her only hope for a friend around here. And now Roberta threw her off the Board. Ann planned to go into town, which was a twenty minute drive from their remote farmhouse, to have lunch at the Spoon 'n' Fork restaurant. She hoped Roberta would join her there so they could talk this out. Whoever heard of someone being asked to resign from a volunteer board? But she waited in the Spoon 'n' Fork, and Roberta never showed up. She ordered her lunch, to eat alone. This would take some thinking. *If Roberta wouldn't even talk to her, what could she do?*

While she was waiting and thinking, Ann picked up a copy of the *Copper Hollow Mercury*. She noticed that the best articles seemed to be written by a reporter named Mitchell Davis. She remembered that she had met Mitchell once. A young man, barely out of college. He had come by Elisa House, wanting to interview the staff. He wrote a nice article about the fundraiser for the shelter. Maybe, she thought, she should have a talk with Mitchell Davis. After all, where she came from, if there was an issue of public interest, you talked to the newspapers. Ann decided she should find Mitchell Davis and have a talk with him. Why not? She headed to the office of the *Copper Hollow Mercury*. What could it hurt?

Mitchell Davis had nothing important to do the day Ann Kiernan came to see him about Elisa House. *Like everyday, he thought.* He had no reason not to spend the afternoon hearing her thoughts about problems in Copper Hollow. But after he heard her stories, Mitchell felt overwhelmed. Who to talk to? His boss? He didn't think that Mr. Reese Babbitt would print anything this controversial, and he knew Elisa House did not want any information about them to be published. The manager at Elisa House told him that any story about them at all would be twisted around in the heads of the men. Whatever he said would result in revenge against the women. The men would see themselves in the article, even if it wasn't about them. So he couldn't write about it. He explained all that to Mrs. Kiernan. It seemed that she was about to cry.

Meanwhile, Joey Anhalt IV was becoming a thorn in the side of Will Pruitt. He was an itch that needed to be scratched, and he kept irritating the defense attorney. Joey Anhalt IV lived in Copper Hollow his whole life. His great-grand-daddy was Old Joey Anhalt, the mountain man. When the patriarch Joey and his family got kicked off the mountain, it was Old Joey who found the copper mine. He got first pick of the land, after that, but Joey's family grew fast. They had more relatives than they could fit on the land, so over time, he and his sons figured out a new business. They learned to run the supplies store. Hardware and supplies is what Joey IV knew, and it had made him reasonably well-off. He wasn't greatly educated, but he had a high school diploma, and he knew what he knew. He owned fifty acres outright. He was a man who never believed in debt, didn't use credit cards, and had no use for e-mail or the Internet. He sold hardware. That's what he did. From this skill, he made a living for his family. Joey had been 52 years old when he met Molly Willett. Molly was one of those pretty little things, young and flirty. She flirted with Joey when he came in to pay his bill at the insurance office where she worked as a receptionist. Joey was a man who was not perfect, and Molly was a buxom dyed-blonde. Stuff happened. A little while after the stuff happened, Molly told Joey they were having a baby. It was his son, she said. She wanted to move into his big farmhouse and quit her job. Joey married her. It was a big mistake for both of them. Shortly after the baby was born, Molly left Joey, went to beauty school with the money he gave her, and got a new job as a hairdresser. She had an apartment in a small town about an hour away from Copper Hollow, and she kept their son with her.

Nobody would call Joey a perfect man – he was a fighting man, for some reason, or no reason. He ended up in the Copper Hollow courthouse every couple of years or so. This meant he was always in need of a defense attorney. Joey was a high-maintenance client. He had a lot to say. He hammered away at each of his points, until the jury believed nobody could make up a story so emphatic and detailed. This made Joey an annoyance to Copper Hollow's rotating prosecutors. Prosecutors tended to believe Joey was guilty, maybe because he was feisty and aggressive. This meant Will always had an uphill battle when he defended Joey. He could never make a deal with the prosecutor. And yet, Joey was never convicted. Juries, Will believed, were an unpredictable element of surprise in any trial, and Copper Hollow juries continually surprised him. Joey Anhalt was a descendant of one of the founding fathers of Copper Hollow. Will realized that meant he was a pillar of the community, and could do no wrong. Who would convict Joey? By the time four generations had passed, everybody, one way or another, was some kind of relative to Joey Anhalt.

His wife left him. Joey got over it, and he learned to live on his ranch alone. He hired help, and sadly, some of his help appeared unsavory and undesirable. But that wasn't Joey's fault. He made do with what was available. He gave his workers drug tests. If they passed, they worked. If they didn't, he chased them off. Even so, some days he skipped the tests because he needed the work hands. This is how Joey ran across Josh Bockenheim's operation. His employees made him suspicious that somebody was drug dealing in Copper Hollow. Joey dug around in dirt, as a regular practice. He made a habit of filling buckets full of dirt, adding water, and slinging mud. It was his normal way. Joey Anhalt, like his ancestors before him, liked to know everything about what was happening around him, and he ferreted out all the details. But Joey didn't need proof, the way Will Pruitt needed proof for a judge and a jury. Joey Anhalt had the luxury of flying off the handle and shooting from the hip, with no proof whatsoever. Joey used those tools regularly, and it was getting Josh Bockenheim mightily annoyed. This is what made Joey Anhalt a constant irritation to Will Pruitt.

Joey said that Josh Bockenheim was bringing drugs into Copper Hollow. No proof, of course. Just Joey sayin' it. Yeah, sure, Bockenheim could sue Joey for slander. But then Joey could bring his "proof" into court. Wouldn't that be a pickle? Now, Joey's claims and his threats to expose Josh Bockenheim's little operation threatened to blow up Will Pruitt's entire world. Will's job was to keep the police away from Bockenheim's organization. These allegations were nothing, Will knew, but they served to stir up the law, and eventually, they might turn into something. Will was sure he could handle it, as long as he remained in the loop for what Bockenheim did. But things just kept getting more and more complicated. Bockenheim did things in very strange ways. Will could suspect, but he didn't know, what Bockenheim was doing. He understood that he should know more; it wasn't right for him to be in the dark about what was going on.

One day, Will asked Bockenheim outright. "Are you running drugs?" he asked.

"No," Bockenheim answered.

But then Will looked himself in the mirror and thought, *If he were, would he say yes?*

"So what are you doing, Josh?" Will asked. And Josh said, "It's classified."

Yet, people who nosed around were coming to the conclusion that the drugs in Copper Hollow came from Josh Bockenheim, somehow, someway. It made Will feel unsettled. Nosing around was a dangerous activity, where classified defense contracts were concerned. Will did not need Joey Anhalt getting in his way and throwing another wrench into this delicately balanced machinery.

Present Day

Paris

"So you see, Andrew," Madeleine told him, "people can be dangerous even when the information they are spreading is not quite true, or is only a small piece of the puzzle. If you give a single puzzle piece to someone who already has five other pieces, they may be able to see a picture you did not even know existed. Or perhaps, they will see something that is not really there. Joey Anhalt was asking questions about Josh Bockenheim because Joey Anhalt is a nosy guy. Just like Mitchell Davis. Just like Ray Plotzky. All these people were nosing around in Josh Bockenheim's business. They were making observations, and maybe those observations weren't quite true."

"You mean observations like the two bullet wounds the paramedics saw?" Andrew asked.

"Right.   Observations that didn't have all the informa-tion in them. On top of that, what Joey did not know is that Will Pruitt was becoming very worried about his own posi-tion. Will needed to ensure that he could keep covering up whatever it was that Josh Bockenheim was doing in Copper Hollow. Every person sees the world through the filter of their own background and experience," Madeleine ex-plained. "People are taught their set of values within their culture, and after that they think of it as Right and Wrong. Will worried that whatever was going on, he could be the person who got caught in the middle. He worried that he may lose his job, or even go to jail."

"When, actually," Olivier added, "a lot of things are not Right or Wrong.   They are True or False. Copper Hollow was a place full of rumor and innuendo. Bockenheim said he wasn't running drugs. But people saw drugs running. If it wasn't Bockenheim, who was it? Everybody knew everybody else, so when something new started to happen, people looked around and saw a sea of their cousins and in-laws. Then they saw the outsider, Josh Bockenheim. Nothing was hidden in Copper Hollow, yet nothing appeared to be black and white. This is a principle that Chance Kiernan under-stood well. He was a man who saw everything in shades of gray. Even the whitest of clouds."

Chapter 12

2006

Copper Hollow

When Chance finally came home again, Ann told her husband everything that had happened. She explained what she learned from her neighbors about the history of the mountain people. She told him about Elisa House, about Roberta standing her up at the restaurant, about being thrown off the Board. But he was distracted, thinking about his mission in war-torn Afghanistan. He didn't hear her. As Ann continued to describe what was happening to her, Chance's mind drifted back to a time when he had been in the mountains. Memories of the people he knew in those days forced themselves into his mind. He could not hear Ann, because he could not stop hearing those other mountain people. The more she said the words "mountain people," the more the memories invaded.

It was 1997. Chance Kiernan was active duty Delta Force. General Dostum, the warlord from the northern part of Afghanistan, had asked for help. Although it wasn't official that the U.S. was working with him, Delta sent a team. Delta was the part of the Army that did the things that had no stamps of approval from Washington's politics on them.

By this time, the Soviet Union had been defeated in Afghanistan. The Taliban had taken control of most of the country. The Taliban were so crazy, they were beating and beheading civilians, normal people in the streets. At least, as normal as Afghans get, with their silly trucks painted like carnival wagons, hanging jingle bells on the side. Taliban are mostly Pashtuns, who somehow got to be crazy religious fanatics, and wanted to force everybody to be as crazy as they are.

General Dostum was an ethnic Uzbek, warlord of the northern Balkh province. At that particular time, he had joined up with Ahmed Shah Massoud. Massoud was the Lion of Panjshir. He was the ethnic Tajik warlord from the neighboring province. Together they formed the Northern Alliance, bent on getting control of Kabul, defeating the Taliban. They'd asked the CIA for help. Washington DC hadn't decided yet if it backed the Taliban or the Northern Alliance, so the U.S. was sending all its aid money to Pakistan, and letting the Paks make the decisions. The Paks, coincidentally, happened to pretty much be the Taliban, but that distinction hadn't registered in Washington. Officially, Delta Force was investigating, not helping or fighting. They had a field outpost set up near Mazar-e-sharif, but it was hush-hush.

Uzbeks and Tajiks are the ethnic cultures in Northern Afghanistan. Their families spread into Uzbekistan and Tajikistan, which were new countries formed with the breakup of the Soviet Union. The Soviets fought in Afghanistan from 1977 to 1989. Their defeat was one of the triggers that broke up the empire. Think about it. If you were an ethnic Uzbek, living in the Soviet Union, and you were told to go fight in

Afghanistan, against your ragtag, illiterate cousins who lived on the other side of the mountain, would you see much point to buying into the Soviet spiel? So shortly after the defeat in Afghanistan, Uzbekistan and Tajikistan opted out of the Union.

Anyhow, the Uzbeks and the Tajiks in the north didn't really see how they were part of Afghanistan, either. They called the Pashtuns, who were pretty much basic Pakistanis, the Afghanis. It was the Pashtuns who made up the core brotherhood of the Taliban. The Taliban said they were enforcing Sharia law, which was the law of Islam, but Sharia wasn't crazy like the Taliban were crazy. The law they were enforcing was more like Pashtunwali than Sharia. It was Nuts Mountain law, not Islam.

Regardless of all that, Washington hadn't made up its mind whether they believed the Taliban was going to be the new government of Afghanistan, so there couldn't be any official assistance to Dostum and Massoud. Whenever there was something Washington didn't want to admit, and the CIA couldn't handle, Delta stepped in. My team consisted of Joe Bridgewell, Pete Rutherford, and Doc Riley. We didn't abide much by rules, in Delta. Uniforms and rank were only for official military business. We were so unofficial, nobody would admit we exist. Anyhow, on this day, Dostum wanted to enter a village that was locked between two steep hills, in close proximity. He said the elders asked him to come in and route the Taliban, who had entered their village. We only found out later that Dostum was a psycho, so at this point, we were going with him on his little excursion. Our intention was to hang back, let his troops do their thing, and only take action if he got in too deep. Besides, we wanted to see the engagement firsthand, for the intel value.

Dostum believed he had the element of surprise on his side, and he took his troops in on foot, with only a supply convoy in the rear. We had our Humvee. I had my .50 caliber sniper rifle. The other guys used Heckler and Koch submachines. We hung back, but not too far back, because we wanted to see the action. It wasn't our war. Apparently, Dostum had either misunderstood the request from the village elders, or purposely misled us and his men. The village had welcomed the Taliban into their homes. His plans had been leaked, and his men walked into a death trap. As we turned our Humvee around, we were met from behind. About thirty Taliban in long beards, helmets, and flak vests, carrying AK47s, approached us. The narrow road and steep hillsides pinned us in. There was no way out.

Joe got on the radio and called for a Bird to extract us, and some Willie Peter, white phosphorus, to create smoke for cover. Before the Bird arrived, an RPG fired from above us on the hills. It landed on the hood of our ride and blew up the engine and windshield. All four of us rolled out and into the ditches. When you're lying in a trench, bullets cracking five feet over your head, you lose your connection to the bigger picture. You know if you hear the crack, it's too high to hit you, but if it's slowing down and losing power it makes a low buzzing sound. That's when you're in danger. Your humanity melds with your weapon. You and the .50 caliber are One.

Firing gives you something to do, instead of quivering in fear. I kept firing. It could have been ten seconds, but more likely it was an eternity. I fired for the eternity it took for the air cover to arrive. Then I crawled through the smoke to a hole under an outcropping in the rock wall. By the time Dostum got a reinforcement convoy in, only two of our team still counted among the living. I carried out Doc's body. Joe car-

ried Pete. As we carried out the bodies of our friends, the local villagers smirked and laughed. It was the last time I would agree to work with Dostum.

After that, I left Delta and took a place with the Defense Intelligence Agency.

Then there was the incident. When Kate died. Kate was murdered. Kate's body, her beautiful body, lying there on the living room floor, blood spreading through the Turkish carpet she had selected so carefully, in our suburban Los Angeles home. It was daytime, sometime between noon and three in the afternoon. She had been wearing sweatpants and her running shoes, ready to go out, with the headband around her shiny brown hair. Someone rang the doorbell, the police thought, and blasted her as soon as she opened the door. It was only luck that the house cleaning service showed up and found her before the boys came home from school.

Ann's voice broke through Chance's reverie. He remembered Kate was not here. He was in his living room in Copper Hollow, with Ann. He shook his head to clear the memory. It was not good for him to think of it. There was no more Kate. Ann was his wife now. Ann was pretty. She had strawberry blonde hair, with soft curls. Her skin was ivory-white, with a few freckles. She had a California-girl smile. But she hadn't smiled lately. He didn't share her outrage at the plight of some illiterate mountain families, back in the 1930's. He didn't care about town politics, or Roberta Bertram, or the lives of drug-addicted mothers. All the same, he took her in his arms and told her she was right and he agreed. It was the best way to calm her and make her smile.

"You're such a good cook, honey," he whispered, taking her in his arms and brushing the hair from her face. "That was a fabulous stew you made tonight. Whenever I'm away, all I think about is coming home to you. Let's get the boys to bed, open a bottle of wine, and stream a movie on the big-screen. I'll build a fire in the fireplace, and you can tell me all the things that worry you. Tomorrow we'll all go for a hike in the forest. You can show me where all these things happened seventy years ago."

As usual, his attention mollified her. She felt safe again. He did it every time.

Chance stayed home for weeks after that, and Ann calmed down. Although he came home every night, he still went out during the day, to "work" at the backroom in The Spoon 'n' Fork with other colleagues in the town. Ann knew there was an amazing communications setup in that room, from the one time he'd taken her to show her where he worked. Sometimes, she knew he was picked up by a helicopter and taken to Washington, D.C. As long as he came home at night, Ann felt comforted. She could deal with Copper Hollow, as long as Chance was home.

As much as she loved being with Chance, she could not talk to him about her fears and worries. She could see that he found weakness unattractive, so she hid her worry behind smiles. The fake smiles appeared to completely fool Chance Kiernan. But Timmy and Jeff Kiernan saw right through them. While she was anxious, they were anxious, and so they pulled farther and farther away from her.

Back to Present Day
Paris

It was at this point in 2006 that Olivier and Madeleine first became involved with Ann's problems. Because she felt isolated in Copper Hollow, Ann reached out to her friend, Madeleine Fontaine, whom she'd met in graduate school at Pepperdine.

"This was how we first came to know about these events in Copper Hollow, Andrew," Madeleine told him.

Flashback to 2006

On Skype, from Copper Hollow to Paris, when Madeleine and Olivier first got involved with Ann's dilemma

Ann and Madeleine talked through the video communications network on their computers, Skype. Evening in Paris was mid-afternoon in Copper Hollow, so Ann developed a routine of calling Madeleine before the boys returned from school. Madeleine was a great listener and sympathizer. Ann told her all the details. Of her marriage, her experiences at Elisa House, her lack of friends, her concerns about Copper Hollow itself. Now and then, Madeleine's boyfriend, Olivier Beauchemin, leaned over her shoulder and listened in.

As Olivier tended to do, he jotted down a few notes and key words from Ann's stories. "When did this happen?" he asked Madeleine. "The removal of the families from the mountain, I mean."

Madeleine looked at her video screen. "Olivier wants to know when the families were removed from the mountain," she asked the video-face of Ann.

"It was Franklin Roosevelt," Ann answered, "so I'd guess the early 1930's. It was the Depression."

"Ahh," Olivier said, leaning over Madeleine so he could talk to Ann directly. "Then the families no longer had food, because they lost their land, and they had to get jobs. But it was the Depression, so there were no jobs."

"Yes," Ann answered, "the families were devastated."

"Now it's four generations later, and the same families live in poverty and suffer from excessive family violence. Is that what you are seeing?" He stood behind Madeleine and leaned in, so that Ann could see both of them on her computer screen.

"Yes, the children have poor diets, they speak a dialect of English that can hardly be understood, and domestic violence seems to be the norm, in too many families."

"Why does that surprise you?" Olivier responded.

Ann looked confused. Olivier had always made her uncomfortable. He seemed brusque and insensitive, calling all the spades black with no thought to the feelings of his audience.

"What other result could occur when you take an isolated society, living separately from the resources of a city, and you emasculate their father figures?" Olivier continued. "Did you imagine that the families would remain happy, when their fathers could no longer bring home a deer from the woods for their dinner?"

Ann hadn't thought of it in terms of the emotional life of the fathers. She sat quiet for a moment and then said, "Honestly, I would have thought they would move to the cities, if there was no work here. I thought four generations later, all those people would have moved away."

Olivier slapped the palm of his hand on the computer desk. "And there it is," he muttered, *Voila!* He walked away from Skype and returned to his own computer.

Madeleine rolled her eyes and took the full computer screen of Skype back. "Olivier meant to say that poor people with no money and no experience outside their culture would never think of that solution. The men would be uncomfortable and feel inadequate anywhere away from their homes. Their mountain culture would be all they knew; they wouldn't be successful if they left and moved to the city. They would feel humiliated, as men, so they would have felt unable to leave. They wouldn't want their women to see that, so they would pressure everyone to stay in place."

"Well, that's apparently what happened," Ann said. "There are only about two dozen last names in the local phone book. Pages and pages of people with the same last name." Her voice developed an edge as she talked about it.

Madeleine recognized that Ann was becoming distressed again, so she switched to small talk, and in a few minutes hung up. She saw Olivier googling on his Mac-Book.

"It was the communications network," Olivier muttered.

"What?" Madeleine asked.

"The reason Roosevelt threw the families off the mountain," he said. "He was building that communications network, to use in the coming war. He threw them off the mountain so word would not get out about it."

"Oh. Okay, well . . ," Madeleine hated to encourage Olivier when he started in on a conspiracy theory. She usually just let him rant without adding any questions that would fuel his enthusiasm.

"Where did Ann say her husband went, on these long trips?" Olivier pressed for more information.

"I think she said he goes to Afghanistan," Madeleine answered. She decided to go to bed, before he got too excited about whatever his new theory would turn out to be. When she left, Olivier was still searching the Internet. He had the look of a hunter, closing in on his prey. At 2 a.m., Olivier bounced onto the bed and woke Madeleine.

"I figured it out," he announced. He had the look of a puppy, bringing his mistress the stick she threw out for him. She patted his head and rolled over to go back to sleep. She loved him.

Return to Present Day
Paris

Over the next weeks, Olivier and Andrew worked together to check their facts about the situation in Copper Hollow, and all its ramifications. They researched the people, the histories, and the actions that were taken. They reported carefully. One thing that bothered Andrew was the role of Josh Bockenheim. Madeleine helped him understand.

"What did Joey Anhalt find out, and what was Ray Plotzky looking into?"

"They were both looking around at the drug problem in Copper Hollow. They suspected that Josh Bockenheim was running drugs, but they couldn't prove it," Andrew answered.

"Bockenheim's operation was classified. Nobody knew what he was doing. It was shielded from the prying eyes of journalists. So the question became, what was happening? If the drugs were there, and everyone pretty much agreed they were, who was doing it? Copper Hollow was a small place, where everybody knew everybody else's business and activities. Who else could have been doing it but Josh Bockenheim? And then, the only conclusion was either Josh Bockenheim was doing it on his own, or it was a sanctioned operation of the United States government, Andrew," Olivier stated.

There was a dead silence. After a while, Andrew said, "So you are saying we can only *hope* it was Josh Bockenheim who was running drugs, all on his own, in Copper Hollow?"

Madeleine nodded. "Bockenheim had a company which had classified defense contracts. Nobody could ask or investigate what he was doing."

Andrew bit his lip. He was thinking about the concept. Classified information from the United States government. So you couldn't ask questions, and you couldn't report. He looked at Olivier, carefully documenting each thing that happened in Copper Hollow, that they knew about. A convincing argument that something was wrong. But when it got to the actions of Bockenheim's company, a wall of redacted documents, shielded by the corporate veil and the classified lockbox. *If Josh Bockenheim was not a bad guy, Andrew realized, he was following orders. Orders to do what?*

Chapter 13
2006
Kabul, Afghanistan

"My navel chord was tied to the apron strings of custom."
-- Afghan poet

After the American named Kiernan and the Pakistani, Hanif, left him in Kabul, Farzam found the house of his mother's cousin, Mosen. Arriving unannounced was polite, in his family. To send word ahead implied that you expected the family to provide you with dinner. Because of his politeness, Farzam was welcomed and offered a place to sleep on a roll of carpet on the living room floor. As part of the ritual of hospitality, his cousins urged him to eat with them, but he insisted that he had already eaten, because he knew the food was limited and valuable for them. He offered to sit with them and talk, but carefully ate only a polite handful, with much exclamation about how the food was wonderful, but sadly he had already eaten. He had money, and was able to purchase his dinner from the street vendors in Kabul.

Wakil, his grandfather, and the leader of his village, had entrusted him with the mission to ensure that the weapons they needed would come in, and the tor they sold would go out, without incident. It had been determined, by a *Jirga*, a tribal council, within his tribe, that he would have this task to find the right trading partner, and he was proud to serve his people. More importantly, Farzam had been entrusted with a secret task. In addition to their tor, the tribe had found emeralds in their mountains. It was Farzam's duty to find a way to market them. To do this, he needed to re-establish their relationships with the mosque in Kabul, so he could make contacts to help him find the traders. The deal which the American and the Pakistani offered sounded good, but the tribe wished to know what other deals might be made, so that they could make a responsible decision. Farzam knew that relationships were everything, in a contract. Words on paper meant nothing, if the man behind the words did not have the right relationship with his partners. Farzam knew this from his uncle, and many times, he had heard stories of how his father died.

But Farzam had heard many things, and one of the things he wanted to know about was the Taliban. This he would learn, through the contacts he expected to make while in the mosque. Learning was an important thing and he wanted to know. He wondered if the American who had brought him here could be trusted; when the American returned, he planned to test the trust. Meanwhile, he would hang around at the mosque, and with his cousins' friends, to learn from his elders.

Kabul City bore little resemblance to the thriving cosmopolitan mecca of free thinking that once attracted the hippie crowd in the 1960's. Then, it was a hub of intellectual discussion, romantic poetry, and shared philosophy, with the stimulating assistance of an unending supply of hashish and a hookah pipe. In those days, Afghan women attended Kabul University while wearing mini-skirts. The drug trade contributed mightily to the local economy, but it did not dominate it. In those days, Afghanistan only provided 20% of the world's heroin. But times changed. Afghanistan's share of the opium market expanded dramatically. Now, since the Americans came, they provided nearly 80% of the world's heroin. And the number was climbing.

Farzam was headed to the mosque that his cousins recommended for him. He had not walked far from his cousins' house, when he heard the shouting and commotion in the street. People screaming. Machine gun fire. He saw a Humvee . . . no, two Humvees, three Humvees . . . and he saw men in United States military uniforms. They were firing machine guns into the crowd of Afghan civilians on the street. Women, children, men, falling as the convoy drove. Blood, and blood-curdling screams. It was six years after the Americans arrived in Afghanistan, five years after the Karzai government was installed, long past the defeat of the Taliban and suppression of the insurgency, long past the assassination of the Lion of Panjshir, Ahmed Shah Massoud. And crazed hollow-eyed killers, in American uniforms with blasting machine guns, were heading his way. Farzam turned back from the street and ran as fast as he could. He ran, ran, ran back to his cousins' house. He slammed the door of the house behind him and struggled to breathe, trying to calm his racing heart. How could he trust the American with his village secret now? He worried.

It was a suicide bomber, Farzam's cousins told him, when he calmed down enough to describe his experience.

The suicide bomber attacked the American Marines, and the Marines reacted by blowing up everything everywhere around themselves. It's what they do, his cousins told him. They go crazy and shoot everywhere. His cousins used the Dari word for "ape-shit." We would stop the suicide bombers, if we knew how to stop them, they cried. We think most of them are not even Afghani, his cousins whined. They're crazy people from all over the world—Arabs, Pakistanis, Egyptians, who knows where else. They came here *because* the Americans are here. They came to fight the Americans. Farzam shivered. Crazy people, provoking men in uniforms with machine guns. On the streets where he had to walk! It gave Farzam much to consider. He longed to get his business in the city concluded and return to his mountain home. Although he thought of himself as a sincere and devoted follower of Islam, he could not understand this crazy business called "suicide bombers." Suicide was an insult to Allah, he believed. The Quran forbade it! It was all upside down and crazy here. Nonsense and curiosities. He had only one mission. It was to get the best deal for his family's farm products and mining resources. He would have to consider how that was best done, and who would be his most beneficial partner.

Cousin Mosen told him they would have to talk to Mullah Aziz, the educated cleric who knew many things. The Mullah would explain to Farzam whatever he needed to know. Again, Farzam set out for the mosque, but this time his cousin accompanied him. "I know this man, and he will be open and honest," Mosen said. When they arrived at the mosque, they entered the private room where the Mullah agreed to talk to them. They shared tea, and sat on carpets. The Mullah's beard was gray underneath, but unsuccessfully dyed black. He wore his turban in the manner that indicated he was Pashtun. His multi-colored robe covered a vest over a long dress. Mosen explained that Farzam was from the mountains in the north, and did not know enough of the history of Afghanistan. The Mullah agreed to educate him.

"Afghanistan," the Mullah said, "attracts historic and cataclysmic events. The magnetic force of the mountains creates a call to Allah that sticks to the flinty surface, waiting for sparks to ignite it. This has been true since the beginning of time. Our nation was conquered by Alexander the Great, a thousand years before the prophet Mohammed, may-Allah-grant-peace-and-honor-to-him-and-his-family. This is what made Afghanistan a Persian nation.

"The land is too hot and too dry in the valleys, or too cold and too rocky in the mountains. Its dryness and sandy soil yields melons, pomegranates, grapes, and cotton. Its people herd goats and sheep. We ride donkeys and camels. The blue gemstones of lapis lazuli and the green of emeralds and the red of rubies underlie our mountains. These are signs of the value deep within our souls.

"We have been at war since the beginning of time. Every person who wants power, wants to rule Afghanistan. But you are interested in what is happening now, Farzam. You want to know what is relevant to your problem."

Farzam nodded. There was so much to know.

"I must start more than thirty years ago, to tell you what is happening now. In truth, we would have to go back thousands of years for a real explanation, but we are merely small bugs on the face of the earth. We do not have the capacity in our heads to understand what Allah has in mind.

We will content ourselves with knowing the last thirty years then.

"Thirty years ago, a column of Russian-made tanks advanced through Kabul city, toward the palace of President Daoud. A company of policemen fired on them, but soon some Soviet-made fighter planes attacked the palace. President Daoud and his brother Naim grabbed their pistols. But they were killed in a volley of shots, from their own forces. It was a revolution, by Afghans against Afghans.

"The new government declared itself to be a pro-poor, pro-farmer, socialist democracy. It signed a friendship agreement with the Soviet Union. It announced in the *Kabul Times* that women would have equal education.

"But the reforms of the new government were not well-received by the tribal rulers, and the mullahs in their villages. They were religious men. They did not agree to the reforms of the central government. Imagine the deterioration in our society if our women were left unprotected, to be whores in the streets and abandon their children. In fact, the tribes did not agree to a central government. We are a nation on paper and on maps. On the land and in real life, we are independent villages and family clans. Our mosques define us, and our families choose to govern their own affairs. Is this what you have experienced in your village, Farzam?"

Farzam listened carefully to the mullah's words. "Yes, Teacher," he answered. "Our village would be deeply offended if the government in Kabul told us how to run our families."

"This is why the government in Kabul stays in Kabul. It's like Las Vegas," he smiled. "What happens in Kabul, stays in Kabul." The mullah laughed, but he knew Farzam and Mosen would not understand his reference to the Las Vegas TV commercial. They had never seen television.

The young men looked confused, and the old man continued. "What the government does in Kabul; that is a theory. No one in the tribal villages pays attention to it. So the new government needed help. They could not get the outer provinces to recognize their authority. The leaders of those areas would not acknowledge their rule."

Of course they would not, Farzam understood. His village followed Ahmed Shah Massoud, who was assassinated by people posing as journalists in 2001, only a few days before the attacks on the World Trade Center in New York. No government in Kabul would overrule what Massoud told them. People selected their own leaders. Villages governed themselves. Fathers ruled their families. This is how Allah ordained it. Who could think there would be any other way?

"The new President," Mullah Aziz continued, "President Taraki, worried that he would be killed. He begged the Soviet Union to send troops to protect him. The Soviets did not want to get involved. They sent some bodyguards, but it was inadequate. So Taraki and his prime minister, Amin, sent their own Afghan troops out to kill everyone who disagreed with them. They killed thousands of local village leaders, who would not bow down to their rule."

Farzam and Mosen leaned closer so they could hear every word. They needed to know exactly what occurred. They did not know this had been done. They did not know the Afghan government asked the Soviets to invade them. This was another outrage. Another reason there cannot be a central government in Afghanistan.

The mullah spoke with more anger in his voice, deep and sharp. "Killing the leaders of the groups who oppose you is a very bad political strategy," he said. "Before long, the followers of the dead men chose new leaders. These new leaders, as a result of their experience, had become radical and vicious. They were called mujahedeen. You could think of them like Devil Dogs. Devil Dogs, leading demon packs. They were enraged, and on the track for blood. Now, the Kabul government really did need help. Taraki pleaded with the Soviets to send weapons, fighter planes, tanks, and troops."

"So the government in Kabul asked the Soviets to invade our country?" Farzam's father died in that fight. He already felt the anger rising. His village would never agree to rule by a central government.

"They did, Farzam," the mullah said. "But the Soviets did not agree to come. At that time, Leonid Breshnev, head of the Soviets, did not want to invade Afghanistan. He dragged his feet, led Taraki on. Taraki didn't know what to do. It isn't known, but there are rumors that it was Taraki who got the idea to kidnap the American ambassador to Afghanistan. He thought that would make the Soviets like him better. Maybe it wasn't him who did it, but somebody did it, and it got things started."

"What happened to the ambassador?" Mosen asked. He didn't know this part either.

"The kidnappers took the ambassador to room 117 in the Kabul Serena Hotel. Their plan was to get him room service and let him take a rest until things got straightened out. Taraki thought the Soviets would help him if he showed he was against the Americans. But the rescuers, who were Soviets, shot up the hotel room. They killed all the kidnappers and the ambassador. Nobody could find out who was behind the plot, because the kidnappers were dead. This started some trouble."

The mullah had talked for a long time, and he was getting tired of talking. He wanted to tell these young men some important points. The most important point was coming next, and he wanted to get it out clearly and emphatically, so they would understand. He poured tea for each of them, then he cleared his throat and continued. In the distance, he heard the call for prayer starting. He wanted to say this before he had to interrupt for prayers. He pushed on, not stopping for any questions.

"When the U.S. President, Jimmy Carter, heard that the ambassador was killed, he stopped sending ambassadors to Afghanistan. He worried that the Russians were going to take over the country, so they could get access to Middle East oil. Instead of sending a new ambassador, President Jimmy Carter signed a covert action order for the CIA. He gave them all the money they wanted. Saudi Arabia matched it. He told them they could send whatever it took to arm the insurgents who would overthrow the Afghan government and chase the Soviets out. He did this before the Soviets were committed to come in. Breshnev did not want to fight in Afghanistan. Breshnev understood what Afghanistan was."

"A formidable enemy who can never be defeated," Cousin Mosen offered, with a smile.

"Allahu Akbar," said Mullah Aziz. *God is great.*

"A very strange thing happened a few months after Carter's order," the Mullah continued. "President Taraki had a prime minister, Amin. Amin smothered Taraki with a pillow, in the bedroom of his own palace. Amin announced that Taraki died of natural causes. Then Amin came out, took off his business suit, placed a turban on his head and put on some traditional Pashtun clothes. He announced that, suddenly, he was a good Muslim. He passed out copies of the Quran, and threw the word Allah into all his speeches. He visited mullahs at the mosques. He declared that all those previous executions were Taraki's idea, and they would never happen again, under his rule. This was all new behavior for Amin.

"The problem was, everybody knew this was not the real Amin. Everybody knew Amin was a high school principal from Ghazni, who went to Columbia University in New York, and had never been a good Muslim. Everybody knew Amin left Afghanistan for nine years, and when he came back, suddenly he was running for Parliament. With his new Ivy League degree from America, and his missing years working somewhere unknown in the United States, he suddenly gets money and power in Afghanistan. As soon as he takes over as President, all the new policies are against what the Soviets want. Amin is suddenly a devout Muslim. It doesn't make sense.

"The Soviets decided Amin was CIA. Whether he was or was not, we will never know, because the Soviets poisoned him. Sadly, he survived. Then they sent a sniper to shoot him. But the sniper missed. So on Christmas day in 1979, the Soviets dressed up their troops in Afghan military uniforms and pretended to be the Afghan Army. First, they paralyzed the communications hub. Next, they occupied the main government buildings. Then they got on Radio Kabul and declared victory.

"It would be ten years before Afghanistan defeated the Soviet Union." The mullah suppressed an outright laugh.

"And then the Soviets were bankrupt, the Uzbeks and Tajiks and Turkomen were disgusted, and there soon was no more Soviet Union." He laughed, please with this outcome. Tears came to his eyes, tears of laughter, as he said, "And the Americans thought Reagan destroyed the Soviet Union, but it was Afghanistan all along." He chuckled and his face lit with victory.

The mullah had to go to prayer now, as they all must. Mosen and Farzam performed their prayers, and left the mosque. On their walk home, Mosen told Farzam some things he knew. "The Americans sent money to Hekmatyar," he told Farzam. "The Pakistanis gave him the money. They gave some money to Massoud, too, but not as much. This is why Hekmatyar prevailed."

That was disturbing news for Farzam. Hekmatyar was the enemy of Massoud, the warlord of Farzam's tribe. The Americans gave the enemy of his village's warlord more money than they gave to his warlord. Maybe if they had given more money to Massoud, his father would have survived the war. A jingle truck came by, and Farzam wondered how much longer he would have to be here in the city. Here in the city, people painted their trucks bright colors and decorated them with bells. The jingle trucks brightened up the day, because everything else was gray and sad. Farzam was already homesick for the mountains.

With the new information he had learned, Farzam decided that he would have to consult with his tribe. He wanted to tell his grandfather, Wakil, about the Marines shooting into the civilian crowd on the streets. He wanted to tell Boba Wakil about the money the Americans gave to their warlord's enemy, Hekmatyar. Farzam Parvanda no longer wished to make an agreement with the Americans.

When the American returned, things would not be the same as they had agreed in the Jirga. The circumstances have changed, Farzam thought. When circumstances change, it is only responsible to change agreements. They would have to re-negotiate. Perhaps the village would cancel the deal. The Americans would think he reneged on the deal, but that would not be true. He simply had new information.

Farzam looked around the streets where he walked. He saw gray and dusty-brown stones. Mud and metal, shaped into boxes, stacked on top of each other. These were houses, in which people lived. Some of them had broken corners, fallen roofs, knocked down facades. The streets also were gray and brown. There were no trees, no bushes, no gardens. At night, he knew there would be no streetlights, no electricity. The stench of garbage, laying open in the street gutters, filled the nose until no one smelled it anymore. Familiarity developed in the senses, so that only visitors to the city noticed the smell.

This was not the powerful and compelling sanctuary of the mountain, which he enjoyed at home. This place had no gardens on the outside. Gardens hid, in the inner courtyards of houses, where the women lived. The beauty refused to come out in public. The society felt that its beauty could not be revealed, lest it be stolen away. Farzam remembered the poetry recited around the fire by his family.

In my ear, a prayer was whispered, 'may the earth behind and beneath you be forever empty.' This must be the earth of which the poet wrote. He felt a piercing agony of emptiness as he understood that these were things he could not change. Like Darya. The feeling reminded him of Darya. Lost. Lost. Too much loss. With a rising anger deep within, Farzam decided that he would keep his meeting with the

American. But, when the American returned, he would be surprised to learn there were now some new terms.

In' shallah. God willing.

Marine Corporal Luke Trout sat on his bunk, holding his head in his hands, as he listened to the confusion and banter in his barracks at Camp Eggers in Kabul. A convoy had come back from patrol. Five Humvees. *Five camels, the enemy called them, on their radio transmissions.* They'd been on a routine mission. The thing was, they'd been pulling too many routine missions, back to back, and not getting enough sleep. Too much was going on, and everybody felt overly tired. They were short-handed, for all they needed to do. With the war in Iraq taking most of the attention, their guys were expected to do too much with too little. They'd been going out on mission after mission, without enough sleep, without enough time to heal their wounds. Sergeant HamHock Hartman was getting punchy. HamHock had a head wound, from that attack last week, and the medics didn't do anything about it. Probably because that stubborn bastard, HamHock, didn't tell the medic his head hurt. Captain Jaggers was starting to think he was in charge, because HamHock was stepping back. Jaggers was taking risks that weren't worth taking.

As the convoy was driving down a street in the city, an RPG, rocket-launched missile, landed smack dab in the street right in front of them. Those damn things are completely hit-and-miss, random firing junk. Everybody knows if you get killed by an RPG, it's because your time was up, not because the enemy was a good shot. So Jaggers, thinking he's some kind of swaggering pirate, stops the damn convoy and gets out of the Humvee! Like an idiot!

As soon as Jaggers gets out of the vehicle, a suicide bomber comes racing from the side of the street, runs up and hugs him. Blew himself up, while hugging Captain Jaggers. Boom. Gone, just like that. Then a bunch of dushmen – the Afghan army's word for enemy – ambushed the convoy. Started climbing all over the jeeps. Jabbering in Persian talk. The team was in shock after watching their leader vaporized. Then the dushmen were climbing up the sides of their vehicles. The Marines stood up and fired their M16s. All around. Even into the crowd. Where the civilians were walking down the street.

Luke knew that in this country, everybody was a civilian. All the dushmen, all the bad guys – they were all civilians. These people didn't wear uniforms and announce themselves as the enemy. How can you fight people who won't wear a uniform and call themselves military? All these people were the enemy, weren't they? Even the Afghan Army. They'd show up for work, get their paycheck, procure their weapons, and walk off. They'd come just to get some money and a gun. Then they'd go join the insurgents. Who could even know which raghead was a dushman? This whole country was straight out of a Bollywood movie.

Now his whole company was devastated. They lost the captain, which was the worst part. On top of that, there was some real worry that the Afghan government wanted to file charges. Some kids were killed in that street, when the Marines fired. Luke wasn't on that particular convoy, but he knew it wasn't the Marines fault. It pissed him off that anybody suggested there would be charges. Didn't they know this was a goddam war? Luke had been in Afghanistan for over three months. He'd been a Marine for more than a year.

Back at Copper Hollow High School, from which he graduated the year before last, becoming a Marine was his life's dream. He'd told his Mom, "You can *join* the Army, the Navy, or the Air Force. But you have to *become* a Marine." It was an identity that represented the super-hero he'd wanted to become since he was three years old, running around the living room wearing a towel like a cape over his shoulders, calling himself "Super-Lukie." His mom called him Lukie, at home. His eighteenth birthday didn't come until August, so she had to sign the paperwork to let him become a Marine as soon as he graduated from high school. It was a proud day for both of them. Luckily, the recruiter had come to the high school when Luke was still a junior. If he hadn't met the recruiter then, he probably would have made some mistakes in his high school years, mistakes that would have prevented him from getting into the Corps The recruiter mentored him, kept him from getting in with the wrong crowd, convinced him that getting a tattoo was a bad idea, admonished him to stay away from drugs, encouraged him to exercise and play sports, and pushed him to graduate with good grades. Anybody can be Army, the recruiter told him. You have to be something special to become a Marine. Luke wanted to become a Marine. It was something he could do with his life that would have real meaning.

In Luke's family, he was the oldest child. His two sisters smiled for the camera, and they all stood together with the recruiter, as Luke got into the van and headed off to Parris Island for boot camp. After three months of boot camp and six months of special weapons training, he came home to visit. Mom, dad, and his sisters all fawned over him, calling him their hero. He felt good. They all took a family trip to the nearest city, to J.C. Penneys to get pictures taken. Plenty of wallet-sized, to hand out to all the relatives. In Copper Hollow, there were lots of Trout relatives. Lots of Ellingham relatives, too, from his mom's side. Few of the cousins had ever made something of themselves, though, as Luke had done. In Copper Hollow, lots of kids graduated from high school, stayed home, and worked at part-time jobs in retail stores or as waiters. Drifting. Waiting. Wondering when their own lives were going to begin. Some took classes at the community college. Some found jobs in construction, waiting at five a.m. for the vans that would take groups of them to construction sites in the city, two hours away. Some worked on their family's farm or their family's auto repair shop. A few went away to college or joined the Army. Many waited at home until the early advent of a baby resulted in a shotgun wedding and a life sentence of continued living in Copper Hollow. But at least this year, only Luke Trout became a Marine. It was glorious, exciting, challenging, and his biggest source of pride. The whole family celebrated his achievement. After training, Luke had come straight to Camp Eggers. Now, he was adjusted to his new life and his new identity as a Marine.

In a little while, that same day, Luke heard the boom of incoming fire. Their camp was under attack. The first two months here, that sound alarmed him. Now, it had become so commonplace, he seldom even looked up from his iPad when he heard it. He was having a hard time processing the loss of Captain Jaggers, so he didn't react when the booming fire started. It was only when HamHock Hartman smacked the metal side of his bunk and barked, "Move out, Marine," that he realized his squad was responding. He grabbed his shirt, pulling it over his tee, and hit the door.

The scene outside was chaos. Incoming fire had stopped, but the rockets had hit a children's play yard, outside the base. Afghan parents rushed the gate, holding their bleeding toddlers, begging for medical help. Both Afghan and American soldiers and Marines rushed to take the children from their parents' arms, and deliver them to the medics. The parents jabbered in their Persian talk. "What are they saying?" Luke asked their interpreter, Juma, who was standing right next to him.

"They're saying they want you to save the boys first," Juma answered, in a low voice so that only Luke could hear.

Luke felt his stomach twist, and then he purposely pushed away the father of a little boy, and lifted a little girl, a wisp of a tiny thing, from her mother's arms. Her one shoe fell off, and her delicate toes dangled over his elbow as he lifted her. Her body was so fragile, nearly weightless. He was afraid he would crush her, holding such a bird-like creature. Her dark eyes opened, and the long eyelashes flashed, as she looked at him. He ran, cradling her, and he tried to brush her hair out of her eyes, when he realized that the blood dripping from her head matted her hair. He got blood on her cheeks when he tried to brush the hair aside. And then she took a deep breath, and her body went limp. He didn't need to run any more. She was gone. But he did keep running, even though he knew. He left her body with the medics, and walked back to his tent.

At his bunk, he pulled off his blood-stained shirt and dropped it on the floor. His squad returned, one-by-one. "The Talibs are going to get their asses kicked when that crowd gets aholt of 'em," HamHock told the group. But Luke doubted it. It would be like the convoy that went out this afternoon. The Marines were attacked by the suicide bomber, and then they were ambushed. But the crowd blamed the Marines for shooting back. Luke believed the local Afghans would say, *"if the Americans weren't here, the Talibs wouldn't be launching rockets."* That's what folks would say in Copper Hollow, and Luke decided folks here were pretty much a lot like folks back home. Would the folks back home be more worried about keeping a son alive than a daughter? Luke thought about it, and he had to say, some would. Whatever happened here today, and tomorrow, it would be the Americans' fault, in the Afghans' eyes. Luke knew it. *Outsiders were outsiders, whichever mountain a person lived on.*

Luke didn't know why he felt despondent. He came here to be a real-life hero, to fight the bad guys, and to help the vulnerable and innocent. But he didn't feel heroic. He felt empty, desolate, and drained. He sat on his bunk, and reached down to unlace his boots. That's when he saw the little girl's blood on his hands. It had gotten there when he brushed the hair from her eyes.

He knew the harm that came to that child was not his fault. But he also knew he had not saved her. He wasn't a hero. He picked his shirt up off the floor and went to the sink. He washed the blood off his hands. He felt a thick, tight clot forming in the pit of his stomach. Then he walked outside and looked up at the mountains. He wasn't in Copper Hollow any more.

BOOK TWO:

THE CONTEXT

Chapter 14
Winter, 2007
Kandahar, Afghanistan

It was slightly before dawn in Kandahar, and the call to prayer of the mullahs blared so loudly that the crowing rooster wasn't noticed. It had snowed the night before. Goats and chickens roamed the streets, punching through the light covering of snow to munch on rotting garbage. The first employees to arrive at the office of the Aid Relief Institute of Kandahar stood on the cement front stoop, jiggling a key in the door. The three women's brightly-colored head scarves contrasted markedly with the gray buildings and white snow surrounding them.

"Let me try," Shannon said, relieving her friend, Linda, from the task that wasn't working. Linda stepped back and let Shannon work. The key turned, but the door didn't open.

"It looks like the deadbolt is on," Shannon said. "From the inside." Shannon peered in the side window. "I think there's a light in the back room."

Linda pushed her head in so she could see the light, too. "Maybe Chuck is in there," she said. "He might have stayed all night and forgot to unbolt the door." Linda, Shannon, and MaryAnn worked for the institute. They delivered snacks to the children at the school. They all attended a church-affiliated college in Ramshead, Ohio. They would get a semester's college credit for their service at the Aid Relief Institute. Their church congregation had collected the money to pay for their apartment in Kandahar. The Aid Relief Institute paid for their flights to Afghanistan and back, and gave them a monthly stipend for food. Other than that, they were volunteers.

Eager to get the work day started, Linda banged on the wooden door with a flat palm. "Chuck!" she yelled.

"Don't make noise," their third friend, MaryAnn, cautioned. MaryAnn had walked back down the three cement steps of the gray stone townhouse-turned-office-building. She was looking up and down the street. "It seems really quiet this morning."

At that moment, a blue Toyota van screeched around the corner. It pulled to a stop in front of the three women. Three bearded men in black, loosely tied turbans, with what looked like a tail hanging out of the turbans, hopped out of the van and bounded up the cement steps. They each grabbed one screaming girl, placing their brown, hairy hands over their mouths. They dragged the girls, kicking and wriggling, into the back of the van, closed the doors behind them, and sped away. In the dark in the back of the van, Linda could see that they shared the van with the large cardboard boxes of Sticky-Sweet Toaster Pies and orange soda that the Aid Relief Institute kept in its basement. The truck drove through the city streets and out onto the Asia Highway. Oddly, at the many police checkpoints along the way, no one stopped it.

Back at the office, it was 9:30 am before Chuck Farley arrived for work that day. He'd been delayed by a feeling of nausea from the hashish he'd smoked the night before. He found the front door dead-bolted, so he went around to the back, thinking he would climb in the basement window. The basement door was unlocked. Chuck was surprised that Mary Ann, Shannon, and Linda were not in the office, so he called their apartment. When they didn't answer, Chuck figured he was not their keeper, so he laid down on the office sofa for a nap. He left the phone on auto-answer.

When Chuck awoke at noon, he played the answering machine. The message announced that the missing girls had been kidnapped. The Taliban were going to take them to "trial" for their crimes. Scared, and feeling guilty for not getting the message earlier, Chuck called the emergency phone number taped inside the top drawer of the reception desk. At 2:30 a.m. Eastern time in Josh Bockenheim's rented house in Copper Hollow, the phone rang.

Josh Bockenheim had been dreaming of a large hotel conference, in which he was the featured speaker. In his dream, the audience applauded just as the phone rang, so he didn't hear the ringing right away. When he finally heard it and answered, he never expected to be talking to Chuck Farley in Afghanistan. The Aid Relief Institute was not a top priority for Josh Bockenheim, at the moment. He had bigger problems right now. He had serious problems, not some niggling annoyance based on a few college girls. He made a note to himself to remove his home phone number from the records of the ARI in Kandahar.

Josh Bockenheim had real trouble in his life, so he found it inconvenient that he was pulled into this distraction over some young women. Josh Bockenheim was an important person, too important to be bothered. He believed in working for a better world, but not with his own hands. He was the top dog, not the underling. His work consisted of making decisions and giving orders. It was performed on golf courses and at dinner meetings. He was the man to whom the presentations were made, not the man who presented. In every action Josh Bockenheim took, he thought his decision was the definition of the moral high ground. If Bockenheim said it, it must be right. Moral righteousness oozed from his pores. His pores, of course, were only one of the perfect features in his perfect Latino-German physique. Except for the thirty extra pounds of baby-fat cuteness, the rest of Josh Bockenheim spoke of aristocratic breeding. Curiously, this breeding mixed Argentinian and German heritage.

Joshua Bockenheim's mother was the daughter of his grandfather's family maid. Joshua's father, Bruce Bockenheim, grew up with his mother, Marissa Sanchez, in the same house. Marissa lived in the maid's quarters. They were effectively, but not genetically, raised as brother and sister, by Marissa's Argentinian mother. This gave Joshua a dark, mysterious look, cloaked in a patrician countenance. His thick black eyebrows and high cheekbones complemented his square jaw and perfect, white teeth. He wore his coal-black hair long enough to see the waves in it. The large gold and onyx ring on his right hand and the circle of gold bracelet on his right wrist added to his exotic mystique.

He was the kind of person who judged others. He had an unusually thick and unyielding nature. For example, when he got the phone call from Chuck Farley in Kandahar, he judged that a few young college girls were not important to his personal world. He judged that these girls were not like him, had no particularly useful purpose for him, did not contribute to his growing wealth, and could wait until a more convenient time for him to take action. It was not important to him that he was the only person in the Western hemisphere who knew these girls had been kidnapped by brutal thugs. It was not relevant to his judgment that he was the person responsible for putting them in danger in the first place. That judgment noted, he turned over and went back to sleep. If asked, he would have justified his action by saying there was nothing to be done until morning.

For Josh Bockenheim, if you were useful to him, you were a good person. If you impeded his mission, you were a bad person. If you neither helped him nor hurt him, you were a piece of furniture. He would sit on you, like a chair, if he needed to. He would eat his dinner off your back, like a table, if it convenienced him. He would use you to store his supplies, like a cabinet, if it unburdened him. And if you had no functional use to him, he would ignore you. It was all about him. Over his formative years, he had noticed that his father, a well-respected and duly-honored finance man, did not get to be who he was by taking the high road. With the keen observation skills of a child who wanted to be loved, Josh Bockenheim strove to be like and be liked by his father.

Josh was a money man. Money was his interest. Just money. Moving it, counting it, concealing it, and protecting it from the grubby hands of the unfaithful. You see, Josh knew, in the marrow of his bones, that those who did not have money were, at their core, morally impure. In his value system, money was the measure of God's approval of a human life. It said so in the Bible, he believed. If God considered you worthy, God would make you rich, Josh knew. Josh Bockenheim was born rich. Thus, by his own measure, he, personally, believed himself to be a worthy human being. No matter what he did or how he acted, he expected that God approved of him. This allowed him extraordinary latitude in selecting his value system. When God is on your side, you feel positively entitled to route the Canaanites out of the holy land. With the power of the heavens behind you, what does it matter that a few heathen meet their death by your hand? And who decides which person is a heathen? Josh Bockenheim decides. He decides, he judges, and he grants himself authority to execute, all while perceiving himself to be the good guy. That's what it is, when you are born entitled.

In the year 1998, Josh set up a military training camp in the Blue Ridge Mountains. He wanted to train Soldiers of God. They could be available to provide private security for people like his father. His father and his father's friends often needed these security forces. The heathen who were not rich, and by implication did not love God, dangerously threatened the wealth and welfare of the rich in many ways. It was because of these dangerous heathen that Josh and people like Josh could never fully participate in the ways of the world. People like Josh needed bodyguards, security measures, and fences at all times, to isolate them from the greedy who tried to steal from them, harm them, and redistribute their wealth. Poor people were poor because they were lazy and did not want to work, Josh believed. Because of the danger that poor people represented to rich people, trained security was a necessity in God's plan. In its first three years, Josh's little security business spent much more money than it made.

And then God sent the events of September Eleventh.

The attacks on America that occurred on September 11, 2001, catapulted Josh Bockenheim's little gang of trained mercenaries into a wildly wealthy alternative security force for the U.S. government. For a decade after the attacks, Josh's company grew. He hired an ex-CIA executive to run the company. His father arranged the meetings he needed to get the government contracts. The meetings, of course, were key. One could not simply pull up FederalBusinessOpportunities.gov and submit a proposal. Of course not. The way things really worked, in Josh's personal opinion, was that you first had a contact, an introduction, and a friend. Then you and the friend wrote the RFP, customized to your company. Then you put it out on the Internet for bid. Then you bid. Then the committee that your friend was on found a way to nit-pick all the other bidders until you won. This was how government contracting worked, and Josh's contacts greased it smoothly. *Anybody who ran a company that had government contracts knew that. The only people who didn't know it were the people who didn't have any contracts,* Josh thought.

Finally, with all his government contracts, Josh was becoming rich on his own, without relying on his father for his wealth. Josh named his company Te, for the chemical element Tellurium, a component of gold, both rare and toxic. As his company grew richer, Josh came to enjoy the benefit of earning his own money.

His success was proof-positive, in his own mind, that God approved of *him*. It was no longer enough that Josh believed in God. He was now convinced that God believed in Josh. Not just of his actions, which his religion told him never earned redemption, but of his *being*, because he believed. He had no doubt that God walked into battle on the side of Josh Bockenheim's mercenaries. God approved of Josh Bockenheim, Josh believed, and therefore, nothing he did was wrong. This was a comforting value system, which he used to keep himself happy, even though his wife had left him, his mother had died, and his father never really warmed up to him.

To please his father, Josh Bockenheim would do whatever it took to merit approval. Josh knew that, in Bruce's eyes, the only merit was wealth. This was the driving force that convinced Josh to expand his mercenary company into faith-based initiatives. The Aid Relief Institute of Kandahar, the ARI, was one of those. It operated under the government mantle of a faith-based activity. This meant it qualified for United States grants, paid for by the taxpayers. More importantly, it offered an excellent cover for his mercenaries to operate. It allowed a cover for truck deliveries, cargo flights, and access to permissions and passes. With the identity of ARI, his mercenaries could go wherever they needed to go, whenever they needed to go there. What could be more convenient? Routinely, he shipped the weapons and the money for his Te mercenaries through the auspices and brand names of the Aid Relief Institute. There was nothing illegal about it. They were his company's mercenaries, and he was using resources of another corporation under his own control. All the same, Josh Bockenheim was cautious, maybe to the point of paranoia, about keeping news agencies away from any of his work.

Shannon, MaryAnn, and Linda stayed tied in the back of that van for the entire work day. Nobody was looking for them, as Josh had gotten a late start on informing the State Department of their kidnapping. The van was parked in an out-of-the-way vacant lot, well outside the city. The bearded men taped their mouths, so they could not make noise to draw attention to the van. They tied their feet and hands and left them in the cold van in the dark, with no food or water. No one spoke to them, not even when the men un-loaded the boxes of Toaster Pies and soda. By the time Josh Bockenheim woke up in the morning, showered, dressed in his expensive suit, and affixed his silver cufflinks, the time zone difference meant the work day in Kandahar was ended. With no one to contact to work on their release, the Taliban went home to their families, and the girls spent a terrifying and sleepless night locked in the dark van. The night was freezing cold, and they had only their coats and the body heat of each other to keep themselves warm. They huddled together like frightened kittens in the back of the van.

By the end of the next day, there was finally some aware-ness in Washington, D.C. that these girls were in trouble. It had taken hours for the Defense Department to contact the State Department, who contacted the government in Kabul, who found an informant who suggested that he probably knew who took the girls.

"They are accused of proselytizing Christianity to school children," the Department of Defense Boss repeated sternly, hands clasped behind his back, pacing in front of the speakerphone in his Washington, D.C. office. He had

Josh Bockenheim on the other end of the line. Bockenheim was in his Copper Hollow office, also known as the back room at The Spoon 'n' Fork. Bockenheim had called his contract boss at the Defense Department to tell him about the kidnapping, that morning, as soon as he arrived in the make-shift office at the back of the restaurant.

"They don't do that, Boss," Bockenheim protested. "They don't talk about Jesus. They know not to do that."

"The Taliban says there were 'sayings' under the soda pop caps. The 'sayings' were Bible verses." Boss leaned into the speakerphone. "Did you ever look there, Bockenheim?"

Josh's voice fell. "There could have been." He went silent for a moment. Then he said, "I forgot about that."

The boss stopped his pacing, sat down in the chair behind his desk, and opened his pencil drawer. "Did you do anything else?" he barked at Josh. "What was the point of the girls taking trips to the schools with orange soda? And why Toaster Pies?"

"Sir, the manufacturer of those Toaster Pies contributes them. It's their charitable contribution to help the war effort."

Boss stopped in the middle of chewing on the eraser of a pencil. "I see," he said. "So Te also contributes, by distributing the snacks?"

"Yes, sir. Our charitable works are part of our corporate philosophy."

There was a long silence. Boss tapped his index finger on his chin, and removed the pencil eraser from his mouth. He didn't quite know what Bockenheim was up to, but there was no point asking. The answer would be bull crap. It wasn't up to him to challenge the motives of a corporate, church-based charity. After a moment, he made an executive decision.

"Bockenheim, getting those women back safely is the responsibility of the United States Government. You are out of it. Stay away. Don't get involved." he said.

"I understand, sir," Bockenheim answered.

"But your responsibility is to keep the name of Te out of the limelight on this. I don't want to open my Google-alert email to find a headline that reads: Abducted women were secretly working for U.S. Defense Department. If that occurs, these girls could end up being charged with spying. That just better not happen."

"Of course, sir."

The boss clicked off the phone, but he knew things were going downhill from here. It was a mistake to get himself involved with Bockenheim. He knew the guy was a crook and a phony. Whenever he swallowed Bockenheim's spiels, they left a bad taste. Now he felt like things could potentially get out of control.

He had to do something about these hostages. He put in a call to Colonel Joe Bridgewell of Delta Force. Bridgewell ran the operatives of the Joint Special Operations Comand, JSOC, who could intervene in this situation, without bringing attention to the role of the Defense Department. After that project was set in motion, he would sit down with the State Department. It would be another long day, with another unnecessary pile of crap, courtesy of Josh Bockenheim. He wondered what it would take to cut that guy loose from his ties with the United States Department of Defense. He made a note to himself to add that task to his top priority pending list. Josh Bockenheim was always more trouble than he was worth.

The congregation at the girls' church in Ramshead, Ohio, held their third press conference on MNN, during their candlelight vigil for the three college girls. Everyone's heart went out to them and their parents. It was so sad that the good work of the Aid Relief Institute of Kandahar was delayed because of this tragic and brutal kidnapping. What kind of people would do such a thing?

The mothers and fathers of the three girls were interviewed on all the networks. Did they want to appeal directly to the kidnappers for mercy? Was it true the girls were spies? If this is resolved, will they go back to Kandahar to continue their good work? If anyone would like to donate money to the Aid Relief Institute of Kandahar, to help them recover from this grievous loss, here is the 800 number for contributions.

Meanwhile, Colonel Joe Bridgewell gave Chance Kiernan his orders. The United States does not negotiate with kidnappers and terrorists. It will not pay ransoms or bribes. Therefore, it was Chance Kiernan's job to discuss this situation with someone who would.

Until Chance Kiernan found someone to save them, MaryAnn, Shannon, and Linda, college students from Ohio, would remain chained to a metal radiator in a stinking, rat-infested basement, where they would sleep on the floor. This was why Chance went to Frankfurt, Germany. Along the main market street, in a residential district of Frankfurt, the American rock music blared suddenly from apartment 38A, above the florist shop. The butcher from the deli, *the metzgerei,* across the narrow, cobbled street, peeled off his sheer blue plastic gloves and laid down his chopping knife to see what was disturbing his customers' peace. His large belly pushed against his dark blue apron, as he plunked his hands on his hips and stared, scowling, at the offending window. An old and wrinkled woman, wearing the black headscarf of a Muslim, stuck her head out the window and motioned for the butcher to settle down. In a moment, the music stopped.

Chance Kiernan, wearing navy blue jeans and a camel blazer, picked up a beer from the row of bottles along the side wall of the butcher's take-out deli. He handed the cashier the money in euro coins, and stood outside at the counter-height tables along the sidewalk, drinking his beer and observing the scene. To his left, the market street bustled with after-work shoppers. An old man in a wheelchair operated his chair like a motor car, and plopped his purchases in the side basket. Overweight women in colorful babushkas selected produce for their cooking pots, one vegetable at a time, their two-wheeled shopping carts rolling behind them like luggage. A young couple pushed their twins in a stroller, the children fussing while their parents continued stone-faced on their way. Two teenage girls entered the tattoo parlor on the corner. A well-dressed woman entered the foyer of the bank to use the cash machine, and a homeless man with one leg cut off at the knee sat on the sidewalk with a begging hat, waiting for her to pass him on her way out with cash. Six bicycles rolled by, their young and strong riders, four men, two women, dressed in business clothes and bike helmets. No Asians or Arabs anywhere on the street. He checked up, and checked down, and checked up and down again. The gray clouds of winter offered a fitting haze for his next task. Chance finished his beer. Taking the empty bottle with him, he crossed the street diagonally and disappeared down the passage of an internal courtyard.

The wooden picnic tables under faded awnings in the enclosed courtyard suggested that the restaurant proprietor knew a better life, and a better place, at some time in his past. Autumn-olive trees in pots decorated the cement yard; a faded checkered red-and-white tablecloth muted the coffee stains. Every table boasted a single yellow daisy in a water glass. But the proprietor's attempts to create a pleasant atmosphere for his guests lost the battle to the graffiti artists who contributed their own form of decoration on this residential part of Frankfurt. Above the colorful scrawls of vandals, open windows in apartment houses emitted squeals from German children, and barks from German dogs. The menu displayed a mix of Italian, Spanish, and German dishes, suggesting that none of them would be particularly well prepared. Chance Kiernan strode confidently past the familiar scene of laughing Happy Hour patrons and quietly entered a private room behind the dark-paneled bar.

Argentina is a place of festivity. Its German community mingled and married the Argentines, over the years since World War II, and along the way, created the man who would one day own this Frankfurt bar. His olive complexion and German name were a point of conflict for Gerst Sanchez; somehow, he always felt he had to prove his German-ness. And though he didn't take this proof far enough to willingly give up his mother's rosary, which he kept in his inside jacket pocket at all times, the conflict felt strong enough to make him want to be considered a friend to a man like Bruce Bockenheim. When Bruce asked to use his back room for a meeting . . . well, why would he refuse? Gerst ensured that Mr. Bockenheim and his guest would have utmost secrecy and luxurious treatment, during all of their meetings together. This would happen frequently with Mr. Bockenheim. Gerst Sanchez, husband of the Bockenheim family maid, father of Marissa Sanchez, grandfather of Josh Bockenheim, was honored to serve Bruce Bockenheim's needs.

Bruce Bockenheim, Josh Bockenheim's father, did not always live in Germany. He only moved here when it seemed prudent to stay out of the public eye; that happened recently, after things heated up with his son, Josh, and the various deals he'd done. He felt inclined to leave his Manhattan apartment, his villa in the Caymans, and his Vancouver ski lodge, all because he had a son who failed to follow the rules of class. It was more than embarrassing; it was consequential, to misunderstand one's place in the social structure. Bad things result from it, like this complication with the Department of Justice.

In Bruce's old age – although he was only 68 – he'd taken to wanting to do some good in the world. He didn't need fallout from his wayward son. The one activity Bruce focused on now was his AlphaZeta fund. This was a hedge fund that, among other things, participated in making loans to third world villages. The loans funded small electric power plants that ran on solar power. The AlphaZeta team calculated the revenue that could be generated through agricultural productivity in the African village. The money from the harvest would be applied to the costs of providing and operating the electric power plant for the village. So AlphaZeta financed the power plant, then collected the debt plus interest from the revenue of the harvest. The villagers traded their work in the fields for electricity. This was an excellent business model, as Bruce saw it. He was helping to develop a new generation of consumers, who would soon want to buy refrigerators, dishwashers, televisions, and ipads. They would be busy working in the fields; this meant they would need these labor saving devices to improve their lives. Before they had the electric power plant and the jobs, they didn't know they needed these things. They didn't work in the fields as much. Bruce was pleased at the value he was providing for these poverty-stricken lives.

Bruce had no regrets in his life, but he did have a worry. He saw himself as a self-made man. Of course, his father had also been wealthy, but in Bruce's circle, if you avoid making a small fortune out of your inherited large fortune, you are successful. In Bruce's worldview, his career was entirely made on his own merit, unrelated to the jump-start of his father's wealth and contacts. He believed that others could be successful like he was, if they weren't shiftless and lazy.

Bruce grew up in the suburbs of Chicago. He attended an all-boys prep school, as his father did before him. Then on to the University of Chicago, through to his MBA, before entering the family business. His father, a simple loan-shark when Bruce joined him, acquiesced to Bruce's ideas to turn the company into a venture capital fund. The elder Bockenheim said he didn't see much difference between venture capital and loan sharking, so he gave Bruce the reins. Bruce expanded into hedge funds, and before long, the large fortune had three more zeroes behind it.

Bruce's father had some iron-clad rules for living and for exhibiting virtue. His mother, Pearl, had trouble carrying children. She miscarried many times during Bruce's childhood, resulting in a final Bockenheim family that consisted only of Bruce and his sister, Laura. The brother and sister grew up in a solid and respectable family, with a stable home, and a stalwart education in the Presbyterian faith. While they were rich by objective standards, Bruce's father was a frugal man, and a committed saver. His family lived in a big house, drove a nice car, employed a few live-out servants, and vacationed in Aruba. But this was modest compared to how much money they had, and what they could have spent without worry. Every family in their immediate contact lived the same way, so the children had only a theoretical concept that poor people existed. They learned of poor people from pictures in books, and an occasional rogue servant's tale.

After Bruce's idyllic childhood, with his doting mother and distant, but attentive, father, Bruce felt compelled to exceed his father's expectations. As the only son, he would inherit the mantle of their business, and he determined to be worthy of the job. Sadly, in Bruce's life, his need to excel overwhelmed his personal life. He spent little time with his family.

Bruce had done only one thing in his life to defy his father, and that one thing proved to be a disaster. Usually, boys of his class were carefully schooled that one must never speak of money, to anyone outside the family. It was rude and humiliating, they were told. It was also dangerous, as talking about your money could set you up as a target. The children had to be taught to keep their mouths shut, lest their innocent information leaks result in a federal investigation. Behind every great fortune is a crime, Bruce Bockenheim understood. Perhaps the crime was merely unethical, rather than fully illegal, and most likely, it was still in progress. Loose lips would sink those ships. This is why the children of fortune are taught never, never, never to speak of money.

As a corollary, it was essential to marry only within one's own social class. Not that a boy like Bruce would be likely to have an opportunity to mingle with any one from outside his social class. All social interactions were tightly controlled, in these circles. Cotillions were held: dances where teenage girls from the right families could be "presented" to society, and introduced to potential suitors. Venturing outside these circles, fathers told their sons, was a dangerous trek which could result in being cut off from the family fortune. Girls of the lower classes were gold-diggers, they learned. These girls were inclined to trick you, by getting pregnant and extorting you for money. You surely could not marry these girls, as they had no idea how to manage a staff, and would consort with the help. This, obviously, would result in the staff taking advantage of you and stealing from you. Or taking pictures and blackmailing you. Or voluntarily signing up to be witnesses at your trial. So the third inviolable rule of class, to be taught to the children, was: do not get friendly with the staff.

First, the children must learn never to speak of money. Second, never to marry outside their class. Third, never to become friends with the staff. These were unspeakable sins, punishable by losing your inheritance. But the highest duty of a first son, after carrying on the family fortune, was to marry well. This meant marriage within the social class. In addition to all of their inherent moral character flaws, lower-class women would dress and behave improperly at social functions, causing you to lose your business contacts. Bruce's father made it very clear that Bruce must select a reputable girl from an approved family – one of the daughters of his father's friends. These were not arranged marriages, of course. Bruce was free to select any of the girls presented at Cotillion.

Unfortunately, Bruce had grown up consorting with the housekeeper's daughter, during some of his mother's illnesses after her multiple miscarriages. He thought he was in love with this lower class girl, and he defied his parents to marry her. While his father did not cut him off, and worked hard to accept his wife, it turned out that everything his father thought about lower class girls was completely true. Marissa Sanchez Bockenheim had no idea how to treat the servants, how to enhance his business functions, and how to entertain his guests. She became a liability to his ambitions, and in a short while, he divorced her. It was not a short enough marriage to keep her from getting pregnant, however, and she subsequently bore a son, whom she named Joshua.

Living up to his obligations, Bruce provided well for his ex-wife and his son. He tried, when he wasn't too busy working, to spend time with Josh. But soon, conceding to expectations for his business, he remarried a woman more suitable to fill the job of his wife. She bore him a second family with another son and two daughters. When Josh came to visit, his stepmother treated him politely but not warmly, and he clearly understood that he was the odd man out. Bruce tried, when he thought about it, to assure Josh that he was a fully entitled first son, a one hundred percent Bockenheim, born in wedlock, and completely loved. But Bruce didn't think about it often enough to make it a really convincing argument in Josh's mind.

Throughout Josh's life there had been repeated problems. He had early incidents with shoplifting, despite a generous allowance that could buy anything he wanted. Later, Josh developed a cocaine habit which required two stints in rehab. But as Josh matured, he seemed to grow out of these things, and Bruce saw something arise in him that was completely foreign to anything Bruce had ever experienced. In his late twenties, Josh turned to Jesus. He married, settled down, and started proselytizing in his daily life. Of course, Bruce had always attended the Presbyterian church. He took all his children there. He considered his church to be excellent values-training and a place to build community and empathy. Josh, however, was doing something completely outside anything Bruce had ever experienced within Presbyterian teachings. Josh started opening his business meetings with a prayer. All his managers had to join in, folding their hands and closing their eyes while Josh entreated God for his blessing on their business venture. *Please, Jesus, let our team win. Spit on the other team and ground them into the dirt.* He prayed about his business dealings, asking God to harm the other team. To Bruce, this qualified as certifiable mental illness. He did note that Josh was submitting business proposals for "faith-based" federal grants, however, so Bruce clung to the thought that this was the explanation for Josh's behavior.

Additionally, Bruce felt guilty about leaving Josh with his mother after the divorce. He should have taken full custody and paid Marissa off, he thought. But that was decades ago. How could he have known the impact it would have on his son? As for Bruce's second son, Stuart had no desire or inclination to follow his father into the business world. Stuart wanted to pursue a career in ballet. So be it. Bruce Bockenheim did not impose his will on his sons. But he worried a lot about Josh, and he started to think it would be better to keep a low profile himself, lest he be dipped in the mud by association. As long as Josh was married to Laura Peabody, he seemed to be maturing. Laura divorced Josh, and after that, Josh spiraled into his Jesus period. It was Jesus, Jesus, Jesus, Jesus, after that.

That's when Bruce moved to Frankfurt. He felt safer in Germany, where he was just a short drive away from his money in Switzerland. He focused his attention on the Alpha-Zeta fund, and let Josh handle his own ventures. To his amazement, Josh's performance in wealth accumulation exceeded his own. The boy must have figured something out. Bruce did not know exactly what Josh figured out, but he had enough experience as a wealthy man to know that it was best not to ask. *A little part of him worried that Josh would answer that it was his relationship with Christ that caused his success, and he frankly did not want to hear that. It was too nuts for Bruce's comfort level.* His bank accounts swelled, and to his mind, that was the definition of success. Success, of course, was the exact same thing as merit, he believed. Therefore, by definition, he was proud of his son, Josh. And he would continue to be proud of Josh, as long as the money flowed.

While the Defense Department worked in the background, and the State Department worked in the public eye, the three college girls from Ohio had nothing to do but talk. They'd been moved from the van after the first three nights. Now they were in a basement of some sort, chained to the radiator pipes. At least they had heat.

The men who held them delivered food and water twice a day. They had a bucket for a toilet, and blankets to sleep on. Their chains were long enough to allow them to stand

and stretch. No one had hurt them. Mary Ann suggested that they exercise, to be ready in case the opportunity came to run.

"Run where?" Linda questioned. "We'd have no place to go. Anybody who found us would turn us in to the Taliban. We don't know where we are. It's cold. We have no cell phones. We don't speak the language." Linda was the oldest of the group, at age twenty-two. She had short brown hair and wore red-framed glasses.

Shannon, the youngest at age nineteen, began crying. "We aren't even sure anybody's looking for us," she whined. She had dirty-blond hair, long and stringy, and a gap between her top front teeth.

MaryAnn touched Shannon's arm. MaryAnn was twenty years old, with a nose too big for her face, medium-length brown curls, and thick eyebrows. "Chuck would have called someone, Shannon. The Taliban probably wants ransom money. Why else would they take us and keep us alive? They're probably negotiating with the company."

Linda chimed in to agree with MaryAnn. "That's right," she said. "We should keep a positive outlook. We should pray."

The girls agreed that they should pray. They adjusted their chains and laid their blankets on the cement floor. They got onto their knees, bowed their heads, and lowered their eyes in submission. At first, they were all silent. Then Linda said, "Which direction is Mecca?"

"Why?" asked MaryAnn, with a menacing tone in her voice.

"If they are watching us, we should face Mecca. So we don't offend them." Linda answered.

"What's wrong with you?" MaryAnn growled. "We're praying to Jesus, not Allah."

"No, she's right," Shannon added. "There's only one God, so Jesus is Allah. We don't want to make them mad."

"Shut up! Shut up!" MaryAnn hissed, in a low whisper. "Allah is Satan, not Jesus."

"Don't say that!" Linda whispered back. "What if they hear you?"

MaryAnn started to cry, too. Big, deep sobs. Shannon added a harmony with her own keening. Linda sat on the floor and dropped her head in her hands. That day, nobody prayed. Nobody hugged each other. All they could do was cry until they fell into dry heaving. Not far away, they heard the sounds of gunfire in the distance. Deep inside, the booms and crackles of conflict gave them hope.

Maybe somebody is coming to get us, they hoped, as the gunfire cracked.

Chapter 15
Winter, 2007
Afghanistan

Not far from the basement where the girls were held, Luke Trout's Puma Platoon joined a British platoon from Camp Bastion. It was to be an offensive attack on a suspected Taliban stronghold near Marjah, in Helmand province.

"Puma Two, we are at the base of Gereshk Hill. We've been engaged by the enemy. No way to determine how many. At least two dozen. We are advancing up the hill on foot. Our vehicles have been abandoned. Request air support."

Corporal Luke Trout heard Captain Mercer call in the request. Help was on its way. Luke grabbed a bottle of water and chugged it. His sergeant, HamHock Hartman, was leading the team forward. The crack of a sniper rifle stirred up a cloud of dust in front of Luke's feet. He froze in place. More machine gun fire behind him, until everything was smoke.

Through the dust cloud, HamHock Hartman's grizzly and worn face appeared, his mouth open, yelling. Ham-

Hock's face had three decades of tough experience showing on it, with the redness of a whiskey bloom making it glow. "Trout! Get the hell out of the open road." He grabbed Luke by the shoulders and pushed him off to the side.

The squad was climbing the hill, grabbing scraggly bushes to maintain their balance. The Humvees had been left behind. "We need to get higher than that ridge across the wadi," HamHock said. "That will keep the snipers from getting a straight shot. We'll go back for the vehicles after the air cover routes them out." They clambered up the hill, slinking on their bellies, dragging weapons and ammo along with them. It became difficult to find cover, and shots from the snipers rang close.

"Their snipers are no damn good," Chil-Beans hollered. "That's the only reason we're alive." Private "Chil-Beans" Ramirez was a Marine from Arizona. He aspired to be a sniper himself some day. That was the thing about Puma Platoon, Luke thought. Everybody had aspirations.

Luke saw a rock outcropping that provided cover and he moved behind it. "How 'bout I take offensive shots from here while you guys move on?" he shouted to HamHock.

"Yeah, go," HamHock answered. "Keep 'em busy. Don't stop until the air cover gets here."

Whoever it was that was attacking them – Al Qaeda, Taliban, the Haqqani network, or some new offshoot of local insurgents – their fighters were not the best Luke had seen. Puma's original battle plan had been to launch an offensive attack in full force, working with the Afghan National Army and the British forces from Camp Bastion. On their way to the meeting point, Puma had been intercepted. Now they were under fire, again in a place where they could not defend their vehicles, and could not move them forward.

Luke could hear machine guns banging away at the Humvees below. Shots created dust clouds all along the hill as the squad climbed. He focused his own weapon on the point where he saw the sniper's flashes. He may not be able to hit the sniper, but he could distract and worry him. Chil-Beans came up behind him, dragging a pack full of ammo rounds. "I almost got my ass shot off getting this to you," he laughed. Luke didn't like the manic sound of that laughter.

"The ANA is already up at the top," Chil-Beans told him, referring to the Afghan National Army. "They've got some injured, from their own surprise attack. It looks like the dushmen picked all our units off one-by-one on the way to the rally point. The Brits had a fan club after them."

Luke reloaded and focused. This was no time for chit-chat, but Chil-Beans kept at it. Luke suspected he wanted an excuse for staying under the rock shelter, and not venturing farther up the hill with the squad.

"We got casualties, too," Chil-Beans reported. "Ham-Hock set up a CCP, *a casualty collection point*, up at the top. Mojo got hit in the leg. Blake got his ear shot off. And Captain Mercer had to be carried up there."

"What happened to Captain Mercer?" Luke asked. This would be his second Captain that got hurt in battle, after Captain Jagger was blown up by a suicide bomber.

"Somethin' weird," Chil-Beans answered. "He's sittin' on the ground staring, not talking. Not bleeding, either. Just a vacant look in his eyes. HamHock dragged him by his legs up to the CCP. Couldn't just leave him sitting there like a duck, and had one hand full of his weapon, so he grabbed and pulled."

Machine gun fire came in and splattered across the top of the rock ridge where Chil-Beans and Luke hid. Pieces of rock blew off behind them, shattering into their space and pounding them. Within seconds, the first line of Puma Platoon responded, sending grenades back at the enemy position. Seeing that the team was established on higher ground, Luke and Chil-Beans made their way up to join them, with mortar rounds and grenade covering their advance. Once they were all in position, they started killing bad guys. Wiping them out. It felt good. Luke got his adrenaline high, and the hormone spike washed through his body like a wave of pure love. The camaraderie of the shared ordeal would bond the men of Puma Platoon forever. Luke would do anything for HamHock Hartman and the squad. Blake, Mojo, Chil-Beans, HamHock, and the Captain. They were his brothers. *This was what love felt like, he realized.*

The fighting continued for about twenty minutes, but Luke would swear it was twenty years. The rawness of battle, the abject fear and the horror of seeing the blood of your buddies, turned him from a teenager to a man of maturity in those minutes. When the air cover arrived, the planes strafed the enemy ridge with bombs, until there was nothing moving and no whimper from that hill. The power of the air response was stupefying in its overkill. Nothing could have lived through it. Not a bird or a squirrel. But Luke was glad. The enemy was dead, and the enemy needed to be dead. The men of Puma Platoon cheered. They were bruised, sore, and broken, and they needed the high of victory. Victory, even more than power, was the aphrodisiac. Luke never felt a happiness like the happiness of victory, shared with his blood brothers in combat. This was why he became a Marine, for this moment and every moment like it. This was the high he needed.

They sent their injured to the hospital at Camp Bastion, because it was the closest. Brayson drove the Humvee with the injured, and McGarrity climbed into its turret, racking the bolt of his M2 .50 caliber machine gun, to make sure they made it home with their precious, injured cargo. Captain Mercer would soon be on a plane to Germany, to be tested for brain injury. The rest of the vehicles met up with them on the top.

"Now what?" Luke asked, ready to go back to base himself.

"Now we go back to Plan A," HamHock said. "We attack. While the rage is running, we always attack. You don't waste a good rage. It could turn inward."

All the drills and rehearsals of training camp cannot prepare anyone for the reality of combat. The high highs of victory compete with the low lows of tragedy and loss. A man's psychology is his initial state. When that initial state comes in contact with raw combat, nobody knows how it will play out. The outcome for each one is unpredictable. Flawless execution of the battle plan does not guarantee victory. In battle, some people panic. Some freeze. Some go numb. Some come into their own, and don the cape of the super-hero. As the battle wore them down, the men of Puma sorted themselves into leaders, followers, and the lummoxes who got in the way. When it was over, they all went back to their field operations camp, sadder and wiser and filled with emotional grief. Their rocket-scarred Humvees seemed to limp into the camp. Every head hit the pillows, too heavy to lift until morning. The next day, as each man got out of bed, they went out into the yard and played baseball. Nothing makes a man feel American like a game of baseball. Baseball, and a raggedy stray dog, with a can of

Near-Beer. Just like home. The men of Puma platoon melted and merged until they became a team. Sometimes, they were just a baseball team. Other times, they were a killing machine, each one a single part, so that no one individual held the responsibility for the kill. This was for the best, for their wives, girlfriends, and mothers, at home. When the team left a field of dead and bleeding bodies, some of whom would inevitably be Afghani children, it was so much better that no one person carried inside him the raw burden of the kill.

Back in that dirty basement, when the shooting stopped, the girls from Ohio felt hopeful that their rescuers would soon be kicking in the door.

"I saw a TV documentary about the Iraq war hostages," Linda said. "The Marines went house-to-house, kicking in doors until they found them. Then they kicked down the door and they hollered 'everybody on the ground, United States Marines.' They could be here soon."

"When we get out of here, I'm never coming back to this place," MaryAnn said. "I thought we were going to be helping people here, but they never cared about what we did for them. After all our sacrifice to come here."

Shannon stopped her sobbing for a moment. "They didn't like the Toaster Pies," she said. "They said they didn't taste good."

"What do you think Chuck is doing right now?" Linda said.

"I know if I were Chuck, I'd be trying to get a plane out of here," said Shannon.

215

"Maybe Chuck is dead," MaryAnn sniffled. "Maybe they killed him before they even took us. Maybe that's why the light was on and the door was locked."

Shannon wiped a tear from her eye. In a quiet voice, she said, "I didn't want to tell this. I thought if I didn't say it, it wouldn't be true."

"What?"

"When we were in the van that first night, and you were all asleep, I opened one of the cartons that said Toaster Pies on it. Because I was hungry."

"But it didn't have Toaster Pies in it, did it," MaryAnn stated. It was not a question.

"No. There were no Toaster Pies. It was guns."

Linda exploded. "You both knew? Why didn't you say anything? Am I the only one who didn't know?"

"I saw it last week, in the store room," MaryAnn said. "I didn't know what to think. I was afraid to talk about it. I was just letting it sink in."

"Did Chuck know?" Linda asked.

"Chuck showed it to me," MaryAnn said. "He didn't know what to think about it, either."

The girls lapsed into a stunned numbness. What was going on? That night, they waited for the man to bring their dinner, but he never came. No one came to empty their toilet bucket, or refresh their water. As the days wore on with no food or water deliveries, the girls fell into a weakened sleep. They no longer smelled the basement stench. The men who had sent the kidnappers did not know that the captors were killed in the fighting near Marjah. This, of course, did not stop them from negotiating for the ransom.

Chapter 16
Winter, 2007
Washington, D.C. and Copper Hollow

Fifty-five year old Kenny Kruger was the grandson of Lorene Ellingham and Earl Kruger. The whole family knew the story of the day their family was kicked off the mountain. They knew Lorene was bitter to the end of her life about it. Earl Pap had been a good man, not so inclined to deal in moonshine, and after a while, he tried chicken farming. Chicken farming changed over time. When Kenny took over the business, after Earl Pap died, Kenny signed up the Kruger farm to be a supplier for Big Bird Poultry. Unfortunate name, for a chicken processor, Kenny thought. You couldn't say it without thinking: *All our chickens are unnaturally large and strangely yellow.* But, Kenny was not the marketing man. He left sales and business to somebody else. Kenny was a farmer. He remembered the dark and dreary day when the Big Bird Poultry representative sat in his living room with the contract.

"I'm happy to welcome you into the family of Big Bird," that lying dick of a sales rep told him. The young fool wore an expensive suit with a white button-down shirt. And cufflinks. The guy had silver cufflinks. He looked about twelve years old, but probably, he was in his twenties. So he sat right there, on Kenny's Sears floor-model sofa, and he put that two-inch thick contract down on the colonial-American style coffee table. At the time, Kenny was too much of a naïve hick to know any better, so he signed it and smiled.

The Big Bird guy smiled, too, when Kenny signed. A big Cheshire cat smile, with two rows of dentist-straightened teeth and whitener on them. He reached over and picked that contract right up, and slipped it into his leather briefcase. "Now, let me review the terms, for clarity," the boy was saying, as if he were talking to a moron, which now that Kenny thought about it, he probably was. Heck, now that I understand it, Kenny said to himself, I'd think I was a moron for signing that contract, too.

The Big Bird boy stood up, briefcase in hand, and slipped one hand in his coat pocket. "The terms are: we send you the feed, and the baby chicks. You raise the chicks according to the procedures we teach you in the video training course we send you. You will provide the housing and equipment. At the end of six weeks, the birds will be ready. We will send a truck to pick them up, and pay you for your output. Of course, since we are paying for the feed and providing the chicks, we expect a specific minimum output. If we get less than that back, we calculate a fee for the feed and chicks."

"And I make $50,000 a year, right?" Kenny asked. He was nervous to make sure that was part of the agreement.

"Per chicken house?" He had loans on those chicken houses, and he needed to make sure this was going to pay them.

"You can. Yes. If you meet your output requirements, and follow our other standard procedures." Suddenly, the boy was in a big hurry to git out. He handed Kenny his big-shot business card, and practically skipped out to his BMW 650i coupe.

It was a year or two before Kenny figured out that he wasn't going to make much money chicken farming. Big Bird kept applying more and more requirements. Kenny had to keep up with the equipment. Then the Big Bird Poultry company got itself bought by some company in Costa Rica. They said Kenny's contract was still in force, but they were allowed to change the terms. And the next thing he knew, Kenny couldn't afford to keep chicken farming. He was complaining at the veterans' association one night, and Ike Romanski told him to come by the house. He said he might know something Kenny could do to fix the problem.

Ike was a big-time chicken farmer. After Kenny went over to Ike's house, and took Ike on as a business partner, things started working out. He kept on chicken farming.

Prosecutor Ed Brentwood sat down to his lunch with Congressman A and Congressman B. They had come directly from a meeting with the Big Bird Company. The Company pointed out that the poultry industry receives more than a billion dollars in taxpayer-funded subsidies, which causes them to raise more chickens than the market demands. To relieve this burden of overproduction, the Company hoped to convince Congress to allow the USDA to purchase an additional forty million dollars of poultry, on top of the more than one hundred and some million they already bought.

These chickens would be served in school lunches and food aid programs. The Company also suggested that Congress could get the money needed for the chicken purchases by reducing the number of inspectors in the plants. This, they said, would allow the industry to speed up the chicken lines, and produce more chickens.

The Congressmen wondered how it worked. The industry produced more chickens than the market needed. If the USDA reduced inspections, the industry could speed up the lines, and produce even more chickens. So the industry association wanted the USDA to reduce inspections, to increase production even farther above market demand. Then, they wanted the USDA to increase the chickens bought by the USDA, to make up for having produced too many chickens. Ed happily joined into the circular argument, adding his lack of knowledge to the group's combined illiteracy.

Congressman A said, "Anyway, what's going on now is there are a lot of empty chicken houses out there. They're shutting them down. The new methods don't require as much equipment." His lunch had been finished for quite a while, but the waitress had not come to take the plate. He sat in front of a dirty soup bowl, with crumpled paper napkins in it. They met at a low-profile, but expensive, diner on Fourteenth Street. The food was mediocre. The service was bad. Ed could not understand why this diner was chosen. It was the Congressmen's suggestion. Perhaps it had something to do with the ability to avoid running into anyone who knew them. Driving back to his suburban office, Ed thought about what they had discussed. He thought about the chicken houses closing. He thought about empty chicken houses. He thought about what he could do that would get favorable attention, for his future career.

Empty chicken houses would make a great cover for meth labs, Ed Brentwood speculated. Ed had an opinion about methamphetamine in America. He suspected that the smartest operators might keep their chicken businesses going. That way they had an onsite facility for laundering the money. With four chicken houses, trucks would be always going in and out, money would consistently flow, and who would know whether the money came from the chickens, or the meth? The chicken business paid its farmers crop-share wages. These weren't yard birds, who ranged free and ate bugs. They were chickens raised by factory farm standards. The processors signed contracts with the farmers. They delivered chicks to the chicken houses, and a short while later, they picked up fully grown chickens raised according to their specs. The farmers bore all the costs of the equipment and houses, and were lucky to make minimum wage when all was said and done. Trucks from the processors came in and out all day. This was Ed's theory. As a prosecutor, he knew one had to start with a theory of the crime. Then he could investigate and find the criminal.

Ed supposed he could try to prove it, but it sounded really hard to get past all the paperwork that would entail. And where would he be after he'd done it? He didn't think the Congressmen were looking to follow this path, it seemed to Ed. He didn't believe they were interested in pursuing drug lords. He thought they were only looking to get the USDA to buy more chickens. *Was it Congress who passed that law saying nobody could take any video inside a chicken house? Or was that just pig farms and dairy farms? It was a law that made it illegal to take videos inside the factory farms, and show those videos for the purpose of exposing the practices inside. Why did they do that? Ed wondered. What was there to hide?* Anyway, Ed realized his future would not be made by cracking down on drug trafficking. It was fairly clear to him that his career would not be improved by pursuing drug lords.

The way Ed saw it, if a local boy needed to supplement his family's income by putting a little something extra on those chicken trucks, the chicken company would never know. It would be something the independent chicken factory-farmer did, not the company. In Ed's world view, local homeboys might believe a little bit of meth-cooking, to feed a man's family, fell in the category of moonshine running. As a prosecutor, this was a theory he was thinking of testing out.

Ed Brentwood suspected this was going on all over rural America. He suspected this was the source of the drugs sold in cities. *After all, marijuana was being grown in the national park, wasn't it? It made all the sense in the world that chicken houses would manufacture methamphetamine, he thought. Hell, why stop at crystal meth? The chicken houses could make heroin, too, if somebody brought the poppies in. It was perfect. The houses were well hidden. More and more of them were sitting empty. They had in-house ability to launder the money and distribute the product, with nobody suspecting.* Nobody except Ed Brentwood. Of course, this was all speculation. He was just adding the data points in his imagination. Nothing Ed thought about this chicken business had any proof whatever. But that didn't stop him from thinking it, and considering what he should do as a prosecutor.

As he drove back to his suburban office, in Washington D.C. traffic, he had plenty of time to brood over his next career move. Who should he go after? What would give him some national exposure? What could he do to make himself look good and secure his federal appointment as a judge? He should stop thinking about things like crystal meth and heroin in chicken houses, he decided. Pursuing that route would not lead to a good end. It was all his imagination, anyway. He didn't know anything. *But, he thought, what else could it be?* He pushed the thought down, telling himself to ignore it. His focus had to be on something more productive, and more likely to succeed.

When he returned to his sixth floor penthouse office next door to the courthouse, federal prosecutor Ed Brentwood still stewed. It was a sunny winter day, cold but bright. Ed pulled the dark blue, floor-length lined velvet draperies shut, closing out the bright sun that came through his floor-to-ceiling windows. He sat down in his leather ergonomic desk chair, and tried to focus on his task at hand. His stomach growled.

Ed had no shortage of high-priority prosecutions, and his budget was tight. He had to pick and choose what to pursue. Crime, it seemed, was prevalent enough in this society that Ed Brentwood held the final say over which criminals would be selected for the prize of a trial, and which would go free.

As a prosecutor, Ed had a meteoric career. He turned forty-five last month. A federal judgeship was his next big move. But he needed to do something notable, something that would make it clear he was an up-and-comer. His plan for today was to select what that might be. What priorities would get attention in the press? Who should he go after that would make the right kind of news, for himself, his career goals, and his friends in Congress? Ed knew that the crime came first, and the prosecution was meant to inevitably follow. But there were thousands of federal crimes on the books, many of them so impossibly vague that they could never be applied the same way twice, as he saw it.

It was naïve to think that the application of these laws was not meant to allow discretion. His discretion, he believed. And in using his discretion, he did not intend to yield to the demands of any special interests. He had important crimes to pursue. He did, however, need to select carefully among the crimes available. Resources were finite and budgets tight. If he selected strategically, the judgeship could be his prize. Ed Brentwood had money launderers and drug runners and organized crime rings, all available for the catching. But would it be better for his career if he caught a terrorist or two? How would it play in the public eye? What impression would his actions leave on the voters? What choices should he make that would increase his political chips? How could he use his budget the best way, the way that would cause him to be the most successful? With nearly nine hundred thousand names in the watch-list database for possible terrorists, where would he begin to focus his effort? There was a lot to consider.

Back in Copper Hollow

Mayor Ray Plotzky, in his desire to do well, took his binoculars and invited his favorite police officer, his friend Charlie Wenzel, out to the airport to poke around.

"What's your idea?" Charlie asked.

"A corporate jet flies in here, and guys from Te unload boxes onto a truck. A closed van. The van drives away," Ray said.

"And this is suspicious? How?"

"Te doesn't have a warehouse here. So where is the van going? The Copper Hollow airport is not the closest airport to anywhere else. Why would they fly in here, and drive somewhere else, when they could just fly directly to the real destination?"

"Maybe it's because the hangers are cheap here. You know. For storing the airplane."

Ray looked his deputy up and down. "Wouldn't you deliver your goods to their distribution point first, before you stored your airplane?"

"Yeah, Ray, I would," Charlie said. "But I'm not that summa-bitch Josh Bockenheim. He don't think like I do." Charlie was your run-of-the-mill homeboy. He din't think in fancy circles.

"I say we follow the van. See where it goes. Not in the police car, though. Go get your pickup and some old clothes first." Charlie and Ray took a few days to coordinate their plan. They didn't know when the planes would come in. There were no flight plans or regular schedules. The plane also did not always have a load for the van. Ray and Charlie had other jobs to do, too. As a deputy, Charlie had to take care of the fighting and the drinking and the petty theft in Copper Hollow, and that could really suck up time. Charlie had to fit this extra activity in, as a favor to Ray. They were both Born-Heres. They cared about everything that happened in Copper Hollow, so Charlie helped Ray out.

Ray and Charlie took turns watching for the plane. Ray left Darrell Monk, and every other officer, out of it. "I don't want Darrell in on this," Ray told Charlie. "Don't even tell him we're doing it."

Eventually, Ray saw the plane, with the van coming to meet it. Charlie brought the pickup and their civilian clothes, and they set up their Copper Hollow version of an undercover surveillance.

"How come you didn't want Darrell to know what we're doin', Ray?"

"Ahh, you know, Charlie. You keep a secret by not telling anybody. No need for more than you and me."

"I hope we're not gone more than three hours," Charlie said. "I promised Bonnie I'd take her to the Pub to hear Whistlin' Pete Fink play guitar tonight."

"The van's gotta be going at least to Wickersville," Ray offered. "That's forty-five minutes one way. There can't be any warehouses any closer than that. So I hope you make it back for your date with Bonnie. A date like that is a big deal for a guy like you."

"Don't bust my chops about Bonnie. I'm thinkin' of marryin' her."

"Speakin' of hot dates, isn't Darrell dating Jeanine Sherwood? Are they an item now?"

"They sure are hangin' out a lot. They mus' be doin' a little undercover operation their own selves."

"What the . . ." Ray exclaimed, as the van they were following pulled off the road into the Kruger chicken farm.

"Yo!" added Charlie. "I didn't expect that."

They couldn't follow the van into the farm, and they couldn't wait for it to come out without being seen. They were done for the day.

"I'm thinkin' that corporate jet didn't deliver some new-fangled scientific experimental chicken feed, Ray."

"I'm thinkin' the same," Ray said to Charlie.

After he dropped Charlie off, Ray considered what to do next. He didn't want to discuss with Charlie that the corporate jet belonged to Josh Bockenheim, and Josh Bockenheim was a very well-connected person with plenty of defense contracts, and lots of influence among authority-holding buddies. Ray was not ready to open up that particular can of worms. Of course, Ray mulled over the idea of asking Kenny Kruger what was going on. What would that do? That would cause Kenny to tell Josh Bockenheim that Ray was poking around, and that would be a bad idea.

So Ray decided his best bet would be to discuss this matter with his good friends, Congressman A and Congressman B. Ray respected them. They were helping him with his own political aspirations. They knew the political landscape. Ray felt confident the congressmen could guide him through this minefield with Josh Bockenheim.

Shortly thereafter, Congressmen A and Congressman B wrote to Secretary of Defense, Donald Rumsfeld. Drugs are funding the Taliban, the Congressmen said in their letter. We must shut down the poppy distribution network. Secretary Rumsfeld responded with his own letter. "Our troops are focused on fighting the Taliban, and we view the drug trade as a law enforcement issue." Even though he really didn't want to engage in the mission creep involved in solving an age-old issue of the worlds' heroin production, all the

227

same, Secretary Rumsfeld decided it wouldn't hurt to get some special operations forces involved in these issues. He called the Boss of JSOC, the Joint Special Operations Command. The Boss called Colonel Joe Bridgewell, who sent Chance Kiernan to try to figure out who was doing what, to whom, where, and when. There were a lot of threads in this carpet, and they only formed a pattern when you saw them from the top. A man like Chance Kiernan was known for his willingness to pull a thread and see what might unravel.

Meanwhile, in Frankfurt, Germany

The men who finance drug trafficking never see the consequences of their actions on the lives of the MaryAnn's, the Shannon's, the Linda's, the Luke Trouts, the Daryas and the Farzams of the world. They layer corporations over corporations, partitioning the transfer of money behind mysteries and paperwork. When Export Business A, from Karachi, Pakistan, sells building materials to a company in Abu Dhabi, at a thirty percent premium markup over the going rate, who is to say that the markup was a payoff for a drug deal in Kandahar, Afghanistan? How would one know if the higher price was not simply an indicator of better quality? The world of capitalism does not prohibit the free flow of money and profit. Auditors do not evaluate the business merit of a deal. They only verify that column A times column B equals column C. Beyond that, auditors are not accountable for the quality of the business transaction. They do not open Sticky-Sweet Toaster Pie boxes on rural trucking routes, or taste the orange sodas to verify their contents. Because of this, no one could follow the money.

The money flowed in and out of multiple corporations through multiple stock exchanges, across multiple national borders. When the money for a drug deal passed from the hands of a buyer to the hands of a seller, it existed in cash. Physical Pakistani rupees, or Afghanistan Afghanis, or United States dollars. But a seller of drugs had many expenses along the journey from poppy fields to heroin addict. Many mouths opened for their "taste" along the dangerous route. It was money that closed the mouths, and guns that ensured they would stay closed.

The poppy farmers are at the bottom of the chain, like farmers anywhere. They borrow money for their expenses of growing. They get the least part of the money in the system. Then someone must transport their harvest to a manufacturing facility, where it can be made into heroin. The transporters have a dangerous job. They travel on routes combed by narcotics agents, looking for them. If they are caught, they are likely to die. They most likely must cross international borders, going across the border to Iran, Pakistan, or the Central Asian states formerly known as the Soviet Union. Or perhaps they can find a way to load their product onto an airplane, and send it to Germany or the United States. It is surely less dangerous to load the product onto an airplane as cargo than it is to drive a truck across the border to Iran. It could be hidden in shipments of carpets, heading to Dubai. Or perhaps it could hitch-hike on a supply plane, returning from delivering its humanitarian aid to the families of the 500,000 starving poppy farmers. Or maybe it could catch a ride on the supply chains of the contractors who supply the NATO forces. After all, the cargo planes come in full, and they go out empty. What could be more practical than to hitch a ride?

Part of Bruce Bockenheim, the part deep inside that he would never acknowledge, knew that the call from the United States Department of Justice would eventually come. No, he said, to Chance Kiernan, when they met in the backroom of Sanchez' restaurant. No, he knew nothing about money laundering. No, he did not actively control his corporate empire. Yes, of course he would cooperate fully with the investigation. Yes, he understood the need for secrecy, and he would comply. There was no doubt that Bruce felt devastated.

Secretly, Bruce blamed himself, for marrying a woman who was not of his social class. Stepping out of his class structure caused him to have a son who did not know the rules of his elite society, down to his bone marrow, as those of his class knew it. If his son, Josh, had followed the rules of his elite class, there would not have been an Aid Relief Institute of Kandahar. No one would have been taken hostage. The money laundering would be business as usual, as it was with banks worldwide, Bruce believed. The Justice Department would not be chasing Bruce Bockenheim.

That one act Bruce took, marrying the housekeeper's daughter, snowballed to this final result. The shame burned. Bruce Bockenheim's first son, Josh, had gotten into another mess, and Bruce would have to bail him out. Chance Kiernan was going to offer Bruce a way to use his means to stay out of jail. All Bruce had to do was use his contacts, his networks, and his money, to get the girls released. He needed Gerst Sanchez to ensure his meetings would be held in absolute secrecy. Thank God there were still some loyal servants in this world, because using electronics to communicate would be out of the question. Gerst would know who to contact, and how to make the arrangements. Yes, Bruce Bockenheim would pay the ransom, and Chance Kiernan would ensure that the Department of Justice found somebody else to pursue. That was among the skills and types of special operations Chance Kiernan handled.

In the basement in Helmand Province, Shannon, Linda, and MaryAnn lapsed in and out of consciousness. Their lives depended on Gerst's efficiency. Luckily for them, Gerst was a competent and efficient man. For the price of the ransom demand, which Bruce Bockenheim paid, the location of the college girls from Ohio was given. Sadly, the contact Gerst Sanchez found did not know the exact location, just the general area. Puma Platoon was called to go house-to-house, kicking in doors. The platoon had gone out on offensive missions, day after day. They were tired, and after too many missions, they had become numb to the suffering they were causing. This happens, when people see their friends' ears blown off, their captain's brain shattered, and their buddies' guts torn from their bodies. In the fog of war, even the best of men lose their ability to remain human, when asked to do things beyond the ability of humanity. The men of Puma Platoon were no exception. They were not worse than or better than the warriors who came before them, or the warriors who would come after them. As warriors do, they started laughing when they killed. They made mistakes, blowing up vans of civilians with children inside. They said "oops," and laughed when it happened. They called their enemies "ragheads," and failed to distinguish between the regular citizens of Afghanistan and the enemies fighting them. They did everything the young soldier, Bradley Manning, saw them do on the videotapes he released to the whistleblower website, Wikileaks. They did it because that's what people do when placed in inhuman situations. It's what people did throughout history, in all wars, on both sides. They were very good people, placed in very bad situations. They were American heroes, doing the job they were assigned. Everybody does it, when they are in war. That's why it is so important, *if you want to keep warring*, to keep videos like that off the Internet. It illustrates why governments have to go overboard plugging leaks. Because if the American public saw the video of Puma Platoon doing their jobs, the public would object to warring. That would not be fair to Puma Platoon. Puma Platoon were, truly and honestly, trying with all their might, to be the good guys. But there are no good guys in war. There are only warriors.

On this particular day, Puma Platoon was searching for the three college girls from Ohio who had been kidnapped and treated so badly. They needed a win, and they needed to feel like heroes. So they went out to be the heroes America needed, and the heroes they truly were. But warrior-mindsets carry a price, and the men of Puma Platoon were paying it.

They had a set of co-ordinates, and a group of houses within them. One by one, they were going to enter those houses and search. But when you knock down a family's front door while the family is sleeping, and you enter their house dressed in SWAT gear, you very seriously threaten and frighten the women and children. Husbands and fathers, when confronted with this sight, their wives and children shaking and crying in front of them, tend to get uppity and aggressive. On top of that, the husbands and fathers look very much like – no, look exactly like – the dushmen who have been attacking these heroes, day after day. They dress like the enemy. They wear their hair like the enemy. They have the same skin color and facial features as the enemy. They talk in that Persian jibberish like the enemy. Their common food and spices make them smell like the enemy. They keep Kalishnikov's leaning against their bedroom walls like the enemy. Who can know whether they are the enemy or not? And so the heroes are on guard.

One of these families is holding three college girls from Ohio as hostages, the warrior team knows. Which one is it? The heroes are wary as they enter each house, weapons drawn. Of course, their new Captain, Captain Jenkins, has carefully explained to them the rules. They are not to harm the civilians. But if a civilian attacks them . . . obviously, they have the right and the need to defend themselves.

Twenty-seven times, the team whose members included Corporal Luke Trout and Private Chil-Beans Ramirez, successfully searched a house without incident. Twenty-seven times, families quivered in fear, but peacefully returned to bed. And then one time, the enraged father in the house grabbed an AK-47 and pointed it at Chil-Beans.

Luke Trout opened fire.

In the end, the father, the uncle, and the oldest boy lay dead. HamHock Hartman was called to pronounce the kill justified, and the screaming mother and grandmother were pushed aside. The wide-eyed children curled into the corner and wailed. They probably were Taliban, HamHock told

Corporal Trout, and Captain Jenkins agreed. That was going to be what the report said.

Fortunately, a few houses later, the team found the girls, locked in the basement of an abandoned house. They were dehydrated and nearly dead. They flew by Chinook helicopter to the British Camp Bastion until they were well enough to be sent to the hospital in Germany.

MaryAnn was the first to recover enough to ask about Chuck Farley at the Aid Relief Institute's office in Kandahar. There was no answer at the office, so someone went to look for him. Chuck Farley was found on the floor of the office. He was dead of a heroin overdose. No one had mentioned him. Josh Bockenheim didn't report him missing. He had no home address on file. Poor Chuck. The man nobody knew, and nobody searched for. He was a casualty of war, who would never show up on any chart or be part of a statistic. He had no one to grieve for him. He was just an employee of a company, not a husband or a father. No one knew who to call to receive his body, and Josh Bockenheim never thought to pay for the funeral himself. What happened to the body? MaryAnn asked. But nobody knew.

Luke Trout was a hero. He was part of the team that found the girls. He was interviewed by the embedded reporter. He should have felt victory, and love, and the high of accomplishment. But in his dreams at night he saw the face of the boy he killed two hours before Puma Platoon found the girls. He saw the grandmother wagging a finger at him and wailing. He saw the mother collapsing in grief. He had that little niggling concern in the back of his head: if these men are so bad, why do their women love them so much? He couldn't reconcile it. He couldn't put the tales he had been told into his frame of reference of home and family. The culture clashed in his mind and made him feel crazy. The price of heroism was rising for this Marine from Copper Hollow.

Back in Copper Hollow

When Chance came home to Copper Hollow late the following Friday night, the TV news was reporting the safe release of the young women. The boys were already asleep. Chance promised Ann that he would stay home for a long time now, weeks. "We'll work through this," he told his wife. When he was home, Ann felt safe again. He didn't need to do anything to make her feel safe. It was his presence that gave her that feeling. Ann believed that her husband held the world together and gave it structure. He was everything she wanted in a man, and even the straight way he walked made her feel safe and calm.

Ann knew her husband played some part in releasing those girls, and that made her feel good. She knew she felt safe when he was here, but she could not bear being alone when he was away. She thought he should call her when he was gone, but he never did. She fixed her mind on enjoying his time here, and building their family. She pushed her anxiety down, from her head into her stomach, where it churned and belched until she thought she needed some form of colorful pills. As she went about her normal day, dragging the boys with her into the drugstore in town, looking for antacids, the boys smacked each other and ran around the store yelling and knocking things over.

In her own mind Ann wasn't a real mother, and it was this thinking that prevented her from knowing that Timmy and Jeff could read her mind. When they read her anxiety, they felt anxiety, too. When boys feel anxiety, they express it physically. Ann didn't know that a happy face doesn't hide a churning stomach from nine-year-old boys. She thought she always had to cry alone, and she thought she could hide her feelings from Chance Kiernan. She thought she could tough it out, and be brave, and put on a happy face until the rain stopped. If Chance had been looking at her, and paying attention, he would have seen the problem. But he wasn't looking. He had big and important problems to address. His wife could not be one of them.

Chapter 17
Spring, 2007
Helmand Province, Afghanistan

In Marjah, within Helmand Province, Afghanistan, the shops in the market bazaar are closed. The doors are shut. There is no merchandise hanging in the stalls. Trash litters the street, as if a festival came through here and left its dirty wrappings behind. Stray dogs roam; an untethered goat ambles along the gutters, rummaging for garbage to eat. Along the sidewalk, a man without legs sits on a wheeled plank, begging for alms. Groups of turbaned men, wearing loose pants and long shirts covering to their knees, in sandals, sporting beards and assault rifles, walk hurriedly along the street. They walk as if they have a war to attend and need to hurry so they won't be late for the opening shots. Expensive cars drive by.

Haji Abdullah Khan emerges from the back seat of his black BMW. The driver waits while the Haji knocks on a door. The door slit opens. Haji is recognized, and steps inside. The driver pulls away. When the Haji's business is concluded, four men from the province are chosen to carry drugs across the border into Iran. If they live, they will be well-compensated for their work. If they are caught by the Iranians, they will be hanged. Their families will select another son to take their places as drug mules. Much cash must finance these transactions. It must pay the border guards, the street thugs, and the government regulators along the way.

But the cash cannot travel with the drugs. It must be kept separate, unrelated, untraced, and untouched by the hands that are tainted with opium. Some of it will finance the insurgents in Afghanistan. The cash must be strained through the *hawala* system, the banking system of the Muslim world, where it may sit on an invoice for building materials, at a thirty percent premium, for a building in Dubai that may never exist. Some of it will pay the employees of Josh Bockenheim, who will deposit it into various companies, where it will be invested in stock exchanges, venture funds, and even charitable organizations. Once it is there, it will transform into pixels of electronic promise, detached from its physical existence, and pregnant with litters of theoretical electronic wealth. The cash that travels through the drug trafficking system may indeed be all the physical cash that exists in the world. The rest of the system of money is merely an electronic concept: promises on debit cards, and burdens of obligation. Money sits as if locked in a piggy bank, but it does not jiggle when you shake it, because it is not really there.

Farzam and his cousins made their way to the town of Marjah, by bus. They were going to find a trader here, who would give a competing bid for Farzam's village products. He was told there would also be someone to bid on his emeralds. They entered the market bazaar, where they were picked up by a driver, who drove a two-door Datsun pickup truck, green. Their driver was concerned about being out after dark. "We must get inside before dark here, Farzam," the driver told him. He seemed concerned about where he would park his truck during the night. The driver took them to the address they gave him, where they were to meet with Atta.

Atta invited them into his house, which was a room behind a rickety shopfront on the bazaar, and told them how the deals would be arranged. "Security is the concern, Farzam," Atta told him. "Ten years ago, when the Taliban was in charge, you could walk down the street with a basket of cash on your head, and nobody would bother you. Then the U.S. and NATO came. They built a large military base. They fought and killed many people, a few of whom were actually Taliban. They chased the Taliban out. Now, you cannot park your car in the streets safely at night. You cannot walk after dark, for fear of the gangs of thieves. And in the daytime? The thieves are the Afghan police, who are appointed by the Afghan government. They stop you on the road and demand bribes to let you pass. If you do not pay, they accuse you of being Taliban and charge you. They take your opium, and turn it in to get the credit for stopping drug traffic. Then they report that the Taliban are increasing, as they have accused you, so they have caught one.

"It is a bad situation, and it is not improving. But the good news . . . the selling of poppy is still a fine occupation, amid a market growing more quickly than ever. Afghanistan provides eighty percent of the world's supply of opium now, when we held only a thirty percent share of the market before the Americans came. So if you work in poppy, you have a future. But, you understand, we advance you the money before you bring the tor to us. That means you owe us, and you must deliver. To deliver, you must either bring us the tor yourself, or you must trust a trader to bring it. If you trust the trader, and the trader does not make it through the mountain roads to deliver safely . . . well, it is you who received the money, and it is you who must repay it." Atta did not have the elaborate look or setup Farzam expected to see for a drug smuggler. He worried that this lack of material presentation represented a lack of success. It would be rude to ask this question, so Farzam remained silent and sipped his tea.

"You understand, I am not a drug smuggler," Atta said, anticipating the question in Farzam's mind. "I am a mere middle-man, collecting the tor to deliver to the laboratory, where it will be manufactured into heroin. This is a job that pays well, so that I can care for my family. But I am not a rich man." He shifted his weight, as they sat on the floor. He motioned to a young boy behind him, for a plate of sweets to be offered to his guests. The boy looked to be about twelve years old. He hurried to comply.

Farzam lifted his eyebrows. There was much to be learned in this business. It was more complex than he had known. "Where are the factories?" he asked Atta.

"No good factories are here in Afghanistan," Atta said. "There are some bad factories here, with low quality. They are used for illicit purposes, to sell to our own people. I do not approve of this. Islam does not allow the using of drugs. It is forbidden under Sharia law." Atta shook his head and waved his index finger in the air. "The factories are in other countries. Iran, some. Russia, some. Wherever heroin is used, there are factories."

Farzam thought about this for a while. He had trouble concentrating as he watched the young boy fawning over Atta. It didn't seem normal to him. Was this boy Atta's relative? There was something wrong. He worried about how this was all lining up. He was still thinking about his village's deal with the American. "Are you saying the factories could be in America?"

Atta reached over to the boy, who was now sitting beside him. He patted the boy's knee. "If the users are in America, then the factories are in America. Why wouldn't they be? The transport of drugs is the most dangerous part. Who would invest in manufacturing of a product and then put the end product in the highest danger? The drugs are manufactured as close to their end buyers as possible."

Farzam considered. *Is this what the American wanted? To take his tor to a factory in America? Would it be safer to trust this route, than to throw the dice with the dangerous men of the drug trade here in Afghanistan?* He would have to consider all these things before he decided which partner to choose.

Atta was not the drug smuggler, but merely the middle man. So there must an actual drug smuggler in Helmand Province, living near the city of Marjah, where Farzam visited now. At the moment that Farzam walked out of the shop in the market bazaar, the wife of this drug smuggler was in the market, purchasing food for her four children and the other members of her family. She was dressed in a fully-covering, light blue burka, with only slits for her eyes. No part of her body was exposed. She wore gloves to cover her hands and socks to cover her feet. Because of the anonymity of the burka, Farzam did not see the second wife of Haji Abdullah Khan, the drug smuggler.

But Darya, the young woman who had disappeared from his village when she was eleven years old, the young girl who was his cousin and his best friend as a child, the young woman whom he thought would someday be his wife, peered through her slits. Darya saw Farzam.

In my burka, you do not see me. I live in a concealed world. But, perhaps, o man of Afghanistan, you think this means I do not see you. This is your delusion.
--- Afghan poet.

It was a few weeks later that Darya woke up excited. This was the day she would go with Abdullah to visit her mother. She had not seen her mother since the day Abdullah brought her here, when she was eleven years old. It was so long ago, she hardly remembered. Now she was a mother herself. She packed her bags, kissing her children good bye. She would be back in a few weeks, she told them. The trip would be too hard for them. They would stay with their grandmother, Abdullah's mother, and his older wife, Naseem. Their routine would not change.

Darya and Abdullah would make the trip in a convoy. Abdullah had business to conduct with her grandfather, Wakil. He was kind to offer to take her to see her mother. It was half a lifetime ago that she left her home. Her mother had no cell phone service. Her mother did not leave the mountains. The trip was very hard. They loaded the cars. Abdullah took many men with him, and arms. Darya wore her burka, of course, and sat in the back seat of the car, next to Abdullah. They traveled in a caravan of four-wheel drive Datsuns, with Abdullah's men.

Darya remembered when she left home, when her mother placed her on the camel and Abdullah took her away. So much had happened since then. She was lucky to find that Abdullah was kind to her. He gave her time to be the child that she was, and did not bring her to his bed until after she began to have her period, months later. They had a wedding then, and the older wives dressed her in beautiful silks. She remembered how awe-struck she felt when she saw the house where she would live. She had never seen such a large house, and so beautifully decorated. Bright colors and parapets everywhere. It was a villa, not just a house, with everything they needed on the inside of it. There was endless food, and music and dancing. Abdullah had plenty of money. He was Islamic, but he was a reasonable man and enjoyed life. He was not a Taliban. Although, sometimes Darya listened to conversations, and she thought maybe Abdullah pretended to be a Taliban, when it amused him.

Abdullah's first wife, Naseem, was forty years old. Abdullah was now forty-five. Naseem had gone to Kabul University. She had a degree in teaching. She told Darya stories about the history of their nation and their people. She said there was a time when Kabul was a modern city, and people from all over the world came there to enjoy its culture. She said women wore mini-skirts then, and worked in all kinds of jobs. Darya liked Naseem, and felt happy when Naseem taught her to read. Naseem had daughters older than Darya was when Darya married, but Naseem would not allow Abdullah to arrange marriages for them yet. She told Abdullah that her daughters must be eighteen before they married.

Naseem taught Darya to speak to Abdullah in a way that he would do as she wished. "It is a skill," Naseem told her, and Darya learned well. In the beginning, Darya felt unsure of herself, and cold toward Abdullah. After her first child was born, however, Darya warmed to him. Now, she would say, she might even love him. It was a learned love, which had its roots in practicality. It made sense to love him, and so she did the rational thing. She was very happy that he was taking her to visit her mother now. Her life was good. In her mind, Naseem was more like her mother now, because she had been so young when she came here. She hardly remembered her real mother. The memory was vague and fading.

After their trip to Marjah, Farzam and his cousins met with the Taliban leader Haji Raj Ahmed in the corridor of the Kabul mosque near his cousin's house.

"This American man you took into your village, the Pakistani Hanif, is CIA," Ahmed told them. "If you are caught with him on the road to Kandahar, you will suffer the same fate as that dog. As a good Muslim, you cannot even be known to talk to such a man."

Farzam was not sure about this. He was not extreme in his views, and he did not believe what the Taliban believed. All the same, he had seen the U.S. soldiers shooting into the crowd, and he did know about drone strikes that killed entire innocent neighborhoods of people. His cousins knew he was hesitant, and intervened with their own views.

"You should pay attention to Haji Ahmed, Farzam," his oldest cousin said. "Ahmed knows how things work, and he is well-connected to Haji Abdullah Khan, who controls the poppy trade throughout the Balkh Province. It might seem that they are interfering with the decision of your village, but it's their experience talking."

Ahmed continued, "I have discussed the situation of your village with Haji Khan. We have a proposal for you. If you and your cousins will come to Haji Khan's house for dinner tonight, we wish to explore a relationship with you."

They went home. Farzam told his cousins he had grave apprehensions about partnering with the Taliban. Wasn't there a new government in place? Would this make them outlaws with the official government of Afghanistan?

"You are misled, Farzam," cousin Afrooz said. "There is no second, competitive outlet for your product. If you try to deal with the Americans, you will be killed as a traitor. You saw why, when you were almost shot on the streets of Kabul as they came through like maniacs! The warlord of your province has sold the trading rights to Haji Khan. All along the way, there will be police and government officials to be paid. It is not all of our people who hate the Americans, Farzam. Many had hope that they would make it possible for the Kabul of forty years ago to return. Then, we had a fine university, and a thriving city. Our economy, even then, depended largely on hashish. The Americans disappointed all of us, and our people hate having armed invaders among us. Still, most of us do not hate. Most assuredly, the drug traffickers do hate them, though. You and your family . . . you are drug traffickers."

Afrooz looked down at his bare feet. The floor of his house was carpeted, their shoes lined up by the door. Farzam's house was made of the mud of the land, so that it was hard to know whether it was a house or a cave in the hill. Afrooz seemed to feel some shame about his cousin's family.

Farzam, to that moment, had never thought of himself as a drug trafficker. He saw himself as a farmer, selling his farm product. The Quran does not prohibit selling poppy. The Quran prohibits using drugs, not selling the innocent plants of the field that some use to make them. Poppies make morphine, too, which is needed for their hospitals. He knew there were bad effects of heroin addiction, but he saw no reason he could not envision himself as a provider of morphine to hospitals. He got a sudden vision of his uncle, forced to sell his daughter, Darya, to pay his debt to a drug trader. The memory of Darya stung. When they were children, they played together as friends. He heard that she might come to visit her mother soon, and that she had children. But he could not see her now. She was a married woman.

That evening the four men walked to Haji Khan's house for dinner. It was a modest house, not a palace, typical of the other houses in this higher class neighborhood in Kabul. His cousins said this was only one of Haji Khan's houses. He had many others. A drug kingpin's houses are his business offices, they told him. Where else could he be assured of privacy and protection? Haji Khan is not here tonight. They would meet only with Haji Ahmed, who would have full authority to make the deal.

After the meal was eaten, and the third cup of tea poured, Haji Ahmed said, "Farzam, I know your grandfather well. I knew your father even better, as I fought alongside him in the Soviet war. Our families are friends. We have much in common."

Farzam nodded; his cousins affirmed that these families were connected through a long history.

Haji Ahmed rubbed his chin under his beard. His lips tightened. His eyebrows pulled into the crease above his nose. His next words would be serious, this action said. "Although I am Pashtun, and you are Tajik, we have much in common. We share a disgust for war and fighting. We seek only peace, to live as our ancestors lived, and to govern our own tribes."

Farzam had to agree. This is what he wanted. He had a wife, back at home. He had a son. His wife was not Darya, but she was his wife, and she provided the nurturing and comfort that stabilized a man. He had learned about this government in Afghanistan. He spit on the government. Government belonged in the village, and the tribe. What could it mean, to think Uzbeks and Tajiks and Pashtuns were all one? Which of the long history of invaders of their mountains had chosen to define these boundaries and call it a nation?

The women arrived with more tea and pastries. The men took them and sipped before talking again. Ahmed said, "I do not call myself Taliban, although there are others who do call me so. I do not have the level of devoutness of those who claim that title. I trim my beard. I play music in my house. I am not the most devout of Muslims. But I am a believer, and I pray." He adjusted his robe, and shifted on the carpet, as if to stretch his leg and keep it from going numb. Carefully, he kept his legs folded with his feet back, toward the wall, not toward his guests. He selected a pastry from the plate, and offered one to Farzam.

"Our land has always been a land driven by hashish," Haji told him. "Before the Soviet invasion, we had a thriving city in Kabul. The Flower Children came here from San Francisco, to buy their supplies. Hookahs and opium. Even then, opium was our economy. Then the Soviets invaded. The Americans fought the Soviets on our soil, by providing money to the Pakistanis to give to our mujahedeen. But

Afghanistan is an imaginary concept, made up by invaders. We are not a nation, but separate tribes. Our tribes choose to govern themselves, not to be led from Kabul. We have our own thoughts of how to manage our affairs."

"I consider myself a businessman, Farzam, as you consider yourself a businessman. I am a Muslim businessman, and a believer. What I believe is that a man should be able to provide for his family through the fruits of his labor and the work of his farm. That is why we pay the government officials. We do it to prevent destruction of the poppy fields."

One of the cousins gave Farzam a nudge. "The poppy fields cannot be burned without repercussion," the cousin interjected. Another cousin said, "Some of our sons will become the government officials who stop the field eradication. It is a risky task, and deserves payment for the danger involved."

All the cousins and the Haji nodded. The payment was for risk-taking on the part of the officials. They deserved the money.

"Why are the invaders burning the poppy fields?" Farzam asked. He worried greatly that they should not have allowed the American to visit their village.

"There can only be one answer to that," Haji answered. "They are idiots. Someone told them this would be a way to remove heroin from the world. To burn the fields of a farmer at the time of harvest. To destroy the livelihood of the poorest peasants."

"As if the traffickers in drugs would not simply pay another poor farmer, in another place, to grow poppy," cousin Afrooz added.

The Haji took control of the conversation now. He had a speech to make, and a contract to finalize. "Now, the Americans. What are they doing here? They know their Osama Bin Laden is in Pakistan, not in Afghanistan. This is why they are not trying too hard to find him right now. It would be complicated for the Bush administration." He put up his thumb to indicate "one," then his index finger to indicate "two." "Did any Afghani participate in the bombing in New York City in 2001? No. Not a single Afghani."

Everyone nodded in agreement. They murmured; it was true. All the pilots in the U.S. World Trade Center incident were Arabs, not Afghanis.

"Now, what is happening?" the Haji lectured. 'Arabs come here from all over the world. To do what? To fight the Americans! Here. On our soil, in our streets! It is our children who live in fear of the crossfire. It is our children whose schools are bombed by drone attacks. Our children are the ones who suffer when the poppy fields are burned."

More food was brought in. Rice pudding with the smells of cardamom and raisins. Haji took a bowl of pudding and slurped. Farzam considered these words and said, "Why don't the Americans leave now, Haji? What is holding them here?"

"Hah!" Haji exclaimed. "The right question." He pointed his index finger and raised it to the ceiling. "Who knows the answer?"

One cousin jumped to the bait. "Because now they are stepping on their dongs," he offered.

Everyone rolled on the floor laughing. If they had access to a Facebook page, they would have taken a picture of themselves laughing and posted "ROFL." The Haji wiped a tear of laughter from his eye, and said, "When the Americans first came here, they believed they were going to get the natural gas from the Caspian Sea. The breakup of the Soviet Union left an opportunity to exploit the resource that was formerly part of the USSR. The US government came here talking for the companies. They wanted to get the gas from Turkmenistan. But they couldn't get it because our warlords would not agree. Before long, the defense contractors arrived. They spent money by bucket loads.

"But who cannot see that the money in Afghanistan is in poppy trafficking? Soon, a new industry arose. Now, the Americans believe they cannot leave until they get the gas pipelines built.

"This has proven to be more difficult than they expected. But in the end, the path will go from the Dauletebad gas field. This is on the border of Iran and Turkmenistan. It will enter Afghanistan at Herat, and travel directly across the Taliban-controlled areas in Helmand Province, through Kandahar, and into the Quetta Province of Pakistan. This is exactly the primary drug trafficking route."

"A very convenient choice," said cousin Afrooz. "The trafficking routes, and the gas pipeline, co-located. One logistics corridor, with truck movements in abundance, and security shared."

The Haji continued. "When the Americans leave, the names of the drug lords will shift and the boundaries of the drug territories will shift, and the method of drug protection will shift. The drug kingpins whom they have installed in the government, who give kickbacks to their defense contractors . . . all those arrangements will be void. The same as we have government officials on the take, they also have business contractors on the take. They have to keep the secret." He sighed, recovering from his laughing fit to become the serious teacher. "Money for poppy finances more than Afghanistan, Farzam," he continued. "It is a major component of the world banking system. The billions of dollars in cash that launder through it represent a number nearly the amount of all actual cash in the world. Everything else is a digital notation, not actual money. These flows of physical cash have the unique nature that they are not so trackable. Little pieces of them can be broken off and distributed around, without an audit trail. Let me make it clear. The motive is the untraceable money, my son. It is just the untraceable money. So war goes on, waiting for the gas pipeline to be built, waiting for the security forces to align."

Farzam's head whirled with the new insight he was getting from the Haji. "And are the American people such monsters, that they would allow this to happen? Do they not know?"

"They are absorbed in their own lives, Farzam," Haji said sadly. "They live in a world where it would take serious effort to know. It is not spoon-fed to them through their daily news propaganda. They would have to work and research to know. While the information can be found, it takes effort, and the people do not care to bother. People everywhere absorb themselves in the matters that impact their families. There is seldom time to look beyond.

"They are distracted, updating their Facebook pages, and text-messaging to their Twitter accounts. They cannot look up from their six-inch screens to see the world alive around them," Haji Ahmed added, with an air of deep contempt. He extended his arm, palm up, sweeping it to indicate the entire world. "This is why Islam is the way to salvation. It is against the rule of Allah to behave in such a way.

251

Their women behave as whores, who leave their families to trollop with strange men."

Farzam left that night believing that Haji Khan was a good man, and a good Muslim. Although he did not speak directly to Haji Khan, the meeting with his representative was the same as meeting with him. Farzam believed a man is known by his representatives. This is why he knew he could not become a partner to the American. Farzam learned that there was no real difference between drug traders, the Afghan government, and the Taliban. Each was a fellow Afghani, looking for the best way to survive in the world they found, searching for a way to give meaning to their lives, and feed the families they loved. Each was a part of the system required to get poppy safely to its market. Afghanistan, he understood from the Haji's viewpoint, was a narco-state. He understood that there was no option to go outside this system and deal directly with the American. At Haji Khan's house, he had been ready to make a deal. But first, Haji Ahmed had asked him to do one more thing. Farzam Parvanda would have to lure the American, Kiernan, into a trap. The trap was being set now. Haji Ahmed would contact Farzam when it was ready.

By the time Farzam returned to the mountains, it would be Spring. In Spring, the mountains cracked under the relentless force of thousands of seeds, bursting to life, becoming new, green promises.

Chapter 18

Present Day

Paris

"So you see, Andrew, the situation in Afghanistan was complex," Olivier said, back in his apartment living room with Andrew Meyers. "Bockenheim the Lesser had his fingers in all the Defense Department pies. He had security contracts through Te, and he also had faith-based grants for the Aid Relief Institute. The ARI wasn't a fake charity. It actually did try to perform some good works. But its ability to drive trucks and deliver cargo provided a cover for Te's mercenary operations. It made it easier for Te to operate illicitly without being challenged. Te could fly supplies for the ARI out of Afghanistan directly to New York. The supplies would pass through customs as cargo for ARI, then be loaded onto Te's corporate jet and delivered to Copper Hollow Airport."

Andrew wasn't listening. He was worried about the call he made to his mother. His mother, back in Pennsylvania, wanted to know what he was doing in France and when he was coming home. She didn't understand why he was sleeping on somebody else's sofa in Paris, when he had a perfectly good job with a paycheck and an apartment in Copper Hollow.

"Was it okay to tell my mom I'm here?" Andrew asked.

Olivier, as usual, had his eyes fixed on his computer screen while he talked. "Yes, of course, you can tell your mom. You're not in hiding. I doubt that your mom is a spy for Te. Besides, you charged your plane ticket. If someone were looking for you, you could be found."

"Then why did I have to leave?" Andrew asked. It was sinking in that he no longer had a job or a paycheck. Where would he get another newspaper job in these hard times, without a good reference?

"You left so that it would be too much trouble for Copper Hollow locals to find you. How long has Will Pruitt been dead? A week? After what happened to Mitchell Davis, I'd never forgive myself if you went missing, too."

"What do you think happened to Mitchell?"

"The only thing I know for sure is that he disappeared right after he took his evidence, wrapped in a nice package, to Will Pruitt's office. He left a message on my answering machine that he was going there. Then I never heard from him again. I called around. I searched online. I can't find him."

"Maybe he just took off, went home, or went into hiding. Did you file a missing person's report?"

"No. Who am I? I'm a guy who lives in Paris. A French guy. Why would I want to draw attention to myself like that? Besides, I write for controversial news outlets like Al Jazeera and Truth Digs. Madeleine asked Ann to call the newspaper and ask for him, but they told her he resigned to go back to school. They said they didn't know where he went."

"Well, maybe that's what happened. What was he taking to Pruitt? Didn't he know Pruitt was part of the problem?"

"None of us knew Pruitt was involved back ther.. Madeleine and I had a little insight into the big picture. Mitchell corresponded with me by email after Ann Kiernan introduced him to us. But these were early days in our understanding of the story of Copper Hollow. We didn't have the benefit of hindsight that we have now. Plus, Wikileaks was just a glimmer in the eye of some hackers in Iceland at the time. I didn't get the full story myself until I had full access to the information from whistleblowers at Wikileaks. Even now, there's a blurry line surrounding Josh Bockenheim. It's not completely clear where he gets his direction. Even today, it's still not completely clear."

Back to the Spring of 2007
The Suburbs of Washington D.C.

In the suburbs of Northern Virginia, in a non-descript office building, surrounded by ten other identical buildings, at the end of a curving driveway leading nowhere else, in an ordinary and unexceptional office park, six cars sat alone in an empty parking lot. Two armed security guards sat behind a wooden reception desk, in front of a gray-on-gray sign that read IATF. Inter-agency task force. It was Sunday. None of the IATF employees were in the building.

In a conference room, stocked with party-sized coffee pot, cups, and swiveling leather chairs, eight men met to consider a problem for the company, Te, and its contract with the United States Defense Department. It was a highly secret meeting. To ensure its secrecy, it was held in this non-extraordinary place, at an unannounced time, where it would appear to be unimportant. The attendees included no secretaries or note-takers of any type. No assistants, no drivers, only the principals. These were people who knew that the way to keep a secret was to not tell anybody. They operated face to face, not through email.

In attendance were the Undersecretary for Defense of the United States, Mark Perkins. United States Congressman Gerald Forbes, chair of the House Intelligence Committee. United States Senator Jim Roberts, chair of the Senate Intelligence Committee. Congressman A and Congressman B, who were merely interested parties. Josh Bockenheim, President of Te, private company with many defense contracts, and Hanif Maluod, agent assigned to Pakistan, Central Intelligence Agency. Hosting the meeting and providing the coffee was Bill Rollins, Governor. The Governor began.

"Gentlemen," Bill said, shaking his full head of white hair away from his rotund face, "we are ready to donate the land in Copper Hollow for the training facilities. The land is public land, owned by the town of Copper Hollow, and surrounded by the national park. This has been arranged in closed meetings in the town and will present no problems. There will be 400 acres, completely shielded by closed off park paths and fences. We have even made arrangements that the area is not discoverable by Google maps."

Laughter all around. Ho, ho, we can outsmart Google maps. We must be really powerful.

The Department of Defense guy, Mark, wiped the sweat off his lower lip with a white handkerchief he pulled out of his pocket. He stuffed the used handkerchief back into his left pants pocket. In a raspy voice, too infrequently used for a man who says very little, he croaked, "Hanif, where do we stand on the agreements with Pakistan's Intelligence Service, the ISI? It seems to me that is always what holds us up."

Hanif turned toward Mark, setting down his coffee cup. Hanif's perfectly groomed hair and expensive suit made him look vastly different than he had looked when he accompanied Chance Kiernan to the rugged areas of Afghanistan. "The ISI wants safe passage for their product," Hanif answered, in the perfect English one would expect from a boy born and raised in Missouri. "Both the product in and the product out. They've made arrangements to deliver arms to the mujahedeen as we have asked. They have product from Afghanistan to sell and they need it to reach its market. Our logistics in Copper Hollow have worked well to date and we want to continue that arrangement. As long as we are able to guarantee this will continue, they will cooperate with the larger picture."

Pakistan's ISI, Inter-Services Intelligence agency, was a long-term player in the Afghanistan conflict. It is rumored to be the largest spy agency in the world. When Washington DC talks to the President of Pakistan, there may be no guarantee that the commitments the President of Pakistan makes will be honored by the ISI; the ISI speaks for itself.

It is the ISI that took the aid money from the U.S. and gave it to the mujahedeen during the Soviet war. Later, after the Soviets were defeated, the ISI decided to fund and train another insurgent group: the Taliban. By that time, the U.S. aid to the mujahedeen had dried up. So the Paks found a new way to fund the Taliban. The insurgents were not the mujahedeen any more. Mujahedeen had taken over the Afghan government. Now, the insurgents being funded were the Taliban. But in Afghanistan, all the various enemies looked alike. Who was Taliban? Who was mujahedeen? Who was Uncle Mansour, the shopkeeper? Who was a drug kingpin? At different times of day, might they all be the same person?

Josh Bockenheim recognized his opening and took it. He appreciated Hanif for setting it up so nicely. "It works well now," Josh said, "but we called this meeting because the Congressman has pointed out there is a potential snag. I see it as a potential opportunity to solve a problem. I've mentioned before that I see a weak link in our operation in Copper Hollow. We can't arm the insurgents on money we can slip unnoticed through the budget of American taxpayers. Without the Soviets as a foil, there's no appetite for arming Afghan insurgents. The Karzai government does not have control of any areas in the north. Only the Pashtuns pay attention to the government. While it helps, to have an official government in Afghanistan, it doesn't give us the freedom we need to get the job done. For my company to perform our duties, we must have the option to allow the Afghanis to pay their own way. They do it by distributing their product, and we offer them the channel to do so. They receive the arms they need to fight the Taliban, which controls every area outside the city of Kabul, the southern area next to Pakistan, and the territory around Kandahar. Our workaround to deal with this is a good solution, but it requires a solid plan with total undiscoverability. To date, we have relied on Copper Hollow's facilities to keep our activities in the U.S. unnoticed."

The DoD Boss snapped back. "Hold on, Bockenheim." He sighed, exasperated. They'd been down this road before. "You aren't suggesting we use drug money for this operation." It was a declaration, not a question. The DoD's official policy, still, was hands off on drug deals. We had a war to fight. Getting involved in drug trafficking would only distract from the mission. Mission creep was expensive.

Bockenheim knew exactly how to answer this question, which was never asked. "Of course I'm not, Boss. I'm merely pointing out that the Pakistanis *will* use drug money for this operation. As usual. This allows us to give them less aid. If we had to pay them for everything we are asking them to do, we would run out of money. Fortunately, they don t ask, because they assume they can take the drug money, and that will subsidize it."

The room went completely silent.

Bockenheim continued. "There is no need to speak. I'm not giving an opinion. I'm reading from your intelligence reports." He pushed a stack of papers across the table. The top few pages went flying over the table onto the floor. "If you haven't read them," he inserted, "perhaps you'd like to review."

The room tensed. Everyone began watching everyone else, to see who in the room did not already know. The DoD Boss pinched his lips together. "And what is it you wanted us to do again? I'm getting fuzzy about why you wanted this meeting."

Bockenheim smiled. "You pay me. You give me a contract that specifies what you want done. Then you check back later, to see that what you asked for gets delivered. Beyond that, you butt out, turn your head, and mark what I do as *Classified*. Protected from prying eyes. All I'm asking for is privacy, so I can do the job."

The tenseness dropped out of the men in the room and thudded to the floor. That was the solution. Nobody would have to say it. Classify Bockenheim's operations. Let him do his job. Keep the nosy press out of the way.

Hanif, speaking for the entire Central Intelligence Agency, added, "If it were not for this unspoken task, you would use U.S. soldiers to take care of this distribution and funding problem. You hire contractors when the U.S. military can't be used, and this is such a case. There is no other reason."

Congressman A couldn't help himself. "It's not like these contractors are cheaper than U.S. soldiers," he offered. Then he laughed at his own joke.

The men all leaned back in their chairs. No, indeed, these mercenary contractors were not cheaper than U.S. soldiers. In many more ways than money. They fidgeted in their discomfort. They laughed in their anxiety. As worrisome as Josh Bockenheim's operation was, it did offer a way to build a firewall around the activities that no one wanted to explicitly state or know. There would be no meeting minutes to identify the participants. It would not be necessary to say the words. No prying journalists or unpatriotic activists could expose the scheme. The unspoken could remain unspoken. Yet, they had each clearly heard.

The training center would solve so many problems. Certainly, it was needed for the expansion of the forces in Afghanistan. It would provide facilities for Bockenheim's operation that could be classified and secure. The local elected officials were on board with it. It would not run into zoning problems or privacy concerns. It was fairly inaccessible. It would kill a number of birds with one stone.

After another minute of silence, the Governor said, "Let's get this training center operating, then."

Josh Bockenheim was more worried than he let on to the Boss. He knew that, back in Copper Hollow, Ray Plotzky was stumbling around looking for ghosts and demons. If Ray kept at it, he might accidentally come upon some actual information. Up until now, Josh never worried about Plotzky. Plotzky had his own agenda, and he never looked where Josh hid. As a backup in case that strategy stopped working, Josh had added Will Pruitt to his payroll. As Bockenheim's attorney, Will would have to keep his mouth shut, and he would be limited in what he could allow to be said in other local cases. Because crap always rolls downhill, Josh decided to ratchet up the pressure on Will Pruitt.

When Josh Bockenheim explained to Will Pruitt that Ray Plotzky needed to be diverted to some other cause, and preferably removed from his position as mayor, Will Pruitt objected with vigor. He couldn't even think of something big enough to prevent the citizens of Copper Hollow from re-electing Ray Plotzky. Ray was kin in one way or another to more than half of them. The old-timers believed the name Plotzky and the name Mayor were one word. "MurrPlotzky" they garbled when they talked. Plotzky's had been the mayor here for four generations, and in this neck of the woods, that counted for something. *What could be big* *enough to keep a Plotzky from being elected mayor in Copper Hollow?*

Well, Will supposed, if Ray were in jail, he couldn't be mayor. But, seriously, why would Ray be in jail? Could he come up with something that could be a local scandal, but not something that would land Plotzky behind bars? Will wasn't completely sure how to pull that off, but he knew he could get some mileage out of all the rumors and whispers of rumors that travelled quickly through the town.

He thought maybe he could slip a few clues to Ed Brentwood, the federal prosecutor for this area. Not clues like Sherlock Holmes clues. Ed Brentwood wouldn't grasp subtleties. More clues like: I know how you can get a great job offer to supplement your current salary. If Ed could be convinced that Ray Plotzky was an actual threat, Ed would use his discretionary power to go after him. That would keep Ray busy and prevent him from nosing around in Bockenheim's business. The job offer to Ed Brentwood was a way to get Ed's attention, so he would use his powers of selection to choose to investigate Ray. There wasn't anything wrong with that. *If Ray wasn't guilty, Ed wouldn't find anything, right? Sure, sure, everybody knew an innocent man had nothing to fear from an investigation, didn't they?* Ray would be busy answering questions and he wouldn't get in the way of Josh Bockenheim. He made the call to Ed that night. It was a perfect solution.

Driving to work in Northern Virginia traffic the next day, on Interstate 66, Ed Brentwood had plenty of time to think. After his evening conversation with Will Pruitt, Ed Brentwood realized there were a lot of people who didn't like all this noise about methamphetamine in Copper Hollow. It was making the state politicians look negligent. Their constituents asked questions. State politics, he believed, would look favorably on him if he shut Ray Plotzky down. He'd been thinking of running a campaign to rid rural areas of corrupt mayors. It was low-hanging fruit, as far as a winning public relations effort for his rising career. There were plenty of rural mayors to choose from, few of which had any idea they were breaking federal laws. Often, they were simply doing what had always been done, as their predecessors before them, and were oblivious to the complexities of the thousands of political technicalities. All he'd have to do is pick one mayor, and fish around into his daily business. He needed to choose some hapless schmuck who had bungled his way into a hornet's nest. In the press, Ed could be the hero who rid the nation of oppressive corruption. It would set him on his path to a judge's seat.

Will Pruitt's call to suggest an alternative career path with Josh Bockenheim? Well, that was icing on the cake. In fact, as Ed understood the arrangement, his federal judgeship would be the meat of his career. His consulting paycheck from Te would be gravy. With a setup like that there would be plenty of dessert to go around. He pulled into his office parking lot, drove to his reserved space, cursed to find that someone else had parked in it, and selected an open space three rows down. As he got out of his leased Lexus, he checked to make sure his shoes were not scuffed, and his pants were tightly creased. Then, despite the aggravation of the parking-space interloper, he practically skipped and whistled into his office.

"Good morning, Sally," he sang to Mrs. Jarvis. Over his shoulder, as he entered his deep and dark office, he called,

"Can you get those USDA representatives on the phone? I have time to see them this morning."

Ray Plotzky would be a good candidate for his first corruption campaign. He went out to the waiting room as soon as the USDA reps arrived. He knew they would come over. They'd been bothering him for months to look for something they could do to help out the dairy industry. Ed Brentwood had a case for them. He got the directions to Copper Hollow, and put in a call to the FBI. *Game on.*

For two more months, Ann Kiernan enjoyed the company of her husband, at home. Nothing bad happened in Copper Hollow, that Ann knew about. Chance Kiernan was home, and he spent his days with her and his boys. This made Ann happy. They went to the movies, they played ball at the park, they took family hikes in the forest. They had dinner together, they planted a garden, they considered getting a chicken coop. Every day was routine and uneventful. Ann loved it. Chance? Not so much.

Chance Kiernan considered quiet time as the calm before the storm. He thought it was highly suspicious. Quiet time made him nervous. Somebody's gotta be up to something, he figured.

As it turned out, Chance Kiernan was exactly right.

Chapter 19
Spring, 2007
Copper Hollow

The Plotzky family owned and ran a heritage farm. They believed farming was done a certain way: the way their family had done it for centuries. The Plotzkys owned two milk cows, four beef cattle, three sows, and one boar. They had fifty chickens, give-or-take, and about a dozen sheep. They kept eight acres planted in vegetables, and enough acres planted in hay and corn to feed the animals. They didn't use chemicals to farm, and they saved their own seed from year to year, to keep costs down. The farm itself was owned by Mom and Pop Plotzky. Ray and his younger sister lived there. Some of the many Plotzky relatives came over to work the farm. Pop figured a farm like that would feed twenty families, and he preferred that they all be Plotzkys. This was the way the family had lived in the mountains, and after they got their share of the copper, they staked out their land and started to farm.

Being mayors of Copper Hollow through four generations didn't change the way the Plotzky's lived. Mayor is a part-time job with a nominal paycheck. Plotzkys continued to be what they always were: mountain men and farmers. Of course, with the girls marrying, a number of Plotzkys no longer had the Plotzky last name, and some Plotzkys had moved away from Copper Hollow. Sometimes, a relative who had moved away would drive back to get their share of the farm harvest. Pop Plotzky turned it over. Why wouldn't he? They was family. Now, the Plotzky family drank their milk straight outta the cow. Why wouldn't they? They always had. Cows needed to be milked. Children needed to be fed. What else would a person do?

On a day shortly after Ed Brentwood had his talk with the USDA, a man and a woman drove a beat-up old dark red Chevy pickup to Copper Hollow, and parked in the driveway at the Plotzky farm. The man wore a flannel, button-down shirt, and a pair of blue jeans that looked like he just took them out of the plastic package at Box-Mart. Nice, ironed creases in them, and a color that hadn't bled in the washing machine yet. He had those wrap-around sunglasses on, and a haircut that made him look like he was in the military on the weekends. The man knocked on Pop Plotzky's front door, while the woman sat in the passenger seat in the car. She was wearing headphones, and bopping her ponytail like she was listening to music. Pop opened the door, but it took him awhile, on account 'a his bum leg and his bum knee and his missus not bein' home at the moment.

"Howdy, Mayor Plotzky," the stranger said, stickin' his hand out to shake. "Name's Grady Pell, nice to meet ya."

Old Ray wasn't mayor any more, but he didn't mind people callin' him that, as an honorary title. "What kin I do ya for?" he asked the stranger.

The stranger didn't seem to know Old Ray wasn't Young Ray, or else he didn't care. "Wife and I come from the next state over, where your cousin Donnie lives?" he made it a question, just like the folks in Copper Hollow would do.

"Yeah," Old Ray acknowledged. He had a cousin Donnie somewhere that wasn't here.

"We wuz passin' through, and the wife tells me she has a hankerin' for some good milk. She's expectin'. Donnie tol' us you was here, and we were wonderin' if you might sell us some. We'd be mighty appreciative."

It wasn't something Old Ray would normally do, but what kind of man would turn down a pregnant woman who asked for a glass of milk? Old Ray invited Grady Pell and his wife, Juliette, to come and sit in his living room. The wife didn't look very pregnant to Old Ray, but who was he to say about such things? He settled them down in his living room, turned on the radio, and went into the kitchen to pour some fresh, whole milk into a half-gallon mason jar. When he brought it into the living room, he handed the jar to Grady Pell. When Grady reached for his wallet, Old Ray said, "No charge, for a friend of Donnie."

"I insist," Grady responded, pulling a five dollar bill from his wallet. He stuffed the bill in Old Ray's shirt pocket. "I can't take it free. It's not right. I was thinkin' for the future. Maybe we can come over here and get it more regular. We only live down the road, right across the state line. My wife sure would love to be able to get good fresh milk for the baby."

Old Ray knew they had plenty, and he didn't see the harm. So he said okay.

And then Juliette March pulled out her handcuffs. She read Old Ray his rights, and told him he was engaging in illegal interstate commerce. The U.S. Marshalls waiting at the end of the road pulled their five cars into the driveway, and a dozen of them rushed out in their fancy new SWAT gear and their automatic machine guns. They pointed those guns at Old Ray Plotzky, seventy-two year old ex-Mayor of Copper Hollow, and shoved him into the back of a van.

At the far end of Main Street, if you take a right, and follow it around until the road turns country, at the corner of the lake and the crossroads, sits a country store and diner. Jo-Beans. Jo-Beans may not be the best restaurant in town, but it is the most popular. Every morning, half a dozen or more old-timers meet there for breakfast. Clem, Al, Red, and Buck are the regulars. Others stop in now and then. Everybody stops in, eventually.

Half the morning they talk about politics. The other half, they talk about sports. It was Red who had the inside track on what happened. "Yeah," Red started, his 300-lb frame easing into the largest chair at the table. "The Feds took Old Ray in handcuffs right thar. Heard he's still locked up."

Al laid his dirty baseball cap on the table, right next to the buttered rolls. "Waren't the Mayor thar?" The Mayor was the younger Plotzky.

"s'pose not, cause nobody seen 'im," Red answered, with his mouth full of fried eggs and hash.

"That don't make no sense," Clem inserted. "Why'd the Feds show up wit'out the Mayor?" As he spoke, he reached

268

across Red's plate to get the bowl of foil packs of margarine. "Whadda they gonna do with Old Ray?"

"Mus' a been drugs," Al piped in. "Don' know whad else they'd bother him for."

"Heard they's talkin' of closin' down his farm. Takin' away the animals. 'Cause he's sellin' the milk."

"Well, that don't make no sense," Red said. "You can't arrest somebody for milk."

"It's gotta be drugs," Buck added, leaning back with the air of a man who had the inside scoop. "My nephew, Ralph Merkel – he's out on parole fer drugs. Makes money turnin' people in. Cops pay 'im. Sometimes he offers to sell weed to the tourists an' then turn 'em in." Buck was happy to be related to someone in law enforcement.

"Who does that?" Red questioned. "Will Pruitt?" He wanted to know, thinking one of his nephews might want to get in on a deal like that.

"No, no, just Ralph does it. Then he tells the poe-leese," Buck answered, motioning to the waitress to bring more toast. "When they come out on parole, Will Pruitt's their lawyer. He gets 'em a deal to be informants. Pays 'em fer what they bring in. They do it all up legal. With a contract. It's 'bout the only job these young 'uns can get. Makes Ralph feel like he's a real cop. Undercover. His mama says he's doin' good work, bringin' money in regular," Buck told the group.

"Well, Young Ray knows this town," said Clem. "Young Ray'll straighten everything out."

"Tha's a fac'," Al agreed. "Ray'll go get Old Ray outta this mess. Whaddaya think he was doin'? Growin' Mary-Wanna?"

269

They all laughed. Hearty, country laughter. Mae poured another round of coffee in their cups, when she brought the extra toast.

"That Old Ray's a wild one, ain't he?" Mae agreed. "Who'd a thought he'd be growin' weed on that farm."

And that's how the residents of Copper Hollow came to say that Old Ray Plotzky was growing marijuana on the family farm. They started tellin' the tale, and nobody could stop the rumor from travelin'. After all, who would be arrested for sellin' milk? And waren't Ray arrested?

The real mayor, Young Ray Plotzky IV, Warlord of Copper Hollow, had to be about scraped off the floor of Will Pruitt's office when Will called him to make bail for his dad. Will had to get out his law books, and show Young Ray the actual law that said distribution of raw milk across state borders was a crime in the United States of America. *How could it be true?* No way on God's green Earth did a thing like that make sense to Ray Plotzky, either the Elder or the Younger. In the government that Young Ray learned about in elementary school, the citizens of the United States were free agents. Nobody told them they couldn't drink milk out of a real cow. *And who would even think of such a damn fool thing?*

Even more, Old Ray was sittin' in jail, babblin' on about how there were three branches of government, and the newspapers were the fourth estate, and the poe-leese were not allowed to set people up. That was called entrapment, Old Ray hollered. He was going to call the newspapers and tell them all about it, he said. But the U.S. Marshalls didn't seem worried about Old Ray's future visit to the newspaper office. They were busy trying to figure out how they could have been so stupid as to arrest the wrong Mayor Plotzky.

Present Day
Back in Paris

Olivier paused as he told the story to Andrew. All of this information could not be known at the time it happened. It only had a context in hindsight. "Here's where we begin to see the role Will Pruitt played," Olivier said. "Pruitt was the Public Defender. He was also Bockenheim's lawyer. When Bockenheim wanted Plotzky out of the way, Pruitt had to figure out how to do it. He didn't expect the FBI to pick up the wrong Plotzky, but he figured it wouldn't matter either way. Young Ray would be just as diverted from his goals by having to deal with this attack on his father. It would still keep Young Ray out of Bockenheim's way.

"One of Bockenheim's contracts included building a training center in Copper Hollow. Te's troops would train military and other consultants. Bockenheim was using ARI, Te, the training center, and he had some involvement in trafficking drugs. But with his arrangements with the Defense Department, it was unclear whether what he did was part of his classified work. Was he working within the constraints set for his task by his classified contract? Was it a sting operation, set up to find the real structure of the heroin market? Or was Bockenheim acting on his own behalf, outside the bounds of his federal contract? Who could know? And would the system in place allow him to stay within those constraints and still be safe? Marking an activity as classified served the purpose of keeping the newspapers away. It also served to keep everybody away who wasn't directly involved. Even Chance Kiernan didn't have full access to what Bockenheim was doing. When the military is doing classified activities, maybe that's okay. But when the military is contracting out those activities to a commercial company? Is it still okay to let them operate without anybody knowing what they are doing? Who was going to look inside the box and figure out where the lines were drawn? Nobody had the insight into the workings of a private corporation, once it had that 'classified' label on it.

"So Ray Plotzky is trying to figure out what he's seeing here, when he looks into the activities at the airport, and it turns out to be a classified operation. Ray doesn't know what that means. He's curious. He doesn't know who to talk to, so he calls the newspaper."

"Ray called the newspaper?" Andrew asked.

"Specifically, Ray called Mitchell Davis. It started out as a call to tell about Pop Plotzky being arrested. But it turned into much more. The more Ray and Mitchell Davis shared what each of them knew about Josh Bockenheim's activities, the more they got worried. Mitchell started rolling things over in his mind. Then he got his bright idea."

"What?" Andrew asked.

"Mitchell's bright idea was to interview Josh Bockenheim himself, and make it look like Bockenheim was the good guy, and Mitchell was going to write an article about his successful company. He thought he would be an undercover agent, going right into Bockenheim's office and finding things out for himself."

Madeleine added, "It seems that Mitchell overestimated his personal skill as an investigative reporter."

"So he was found out when he got into Bockenheim's office?"

"Actually, he never made it into Bockenheim's office. He couldn't get the appointment in time."

"In time for what?"

"In time for Chance Kiernan to save him," Olivier answered.

Madeleine entered the room at that point, with a bottle of wine and three glasses. "This is a question which Ann Kiernan needed to answer for herself, too. Was Chance Kiernan going to save her from the perils of Copper Hollow? She needed to know that before she could decide if she would continue her marriage. When Ann married Chance, she did not fully understand who he was and what he did for a living. One cannot easily grasp the concept of life in the bed of an assassin."

She poured the wine. Andrew sipped and stared at Madeleine's seductive beauty. *What exactly did she mean "an assassin?"*

Chapter 20

Summer, 2007
The Hindu Kush Mountains, Afghanistan

Chance Kiernan was frankly happy to be going back to Afghanistan again. His absences from home, since they moved to Copper Hollow, had been extensive. After he'd gotten the hostages released, however, he'd been home for months. He missed the action and was eager to get back into it. The men who took the hostages had a beef with Josh Bockenheim. They basically thought he was an a-hole, and wanted him to take his Toaster Pies and go home, away from Afghanistan. Chance could see their point. He was pretty well coming to that conclusion, too. The question for his mission became: how much of what Bockenheim did was legitimate? He knew there was a mandate to get a fix on the drug operations in Afghanistan, and he knew Bockenheim was assigned to that team. But where did Bockenheim cross the line? With Bockenheim, you couldn't ask him. You could never believe his answer. Was it Bockenheim himself, or someone under him? Or, for that matter, was it someone above him? Did his father, Bruce Bockenheim, who actually controlled the purse strings, order this, or was the father duped by it? Kiernan didn't know, but he couldn't reveal himself as a complete skeptic yet. He needed the evidence first. One thing Chance Kiernan hated was to catch the little guys, and leave the big guys free to run off with the prize.

He waited in Kandahar for almost two weeks, when he got the message from Farzam, through Hanif's channels. There was a problem with the deal. They had received the arms, yes, but they would be unable to proceed with the transfer of the tor. They had decided to cancel the arrangement. Now Chance and Hanif would have to go back to the village to meet with the tribal council. Perhaps they could be paid for the weapons, which had already been delivered, at some time in the future.

Wonderful. How screwed up was that? First, he has to clean up Bockenheim's mess with the Taliban, and now this. He had assembled a convoy, but their cover story required that they travel without U.S. military. Fighting had heated up along the northern road. They would not be able to make the trip without security. He was going to be dependent on Te's security guards. Damn that Josh Bockenheim. You want to get free of him, but you need him.

They took six armed guards from Te, the translator, the porter-guide, the driver, Hanif, and Chance. Plus food, gear, and tents for an overnight stay. Three cars. Their hosts were less than welcoming this time, so they could not count on lodging and hospitality. Because of the short timeframe, they hurried to assemble everything they needed. On top of that, they would now be travelling from Kandahar, where he had been called to deal with the hostages, instead of from Kabul. The trip would be longer, and the roads more dangerous.

They left Kandahar at first light. They would travel north, through Ghazni, and on to Kabul. They would stay overnight in Kabul. Chance and Hanif would stay at the Serena. The Te men always stayed at the Gandamack Lodge. The Gandamack boasted a restaurant that was "rice-free;" the Te men said they needed a break from rice eating. They also enjoyed the history of Gandamack. It was reputed to have been the house of Osama Bin Laden's fourth wife. In Kabul, they would refresh supplies for the convoy, and head north to Farzam's village the next morning.

Chance and Hanif sat in the middle car, with the translator-driver and the porter-guide. The Te guys took the head and the tail cars, their weapons array of SCARs, M4s, and M16's impressively displayed in the ready position. Chance was satisfied with his personal Glock 19. He knew Hanif carried a Beretta, which was also Chance's backup pistol. It would be a long drive, through hours of gray and brown nothing, on the A-One road to Kabul. The dust-covered and sandy landscape showed nothing but isolated tufts of scruffy green brush, a few variegated lizards here and there, and brown mountains in the distance. Occasionally, as they rode, they saw a camel train or a donkey convoy. Few cars passed by. Chance watched an eagle for a while. The air had a denseness to it, with the smell of dry heat and sand. The temperature hovered around 88 degrees. The open tops of the Land Rovers helped to cool them, as they rolled along at 80 miles an hour.

Chance generally shied away from any form of small talk. To ask a personal question of someone else implied that one would entertain receiving a personal question back. That was not Chance Kiernan. He did not answer personal questions, and so he did not ask personal questions. But he did wonder about Hanif's background and history. He had not asked before, but this time, he felt it might be mission-relevant.

Hanif pulled a foil-wrapped *mantu,* a meat dumpling, out of his man-bag. He offered one to Chance. As Chance unwrapped it and bit into the juicy, curry-flavored lamb in a bean filling, he asked, "What part of Pakistan are you from?"

"The part that's in St. Louis, Missouri," Hanif answered.

Chance should have known. But Hanif's wife wore the *chador,* head scarf, at all times, and spoke with a thick accent, so Chance continued, "And your wife? Where is she from?"

Hanif finished chewing and swallowed before speaking. "She's from Kansas City. We met at Yale."

Chance gave that some thought, then he decided to go for it. "Sooo . . . why does she speak with an accent?"

"She is also an employee of the Company," Hanif answered. "The accent has its purpose."

What possible purpose could there be for an American woman from Kansas to endure the disdain of her neighbors in Copper Hollow by pretending to be a Pakistani? Another data point, Chance thought. To add to many data points. He doubted that further questions would pass the "need to know" test, so he settled down to his own thoughts. As they approached Kabul, they smelled the stench of human waste and garbage before they saw the city. Sparrows and doves led the way.

The next morning, after a solid night's sleep and an opportunity for hot showers, Chance had a breakfast of steaming naan and *chakka,* yogurt cheese, with sweet chai. The group reassembled, ready for a half-day's ride.

As they left Kabul, they followed the north road, the Asian highway, AH76. They were about an hour and a half out when they were stopped at a government checkpoint. It appeared to be a temporary stop point. Just a group of police, some road barriers, and a tent with a barrel fire for the police to cook, along with a water barrel for them. They had some carpets to sit on, and a few police cars. Chance smelled their goat kebabs grilling over the barrel. They had two hefty police dogs, who barked ferociously and pulled on their leashes.

Of course, since they were not travelling as U.S. military, there were questions from local Afghan police. Why are you going north? What is the purpose of so many security guards? Who are you going to see? Why? There had not been a police checkpoint here the last time they came through. Their guide, for some reason, seemed to get the answers to the questions all wrong. Chance expected that the police wanted money. He told the guide to offer what they had, but the police seemed to think that was not enough. The trip had been arranged too hurriedly, Chance understood. He hadn't gotten his backup plans in place. Eventually, after much conversation in Dari, with some side arguments in the Pashto language, the guide told them the police wanted them to go back to Molamanjay, to the police station. The police said this road was too dangerous for travel, that only drug smugglers travelled this way, and that if they did not turn back, perhaps that meant they were drug smugglers. The police moved toward the convoy.

Chance apparently had his back turned when the action began. He must have been looking in the wrong direction, because the next thing he knew, he heard shots fired. He didn't know who fired, whether it was the police, or the men from Te, but suddenly, one of the Te guards jumped into Chance and Hanif's car. They left their driver and guide behind, who were rushing to help an Afghan police-man who laid on the ground. The Te men screeched the cars out, guns pointed in every direction, yelling "go, go, go, go" and driving off to the Salang Pass. There would not have been another way to get to their meeting. From a mis-sion standpoint, the men from Te took the mission-critical action.

"Now how do you think we're going to get back through this way to come home?" Chance yelled into the open air.

"We'll have to keep going north," Hanif answered. "Into Tajikistan."

Damn, damn, damn, Chance thought. We'll be stuck here for a month.

In the village of their destination, Darya is visiting her mother, with her husband, the drug smuggler, Abdullah. Her mother wept when she took off her blue silk burka. Tears of joy. It had been nearly half her lifetime since Darya had been here. She left when she was eleven. Now, she was returning at twenty-one. Her mother looked so old now, with graying hair and a wrinkled face. She seemed smaller and stooped, not like the tall giant Darya remembered. Darya hugged and kissed her mother warmly. She remem-bered her mother's smell more clearly than her face. That smell brought back floods of memories. Tears from the memories flowed, from deep within her belly, as she re-membered the day Abdullah took her away. It was a great bruise then, but it seemed unimportant now, so many years later.

While Darya kissed her mother and greeted her aunts, she saw her father, standing in the back of the kitchen, watching with that same sad, regret-filled, hang-dog look he had the day she left him. He sold her. He sold her to pay his debt to a drug dealer. She had been an opium bride. But it worked out for her, this time. She had been lucky.

She pulled away from the women to go to her father. She hugged him as he wrapped his big bear arms around her and wept, deep sobs of sorrow. Darya cried, too, but for him, not for herself. "Baba," she whispered in his ear, "I am a woman, with my own children now. I am fine, and everything is okay. " She pulled back, and held his face between the palms of her hands. She looked into his eyes. "Baba," she said sternly, her face brightening and beaming with a big smile, "I have learned to read!" She didn't know if he was happy for her, or confused, but she was happy, and that made him smile.

The homecoming festival lasted through that first afternoon and evening. The village turned out for the party, and they roasted a lamb over an outside spit. The women fried raisins and carrots with honey for a pilau. The sweet fragrance of cardamom simmered in chai, filling the kitchens with the scent of joy. The men danced around the fire, some of them swishing swords elaborately through the air. Drums and reed flutes danced with the men, blending the cool night air into the warmth of the fire. Genuine love, tempered by the steel bonds of community, wrapped Darya in its woolen cloak, and she finally fell asleep, completely fulfilled.

While Darya remembered this uplifting sense of belonging, this warmth of community, and this depth of bonded love, she did not remember this poverty. When she left here, she was a child. She had no memory of the work of a woman in this place. She did not remember the trips to the well for water. She did not remember building fires to boil water. She did not remember hand-sorting the rice and beans to remove the stones. She did not remember the difficulty of storing food with no refrigerator. Her life in Marjah was the life of a princess in a castle, compared to life in this village. She wished she could take her mother and father back to Marjah with her. But they would be feral cats in a cage.

She told her mother about Naseem, Abdullah's first wife, and how kind Naseem was to her. Naseem had taught Darya to read, and brought her books of history, and was going to get her a computer, and an Internet account, and her own cell phone. But this, her mother did not understand. Her mother wanted to know that Darya was being a good mother and an obedient wife. That was her wish for her eldest daughter, and her only dream. Darya felt happy that she had left this place, and blessed by Allah to have Naseem and all their children.

As the convoy with Chance and Hanif entered the Salang Pass, the men of Te spun into high alert. Chance watched as the cars climbed, clinging to the side of a straight mountain, next to a thousand foot drop. At the bottom, the river raged. From here, on the narrow, unpaved road, the Lion of Pansjhir defended his valley during the Soviet invasion. The Lion of Pansjhir, Massoud, had been assassinated a few days before the events of September Eleventh in New York.

Chance realized this would be a bad place to be attacked. He envisioned the danger ahead. One narrow opening, flanked by high mountains. A sniper could sit on top, and the target would have no escape. When he heard the shots crack, it was too late. The first bullet smashed into Hanif's forehead. Chance ducked under the back of the seat, as he heard the second, third, fourth bullets crack straight to their targets. There was no way to pull his own gun and shoot back. The nature of the pass and the mountains made the snipers untouchable. He rolled out of the car, trying to keep the sides of the car between him and the bullets. Then the snipers hit his driver, and the car plunged off the side of the mountain, down the cliffs, into the river below. Before the car went over the edge, Chance rolled his body into the gutter and crawled to pull himself under a rock ledge on the mountain side. He could see the black turbans of the Taliban, and their long robes, peeking over the mountain top. Then an explosion, and the first car in the convoy blew up. The third car jerked into reverse and started backing down the mountain, the way it came. With all the convoy gone, he was left alone, under the rock ledge.

He waited under that ledge until dark. Then he pulled out his satellite phone, and crawled to a place where he could get reception. "I need an extraction," he said to Joe Bridgewell. "Here are my coordinates." An hour later, he heard the flap of the helicopter, grabbed the rope extended, and pulled up into the cab. Hanif's body had been forced over the side of the road, down the mountain cliffs, where it could not be recovered.

When Abdullah's men returned to Farzam and Darya's village from their assigned mission, they reported their success. They unwound their black turbans, and re-established their dress as Pashtuns. They were Taliban if they chose, not Taliban if they chose not. Abdullah smiled at Farzam. Man to man, their deal was sealed.

Present Day
Paris

"So basically," Olivier continued, "we have Chance Kiernan running a fake drug deal with real Afghan smugglers, but we don't know if Josh Bockenheim is completing the deal for real. Then Will Pruitt gets pressured into setting up Ray Plotzky as collateral damage. He pushes the buttons on Ed Brentwood, and takes advantage of a human flaw in a flawed system. He does it to save himself, at Josh Bockenheim's urging."

Madeleine added, "Will Pruitt was also collateral damage, but there was much more. When Mitchell Davis disappeared, that's what really set Olivier into high gear to find out what was going on here."

Chapter 21

Summer, 2007
Copper Hollow

When the FBI raided the Plotzky family farm, Mitchell Davis jumped at the opportunity to make a splash with his reporting. At last, something worthy to write about! He'd had some discussions with Mayor Ray about Bockenheim and the Ohio girls. He looked forward to really delving into what was going on. This ridiculous arrest of Old Ray seemed astoundingly suspicious. To Mitchell's dismay, the editor of the *Copper Hollow Mercury* decreed that this issue would be downplayed. "We're going to report it, but we're a small town paper," editor Reese Babbitt soothingly and quietly explained. "We don't want to do anything to stir people up. Keep it short and let that story die off. Write about this terrific new federal grant we got to expand the airport instead." Whoopie. A dry fact piece about goody-two-shoes stuff, Mitchell thought. Imagine all the avid readers who will want to know about this federal grant for a private airport that nobody uses.

With his talent suppressed, Mitchell's enthusiasm melted. His editor wouldn't let him write the piece about the FBI sting at the farm, and if his end-game was to be hired by a big-name paper, he needed front page bylines in the *Copper Hollow Mercury*. But if something didn't change around here soon, he might have to change his goal and try to get an independent piece published in Rolling Stone. Long term, he'd find another way, but for now, Mitchell was a believer in doing his best. He packed up his notebook and his tape recorder, and headed out to the airport.

If he had to write an article about the expansion of the airport, why not start at the beginning? What the heck was an airport doing here in the middle of nowhere in the first place? Why expand something that didn't have much use even when it was small? What was over there? Nine twin-engine Pipers and Cessnas? With no schedule of flights and no public access? Hey, wasn't that airport privately owned? Why would a federal grant pay for a chain link fence for a private airport? Maybe there was a tidbit in the grant document that would give this story some life.

As he drove to the outskirts of town, Mitchell thought about the people in this town. There were no street lights outside of the main street in the one town. There was no high speed Internet outside of the cable tv area in a three mile circumference on the main street. Most places outside of the town didn't even have cell phone service. He'd be driving around in the woods, and realize if he broke down, he couldn't get a cell signal. He'd see a twelve-year-old boy coming out of the forest carrying a rifle. Hunting was the sport here. It was the activity. And he had a suspicion, it was also the way many of these families got food. There was a river. It had small-mouthed bass and catfish in it. *Hunting and fishing, as a way to survive, Mitchell thought.*

He pulled through the airport gate and parked behind the small office. Lots of packages came in and out. Loads of shipping activity. And, of course, the corporate jet.

A corporate jet. Mitchell sat quietly, mulling. So, where's the corporation? he thought. Mitchell carefully reviewed the facts. There were no factories in Copper Hollow. There were no corporate offices here. No distribution centers. No jobs. No business activities of any type. But there was an active airport, moving packages in and out. On twin engine planes, privately owned, with a chain link fence around them. All this place had was hundreds of chicken farms. Chicken houses. Rows and rows of them. And nothing else. Nothing else. Did chickens travel on airplanes? There was nothing here but chicken houses.

To clear his head, and get some fresh perspective, Mitchell decided to see the airport from a fresh angle, to observe some of its activity. Sometimes, he liked to just get the feel of a place, to see if it would tell its own story. There was only one runway. He counted 24 hangers. How many of them had planes inside? He couldn't tell. All the doors were closed. There were no people around. There were no planes coming in or going out. He had checked earlier and found only twelve issued pilot licenses. He got back in his car, and drove around the back of the airport, to the hill behind, where the woods began. He wanted to see the runway and the area where the planes would come in from a different vantagepoint. As he parked his car and walked to the knoll, he saw that he was not alone. Juliette March, FBI Special Agent, was sitting on the ground with her binoculars. "Hello, Mitchell," she said. "Working on something?"

Juliette watched Ed Brentwood sizzle, hot-to-trot on the Mayor Plotzky scandal. She was assigned to the team, along with a more experienced FBI agent, and a USDA agent. Ed, as the federal prosecutor, directed the focus of the investigation. At first, the case had been about bringing down a family farm. *To prevent agro-terrorism, she supposed. All those dirty vegetables.* The image of the U.S. Marshalls in SWAT gear, pointing their red-dotted guns at half-lame old Ray Plotzky would have seemed comical, if it weren't actually cruel. But she tried to forget that image, and focus on her actual job of enforcing the law. The Mayor Plotzky investigation widened. It was clear that Brentwood was trying to pick the person, and find something to pin on him.

Juliette was young enough that she wasn't entirely opposed to this method of prosecution. There were times, she'd been taught, when you couldn't "get" the bad guy unless you targeted them. In the Post 9/11 FBI, sting operations were expected and had become a regular practice. Juliette was flexible about that. She was willing to believe Ed Brentwood knew more than she knew. She was willing to believe it was okay to pick the person first, and find something to charge him with later. Setups and entrapment had become a standard tool for the FBI, ever since they needed to show results in the War on Terror. Time and again, the FBI had posed as someone who wanted to conduct jihad, enticing a vulnerable person to agree to join in. Then they would arrest the person and publicly announce that they had thwarted a terror plot. It was a terror plot that would never have existed, but for the FBI's enticement. Juliette didn't grow up during the Cold War between the U.S. and the Soviets. She didn't know these were the tactics the U.S. decried when they were practiced by the Soviets. She didn't know these were the indicators that America was lost. She would be patient and follow orders, as she had been taught to do. Her drive to do well embedded inside her personality, and it overpowered her drive to do good; she followed orders.

Once again, Chance Kiernan was home. It had been a harrowing journey, from which he narrowly escaped. It resulted in the death of his partner, Hanif. There was not even a body to bring home to Hanif's wife. He went to D.C. to be debriefed on the entire debacle, including his opinion of Te as a team member. He'd been away for more than a month. As wonderful as it was to be home, to see his boys again, it was less inviting to see his wife. Ann Kiernan was extremely unhappy.

The first thing Chance did when he got home was take the boys to the animal shelter and let them choose a dog. Two dogs. Each boy got his own. Then he spent the whole weekend playing ball with them, and watching football with them. He was not in the mood to deal with Ann's sad, snappy, tearful, and desperate need for conversation. Not now. Not after what had just happened. He wasn't ready for Ann. He could not tell her what occurred; he could not explain to her how he felt; he could not divulge national defense secrets. She, on the other hand, felt compelled to talk.

"I think the boys and I should move to Fairfax, Virginia," she said. "There are good schools there, nice houses, and a reasonable environment. You aren't home, so it shouldn't matter to you. We'll live near your headquarters office."

Ann wasn't wearing a burka, but that did not keep her husband from failing to see her. It did not keep his mind away from Hanif's death, Te's role in killing the Afghan policeman, Bockenheim's little toaster pie operation, or Farzam's betrayal. It did not keep him from reliving the narrowness of his rescue, or the sting of his failed mission. These were the things preying on his mind, as his wife complained of her solitude, her lack of friends, or her inability to make a life for herself. So Ann kept talking, and Chance kept thinking of more important things, until Ann said, "And all over the town, there are FBI agents."

He looked up. "How do you know?"

"Know what?" she said. She had already moved on to a delineation of the types of women she met.

"Know that they are FBI agents," he clarified.

"They're sitting at the bar at the Parkside Inn," she answered. "Who can't tell the difference between an FBI agent and a resident of Copper Hollow?"

And as quickly as she said it, Chance grabbed his jacket and left.

At the bar at the Parkside Inn, Chance sidled up to the woman with the dark, collar-length hair, the light makeup, no jewelry, white blouse, and black suit. She wore 2-inch black heels and stockings. Her purse was modestly discrete, black, and small, with a shoulder strap. No nail polish. He flashed his telephone company executive ID badge. He was wearing his snakeskin cowboy boots, jeans, and suede brown jacket.

He stuck out his right hand and smiled. "Chance Kiernan," he said. "It's nice to meet you, Agent."

She looked startled.

He said, "The agency never has figured out that you people dress funny." He gave her his best Irish-rake smile.

Juliette March hesitated, looking around the bar to see if her boss was in the room. "I guess the telephone company would not really assign an executive to work out here, would they." It wasn't a question, and she motioned to take their drinks to a booth in the back. Their conversation became more intense, interspersed with cell phone calls to their respective bosses. At their most impassioned moment, when they were both focused on the intensity of their missions, for the work that they loved --- at that exact moment when their impassioned eyes locked, Charlotte Trout entered the pub. Charlotte didn't know that the handsome man with his eyes riveted on the attractive female FBI agent was Ann Kiernan's husband. But she wanted to know who he was, because she hadn't seen him around here before. He was handsome, charming, masculine, and potentially available. So Charlotte watched him.

During the weeks that Chance adjusted to life back home, he continued to work with Agent March. Ann seemed to calm down, now that he was home. He took her out a few times, and he spent most evenings with her and the boys. But during the day, he went out to work. At the Parkside Inn. With Juliette March.

Juliette and Chance laid claim to the last booth in the back corner at the Pub at the Parkside Inn. They were there so often, other patrons stayed away from that booth, out of territorial respect. Juliette had gotten her boss to open a Bockenheim case, and arrange for a clearance level so that she could talk to Chance. It tied in with whatever was going on with Ray Plotzky in some way, Juliette was sure. Juliette's FBI boss was not Ed Brentwood, of course. Ed was the federal prosecutor, who called in the FBI. Juliette successfully convinced her boss that there was some connection between the investigation of Ray Plotzky and the activities of Josh Bockenheim.

Juliette had a room at the inn, and if she and Chance had to discuss details that they could not afford to have overheard, they would move their discussion to her hotel room. They couldn't use Chance's kitchen table, because his family was there. They couldn't use the back room at the Spoon 'n' Fork, because the owner, Milton Fork, was clearly an employee of Bockenheim. There was no other office space for the TDU and FBI business here, and Copper Hollow was so far away from any other town, that it made sense to make use of the hotel room. So at times, a local resident of Copper Hollow would see Mr. Kiernan, from the telephone company, and that lady FBI agent, entering her hotel room together.

"From what I can put together," Juliette said to Chance, at the desk in her hotel room, her laptop open in front of her, "Bruce owns the top-level holding company. Call that Company One. Then if I'm reading these Securities and Exchange Commission reports correctly, Company One has a majority ownership in Companies Two, Three, and Four. Companies Two, Three, and Four each have minority ownerships in Company Five. But, taken all together, their combined votes actually control Company Five. Effectively, that means Bruce Bockenheim controls Company Five."

Chance spent his career doing action tasks, not reading SEC reports. He didn't quite follow her excitement. "So what?" he asked. Then he said, "Wait a minute. Companies own the stock of other companies? It's not people?"

"That's the play," Juliette said. "If one company owns another company, which owns a third company, which owns a fourth company, it isn't too long before the ownership records and the audit trails short circuit. Pretty soon, the actual ownership gets obscured. All the reporting and regulating done by the Securities Exchange Commission loses its bite. Even though Bockenheim has effective control, the ownership is held by three different companies, making it appear that no one entity is pulling its strings."

Chance began to be interested. He asked, "So let's say you had a government contract that needed to be put out on a competitive bid. Three companies bid, and one wins. But all three companies could effectively be owned by Bockenheim, meaning he wins no matter which company is selected?"

"That's one of the uses for this structure. It also allows a lot of flexibility for tax reporting. Expenses and prices can be transferred from company to company, changing the effective profit levels. Accounting is an art, not a science. Some of these people are real artists." She pushed a stray hair back where it had fallen across her face. "Add in that he's got a hedge fund in the mix. That means he regularly places bets on both sides of an argument."

Chance suddenly became aware of the citrus scent of her perfume, the clean line where her bra showed through the whiteness of her starched shirt, and the faint promise of cleavage, somewhere behind it. The more she talked, the harder it hit him. He leaned over her shoulder, where he could smell her hair. So he could see the computer screen, he said. His arm rested on her back. His thigh touched her thigh.

She fidgeted and brushed him away. She was working. "Listen, I'm getting a thought here," she said, oblivious to his rising libido. "Te, Josh's company. How is it that Josh got them out of trouble when you left the Salang Pass?"

"I assumed he paid the officials to keep it quiet," Chance answered, working at pulling himself together.

Juliette could have been elected Ice Queen. She had no recognition of his rising discomfort. She did not miss a beat in her discussion. "Would they do that?" she continued. "I mean, yes, we know they accept bribes, but think about them as people. Taking bribes to keep drugs running is one thing. People do that because it's about money and things. It's not about people. Taking bribes to let a foreign defense force kill your own men is something else. Would they do *that*?"

Now he was beginning to fall in love with her. She was good at her job, focused and sharp. Powerful. Skilled. Seductive. He thought about what she said. He thought about how she said it. Then he shook himself out of the spell and said, "You're right. You're onto something. Money would not be enough. Something else had to have been offered in payment."

It was past lunchtime, so they moved downstairs to the Pub, to brainstorm over the pulled pork sandwich and a bottle of Merlot. Chance was counting on the wine to break through that ice. After a few rounds of speculations, and half a plate of French fries, Juliette said, "A favor. That's what it is. A favor. Josh Bockenheim must be doing the Karzai government a favor that they can't get done any other way. That's got to be the reason they tolerate him It's a quid pro quo society."

The puzzle pieces clicked into place in Chance's mind. He knew what happened. Juliette gave him the final clue. He looked at her pretty face, with the sunlight hitting her right side, and the wine glass rising to her lips. She was beautiful, brilliant, ambitious . . . if he could have, he would have taken her to bed right then and there, but he was in a hurry to find Josh Bockenheim and get some answers.

At the moment that Chance Kiernan was most passionately discussing this situation with Juliette March, staring into her eyes with all the blazing intensity that a man and a woman who love their work can exhibit, Charlotte Trout brought her sister, Sherry Sherwood, to see the attractive man, who was always in the pub with the FBI lady. Sherry needed just three minutes of watching the two of them, before she rushed to her car. She wanted to drive over to Ann Kiernan's house. This is the kind of sad news that should be delivered in person.

Chapter 22
Fall, 2007
Copper Hollow

In Copper Hollow, the citizens believe the Mayor runs the entire government. President of the United States? That guy's a theory, in a place far away, where no one from here has ever gone, or will ever go. Sheriff? That's the guy from far away who puts the young men of Copper Hollow in jail. County Commissioners? What's that? Never heard of it. But Mayor? The Mayor of Copper Hollow was King. The Warlord. One of the Ray Plotzky's had always been the Mayor. That was a given, in Copper Hollow.

When the schools offered free breakfast, in addition to the free lunches, for the forty-five percent of Copper Hollow children who lived below the national poverty level, the people said, "When is the Mayor going to offer free breakfast and lunch on Saturday, too?"

When the food stamps program was cut by the federal government, and the local food pantry run by the churches had no more to give, the people said, "When is the Mayor going to fill the food pantry?"

When the town council voted to cancel the May Festival because of budget constraints, the people said, "When is the Mayor going to bring the festival back?"

The people of Copper Hollow, or the people of feudal England, or the people of rural Afghanistan, all looked to a warlord leader to protect them. Ray Plotzky was the warlord of Copper Hollow. Until the FBI started threatening to shut down their family farms, no one would bother to run in an election against Ray Plotzky. But the actual indictment of Old Ray hit the front page of the *Copper Hollow Mercury*. The paper reported that the USDA was investigating, and they were considering destroying all the farm animals. Everybody's farm animals, in all of Copper Hollow, the rumor said. The sheep might have Mad Cow Disease, the rumor told them. The pigs might get out and run wild in the forest, endangering humanity with an abundance of pork, they said at their family barbecues. The spinach might have e coli, they whispered in the grocery store. The corn and alfalfa seeds were being re-planted from one year to the next, and perhaps the actions of the wind would cause them to have the patented genes owned by the Monsanto company in them, which would be a horrible crime against patent law, they buzzed at town meetings. The world needed to be protected from this madness of unscientific, sustainable farming. U.S. trade was at stake, the town councilmen said, and Europe must not be allowed to find out that there were people in the United States of America who did not eat factory-farm food. The stock market would crash, if Europeans knew this, said the newscaster on the local radio show. Public confidence depends on our exhibition of certainty in the safety of our large-scale corporate farming model, Ed Brentwood announced in a press release about the Plotzky farm. The USDA makes it a goal to harass and eliminate un-scientific anomalies like the Plotzky farm, Ed confided to Mitchell Davis, of the *Copper Hollow Mercury*. "In the interest of public safety, of course," he added.

The former mayor of Copper Hollow, Old Ray Plotzky, father of the current mayor of Copper Hollow, has been charged with crimes of Interstate Commerce, the newspaper reported.

Not too many people in Copper Hollow knew what Interstate Commerce was, but the rumors told them it was drugs. "Imagine that," people said. "All this time Mayor Plotzky is out talkin' 'bout how bad drugs are, and all along, he's been growin' Mary-Wanna on his farm."

Some other people came along and said, "No, it's about milk. Old Ray was selling milk across state lines, and that's against the law."

But most people looked at these other people like they had two heads. For the law to send SWAT teams to arrest somebody who was selling milk to people was such a ridiculous, crazy thought, nobody believed it. It couldn't be milk. It couldn't be farm products. If milk and farm products were going to become illegal in the U.S.A., then what would happen to them and their farm families? It was a thought so horrifying that they couldn't allow it to sit in their heads. So, they did what people do when they can't stand to hear something: they denied it. It's drugs, the rumor mill insisted, although it wasn't drugs, and there was no reason to say it.

"They's talkin' 'bout sendin' troops in to kill all Ray's farm animals," Clem said, sitting at Jo-Beans one morning.

"Why's that?" asked Buck.

"He don't have no papers," Clem explained. "He never filled out the forms to make 'em legal. And he's been passin' out the meat to half his kinfolk in the Holler."

"Wull, so what?" interrupted Al. "Wha's that got to do with killin' the animals?"

"They got doctors at the USDA. Vets. The vet says if he don't get paperwork, it's a health hazard. So they's sayin' they can take all his animals, and scrub his farm down with Clorox. Then they's sayin' they have to scrape the topsoil off his land, to clean it up."

"That's too nuts, Clem," Red said. "Even I ain't fallin' fer that story."

"No, it's true," Clem responded. "They found out he got a goat from Jody Marigold, when he went to Mexico and brought back that whole herd. So the USDA says all the animals could be sick and they have to be destroyed. Or else somethin' bad will happen."

"Like what?" said Red. "Them goats came here twenty years ago. We all have offspring from that herd. They ain't sick."

"I heared they's lookin' fer people who have the goats. Said if you had 'em, they's takin' all the animals off your farm."

"Even yer dogs?"

"Yeah, the dogs, too."

The four men sat silent, chewing on the words.

Then Buck said, "That ain't true. It's a rumor."

Red agreed. "Old Ray prob'ly put that rumor out to cover up his Mary-Wanna story. Like you said."

Clem nodded. The story about the federal government taking their farms couldn't be true. They wouldn't hear it. They couldn't hear it. It must never happen here. *Not again.*

And so the rumor quickly spread that Old Ray was growing MaryWanna on his farm. The plants which never existed except in the minds of four old men sitting at a coffee shop became Copper Hollow Legend. *It had to be, the residents agreed. Who would believe the federal government would arrest a person for growing food? Who could dare to believe it, without recalling the tremors of those family tales from long ago? And so the residents didn't believe it, and wouldn't believe it, and the rumor of the Plotzky marijuana farm lived on.*

The persecution of Old Ray, and the subsequent rumors of drugs on the Plotzky farm, made a chink in the armor of Copper Hollow's Young Warlord. It made Mayor Plotzky vulnerable. For the first time in the history of Copper Hollow, when the Mayor election came up, some other young local men who dared to wannabe signed up to participate. Of course, Ray held the coveted Republican spot, so everybody else had to run as an Independent. In all, six candidates were on the ballot. One Republican, five Independents. *There hadn't been a Democrat in Copper Hollow since Franklin D. Roosevelt, the locals were proud to declare.* The election festivities provided a focal point for festivities. The campaign raged from the time of the country fair in August through to the Tuesday in November when all the voting citizens went to the polls. Election years in Copper Hollow were a time of good old country American fun.

Ray Plotzky lived his life around elections. His dad's, his grandpappy's, and his own. These were the traditions of the

Plotzky family. Other families may have structured their relationships around holidays, but Plotzky family gatherings centered on the annual backyard barbecue campaign fundraiser. Why not? A Plotzky had been the Mayor for four generations! An election requires the accessories of festivity. There must be yard signs, bumper stickers, buttons, and ads. Halls must be rented for campaign speeches. Invitations must be printed for champagne kick-offs. Volunteers must be provided late-night pizza. Ray could count on getting his campaigns financed by holding one barbecue every year. In four years, he'd have enough donations to pay for his next campaign.

This year, the citizens of Copper Hollow had six mayor candidates. This provided the population with a vast array of spaghetti dinners, backyard barbecues, and buffets at the Spoon 'n' Fork. Yard signs bloomed like chrysanthemums along the streets of Copper Hollow. America was free. Ray, meanwhile, was deeply confused. He'd never had a competitor in an election before. Some of his competitors were guys he thought were his good friends. Now that the chips were down and he was up against hard times, they were running against him! On top of that, Ray was really, really scared. Because of the charges against his dad, Ray would have to pay for lawyers. Lawyers cost big money, and Ray never had big money. So even if his dad was innocent, this was going to ruin him. He had gut wrenching pain and paralyzing fear on his insides. He kept on being the mayor of Copper Hollow while the campaign raged around him. He could not, however, paste on a smile and run in the race. He mortgaged his house and depleted his savings. Even a small federal prosecution costs a fortune in lawyer fees.

On the day of the election, Ray stayed home. His friends and family advised him to stay away from the polls. "It's super-charged out there," his brother told him. "Somebody might get crazy if they see you." So Ray stayed home, worried about his dad going to jail, sick to his stomach with grief.

Nearly seventy percent of the registered voters of Copper Hollow showed up at the polls. When it was all over, at eight o'clock that night, the vote count for Ray Plotzky was thirty percent. His nearest competitor had twenty-eight percent. The other four candidates split the remainder fairly evenly. With thirty percent of the vote, Ray Plotzky won. He was re-elected.

Mitchell Davis was unimpressed with the results of the mayor's election. He'd gotten tired of Copper Hollow. It wore on him. He was tired of his boss wanting to write only happy stories. He couldn't see how his career would be advanced this way. He had spent a lot of time researching the airport activities. His boss highly discouraged it, but he'd taken his weekends and evenings to do most of it. He had no social life in Copper Hollow anyway. Now he had plenty of data on the comings and goings at the airport, and he thought he was on to a real story. He knew about Josh Bockenheim's company, Te, and its defense contracts. He knew the corporate jet belonged to Te. He knew there was a training center planned to be built in Copper Hollow. He knew the Aid Relief Institute of Kandahar was a Josh Bockenheim company. Most importantly, he had scored an interview via Skype with the three college girls who had been taken hostage from the ARI. They were back in Ohio, but they had agreed to talk to him via video on his computer.

Mitchell planned to headline his story: "Small Town Airport Plays Big Role in Afghanistan War." He was going to write about Josh Bockenheim, War Hero. He had discussed this with Mayor Plotzky, but the Mayor was pretty distracted these days, mostly, and they hadn't kept working on it.

Josh Bockenheim runs a defense contract that delivers chickens from Copper Hollow to the poor people in Afghanistan, the story was going to read. Then the Afghans pay him in chicken feed and he brings it back. Josh's faith-based contract with the U.S. government allowed this to happen, Mitchell planned to say. He hadn't landed an interview with Josh Bockenheim yet, but he put this all together based on his own observations and his research. Since it would be a happy, positive story about Copper Hollow, Mitchell expected that Reese Babbitt, his boss, would approve it for the front page of the *Copper Hollow Mercury.* Then, Mitchell believed, his interview with the released hostages would make his story national news-worthy.

Mitchell knew this wasn't the big break he was looking for, but it would be a front page byline. The recent hostage rescue of the three girls from Ohio would save it. He finished his story, planning to go over it with the girls on the Skype call. He felt sure they would want to know about the bigger picture of Te. When the time came for his scheduled call, he left the office and went to his apartment, for privacy. MaryAnn, Linda, and Shannon sat on the sofa at Linda's parents' house. Their parents stood behind them.

The call went well. He got some great detail about the ordeal they went through, and the circumstance of their rescue. He told them about the story he was writing, and the hero, Josh Bockenheim. Twenty minutes after he hung up from the video call, his cell phone rang.

"Mr. Davis," a scared and quivering voice said. "It's MaryAnn. We all discussed it, and decided to tell you. But you have to promise no one will know it came from us. Our parents don't want us to tell. Promise me no one will find out."

Whoa! Mitchell thought. *Jackpot!* "Of course," he said. "I will never let anyone know my source. I promise." Even as he said it, he felt manipulative. It was a ridiculous promise. Of course it would be clear where he got the information.

The very young MaryAnn seemed satisfied with the promise from the very young Mitchell Davis. "When we were locked in the van, there were boxes there from the Aid Relief Institute. They were our toaster pastries, it said on the box. But we opened the box because we were going to eat them."

"Yes?" Mitchell said.

"Remember your promise. You have to get this information to the right place."

"Yes, I promise," Mitchell encouraged MaryAnn to continue.

"The boxes didn't have toaster pastries in them. They were boxes of guns."

Mitchell Davis hung up the phone. He did not know what to do. Who should he tell? Who could he tell? Was this his big break?

Mitchell Davis spent most of his days on the Internet, chatting with other aspiring or experienced journalists. Reporting in these days, real investigative reporting, could no longer be done in mainstream newspapers. The papers shied away from uncovering government misdeeds. Mitchell knew that, but he wanted to establish himself in journalism. He expected that he would ultimately get his "branding," as a real reporter. Then he would break out of mainstream newspapers and blog professionally, with his own following. When he ran into that FBI agent, Juliette March, behind the airport, he knew he was onto something. Luck was with him.

He made every attempt to interview Agent March about why she was there. As a friendship offering, he spilled his guts. Everything he knew, suspected, or speculated about what was going on with the airport grants, the drugs, the mayor, and the town. He blabbed it all to the FBI agent like it was his first time talking. He laid out all his opinions, all his speculations, and all his wild-ass conspiracy theories. Juliette March listened with interest, but sadly, in Mitchell's mind, she did not reciprocate by giving him information about her operation. Although her tight-lipped response was disappointing, Andrew felt encouraged that he had seen Juliette there. It meant the FBI was investigating the same thing he was investigating.

Obviously, once he heard about the guns, Mitchell knew there was no point in taking his suspicions or his story to his editor at the *Copper Hollow Mercury*. He knew the editor would squelch the story immediately, if it wasn't a happy hero story. Instead, he decided to ask for some help from more experienced journalists, whom he knew would be monitoring certain Twitter accounts. @IndieJo, he tweeted. He posted a web page on his own account, with all the information he knew, and speculated, about the airport and the activity in Copper Hollow. He talked about the history of Copper Hollow, but he held back that final piece of information that he had gotten from the Ohio girls. He was saving that, for when he got to the right person. Then he created a bitly link, a special link that would shorten the address of his web page to the Twitter-size of 140 characters. *@IndieJo cn u hlp?* he tweeted, adding the shortened link to his page of information. It took less than four minutes to get his first tweet back. *@Mitchell Davis u r looking at a drug deal.*

It took a full fifteen minutes before he got a private message in his Twitter inbox. *Look up the OSS*, it said. The message was from a French journalist, Olivier Beauchemin. He'd heard of him. He had bylines in *Le Figaro*. It excited Mitchell that someone so prominent would respond to him. But wasn't the OSS a European organization? What did it have to do with Copper Hollow? He began his research eager to share what he learned with Olivier Beauchemin. And this is how Mitchell Davis got onto the path that would lead to his trouble.

Once he got together with Olivier Beauchemin, his fate was sealed. He put in a call to Mayor Plotzky. The two of them together were going to figure out what was going on in this crazy town. It was Oz, and they were the Tin Man and the Lion, looking for the Emerald City. Mitchell set out for Mayor Plotzky's house, his notes in hand.

305

Chapter 23
Christmas, 2007
Paris

When Bruce Bockenheim finally got Chance Kiernan on the phone, he swore he had the final and complete results of a thorough investigation into any and all allegations of wrongdoing of the conglomerate companies of Te. This exonerating information could only be disclosed to Chance in person. This would end all discussion of Bruce being involved in money laundering. It would completely clear both Bockenheims of any hint of wrongdoing. Since Bruce was a very busy man, and had to attend many very important meetings, Chance would have to come to him. The most convenient and earliest time would be in Paris, at his Alpha-Zeta board meeting, next week. Not only would he give Chance a complete briefing, but he also had some tips about who attacked the convoy in Afghanistan, and what was behind it. He could identify and lay out all parties and motives involved. But only in person. Secretly.

Through the contacts he specified. *Because if it were known that he was divulging this . . .*

Chance got the picture. Yes, he would come to Paris.

Because Ann Kiernan was so distraught, after her visit from Sherry Sherwood, when Sherry suggested that Chance was meeting Juliette clandestinely, he suggested she hire Charlotte Trout to babysit, and come to Paris with him.

On the day that Hanif's wife and son posted the For Sale sign on the front door of their home, and told the neighbors they were going to move back to live with her family in Pakistan, Ann and Chance Kiernan boarded Air France to Paris.

Every idea that is important to the world has its personal connection to Paris. Olivier would say that, Madeleine thought, and she somewhat agreed. Although, her American friend, Ann Kiernan, looked confused when she heard it. Ann was new to Paris and oblivious to the well-known fact that Paris was the philosophic capital of the universe. Despite the three days of profound and compelling idea-tossing they'd spent together here, Ann seemed naïve in her world view. She was still susceptible to belief in the public utterances of government spokesmen. Ann, for example, thought it was critically important that she vote in every election. Madeleine voted, yes, but only as a social entertainment, with her friends. For party conversation. Madeleine didn't expect her vote to change anything, nor did she believe it mattered who won. It didn't matter in France, or in Germany, or in Russia. And least of all, it surely didn't matter in the United States of America. *Les Etats-Unis.* As Madeleine sat waiting for Ann to meet her, she went over in her mind what she was doing there, and what she would say to Ann. Madeleine tended to think things through extensively. Ann had asked Madeleine to wait for her in the farthest left pew in the Church of Mary Magdelene, in the center of Paris. Madeleine was there at the appointed time, waiting, but Ann didn't show.

Let's get this straight, once and for all, Madeleine thought. In the Eglise de la Madeleine, in Paris, Mary Magdalene's statue behind the altar is either full-term pregnant, or bending over backwards to do the limbo. This is a womb "en plein avec bebe." Ready to pop. Five angels accompany her, two of whom appear to be preparing to catch the child as its born. A woven baby blanket is waiting at her legs. This isn't the standard Queen Isis with dwarf-god-child that portrays many of the Mary-Jesus statues of Christianity. It is a depiction of the French concept of goddess. And this windowless Greek temple in the heart of Paris illustrates it en plusieurs forte. To the utmost.

Ann always argues with me about French culture, Madeleine thought. Ann and her husband, Chauncey Kiernan (they call him Chance), live in the outback rural forests of the Blue Ridge mountains, where I suspect that rogue husband of hers is hiding from something or somebody. Maybe he's hiding from an armed team of government agents. He's creepy and mysterious enough, if you ask me. My husband, Olivier, is the total opposite. Where Chance is the brusque cowboy, with the ex-Special Forces hollow eyes, Olivier is an emotional idealist. Olivier is a journalist, free-lance. Which means he doesn't make money every month. He follows stories and hunts down leads. Mostly, he sits in cafes and philosophizes until he gets a lead. Then he tracks down the facts and tries to sell the story to his contacts at Le Figaro or Les Observateurs, or some underground subversive rag. Sometimes it works, but mostly, we're lucky I have a steady job at the Bourse, the French stock exchange. Olivier and Chance don't get along, so Ann and I tend to meet without our husbands. Olivier pries and asks questions, but Chance is the type that doesn't answer questions, even if they are harmless matters of polite social interaction. Ann thinks Chance doesn't talk about his work because it's government-classified. I'm not sure I'd accept that as an answer. I think he's spookier than a spy. And speaking of Ann's gullibility, why did she want to meet here, at Eglise de la Madeleine? She's not exactly a paragon of religious virtue, and God knows she doesn't think I am. So why am I sitting here staring at pregnant Mary Magdalene?

I waited at the appointed time. Waited past it. And then I saw Chance Kiernan enter the church with a large group of parents bringing their children to be baptized. He wasn't with the group. I think he was just using the group for cover so he wouldn't be noticed. He peeled off from the crowd, and I watched him make his way quietly along the dark aisles along the side. The light was low, so if I hadn't seen him come in, I wouldn't recognize him in the shadowed recesses. My first thought was to wave to him, but then I realized Ann must have known he was coming. She meant for me to see him. But why didn't she tell me? And where was she now?

For a moment, I lost sight of Chance while the group of parents pushed toward the baptismal font. I was about to get caught up in the whole "casting-demons-out-of-babies" drama when I saw him again. A priest wearing white vestments and a gold scarf pushed open a door marked "Prive" (private) at the back of the altar. Chance Kiernan was walking through it. Where was he going? Why was he here? More importantly, why was I here?

I decided I'd had enough mystery. The priest baptizing the baby launched into a sermon about how babies need to be taught their humanity. I decided I'd better leave before the nausea hit. Outside the church, I descended the long staircase and headed for the nearest brasserie. Ann was inside, waiting for me. She already had a glass of Bordeaux. "You saw him?" she asked. I pulled up a chair and beckoned for the waiter.

In a private back room of the Church of Mary Magdalene, in the center of Paris, Bruce Bockenheim sat next to the priest. Chance took the seat across the table. Bruce's age spots showed mostly on his hands, but they were creeping onto his forehead now, and the wrinkles around his eyes and mouth looked deeper than they did when they talked nearly two months ago. At that time, Bruce had learned he would be pursued by the Department of Justice, but that he could do himself a lot of good by working with Chance. He had agreed, including making the payment to get the hostages released from the Aid Relief Institute.

When they were seated, Bruce offered Chance a sherry. Chance refused, but Bruce got up and poured himself one. "For my health," he said.

After a slow walk from the liquor cabinet back to his chair, Bruce spoke carefully and deliberately. "My friend, Father Mandeville, is also my attorney," he said, with a nod to the priest. "He is doubly sworn to secrecy, as he is also my priest, my confessor. He will review any documents we sign or agreements we make. Is this clear, Agent Kiernan?"

"I understand," Chance answered pleasantly. He hadn't bothered to inform Bruce that he was a contractor, and not technically an agent of the U.S. government. He had no authority whatever to commit the U.S. government to a deal. But, it seemed imprudent to bring it up now.

"Then here are the results of my investigation," Bruce continued. If he was aware that Chance could not make a deal, he didn't show it. He put on his best poker-face eyes and spoke evenly, without emotion.

"When a system depends on cronies," Bruce began, "as the system of business anywhere in the world does, there comes a time when favors are called. In a hierarchy of men, these favors can be serious matters of life or death As it turned out, the shooting of the Afghani policeman in the Salang Pass, that day when you witnessed it, was not the only time the men of Te have shot Afghani citizens. It happened before, in Kandahar. And another time before that. The Karzai government discreetly contacted the Defense Department, demanding that Te's men be tried for murder. In the negotiations which followed, the U.S. Defense Department agreed to allow Te to carry the materials which Karzai wanted to a specific location in the U.S., unobstructed. The manufacturer of the heroin was the U.S. government. They said they would turn it into morphine, for hospital use. Maybe they did. I have no record otherwise.

"This is set up as a second distribution system for the heroin, outside the one the Taliban used for their funding. It funded the Afghan government, who could not raise enough revenue to keep the kleptocrats happy. This was a preferred operation, as it took poppy off the streets, and kept it from funding the Taliban. It takes enormous funds to grease the palms of the new elites in the Afghan government. What other explanation is there for more than fifty billion taxpayer dollars spent on training Afghan troops? If Te stops carrying the product out to the U.S. factory, the

311

men of Te will be tried for murder. The U.S. will be accused of operating the drug trade. So, you see, Mr. Kiernan, I am not a money launderer. I am a patriot, carrying out a mission for my government. Like you."

Chance suspected Bruce knew he wasn't authorized to do anything. That's why he admitted to nothing and denied all knowledge. But he realized now how dangerous the situation had become. Men are killed daily for interfering in the transfer of heroin, and for uncovering its associated money trail. It occurred to Chance that this room, in which they met, was both heavily guarded and fully video-monitored.

But while Chance met with Bockenheim and the priest, Mrs. Kiernan was opening up her fears and anxieties to her friend. "Madeleine, I'm about to go crazy," Ann confided. "My husband must have another woman. He must. I've been told she's an FBI agent. I'm left to raise his children, who honestly don't even like me. I'm living in a place that is so foreign and completely weird, that I can't even make any friends. There's no possibility for me to work there, because there is no work, and when I try to volunteer, I get rejected! I tried to tell Chance I was unhappy, and he came up with this idea for me to come to Paris with him. But now that we're here, he still leaves me alone all day! So I started following him." Ann's voice broke as she told her story to her old college friend, Madeleine, in the Paris café.

Madeleine knew this was a serious situation for Ann. The Ann she remembered was vibrant, fun-loving, and care-free. This woman was near breaking. Over a man? Over something as trivial as a cheating husband? Madeleine doubted that a cheating husband would be this serious a

312

crack for Ann's psyche. A cheating husband may be a cause for some action, but not for depression and tears. Anger was an appropriate response, Madeleine thought, but desperation? Definitely not. Women sometimes blamed a man when the problem was rooted in deeper issues.

"We're in no hurry, *ma cheré*," Madeleine told her friend, reaching over to pat her shaking hand. "We will talk here as long as you wish. Then we will go to the shopping mall, Printemps, and buy makeup and perfume and jewelry. You will use your husband's credit card until it squeals for mercy. That will be some small satisfaction."

By the time the waiter came to collect the bill for their afternoon bottles of wine, Madeleine had convinced Ann to tell her story of Copper Hollow to Olivier, whom, she said, would know exactly what to do about it. They went home to Madeleine's apartment. Ann talked for hours, and told Olivier everything she knew about the events in Copper Hollow, the FBI presence, the investigation of the mayor, and Chance's trips to Afghanistan. She told Olivier that Chance was a contractor for the Defense Intelligence Agency, which was the story she was told. She told everything she knew about Mitchell's research and Josh Bockenheim. Ann was still with Olivier when Chance returned to their hotel room. She had left no note, and she did not answer when he called her cell phone. By the time she returned, hours later, Chance finally realized his marriage was in jeopardy.

That could be a problem, Chance Kiernan thought. Ann already knew too much.

After Ann left Madeleine's apartment, Olivier took Madeleine by the hand. He led her to the sofa, and they both sat down, facing each other. Olivier held Madeleine's hand, to soften the impact of what he was about to say. "I worry," he told his true love. "Your friend and her husband. I fear that she knows too much. Her husband thought he was marrying a bimbo. Men like this can underestimate, when it comes to women."

"Do you think she's in danger?" Madeleine questioned.

"I have been in touch with a reporter from Copper Hollow. I think it would be prudent for Ann to be cautious," he answered.

"Cautious about her own husband?" Madeleine said.

"Cautious," Olivier said. "Cautious about everything. She is sitting in the midst of a swirling snow storm. I suspect that Chance Kiernan is the key to calm the winds. Or the catalyst to blow the roofs off all the chicken houses in the Holler."

BOOK THREE:

THE IMPACT

Chapter 24: Ray

Winter, 2008

Copper Hollow

The election was over, and newly re-elected Mayor Plotzky breathed a sigh of relief. Surely, he could expect this foolishness about his Pop's arrest to be behind him now. Surely the investigators would go away and let his family alone. He had felt certain that his family had been targeted because of all the good work he had been doing and his political rising star. *His dad was a pawn, in a scheme that was meant to get him.* That's what Ray believed.

Before this happened, friends in the Party had suggested he might have a bigger future, beyond Copper Hollow. He'd been talking about possibilities. Then this trouble came out of nowhere. It had to be related to his political aspirations. It had to be. It was too crazy to be anything else. *But if the bastards who did this think they can bring down Ray Plotzky, they have another think comin', said the Warlord.*

Ray decided that now he would put some real effort into tracking down what Bockenheim was doing, and how it tied in to the drugs in Copper Hollow. He would call in his friends. He would sit down with Charlie and Darrell, his best friends, who happened to be police officers, and see where they were on the tracking of the drugs in Copper Hollow. Someone had targeted his family, and ensnared them in a trap. He was sure of it, and it wasn't over yet. They had ruined him financially, and tarnished his reputation. But he wasn't going to stop fighting. He was a leader here, and he had friends. He had his second wind, after the election, and he was ready to pull himself back together and lead the charge.

The Copper Hollow jail, right next door to Ray's courthouse mayor's office, overflowed with petty thieves, embezzlers of money from the cub scouts and the church bake sales, bad check writers, fugitives from bar brawls, wife beaters, drunks, and drug abusers. As usual. But there were no drug lords in there, and Ray was sure there was at least one lurking nearby. He felt compelled, even driven, to make it his mission to catch him. Especially now, now that he believed the drug lord had launched an attack on his family.

"Listen, Ray," Charlie told him, while they were staking out the airport once again. He peered through his binoculars, rather than look Ray in the eye. "I don't see how Bockenheim could get the USDA to send a SWAT team to your house. It's not related."

Ray was having a little trouble figuring out how that could happen, too, but he had this niggling suspicion that it did. Ray lived with his parents and his younger sister. Pop had been shot while on the job, by a farmer who decided he was trespassing. The way all the families felt about trespassing, you'd think Pop Plotzky would have known not to do it, but he'd gotten to feeling a little entitled, being the Mayor, and that was a dangerous flaw. He had gone on disability early. Young Ray took over as mayor, and kept the family afloat. He'd both worked the farm and run the Holler as mayor, for the last fifteen years. Things had been going well, and Ray was looking to maybe getting married to Amy Clancey sometime. Sometime, but he din't know when. Then this trouble hit.

Pop was out on bail, but the constant pressure about the federal charges was making his mother look gray and fragile. It was making Pop turn sour and disagreeable. It was spending his sister's Hope Chest fund, for when she finally got married. All the money was going to lawyer's fees. Ray soon found out that being re-elected didn't stop the investigation. He could not understand what this was all about. They were turning his life inside out looking for something, but what? Why him? Ray realized this attack on his Pop wasn't about Pop and it wasn't about milk. He listened to the questions that the FBI asked, and he heard what the neighbors said, and he realized they were after him. The Mayor. That wasn't what the law was supposed to be about. It wasn't the America he knew.

Ray was completely convinced there was nothing to find. He'd loved his job as mayor. He'd been proud to carry on the heritage left by the Plotzkys before him. He'd done everything by the book, as far as he knew. He had to admit, "the book" he did things by was the book of how things were done in Copper Hollow. *If that was a little different than the book of the FBI and Washington, D.C. . . . well, he thought, it must be different, because nothing in my book would target a man first and think of something to charge him with later, like the FBI was doing to him.*

Through it all, Ray kept thinking this had something to do with the drugs in Copper Hollow. While Ray suspected the strange activity of Josh Bockenheim's corporate jet deliveries to the chicken farm, he couldn't prove anything. He

319

didn't have the authority to stop the van and look inside its boxes. He didn't have the right to go onto Kenny's chicken farm without being invited. He did pull the electric and telephone bills for Kenny's farm, but they didn't mean anything to his case. *How come I'm constrained to stay out of Josh Bockenheim's business, but the FBI can scratch around asking all my old high school buddies about the times I ditched study hall? How come they can snoop around and talk to my neighbors about who my friends are and where I go on vacation?* It all seemed surreal to Ray, but he loved the United States of America and he told himself that an innocent man had nothing to fear from investigation.

An innocent man could have his whole life exposed, and it wouldn't matter, Ray thought. They could listen in on his phone calls, read his e-mails, and hack his Facebook page. So what? Ray Plotzky had nothing to hide. Nothing to fear from federal snooping.

There wasn't really a whole lot for a mayor to do in Copper Hollow. Ray should have had plenty of time to investigate this drug issue. Before the investigation by the FBI into his activities started, Ray spent a lot of his time kicking off charity fundraisers. He was the guy who stood behind the barbecue grill and talked to people about giving money for that little boy who needed a bone marrow transplant. He was the auctioneer at the United Way fundraiser. Ray was very popular in this county. He was a political rising star. He had big future plans. He'd been certain he would one day run for higher office, on a state level.

Now it was getting hard to hold his head up. People talked about him in whispers. Many of his regular friends turned away when they saw him in the streets. The way the neighbors saw it, if you were accused, you were guilty.

People who knew Ray and supported his efforts all his life, were starting to wonder. Folks believed the Feds would not spend all this money and time on an investigation if there weren't some truth to it. Because of the act of the investigation, folks were buying into the thought that there must be something wrong. Ray Plotzky was becoming a pariah.

Ray tried to keep his spirits up. He told himself, and anyone who would listen, this was all a mistake. He wasn't guilty of anything. All the same, he worked under a cloud of suspicion now. Even if his pop went to trial and was found not guilty, people would always believe he'd done something wrong. It was getting harder and harder to do his job because he felt uneasy about who to trust. The citizens were turning against him, as more and more talk about his family's court case fed the local gossip mill. Gossip said it was drugs they were after, and that was so ridiculously false, he didn't know what to do about it. *I'm the guy who is after the drug lords, he screamed to himself. How can they turn this around to make me the drug lord?* He won the election with 30% of the vote, but that was down from his usual 80%. His approval rating was plummeting because of all the talk. People thought that a man accused was a man guilty. They thought that the act of investigation meant there was something wrong.

Ray's ulcers were flaring. The money he paid his lawyers was mounting. The worse thing was, it looked like he was going to have to sell his house to pay the lawyers. And that, sadly, was the house where he had grown up, and which belonged to his mom and dad.

His ulcers acted up, and the doctor said he was going to have to go into the hospital soon. He was having a lot of stomach trouble today, but this was the day he had an appointment with Joey Anhalt. Joey was the owner of the local hardware store. On a regular basis, every now and then, Joey made himself a royal pain in the butt. Joey was a guy who snooped around in other people's business. He was always complaining that somebody was doing something wrong. This time, however, Ray wanted to hear what Joey had to say. He thought maybe Joey could offer a lead into this drug business.

That afternoon, Joey Anhalt IV sat in Mayor Plotzky's office and cried. He had to wait two days to get this appointment with the mayor. He had gone to the police right away, but everybody knew the Mayor of Copper Hollow was kin to everybody and could get to the bottom of things. So Joey called Ray.

Little Brian Anhalt, Joey's son, was six years old when Joey got the anonymous phone call. The female caller told Joey that Joey's ex-wife, Molly, was leaving Brian home alone at night, while she was sneaking out to see a boyfriend and take drugs. If you want to know more, the unknown voice said, go ask Ralph Merkel. The caller hung up. Joey didn't doubt for a minute that the caller was real. He didn't think much of Molly, after their divorce, and he was ready to believe she was guilty. He jumped in his truck and raced to her house to confront her. But nobody was home.

In his distress at having to wait two days for an appointment, Joey had gone to Ralph Merkel's farm. The anonymous phone tip he had received about his ex-wife's drug dealing told him to ask Ralph Merkel for more information. Old Ralph swore he din't know nothin' about any phone call and he din't know nothin' about Molly. They were sitting outside in Merkel's driveway, Joey in his truck and Merkel just off his front porch with a bucket of chicken feed in his hand. Just by coincidence, a beatup old cherry-colored pickup pulled up behind Joey at that very moment. It had FARM written on its license plate, which meant it wasn't supposed to be driving in the streets, where it had just come from, because it wasn't licensed.

"This is my grandson," Merkel said. "His name is Ralph Merkel, too. Maybe he knows somethin.' "

The younger Ralph Merkel had a scar down his left cheek straight to the jawline. Two missing teeth suggested, at his age, they'd been knocked out of his mouth in a fight. "I know what Molly's been doin'," the young Ralph told Joey Anhalt. "Gimme a drive into town and fi'ty bucks and I'll show you where she's doin' drugs." Joey figured Ralph was down on his luck, so he agreed.

On the way into town, Joey learned that the young Ralph didn't own a car. He didn't have a job. He lived with his mother, but often stayed at his girlfriend's house, Mavis Ellingham. He borrowed his grandpa's farm-use truck, when the old man felt inclined to lend it.

"That thar's the place," Ralph pointed as they passed a house where a middle-aged bald man with a substantial paunch was crawling on his roof installing Christmas lights. "That guy rah't thar, he's her boyfriend. Name s Jim Thorpe."

Joey slammed on the brakes. He caught himself in time to prevent his arm from lashing out to smack Ralph on the nose. "What the hell?" he screeched. "How's the guy's name Jim Thorpe?" Ralph stared at him with a blank look, like he'd never heard the name of the famous sports figure in any other context.

"It's what he says," Ralph coughed while he talked. "He's the drug dealer."

"Ralph," Joey said. "That is not Jim Thorpe. Jim Thorpe is a famous sports figure. It ain't him, and there ain't nobody else in Copper Hollow with that name."

Ralph shrugged. "I jes' go by what he says. Anybody kin have whatever name their mama gived 'em."

Joey cried the whole time he told this story to Mayor Plotzky. The Mayor patted his shoulder, handed him tissues, and said, "We'll get you hooked right up with the police." He walked Joey over to the office of Charlie Wenzel. "Can you help out Joey?" the mayor said.

"I already came into the police, Ray," Joey said. "I already got a case officer. I'm askin' you to get involved personally, beyond what the police is doin'. Like, frankly, because they ain't doin' nothin'."

Ray hesitated. He wanted to hear every detail of Joey's problem, and he wanted to know everything about it, but he wasn't the local police, and he knew the Sheriff wouldn't like to see him in the middle of police business. It was one thing for the mayor of a town to pick up clues and watch for unusual actions. It was another thing altogether to interfere in a specific case. Ray was very aware that the FBI was watching his family. He wondered how it was going to look if he started getting smack in the middle of Joey's case. Ray knew Joey had a tendency to make things complicated, and he worried that maybe he would get tangled up in something that wouldn't look good from the outside. Charlie Wenzel came to his rescue.

"Yeah, Joey, I heard about your case from Darrell Monk. We're gonna work on it. I'll call him over and you sit down and tell us the whole thing from the beginning to end, and we'll do the job for ya. Ray don't have nothin' to do with this."

Ray let out his breath and nodded a thank you to Charlie, then he patted Joey on the back and went back to his office. He wanted to know what was going on, but he didn't want to step in the middle of it. Charlie would keep him informed, he was sure.

When Darrell Monk arrived, Joey eagerly described every detail of his problem to Monk and Wenzel. To emphasize the deeply serious nature of the danger to his baby boy, he made an appointment to go get the younger Ralph Merkel and bring him in as a witness.

The next day, when Joey brought him in, Ralph Merkel the Younger told Officer Darrell Monk about the drug dealer, Jim Thorpe, who was installing Christmas lights on his house. Officer Monk agreed with Joey that "Jim Thorpe" was undoubtedly not the man's real name. They were in the county jail at the time, in Monk's small office, furnished in police green and beige. Officer Monk denied knowing Ralph Merkel. He said he'd never met him before.

"We're going to handle this," Officer Monk told Joey. "Don't worry about it anymore."

Joey immediately ran back to Ray Plotzky's office. "When are you going to do something?" Joey hammered away at his points. "Why can't we go out there this afternoon and take my baby boy away from Molly?"

"Hold on, Joey," Ray answered. "We don't have any proof. We can't just go over there. First off, Molly don't even live in Copper Hollow. There's a court process on stuff like this. You have the police workin' on it. I can't do anything more than they can." Part of Ray felt bad about turning Joey away. He knew the reason Joey was asking him to get involved. He knew that last year, he would have stuck his nose into it. Ray normally had his nose stuck in everybody's business in Copper Hollow. But now, with the investigation going on, he figured he'd better stay back and follow the straight and narrow. He'd been warned before to keep out of the business of the sheriff's office. Sheriff Freel may not have an office in Copper Hollow, but he ran a tight ship. Monk and Wenzel could take care of it. It was their job.

Joey left, but Ray knew him well enough to know he would head straight to Molly's house on his own. He called Officer Monk. "He's goin' ta get himself in trouble," he said to Monk. "You know he flies off the handle too quick."

Ray didn't want Joey to get himself in the kind of trouble that Joey had a tendency to get into. He actually would have liked to work on the case himself, but right now he was feeling pretty sick in his stomach. He needed to go home, because he also had to think about raising some money. His lawyer bills were going to be much higher than his savings account. This afternoon, he would look into mortgaging his house and selling his vacation cabin. He would do that from his sick bed. He felt his ulcers raging.

Back in his headquarters, at the Spoon 'n' Fork, Josh Bockenheim could not believe the election results. "How could that happen?" he asked Will Pruitt. "The guy's entire family is practically under federal indictment," Josh swore. "What do we have to do to this guy to back him off?"

"I hate to say it," Will answered, "but Ray Plotzky could be re-elected in this county even if he were actually *in* jail. Plus, now we've made him mad. He could go all out trying to track down who was after him. He has enemies, though. We'll beat the bushes and get more of his enemies to crawl out of the woodwork."

"I've got some resources I can put on it," Josh added. "I'll see what needs to be done."

Will worried about what Bockenheim meant by that. He never let on how closely entwined his world was with Ray Plotzky's world. He worried that if Plotzky went down, he would not be far behind. *Not because he deserved it, of course. Will Pruitt never did anything wrong. But it wouldn't take much for the FBI to expand its investigation into the activities of Josh Bockenheim and the attorney who knew about them. Will worried that Bockenheim was so isolated by his family wealth that he did not know what could happen to a pawn caught in the middle of political fights between government agencies. Will would be the pawn, he believed, not Bockenheim, and so he felt the pain of Bockenheim's naivety. The chess king never thinks about what happens to the pawns who get sacrificed for them.*

That night, Josh Bockenheim paid a personal call to Will Pruitt's house. He had never been there before. He insisted that Will find a way to get Ray Plotzky out. If he had not been able to stop him from being re-elected, then Will would just have to figure out something else. Josh noticed Will start to shake when he said that. Just in case Will was not up to the job, Josh called Chance Kiernan to a meeting at his place.

Chance did not enjoy being summoned by Josh Bockenheim. First, he thought Josh was a runny-nosed little snot. Second, Josh was not his boss and did not pay his checks. His checks came from the Joint Special Operations Command, to his own company. Okay, maybe they come from a shell company set up by the Terrorism Defense Unit to pay his checks, but that was a detail. Lots of different agencies jiggled and juggled line items in the budget. The important thing is, the checks didn't come from Josh Bockenheim. Te was another defense contractor, just as he was. He didn't want to seem petty about it, though, so when Josh called him, he was more interested in what Josh was up to than in fluffing his own ego. He agreed to meet at the Spoon 'n' Fork.

When he arrived, Josh Bockenheim proposed that they cooperate on a project to meet their interlocking goals. In light of the unfolding dilemma in Copper Hollow, and the results of the election, Josh Bockenheim suggested that Chance Kiernan kill Ray Plotzky. "This *is* what you do, isn't it, Mr. Kiernan?" the little snot said.

Chance had the self-control and the ability to avoid smacking Josh Bockenheim into next week. He didn't, however, choose to use it. After he knocked Bockenheim out of his chair, he left the room immediately. He called Washington D.C. "Send me a helicopter. I want to talk," he told Joe Bridgewell. He intended to straighten out what this Bockenheim character was doing, and he wasn't going to tolerate it any more.

After picking himself up and dusting himself off, Josh needed a moment to catch his breath. Apparently, Chance was refusing the assignment, he concluded. Josh would have to reach into his bag of tools and find another lever. He had a number of resources on his payroll. There was Will Pruitt, his lawyer, yes. But there were others. They were his levers, in place and on retainer for when they needed him. When he pulled that second lever, Joey Anhalt got another phone call. Officer Darrell Monk made the call.

"We aren't going to be able to do anything about your case unless we catch Molly in the act of using drugs," Officer Monk said on the phone to Joey. "But if you go find this Merkel guy, and bring him back in here, we can set something up to catch her." Merkel and Joey came in to see Monk alone. Monk outlined a "sting" operation, which involved Ralph Merkel wearing a wire, and going to meet with Molly and her boyfriend, the pseudonymous Jim Thorpe. As Joey listened, he realized this sounded complicated for a boy like Ralph Merkel. At one point he interrupted to ask Monk if Ralph is going to be paid for this work.

"After the bust goes down, we'll put in a voucher to the state and he can get paid," Monk answered.

After they left Monk's office, Ralph asked Joey for money. "I'll pay yer back when the state pays me," Ralph said. Joey figured Ralph could easily back out, become unreliable, and screw up this job. He believed that Ralph and Monk had never met before. He understood the plight of the unemployed men of Copper Hollow. He gave Ralph three hundred dollars cash.

Two days later, unbeknownst to Joey, Ralph Merkel was wearing a wire to tape Joey, not to tape the "sting" on Jim Thorpe. In their private conversations, Joey "helped" Merkel understand the details he needed to know to carry out the sting. Joey believed he was helping the young man, his friend's grandson, follow the instructions of the Copper Hollow police department. Monk told both of them these details, but Joey repeated them, for a man he saw as dull-witted and slow. Merkel continued to ask Joey to tell him what to do. Joey wanted to help Merkel, whom he saw as slow, slightly dim, and inexperienced. Joey was also in a state of distress. His child was in danger, he believed, and he must help his baby. Joey had no idea that the young Merkel was a seasoned felon, out on parole and working a complex "double sting," which included surveillance on Joey.

Thus began a full month of what Joey believed was a "police sting" that was meant to lead to a "drug bust." During the month of December, 2007, Merkel, Monk, and Joey Anhalt, had many conversations about this pending "bust." Pieces of those conversations were recorded by the wire Ralph wore, but only the pieces where Joey explained to Ralph what Monk wanted him to do. The tapes were being edited to make Joey sound like the drug dealer. In Will Pruitt's office, Jeanine Sherwood edited the tapes. In the revised version, both Joey and Ray Plotzky were going to be set up to look like the dealers. Josh Bockenheim was a man who liked to cover his bases. He was the chess master, and he saw nothing wrong with manipulating or sacrificing his pawns.

Mitchell Davis finally knew something. He called Ray Plotzky and they agreed to meet. Mitchell Davis and Ray Plotzky sat at Ray's kitchen table and laid out what each of them knew. Ray pulled out his notebook of the comings and goings at the airport. Mitchell shared his information from the college girls in Ohio.

Ray started to get really, really angry. He was adding two and two. His lawyer bills were mounting, his father was distressed, his mother was crying. And this summabitch Bockenheim was the problem, he figured. He wasn't going to stand for it. He absolutely, positively had to do something. But the absolute enormity of an investigation by the FBI and threats from the USDA churned his stomach. The pain in his gut made him weak, and he couldn't think of what to do. His calls to Congressman A and Congressman B went unanswered. He wanted to do something, but this was all more than he could bear. The Warlord of Copper Hollow was defeated. He had no clue about what to do or where to turn.

Chapter 25: Luke
Winter, 2008
Afghanistan

With the sun's hand on my shoulder, I tear my feet away,
a thousand and one times, from the things I leave behind me.
- Afghan poet

Darya felt sad to leave her mother and father's village. But, she was glad she had gone to see them. She hoped they would be able to travel to visit her. Secretly, she hoped they would someday move to her house, and live with her family, and meet Naseem. She was home again now, and happy to be home. Today, she and Abdullah's first wife, Naseem, were taking some of the children with them on a visit to the market, shopping. The women wore their burkas, for safety. There were many Taliban in Helmand Province, and it was important to be protected. Abdullah told the women he had many enemies. It would be unsafe to walk the streets in just their *chadors. Head scarves.* Darya knew that Abdullah did not like the Taliban, but he partnered with them. For his business. The Taliban provided security, and Abdullah paid them for doing this. Abdullah was both successful and powerful. He travelled for his business. He had even been to New York. Abdullah was an important international business man, and even the Americans met with him. It felt good to be part of a rich family. Darya felt proud to be Abdullah's wife.

The women and children walked along the dusty streets, heading to the Loy Chareh bazaar. This market was in the center of Marjah. It sold melons, grapes, pomegranates, grains and spices, as well as cooking equipment and household items. The six children ran ahead, behind, and around their mothers, kicking at stones, chasing each other, squealing, and laughing, as children everywhere do. They passed donkey carts, loaded with grains and supplies on their way to the market stalls. Talibs, in their signature black turbans and long beards, prowled the side streets, appearing to patrol, investigating imaginary demons. When the women saw the Talibs, they called the children to their side. A man with a wispy beard, a *pakol,* flat cap, and curled-toe shoes, talked on a satellite phone by the side of a collapsing building. Ahead of them, the women smelled the promise of the fragrant yellow and orange spices at the food market, well before they could see them.

A mangy dog appeared in front of them, and Darya's five-year-old, little Malala, ran after it. Darya quickly chased her, grabbing her hand and pulling her back to the group. The older boys found sticks and hit rocks into the street, creating their own version of a ball game. Pigeons flocked around them, lifting off noisily as they hit the ball, then re-assembling and landing again, to gather the crumbs of *naan,* bread, which had fallen off a cart into the street.

Looking handsome in his baggy *shalwar kameez,* loose pants and overhanging long shirt, ten-year old Asa was Naseem's youngest child. Darya smiled as she saw him lead the younger boys in the game. As they walked along, Asa saw a construction fence across the road. Behind it was the allure of heavy equipment, too inviting for a ten-year-old to resist. He jumped and skipped over to the fence, calling to his brothers to watch him. "No, Asa," Naseem called. But he was fast. He jumped over the fence. The women stopped. They would have to wait for Asa to run around to the fence opening at the street corner, behind them.

It was a beautiful day, not too hot. Darya felt joy as she waited with her family.

Corporal Luke Trout, son of Charlotte and Jimmy Trout, of Copper Hollow, USA, and proud member of Puma Platoon, Lima Company, 3rd Battalion, 2nd Marines, got into the right passenger seat in the first convoy car. It was an open jeep, for easy in and out, and for the ability to shoot in any direction. This was a routine patrol, heading out to the market in Marjah. Checking for Taliban. His sergeant drove, because Jake "HamHock" Hartman liked to drive, and nobody saw the point to fight him for it. HamHock always told them, when you're driving, don't stop. These ragheads trick you. They lay down on the side of the road, pretending to be hurt. Then when you stop to help them, they hit you.

This morning, everything was quiet. About two blocks from the bazaar, just as the pigeons appeared on the streets, looking for garbage, Luke's squad saw a man talking on a satellite phone, lurking by a dilapidated building. Behind him, they saw two Talibs, in their black turbans, robes, and long beards. They were all looking toward the buildings, when three boys, children eight to ten years old, jumped on the hood of the car and spit on the windshield.

Sergeant HamHock, however, did not see a group of rowdy little boys. Sergeant HamHock saw a devious Taliban trap that threatened his team. He didn't slam on the brakes, to grab the boys and straighten them out. No, these were not mischievous little boys, in HamHock's eyes. These were Taliban in training. He couldn't afford to brake and get out of the car, the way Captain Jagger had mistakenly gotten out of the car that time in Kabul, when Jagger was blown up by a suicide bomber. HamHock was not going to make that mistake. He didn't brake.

He gunned it. The boys fell off the hood. The wheels of the jeep ran over Asa's leg. Luke Trout saw the little smile on his sergeant's face, when he stepped on the gas instead of the brake. *Ragheads,* he heard HamHock whisper, as Asa screamed.

It was the Talibs who ran to help Asa, and the man with the satellite phone who called for an ambulance. Luke Trout vomited out the side of the Humvee.

For weeks, Darya's household grieved as Asa recovered from his injuries. He had lost his right leg below the knee. Abdullah would get him a prosthetic leg, and pay for the best doctors, but the boy hurt. In his loss of innocence, he was not a child any more. It pained Darya to see that he was no longer carefree and happy. Abdullah, too, changed. He no longer allowed the women and children to leave the house. They had an inner courtyard garden, and they took their fresh air there. Abdullah began having more business meetings in their house. He seemed more serious, more intent on something. One evening, he took Naseem to the meeting with him.

This was very strange, Darya thought.

She eavesdropped at the door, but she could not understand what was happening. When Naseem returned, her face looked pale and frightened.

"What is it?" Darya asked her.

"Abdullah has made arrangements. I am to become a member of Parliament, in Kabul. There is a quota for women in the government. A woman has resigned, and the agreements have been made for me to take her position, until the next elections." Naseem was clearly both excited and afraid. "Abdullah says it is time for our family to participate in this Karzai government. To protect our business interests, and to make our family safe. He will buy a house in Kabul, and I will live there, with his brother and his brother's wives, when it is necessary to go to Parliament meetings."

The women grieved. Their lives would change. Naseem would leave them, for a time, and she would be in great danger. Darya didn't like what was happening. A woman shouldn't be in Parliament. It was not safe.

That night, while the family slept, a team of Marines knocked down the door of a house less than half a kilometer from Darya's house. They shot the two men in the house, leaving four widows and twelve fatherless children.

Abdullah told Naseem, "When you are in Parliament, you will call me to ask how to vote." His lips tightened when he spoke, and his eyes blazed.

Naseem agreed that this would be the right thing to do. Votes had no meaning if the proper arrangements were not made to enforce them. Abdullah had the look of an enforcer now. Every day. His face no longer smiled.

Marine Corporal Luke Trout yelled over the clatter of the gun turret on their Humvee, "Woo hoo! Look at those mountains!" He stood up through the hole in the roof, manning the machine gun mounted on top. Their convoy headed north, from Marjah deeper into Helmand, along a narrow road flanked by steep hillsides. The team was on its way to a meet-and-greet with village elders. Looking for Taliban. Gathering info. Building rapport with the population. Villagers lived in the tough mountain towns, groups of illiterate tribes clinging to flinty earth on a treacherous hillside.

Their team of five included the doc, the sniper-grunt, the commander, the machine gunner, and the Pashtun interpreter. The interpreter would ask the village elders, over cups of tea, sitting on carpets on the ground, if Taliban were in the village. The elders, of course, would say no. But that other village, over there, the elders would say. That's where the Taliban is. You should leave here and go over there. They would leave, and the Taliban would shoot at them as they left the village. It was always the same. At this point in the war, Marines were advisors. Army fought. Marines trained the Afghan National Army. Luke Trout was part of a training team, settled into an outpost meant to block the exit from a key valley. Taliban, of course, would walk around the back trails, avoiding them.

The Afghan company they were embedded with was theoretically in charge. In practice, though, the team looked out for themselves. Afghan soldiers, called Askars in the Pashto language, had a turnover problem. Every month, they would collect their paychecks, and those who felt they now had enough money, would declare themselves on leave. They would come back, maybe, when they needed money again. The Army was a job for them, not a calling. They did not care about the mission or the ideology of it.

They weren't fighting for some lofty goal. They didn't see the job as worth dying for. Most often, if a firefight broke out, they would hide or run away. Even Luke Trout knew that was not a problem that could be fixed with more training. If the Afghan Army didn't buy into the mission, no amount of training was going to get it ready. They had nothing to fight for.

Their outpost was a basic flat rectangle, with some gravel mixed into the dust to keep the mud down. They surrounded it with barbed wire. Behind the barbed wire, they placed burlap bags filled with dirt, as high as a person, to serve as bullet-proof walls. Each corner had a cement tower for the sentry. Everybody lived in plywood barracks. Ropes hung from the walls to store your gear. It was a mini-fort, built quickly on the frontier, with a mess hall and a field clinic. The American section of the outpost had satellite Internet; everybody tried to Skype their messages home as much as possible. The Afghans seemed to spend most of their days with cell phones mashed against their heads, jabbering away about their families and villages.

Trout learned that Taliban was a word that really deserved a small "t." It referred to a whole collection of Afghanis with a grievance against the Americans. Some were warlords and drug smugglers. Some were villagers, angry at a drone strike that harmed their loved ones. Some were opportunists, seeing a way to profit from the spoils of war. Some were illiterate teenagers, angry over the burning of their family's poppy fields, joining together in gangs. A few were actually the official Taliban, jihadists imported from Pakistan, determined to install a militant perversion of Islam. Basically, Trout learned, if they shot at Americans, our side called them Taliban. They might call themselves Taliban, or they might call themselves Men. Men who were deeply angry at the invaders, and the cost of invasion. Men who were blowing back at the blowhards. Men who were outraged at the citizen body count. Men whose fathers and sons and family had been collateral damage in a pointless war. Counting them our way, the population of "taliban," with a small t, was exploding.

One night, the team went out on a specific mission. The town of Marjah was a heavy Taliban stronghold, their intelligence said. They had a specific name and address of a reported top leader. They knocked the door down on the house in the middle of the night, emptying the rooms of the women and children, forcing them all into the inner courtyard. Two men were in the house. The team commander saw black turbans and those man-dresses the Taliban wore. Was that the uniform of the Taliban? Or was it what everybody wore, in this tribe and this village. Who could know? He ordered the team to shoot if they felt threatened.

It was Marine Corporal Lucas Trout, who fired the bullet that killed one of the two Taliban in Darya's neighborhood. The man moved too quickly, and Luke felt threatened. He shot a father in front of his children, in their own home, in the middle of the night, on the strength of a report from a neighbor, or from an anonymous source from who knows where. For all Luke knew, the report could have been from a rival dumpling vendor, who wanted to get rid of his competition.

Three little boys hid behind their mothers' chadori, when the military team banged into their house in the middle of the night. Trout made a clean kill of an unarmed man, with his children watching. He didn't know the man was unarmed. The man made a quick move while Luke was holding a gun on him. It happens.

This was war.

This is war.

Luke Trout, the boy turned man from Copper Hollow, was a warrior. But deep inside, that is not what he signed up to be when he became a Marine. Luke Trout, like many of his fellow Marines, thought he was signing up to be a hero, not a warrior. His goal was to help people by defending them from evil. The faces of those little boys hiding behind their mother's skirts did not look like the faces of evil to young Luke. They looked very much like the little boy who spit on his windshield, and lost his leg over it. Their eyes stung him to his inner gut, and this, ultimately, resulted in stomach trouble. When Luke arrived at the medic tent at his Forward Operating Base, he didn't say, "I can't look in the mirror without seeing the haunted eyes of those little boys when I shot their unarmed father." Instead, he said: "My stomach hurts."

The medic gave him some pills to settle his stomach, and sent him back to the field. Perhaps the medic didn't know that the stomach and the mind are tightly connected.

Chapter 26: Joey
Winter, 2008
Copper Hollow

Day after day, Joey waited nervously for news from the police. He called Monk frequently, stopped by the office, wondering if there were any developments. Officer Monk said, "Yeah, Joe, we made one buy from Molly. But we're working on another one."

"You made a drug buy from my kid's mother," Joey said. "So why din't you arrest her?"

"We gotta get this Jim Thorpe guy, too. It's no good to stop at the bottom. We got a coupla buys from him, but Merkel's got some things in the works where we can trace where he's getting his supplies."

"No, no, no, no," Joey protested. "We got a little kid at risk here. You go get my kid out of that house, then you can get back to your drug sting with this Jim Thorpe. You can't lolly-gag around with my kid in danger."

"I gotta talk to Will, Joey. I don't have the authority to bust up this sting. We put a lot into this."

"Will? Why you talkin' to Will? Wha's Will got to do with it?" Joey said.

"Will's runnin' the sting," Darrell told Joey. "He's got the whole plan laid out."

"Whadda you talkin' about?"

"Will's been put on the special task force, Joey. He's helpin' out. We need more manpower for somethin' this big. There's a lotta paperwork, because we're gettin' money from the state in a grant. We don't have the budget for a big sting like this. If Will don't fill out the paperwork, we can't pay Merkel."

"That's nuts stuff, Darrell. I'm gonna go talk to Ray Plotzky," Joey said. In Copper Hollow, that's what you did when you had to get somethin' done. Same as in the Panjshir Valley in Afghanistan. Whether it's the Afghani villagers calling for the Lion of Panjshir, or the Born-Here's of the Holler ringing the Mayor on the phone, you talk to the warlord if things ain't right. This is tribal tradition.

Mayor Plotzky, sadly, was out sick that day, so Joey went home and did nothing. He had to. The warlord wasn't in.

Meanwhile, as the month of December progressed, Merkel stopped by Joey's place, mentioning that he was helping the police with the sting, but he can't be much help, because his car broke down. He needed parts. Could Joey loan him some money to fix his car? In his eagerness to keep the investigation from stalling, Joey helped out with money for Merkel to buy a new motor. Merkel continued, on a regular basis, to ask for a little money here, and a little money there, prompting Joey to keep a diary of how much he had paid Merkel. He hoped that maybe when Merkel got paid for working on the sting, Joey could get at least some of his money back. He checked with Monk about the money again, by phone.

"Darrell," Joey said, "I'm givin' Ralph a lot of money to keep his car runnin'. It's addin' up. How much are you guys gonna pay him?"

"Ahh, hell, you can give him whatever you think is reasonable, Joe," Monk answered. "If he needs a bonus, that's up to you. We'll settle it all out with the state when this is over."

"There's no set amount the state's gonna pay him?" Joey asked.

"Nah," Monk said. "This is up to our discretion. I figure you can dole it out however you want. If he has to keep a car running, you can go with him to keep the costs down. Just keep records and you can hand it in at the end."

In dribs and drabs, Joey handed out money to Merkel. Joey's helping the police. He's participating in a sting. He's doing good. He's saving his little boy. Monk tells him they are going to do the bust on New Year's Eve. Joey thanks God this will be over soon. He gets down on his knees and prays, to save his little son.

Two days before the big "bust" is supposed to go down, Joey gets a call from Merkel's girlfriend, Mavis Ellingham. "Merkel and Jim Thorpe got in a fight," she says, "and now they are in jail. They need $5,000 bail, or they won't be out in time to go to the bust." Joey calls Monk five times in one day, begging him to respond so that this can get settled. When Monk doesn't answer, Joey worries that the bust won't happen, so he turns over the money to Mavis for the bail for "Jim Thorpe" and Merkel. By this time, Joey has paid Merkel nearly $15,000 in bits and pieces. He has discussed this money and these payments with Monk time and time again, pressuring for an answer on how this can be settled out. Monk says it's all going to go in the paperwork for the state. On New Year's Eve, having gotten visitation with his child for that night to make sure the child is out of harm's way, Joey settles in at his house to wait for the sting to go down. That New Year's Eve night, Joey secretly sends some friends over to drive by "Jim Thorpe's house" to see if there are blue lights flashing.

But, there are not. The house is dark.

The "bust" fizzles.

Josh Bockenheim's order came through Defense Attorney Will Pruitt to Officer Darrell Monk, who made the call to Joey Anhalt on January Second. The way it happened: Josh pushed and pressed on Will, for no good reason, except that he wanted Ray Plotzky put away. Will felt the pressure, but he couldn't do anything to Ray, and he was getting overwhelmed, so he started worrying. The more he worried, the more he was afraid he would get himself on the wrong side of the feds. The more scared he got, the more he thought Joey was hammering on him. He truly worried that Joey was going to force the issue with Ray, and uncover the whole operation. Joey Anhalt knew, Will believed. Joey was dangerous. Will was losing his grip, so he did what people do when they feel bullied and get scared. He turned around and looked for somebody else that he could bully in turn. Will offered Darrell Monk money to help him follow through on his plan, and this whole big mess got started. Flawed people are the only people there are, and when they feel pressure, they do unreasonable things.

Monk called Joey on the phone. "We had to call off the bust," Monk said. "There's too much talk about a sting in the works. The drugs in Copper Hollow have dried up. There aren't any more. But we have an idea of how to get them going again. Ralph Merkel is going to come over to your house and work with you on this."

Joey was at home, in his big farmhouse, where a house-keeper came daily to keep it spotless and well-ordered. *Merkel?* Joey thought. *Ralph Merkel is going to take the lead and explain to me what the police are doing? What is he, a police officer now? All this time, I've been spoon-feeding Merkel what Monk said, and now Merkel is going to run the operation? The police say the drugs have dried up, but they're going to get them started again? Is it me? Am I the one who's nuts?*

Merkel showed up within the hour, knocking at Joey's kitchen window, peering inside to get Joey's attention. Merkel didn't seem to know that normal people knocked on doors, instead of peering in windows. That was just something he'd always done. He always peered in windows.

Joey let him in the kitchen door, and set a cup of black coffee in front of him. He sat at the kitchen table and kicked a chair out to let Merkel know it was okay for him to sit down. "Monk says you should watch Molly on your own," Merkel stammered, really fast. "They don't have the man-power to do it. Monk said to tell you it's real dangerous, her havin' those drugs in there. Kids have died eatin' that stuff. He says if you want to hire me, I can do it. But you have to pay me direct, because the state says they're pulling out of the sting."

Joey was a distraught father, all right, but he was finally getting the picture. "No, Ralph, I don't need your help," he said. "I'm not going to hire you."

Ralph looked worried. He wiped his mouth on his sleeve. Joey saw the prison tattoo. "I know a way to get some drugs in here," Ralph said. "I'm meeting a guy at the Box-Mart parking lot tonight. If you meet me there with the money, I can get this started again."

"No," says Joey, on the audiotapes Ralph was making of him. "I don't do that. That's your deal, and it's all on you." In Joey's mind, he pictured the video cameras on the street lamps in the BoxMart parking lot. Ralph was setting him up, he realized. And that meant Monk was setting him up. The realization set in slowly. He was the victim.

But what about Molly? What about his son? He understood that he had to pull away from Ralph Merkel. But he wasn't ready to shut Merkel out, because Monk kept sending him over. He was the kind of person who always had to hammer away at every little point, until he got to the truth. He was sure something was going on with Molly and his little Brian, and he had to find out what it was. So he listened when Merkel came to see him. Which Merkel did. Over and over. Showing up at the kitchen window. Peering inside.

Merkel couldn't get any more money from Joey, so he changed his tactics. Now, Merkel started telling Joey about the murders he had committed. He named two, with details and specifics. Getting desperate to convince Joey to buy in and pay up, Merkel told Joey he'd personally had sex with Molly. At her house. He added details that convinced Joey it was true. Joey turned purple on the inside. His eyes blazed with rage.

Joey went apoplectic. Now, he realized, his child's mother was consorting with not just drug dealers, but also this convict-turd, and murderers. He increased his phone calls to Monk, filling Monk in on all the details Merkel told him about these murders. "What are you going to do? What are you going to do?" he entreated to the Officer. But, Monk seemed unconcerned. "I have to ask Will," Monk repeated, for the umpteenth time. Joey worried and stewed. Why won't anybody help him get his child out of that frightening place? Again and again he left messages at Ray Plotzky's office, but Ray did not call back.

One day Merkel came to see Joey, with more details about the abominations of the drug dealing "Jim Thorpe". Joey thought about his child, stuck in the middle of that mire. His mind could not get off the murders Merkel had told him about. "I'd like to tie that guy to a tree and take a baseball bat to him and shoot him," Joey said, on the wire Ralph Merkel wore to entrap him. He was too involved to understand that everything about this deal was a setup. He had no way to understand that Molly was not doing any of these things. Molly had no idea this was going on. But Joey Anhalt had just said on tape that he wanted to kill Jim Thorpe. And Ralph Merkel was ready to testify that he had been paid to do it. Dutifully, Jeanine Sherwood transcribed the tape. It was murder for hire, she reported to Josh Bockenheim. And Bockenheim smiled.

Even though Will Pruitt thought the problem with Joey was under control, he still felt nervous about Ray Plotzky. It wasn't enough just to have Ray's dad under indictment. It wasn't enough to have the feds seize the farm. Ray was still talking. Ray was still investigating. Ray was still fighting. He had been weakened, but not fully incapacitated, and he was now a raging injured bull. Bockenheim wanted it ended.

Will had to do more. He thought of a plan, and then he called Ray to his office. When Ray arrived, Will handed him a yellow envelope marked Classified, which Will had taken from Josh Bockenheim's office. "I think you'll be interested in what this says," Will told Ray. It was a gamble, Will knew, but he was fairly sure he knew Ray well enough that it would pay off. Ray would take that envelope to Mitchell Davis. Will was sure of it. And then this whole problem would be over, and Ray would be out of the way. On the one hand, Will felt bad about doing it. On the other hand, Will knew this all had to end.

Chapter 27:
Darya and Farzam
Winter, 2008
Afghanistan

For months, Abdullah had been distracted, travelling back and forth from their home in Marjah to Kabul, to work with Naseem. Darya had taken on more responsibility for the household management. She had to hire some Hazaras, the ethnic group in Afghanistan whom Pashtuns consider a servant class, to help with the cooking and entertaining, and it bothered her to have servants in the house. She was uncomfortable telling others what to do, but she needed help with all the entertaining.

She knew Abdullah had wild mood swings, and intense, arguing, emotional dinner meetings at their house. He was particularly kind to Asa, and sought out the boy to spend time with him. She often eavesdropped on his phone calls and meetings. She wanted to learn.

One day, Naseem returned home. Naseem called the women together: Darya, Abdullah's mother, and the older daughters. "Abdullah has decided," Naseem said. "We have learned much in the Parliament. I have told him everything I learned there. Over the years, Abdullah has helped the Americans, when he thought it was good to help them. He has put many of his competitors out of business through this help. It was good business. But when the Americans interfered with his business, he has thwarted them. Now, after Asa's injury, he is angry and wants the Americans out." Naseem spoke confidently and carefully. She wanted all the women to understand the family circumstance, so that they would not accidentally mention family business to other women. Naseem seemed wiser now, more worldly. A lot had happened to her in her time in Kabul, working next to men.

"Abdullah has taken much time and careful consideration for his decision," she continued, "and we must be extra kind to him, as he is greatly distressed. He has discussed this with others, but some cannot know, and this is why we must not speak of it in front of the children, or outside our home. Not to our friends or neighbors at parties. Not at the beauty parlor. Not at the mosque. It is secret. We must keep everything about Abdullah's actions secret. If you hear others speak of Abdullah, you must tell me immediately."

Darya moved in closer to Naseem. She wanted to understand everything. She worried that there would be more change in their home. The women all sat with their knees forward, politely curling their legs and feet behind them. "Abdullah is going to change our family business," Naseem said. "We are going to move out of poppies, and set up new lines of production. It is for the best. I learned about this in the Parliament. We will get startup money from the government. I have talked with Abdullah about this for a long time. But there is a danger."

Darya waited to hear the danger. She did not fully understand, but she knew about danger.

Naseem continued. "Abdullah has worked with the American CIA. Sometimes, he has worked for them. Once, he went to Washington D.C. to talk to them, and he has been to New York City twice. His business partners must not find this out. We must not talk about where he is, or what he does, or any details of our family. He is going to call the CIA, and tell them of his plans. He will offer to help others move out of the drug business, too, in return for his amnesty. This is the best way to get the Americans to leave, he believes."

Darya understood. She felt uneasy about this change. Abdullah was trusting the government. Abdullah was working with the Americans, whom he hated. Was this a good idea? She had no experience in the world of men and work, but she did know their lives were going to change.

In Farzam's village, there was much concern over who would be their leader when Boba Wakil died. He was quite old and his bones were getting rusty. A successor had to be chosen. The village had been followers of Ahmed Shah Massoud, but he was assassinated in 2001, right before the attack on the World Trade Center in New York. Then much happened, as the American war replaced the Soviet war, and the Taliban guarded the drug trafficking routes. Now, concern built over how they would live with a government in Kabul, led by Pashtuns, when they were Tajiks.

Farzam returned to Kabul, where he could learn more and prepare his village for the next phase in the long history of tribal Afghanistan. Let no one be misled: Boba Wakil ran

Farzam's village. The government in Kabul was not in charge. Like any great leader, Boba Wakil needed information. Farzam's job right now was to get that information and bring it back home. As always, he returned to the Mosque, where information flowed.

"Do not be misled," Mullah Aziz said. "The Taliban are not against the growing and selling of poppy. They are against the using of poppy products by Muslim people. But growing and selling it to the West is a fine idea, within the Taliban's authority. This will further weaken their society and contribute to their inevitable defeat. This is why the Taliban offers villages like yours a means of protection."

"Allahu Akbar," Farzam said, the way Christians say "Amen."

To be accepted as part of the group, Farzam needed to participate in an insurgent activity. This would be how he gained credibility, and how he would be perceived as trustworthy, so that he could get more information. The Mullah said he would have to attend a training camp first, so that he would know how to use weapons and learn the techniques of insurgency. This, Farzam could do. He was brave; he wanted to serve his village and honor his grandfather, and his father who had fought before him. Before gaining entry to the training camp, however, Farzam had to prove himself. He must bring the American, Chance Kiernan, back to Kabul. He had done that job, when he brought Kiernan and Hanif to his village. Hanif was killed in that ambush, but Kiernan survived. The Mullah wanted Farzam to bring Kiernan back, so they could try again. It would be a good thing to kill this American. He was much trouble.

"If you do not want to bring the American back here, there is an alternative to attending the training camp," Cousin Mosen told him. "You could join the Afghan National Army. The Americans would train you in their techniques. Then you could desert, as soon as you were trained. It's nc problem. It happens all the time."

Farzam considered the situation, and decided that he was willing to bring the American back. He'd been impressed by Haji Abdullah Khan, and wanted to be more like him. Abdullah wanted to kill the American, but had ended up only killing one of the two, the Pakistani Hanif. Perhaps Abdullah would be impressed if Farzam succeeded at taking out the other one. Farzam's instruction was to contact the American and propose that they proceed with the meeting that was aborted when Kiernan came to the village, because of the unfortunate attack by unrelated Taliban terrorists the last time. To convince the American to come, he was to say that his grandfather would be in Kabul, and he would not have to come to the village to meet him. They would meet in Kabul.

The Mullah told Farzam that Kiernan would undoubtedly stay at the Kabul Serena Hotel. "The Haqqanis are planning an attack on this hotel," the Mullah said. "It will coincide nicely with their plans. Tomorrow, you will meet one of the leaders of the Haqqani network. You will sit in on meetings where we go over our various plans of attack."

When they left the mosque, Cousin Mosen said, "The Mullah trusts you, Farzam. That is why he is letting you come to the planning meeting. Abdullah has recommended you to him."

"I feel that as an honor," Farzam said.

The snow in Kabul was eight inches deep on the streets and sidewalks. It stressed the traffic flow. Farzam and Mosen walked most places they wanted to go. Farzam liked Kabul in the wintertime better. A snow-covered city looked far better than a garbage-covered one. The frozen air suppressed the smell.

They walked to dinner at Cousin Mosen's house, which is where Farzam was staying while he was in Kabul. Mosen's family was doing well, primarily because Afrooz, Mosen's brother, had gotten a good job working for the Ministry of Mines and Industry. "Copper may turn out to be a bigger business for Afghanistan than the gas pipeline or even the poppies," Afrooz said as they sat in a circle on the mat on the floor for dinner. "The Chinese have petitioned to begin mining at Balkhab. They'll put in a railroad first, which would be an excellent incentive for us to agree to the mine."

"Can you imagine taking the train from Kabul to your village, Farzam? What a change that would make in the life of your village," Mosen added.

"Balkhab is in the wrong direction for me," Farzam said. "Our village has no copper. But perhaps the Chinese would like to consider mining emeralds."

"You have emeralds, Farzam? You are looking for a market for them?"

"You work in the Ministry, Afrooz. Perhaps you could help me with that."

"I know the Haqqanis want an emerald mine. If you had an emerald contract, it would make it easier for security in the transport of your tor. It could simplify many of your transactions."

"My tor is already under contract to Abdullah. Haji Khan."

"Oh, Haji Khan will work with the Haqqanis. He frequently contracts with them."

"This will be very good for my position, Farzam. If I can make a deal with the Haqqanis, it will be a favorable thing for my job in the ministry. Of course, we will have to cut a piece out for certain middlemen."

"Of which you are one?"

"I am a very small one. There is one at every layer of government. But it can be done this way, and it can't be done any other way."

"Then we do it this way," Farzam agreed. "I will partner with the Haqqanis and with Haji Abdullah Khan. But first, let me contact Chance Kiernan and lead him to believe I will partner with him. That will get him to come here and walk into the trap."

"We have electricity from eight a.m. to ten a.m. tomorrow. You can use the Internet then."

"Excellent," Farzam said. "I have his email address."

Farzam contacted the fake business email that would send Chance Kiernan to see him. Then he prepared to visit the madrassa to learn the strategies of jihad.

Chapter 28: Mitchell
Winter, 2008
Copper Hollow

Mitchell Davis felt paralyzed. His original story about the hero, Josh Bockenheim, was overturned by the Ohio girls' revelation. He felt afraid to contact Bockenheim. He decided to discuss the situation with his editor at the *Copper Hollow Mercury*, Reese Babbitt. Babbitt, as Davis suspected, squashed the story completely. That's what had happened to him every time he brought what he thought was a big front page scoop to the attention of his editor. As soon as the story turned away from a happy hero piece about Bockenheim, his editor trashed it. Now, thanks to the pure importance of the story, he wouldn't get his front page byline. His career would never take off.

"I'm miserable in this job," Mitchell e-mailed to Olivier, from his home computer. "But I promised the girls in Ohio that I would take their story to someone who would look into it. I took what I knew to the mayor, and he showed me an envelope with financials in it from Josh Bockenheim's operation. The problem is, I didn't know what to make of what he gave me." He was sitting in his studio apartment: one large room that served as kitchen, living-room, and bedroom plus a small bathroom. It was a third floor walkup on Copper Hollow's Main Street. The rent was subsidized, but he still could barely pay. His brown cloth sofabed came from the Thrift Store. His coffee table doubled as his dining room table. He took his meals mostly on the coffee table, while watching reruns of Jon Stewart as his evening news show. Usually, he ate pizza or sandwiches. Socially, his entire network of friends consisted of online relationships, in chat rooms and multi-player games. He had no friends in Copper Hollow, and his family had been estranged long ago. All evening, he searched on the Internet, trying to decide who to tell. That night he got a call from Ray Plotzky. "We have to get together," Ray said. "Tonight. I have something else to show you."

After meeting with Ray the night before, Mitchell felt eager to get on with his project. At nine a.m., he showed up at the office of Defense Attorney Will Pruitt. He wanted to hire Pruitt to represent him, in preparation for selling his story freelance. He knew this information was explosive, and he felt he needed a lawyer to protect his interests and keep him out of trouble. In Copper Hollow, there was only one lawyer. With the information Ray Plotzky had leaked to him last night, he was ready to go all the way to Rolling Stone magazine, or maybe even the New York Times. Jeanine Sherwood greeted him at the door. Mitchell sat on the visitor's sofa. "You don't have an appointment, Mr. Davis. I doubt if Mr. Pruitt can see you now," Jeanine said, flexing her gatekeeper power.

"Please tell Mr. Pruitt that I'm working on a front page story for the *Copper Hollow Mercury* about Josh Bockenheim. Tell him I've got new information from the girls who were rescued in Ohio."

As soon as he said it, he realized his mistake. He told the girls he would disguise the source of his information. Instead, he'd blurted it out at the first opportunity. He hadn't even waited to be pressured for it. He'd told it to a secretary, simply for the purpose of getting access to his own attorney. This is why he needed to work on a big paper, he thought, where he could get someone to show him how newspaper work is done. *But maybe newspaper work isn't done any more,* he thought. *Maybe his career aspiration is futile, and he's just chasing a unicorn.*

In a few minutes, Jeanine returned and invited him into Will Pruitt's office.

"Where are your notes and who have you told?" attorney Pruitt asked him.

And the next morning, Ed Brentwood was preparing an indictment against Young Ray Plotzky, for espionage against the United States of America.

Present Day
Paris

"That, sadly, is all we know about what happened to Mitchell Davis," Olivier added. "He went to see Will Pruitt with his story, and we know that because he said in his email that he was going there. After that, the trail is cold. There were rumors about what happened to him, however, and from this point on, we will talk about the rumors."

"What about his editor, Reese Babbitt?"

"Babbitt received an email resignation from Davis' computer. I doubt that Davis sent it. He would have mentioned resigning from the paper in his email to me. It's been more than five years, Andrew. I think he would have turned up. Mitchell wanted a journalism career. I could have helped him with that, so I can't see why he would hide from me."

Madeleine entered the room. "We know that Jeanine resigned from Will Pruitt's office shortly after Mitchell disappeared," she said. "We suspect that's when her blackmail checks started coming. She knew that Mitchell went into a room with Will Pruitt. She also knew the topic, and she was the girlfriend of Officer Darrell Monk at the time."

"After Mitchell disappeared," Olivier added, "Ann tried to find him. She looked for his parents. She traced back to his college. But she could find no one who had heard from him. Mitchell had no living parents, but he had a stepfather and a stepbrother. They both denied any knowledge of his whereabouts. His former college friends hadn't heard from him, and his online profiles had all been shut down. He was gone."

"Wait. Does that sound like maybe he went into the Witness Protection Program? I mean, he disappeared while preparing to bring testimony to a prosecutor, right?"

"No, he disappeared while hiring an attorney so that he could blow a whistle, Andrew. We'd hoped, in the beginning, that he had gone into hiding. That's why we thought it was important for Ann to get Chance Kiernan involved."

2008
Copper Hollow

Chance was not home again. This time, Ann Kiernan did not know where he went or how long he would be gone. He left the day after Christmas, the very week the boys were off from school and needed him to be home. *Why couldn't he wait another week?* Ann thought. *What was so urgent that he could not postpone it a few days?*

Ann Kiernan still worked on her marriage, and whenever Chance was in town, she tried to keep things light and happy. But Olivier was right about Mitchell Davis. He was snooping into things she and Olivier had gotten him started on. They were obligated to look for him.

Her attempt to find Mitchell through his office at the newspaper failed. Next, she visited his apartment building to talk to the landlord. The landlord said his friends had come over to empty out his place and take his things. The landlord had received an email authorization, and the friends had brought a check from Mitchell to cover breaking the lease.

"A physical check with Mitchell's signature on it?" Ann thought this would be a clue.

"Uhh, no. It was a cashier's check," the landlord remembered.

Okay, Ann thought. *That was a clue, too.*

She told all this to Madeleine. Madeleine said, "You have to ask your husband to find out what happened to Mitchell," Madeleine told her. "Even Chance Kiernan will understand that it's not acceptable for U.S. citizens to disappear in the night without a trace. Who can live in a society where that happens? You can file a missing person's report."

Ann wanted to do it, but her relationship with her husband was tenuous. She felt reluctant to make things worse by bringing up issues that might be related to his job. After all, she knew he met with Josh Bockenheim and travelled with him.

"Madeleine," she asked. "You don't think Chance is involved in what Josh Bockenheim is doing, do you?"

"I think you would know better than I," Madeleine answered. "Is he a sneaky drug dealer who smuggles arms to the people the U.S. is fighting?"

Ann laughed, but it was nervous laughter, not happy laughter. "No," she said, "he couldn't be. Where's our swimming pool and fancy mansion? You would think a drug dealer would live better than we do."

"Well, there it is," said Madeleine. "*Voila*. Ask him to find Mitchell. Go file a missing person's report while you're waiting for him to come home."

Ann felt better after talking to Madeleine, as she usually did when her friend helped her sort through her thoughts and feelings. She dressed in black slacks and a periwinkle blue silk blouse. She fixed her makeup and added some gold jewelry. She wanted to put on a bright face and a happy outlook, at least on the outside. These feelings of a heavy burden couldn't defeat her. She would go to town now and file a missing person's report.

Chapter 29: Ann
2008
Copper Hollow

First, Ann dropped the boys off at a matinee in the town. That would give her two hours to talk to the police. The distance from her house to town required that she bring the boys with her, when there was no school. She would be gone for too long, and arranging for a babysitter out there was difficult. When the boys were inside the theater, she drove a few blocks away to the police station. She parked near the front door. The office was a trailer, plopped on a sparse plot across the parking lot from the jail. Someone had planted a few geraniums by the door, attempting to cozy the place up. Entering the front door, she saw a half-dozen straight-backed chairs arranged around a low thrift-shop coffee table. An array of old magazines were arranged in a fan on the table. The multiple addresses on them indicated the employees must have brought them in from home. A self-serve coffeepot sat on an end table in the corner, with one pot for decaf and one caffeinated. Labels taped on the pot said: Leaded and Unleaded. A tube of Styrofoam cups, sugar packets and powdered creamer lay to the side. To the right of the visitors' area, a wooden counter-top protected the employees from the visitors.

Flo, seated behind the counter, looked up from her typing and adjusted her half-frame glasses when Ann walked into the office. "What can I do for you?" Flo asked. There were no other visitors. If there were other employees, they were behind the wall where Ann couldn't see them. She saw nothing but empty gray metal desks in a dark room.

"I want to file a missing person's report," Ann told the thin woman with gold hoop earrings and long fingernails painted with blue nail polish. Ann noticed that her fingernails got in the way of typing, and forced her to roll over the keys with straightened fingers.

"Who's missing?" Flo asked. She didn't reach for any forms to fill out.

"It's Mitchell Davis," Ann said. "From the *Mercury.*"

"He's not missing," Flo said. She turned back to her typing. "Reese got an email. He went back to school."

"Well, I heard that," Ann said, "but I'd like to verify it."

Flo looked up. "We don't track people down just so somebody can keep in touch with them. If he wanted you to know where he was, he'd of tol' ya."

Ann felt that familiar annoyance she'd felt ever since she arrived in Copper Hollow. She couldn't quite put her finger on why the locals made her feel like slapping them silly. "I believe that Mitchell may not have gone back to school. I think it's possible that someone else sent that email to Reese. I'd like to formally and officially file a missing persons' report, if I may," she said, with an air of haughty-city-person in her voice.

Flo gave her a country frown. "You know we don't have any crime here," she said. "Nobody's ever been kidnapped in Copper Hollow. I think once, about ten years ago, there was a body dumped in the Park, but city people did that. The only violence we have here is domestic. Did Mitchell have family here? Because that's about the worst threat in the Holler." Her tone suggested that Ann was a lunatic.

Ann gritted her teeth, fought an urge to run out the door and drive to California. "May I please speak to a detective," she said.

"Okay, well, that would be Officer Monk, then," Flo said, with a dismissive air. "He's the only detective we have." She pushed a notepad and pen across the counter. "Write down your name and phone number and I'll let him know what you want."

Ann wrote a long note to the officer, explaining her concern that Mitchell couldn't be found. She handed it back to Flo and took a seat. When she sat down, Flo said, "The officer ain't here, honey. I'll give him the note when he comes in, and he'll call you."

Fine, Ann thought. *Fine. I drove in here, a thirty-minute drive, and now I'll drive back home again. Six dollars worth of gas, when I could have made a phone call.* Money was tight, in the Kiernan household. Now the boys were in the movie theater, and Ann would have to wait for them. She would need something to do for the next two hours. BoxMart was the only shopping venue in Copper Hollow, and the Spoon 'n' Fork the only restaurant. She could go to Jo-Beans, but that was more of a truck stop than a restaurant, in Ann's view. Ann decided to stop by the library to get a book to read, then spend the time in the Spoon 'n' Fork.

As she entered the café, Sherry Sherwood was leaving. She'd been with a group of ladies from the Red Hat Society, and she wore her wide-brimmed red hat and a purple dress. Sherry quickly said good-bye to her group and followed Ann back into the lunch room. "Ann," Sherry called, stepping quickly and touching Ann lightly on the arm. "Ann, you are not going to believe what's going on with Mavis and Ralph. They're getting married!" Sherry waved the waitress over and invited herself to sit down at Ann's table. She ordered herself a frozen margarita, with salt on the rim of the glass.

Ann was really not in the mood for an afternoon with Sherry, but she was trapped by her own value system into behaving politely. She smiled at the waitress, who had finished taking Sherry's drink order. "I'll have a turkey sandwich and an iced tea," she said. When the waitress left, she turned to Sherry. "I am definitely surprised to hear about that wedding," she said. "It doesn't sound like a very good thing for Mavis' seven-year-old son, Johnny Ellingham."

"Oh, it's no problem for Johnny," Sherry poo-pooed, waving her hand in a downward don't-worry-about-it stance. "He's moved in with Mavis' parents. Gramma Ellingham will make sure Johnny's fine." Then Sherry leaned in, in a conspiratorial gesture, toward Ann. She put her hand up to the side of her mouth, to keep the secret. "Ralph's come into some money," she whispered.

Ann took a sip of water, using the skill of silence to encourage Sherry to ramble on with more secrets and revelations.

"Ralph's got her a diamond ring, and he's booked the Parkside Inn for a wedding reception. They've been looking at double-wide trailers. They're going to park one on the Merkel family farm."

It was an interesting phenomenon in Copper Hollow. A lot of families had big spreads of farmland. They'd put numerous families on the same spread, without dividing it formally into individual plots in the county records. As they built different cabins and trailers for each new family, they all hooked into the same well and septic. As time passed, some of the younger families would leave Copper Hollow to look for work. They wanted the money from their house, so they'd partition off their piece to sell it. This resulted in houses being sold that shared a well and septic on some other person's land. It had been going on like this for thirty years or more, ever since septic systems came to Copper Hollow. That Mavis and Ralph would be joining the trend seemed somehow normal. In Ann's mind, it anchored the concept that this wedding was real.

Her sandwich arrived, and Ann decided it was good luck that brought Sherry to her table. "How did Ralph come into money?" she asked Sherry, as she bit into her turkey and lettuce.

"He has a job with the police department," Mavis said. "He's a contractor." She lowered her voice again, to add a conspiratorial asterisk. "He just got a big bonus."

This caused a raised eyebrow to plant itself in Ann's mind. *Ralph Merkel works for the police department as a contractor and he just got a bonus big enough to pay for a diamond ring, a wedding, and the down payment on a trailer. That is, frankly, a completely ridiculous concept,* Ann thought. Sherry clearly didn't see the flaw in that story, so Ann didn't point it out. Ann had met Ralph. He's covered in tattoos, his hair is always too long and greasy, he's completely unskilled, and he has the impulse control of a feral cat. "Has Mavis been back to Elisa House, Sherry?" she asked. "Is Ralph still hitting her?"

"Oh, goodness, no," Sherry answered, bubbling with enthusiasm over the good news. "The mayor put a stop to that. It was good you got him into it. Ralph hasn't laid a hand on her since Ray Plotzky had a talk with him about it." She lowered her voice, back to the camaraderie of two conspirators. "In fact, Mavis thinks Ray helped Ralph land this job. Ray says when a man has a job, he's not so likely to act out. Ray is always helping people out that way."

Ann looked at her watch. Still an hour before the boys would be ready to go home. Maybe she could get some real information from Sherry. "Do you know Mitchell Davis?" She asked. "From the newspaper?"

"No," Sherry said, "but my husband, Tommy, surely does. Tommy knows everyone who runs this town, and he's good friends with the editor of the paper, Reese Babbitt. You know," Sherry continued, without even a pause for a comma between her sentences, "Reese Babbitt says they were really after the mayor all along, when they locked up his Pop. And they only wanted the mayor so they could get Congressman A. It was all politics, you know. The prosecutor was a Democrat, and he was after Republicans."

Ann wondered if she personally had the stamina to keep talking to Sherry. She could tell by the look in her eye that Sherry was having thoughts about ordering another margarita. She decided to try to guide the conversation.

"I've already talked to Reese Babbitt," Ann said, "and he told me that Mitchell went back to school. But he didn't know how to contact Mitchell. Do you think Tommy would be able to find a phone number for Mitchell? Maybe Reese would look harder if Tommy asked." She reached into her purse and found a pen. Then she wrote her name and phone number on a napkin. As she gave the napkin to Sherry, she said, "Do you think Tommy could do that?" She knew Sherry would never admit that Tommy couldn't do something.

Sherry's chin quivered. "I'll ask him," she sniffed.

Now I've done it, Ann thought. *If something bad happened to Mitchell Davis, I have just alerted the people who did it that I am on the trail.* Sherry would tell Tommy, and Tommy would talk until somebody who was involved heard the babble. Tommy would hand over her name and phone number to whomever that might be. She felt the regret already.

At home that afternoon, Ann got the phone call from Officer Monk. "Flo tells me you don't believe Mitchell Davis went back to school," Monk said in a tone so pleasant and welcoming his words didn't threaten.

"Thank you for calling, Officer," she said. "I'm concerned because Mitchell was working with a friend of mine on a story. He was excited about publishing it, and it seems out of character for him to disappear in the middle of a project that would be important for his career. I think it's unlikely that he went back to school without explaining that to my friend." She chose her next words carefully. She had not forgotten her training at ENRON. "Mitchell wanted to check some facts before he turned the story in. He went to see an attorney, Will Pruitt. Then after that, he disappeared. Mitchell emailed a copy of the story to my friend in France."

"Well," Monk responded, "I can ask some questions, see if I can get a forwarding address or find his family. But it's not illegal for someone to go missing of their own accord, Mrs. Kiernan. If Mr. Davis didn't want your friend involved in his life, it's not up to me to give you his new contact information."

"That's not what happened," Ann snapped. "If he's missing, something is wrong. He didn't walk out on his friendship and his career."

Monk was quiet a moment. "I'll take a look into it," he told her, with an air of calm and kindness.

Ann didn't share Monk's feeling of calmness. She dialed Ray Plotzky.

Ray Plotzky hung up his home phone, where he'd been talking to Ann Kiernan from his sick bed. She had called to tell him about Mitchell's disappearance. He was using all his strength to put on a good face through his misery. Ray was becoming progressively ill. His lawyer made arrangements to accept his hunting land, as a partial down payment. Life ahead looked increasingly bleak, as his lawyers reported the prosecutors were going for the maximum penalties possible, and he was being charged with espionage. He didn't understand it. What were they talking about?

Nobody can imagine how hard it is to have your world turned upside down by an unjustified persecution, he thought. One minute you're on top of the world, making plans for a big future, feeling like a success. The next minute everyone reviles and hates you and your family suffers. Your future could be a life in jail, and all your money is being sucked down by lawyer bills. The best case is that he'd go broke from paying lawyers.

He was trying to keep doing his job and hide the pain. He realized he should have told Mrs. Kiernan that he knew all about the story Mitchell was working on. All he could think was that he had to solve this whole problem himself. After all, he was the Mayor. Everybody counted on him. There was something that had been bothering him, ever since Joey Anhalt sat crying in his office the other day. He had turned Joey's case over to Officer Monk. Even so, he felt something wrong, so he pulled the file folder from the office and brought it home. He'd been home sick so frequently, he thought he could spend some time studying and thinking about it. For safekeeping, he'd locked it in his bank box. There was something in that file that didn't add up, and he needed time to think of what it was. He pulled the file out again now, and went through it page by page. Then he remembered what was odd. There was a scribbled note on the back of one of the pages. It was the routing number for Jeanine Sherwood's bank account.

Chapter 30: Juliette
Winter, 2008
Copper Hollow

In the back room at the Spoon 'n' Fork, where he had cornered Bockenheim alone, Chance Kiernan should have remembered that he did not have the authority to put his hands around Josh Bockenheim's neck and squeeze. But there was no one else in the room with the two of them, so he allowed himself the pleasure.

"How did you get the Te guys out of the Salang Pass, you little shit," he said. He at least had the self-control to know not to leave visible bruises. If there had been a toilet nearby, he would definitely have practiced some high-school-style waterboarding. Bockenheim was considerably less athletic than Chance Kiernan, and flailed his arms trying to get free.

Chance eased up, but kept a solid hold on Josh's neck. "Talk," he said, "and say things I believe, or I swear you will disappear into these hills and never be heard from again."

Josh's eyes went wild, darting this and that way, looking for an escape route. "The minister, Mansour Shah. He owed me a favor. So I called him, and I paid, and he got them out."

"What did you do that he owed you a favor for?"

"I did him a favor, and he was repaying it."

Chance squeezed the neck again.

"I helped him with a problem he had. We were in there, pretending to be drug smugglers, for the job. I couldn't say no to his favor, without blowing my cover as a drug smuggler."

"So you actually became a drug smuggler. For real."

"Just with this one guy. Just Mansour. He needed me to bring the tor out, and get it to the factory."

"You built a heroin factory?"

"No, no, no. I didn't build it. It was already here. It was already operating in Copper Hollow. I just made deliveries to it. I didn't change anything about the structure. The drugs were here before I came."

Kiernan smacked him anyway, just because he was Josh Bockenheim. Then he called Joe Bridgewell and told him to send a Blackhawk. He and Mr. Bockenheim needed a meeting with the Top Brass.

The Blackhawk landed at the Copper Hollow Airport. With his binoculars, Officer Charlie Wenzel saw Chance Kiernan and Josh Bockenheim board it. He called Ray at home, to report that the telephone company guy was working with Bockenheim.

"Mrs. Kiernan's husband? Are you sure, Charlie?" Ray asked.

"Yeah, I am, Ray," Charlie answered. "It's definitely Chance Kiernan."

Too many data points, and none of them were forming a pattern. Ray didn't feel well, and in his distress and illness, he tried to think, but nothing happened.

Josh Bockenheim, and his petty talk about assassination, was braggadocio, Colonel Joe Bridgewell told Chance. Josh Bockenheim is a fool, not a murderer. His take on Josh is that Josh knew Chance would not do what he asked, and it was all display and posturing. They needed Josh. He had his fingers in too many pies.

But never mind all that, Colonel Bridgewell said. More important than any soap opera gyrations in Copper Hollow, the CIA had identified the person who ordered Hanif killed, in the attack on Kiernan's convoy at the Salang Pass. Chance needed to return to Paris. Bruce Bockenheim had new information. He was cooperating, helping the CIA find the mastermind behind these Taliban attacks. He knew, but only because his vast network of contacts could find out. Only because he was involved in the flow of money behind so many of the transactions. Words here and there had to be checked out, to separate the braggadocio from the actions. Chance should pack for Paris again. Bridgewell would call him on short notice, when it was time. CIA was picking up clues and needed some time to get them sorted. While Chance was home, he could spend more time with his family. Get things calmed down with Ann. Wait for the phone call. Live a quiet life. Don't talk to Josh Bockenheim, it's a waste of breath. Don't worry about what Bockenheim is doing, he may be an idiot, but he's an idiot on a leash.

So Chance stayed home, and this gave him more time to learn about the situation in Copper Hollow. It was all over the town, in gossip and tall tales, and in the *Copper Hollow Mercury*, and all about the mayor. It could be that all this talk in the paper was not related to anything touching on Kiernan's mission. But the noise was becoming deafening, and Chance Kiernan paid attention when odd circumstances appeared. Chance Kiernan stayed alive because he stayed hyper-vigilant. Things that didn't make sense caused him to investigate them. This business with the excessive investigation into the mayor was finally way too fishy for Chance Kiernan to ignore. At least, as long as he had to be sitting around doing nothing, he might as well dig around in the dirt.

Juliette March was the person best-positioned to provide Chance with information about the Ray Plotzky situation, so he would work with her. Ann would have to get over her jealousy. To prevent the eyes and ears of Copper Hollow from sucking in the glory of scandal, however, Chance worked with Juliette in a basement office at the Copper Hollow courthouse. The office had been provided to them by Will Pruitt. It was a much better idea than meeting in Juliette's hotel room. Occasionally, Will stopped by to ask how things were going on the case against Plotzky.

Juliette felt conflicted. "Plotzky is overwhelmingly charming, and he has endearing ways," she said, in response to Will's question. "If we keep digging, we'll find dirt we can use. There are plenty of possible pathways to bring a vague espionage and conspiracy case."

Chance sat across the table from Juliette in the cinderblock basement room. They each had a folding chair. The table was a plastic indoor-outdoor folding top, like you could buy at a discount store. The cinderblock walls were painted cream on the top half and gray on the bottom. It didn't matter. Juliette had her laptop connected to the web, so she had everything she needed. All her documents were offline, and from here she could pull up research on federal law.

Will leaned against the doorway, an uninvited guest.

"What is the need for finding something for which you can prosecute Ray Plotzky?" Chance asked. He didn't mean to suggest that this was a bad idea. He only wanted to know.

"Ed Brentwood wants him out," Juliette said. "I don't know why, but I've seen this before, even in my short tenure as an agent. If there is a good reason, based on national security, I'm not privileged to hold a clearance high enough to know it. All I've been told is to build a case against Plotzky, using whatever resources I need to do it. Brentwood has already filed an indictment, but now we have to back it up."

"Sometimes that's how things are," Chance said. Chance was a man with a very high tolerance of uncertainty. "Is this man guilty?"

"Sure, he is, Chance," Juliette said. "I've got four thousand federal laws at my disposal. They are as vague as the United States tax code. There isn't a person alive who isn't guilty of at least one of them. The job is to find the one that fits best. Now, usually, I don't mind doing things this way. Usually, I can see what the person is actually guilty of, and it doesn't bother me at all to pick something else to use to convict him, if that's what it takes to get a conviction. It's like prosecuting Al Capone for tax evasion. You have to use what you've got in the law. But this guy . . . whatever he is guilty of, he seems to have bungled into it. It really doesn't look like he's purposely done anything wrong. My concern is that we're spending an incredible level of resources on a guy that the people like."

"So your problem is that you disagree with your boss on his selection of priorities," Chance stated, matter-of-factly.

Juliette looked up from her computer to see if he was making fun of her. "I would say that I am concerned that my boss may not have all the information, thus causing his decision-making to be insufficiently analyzed."

It was very important, in the FBI and the TDU and whatever other three-letter agencies hung around in the halls of government, to follow the chain of command. Juliette didn't want to be quoted as being disagreeable within her hierarchy's silo.

Chance said, "Can you get Ed Brentwood to drop the case? I mean, you've looked into it thoroughly, and it doesn't look like something worth pursuing. Can't you tell Brentwood that?"

"I have tried," Juliette answered. "I've talked to Brentwood about this enough times that he's shutting me down about it. I think if I bring it up again, he'll file a complaint through FBI channels."

"Then," Chance said, "it's up to you to put together a briefing for your boss explaining your concerns. If you don't think there's a case, you have Powerpoint on that laptop. That's what it's for."

"Is that what you do when you have concerns up your chain?" Juliette asked.

"No," he answered. "I'm suggesting it's a tool for you. I have other tools. I don't take a job if I can't get a security clearance high enough to understand what it's about."

He was just settling in, starting to think about how backwards this business of the mayor's investigation was, when he got an emergency call from his answering service. Farzam Parvanda was contacting you. He wanted another meeting, this time in Kabul. *Good, thought Chance I've been home in Copper Hollow long enough.*

Chapter 31: Chance
Winter, 2008
Afghanistan and Copper Hollow

Chance Kiernan was in the Kabul Serena Hotel. He'd come here in response to Farzam's call, but he combined the trip with an information gathering mission with a Taliban informant who was inside the Haqqani network. He expected to discuss the village *tor* arrangement with Farzam and his grandfather Wakil while he was here. He invited Farzam and Wakil to have dinner with him in the hotel. Farzam requested that they have an early dinner, then walk to his cousin's house for their private discussions.

It was 5 p.m., and Chance was in the lobby of the hotel, waiting for Farzam. A soldier of the Afghan National Army entered the lobby alone, carrying his AK-47. In the parking lot outside, Chance could see some kind of confrontation going on with the guards. His body went into alert mode. The ANA soldier opened fire first on the hotel receptionist. At that moment, a blast went off in the parking area. Two suicide bombers had blown themselves up right outside the door. Glass from the lobby windows shattered and blew into the building. Chance ran after the soldier with the weapon, as he heard more gunfire from various places inside the building. He ran through the hotel corridors and into the gym, where the shooter had found and murdered a news reporter. By the time Chance Kiernan disarmed the shooter and turned him over to the guards from NATO who arrived shortly thereafter, four people were dead. This was Chance's second scheduled meeting with Farzam which had ended in an ambush. He was getting the hint. He called Joe Bridgewell and aborted the mission. He said he would be going home now. There would be no more work with Farzam's village.

Once again, Chance Kiernan returned home. He had a lot of catching up to do with Timmy and Jeff. Against Ann's objections, he took his boys out of school to go with him on a camping trip into the forest. There he set up targets and gave them air rifles, to teach them to shoot. It was partly a way to decompress and re-enter the real world for himself, and partly a way to relate on his own level with his boys. It was only the boys, their dogs, and their dad, deep in the forest, all alone. He wanted them to know who he was; the forest eliminated the distractions of civilization. He taught them things few other fathers know: how to build a shelter in the forest, how to track deer, how to live in the wilderness, how to purify water. The boys loved it. After three days, he brought them home safely. The next day, they went back to school. Then he hired a babysitter for the night and took his wife to the Copper Hollow airport. There they had a private pilot waiting to take them to Washington, D.C.

Chance had made reservations at a five-star restaurant, and gotten a room in a five-star hotel. (He would, of course, go to the office the next day, so that he could submit an expense report for the trip.) At dinner, he gave his wife an exquisite emerald bracelet, which he purchased in Afghanistan. As he gave her the bracelet, in the fancy restaurant, with the candlelight, the tablecloths, and the soft music in the background, he told her she was his only love. He told her she was beautiful, she was intelligent, she was a wonderful mother, she was a fabulous wife, she was his reason for living, she was his motive for sacrificing to keep our country safe. Like it always did, his method worked. Every resentment, every disappointment, every antagonistic feeling or thought Ann harbored melted away. Once again, Ann was madly in love with Chance Kiernan. Her hostility was forgotten so thoroughly, she couldn't even command it to return. She responded just as he expected she would.

In fact, Ann was so smitten by the moment, so unwilling to ruin it by bringing up anything negative, that she failed to mention the problem with the missing Mitchell Davis. She had Mitchell's article with her, right there in her purse, folded up. She knew it implicated a man who somehow, in some vague way, worked with her husband. She knew she had put the word out to Sherry Sherwood that she was looking into this. But she didn't want to ruin this time, this precious time, with the man she loved. So she put it off. She waited. She would wait for a time when things were more settled, after he got adjusted to being home. She would enjoy the moment, and they would be in love again, and their home would be happy. She would find another time to tell her husband that the walls were closing in. Next week, or next month, or when the time was right.

If Madeleine had known that Ann did not tell Chance Kiernan about the search for Mitchell Davis, Madeleine would have called Chance herself. But Madeleine didn't know, and Olivier kept searching through the Internet for a lead. Olivier had been working with an organization called Sunshine Press, in Iceland. The concept behind Sunshine Press was that the world's governments were keeping secrets, and those secrets most frequently related to atrocities committed by the government itself. Olivier was passionate about Sunshine Press, and volunteered many hours to helping it get started. Many unpaid hours, Madeleine noted, but she could not complain because she understood his passion.

Sunshine Press would eventually become WikiLeaks. WikiLeaks had no funding mechanism except to ask for donations. It began by posting equipment expenses in the Iraq and Afghan wars. Then it moved on to posting video footage of a U.S. airstrike in Iraq that killed journalists. Within a year of its founding, it had over a million leaked documents in its database. The leakers were purported to be people with a conscience, working for corporations and governments who did things that enraged their employees. If it seemed wrong, and you saw it, you could post the documents of proof to a secret place which would not be traceable back to you. This reduced the risk in whistleblowing.

From the beginning, WikiLeaks had a hard time staying operating. Even without paying salaries, it needed a few hundred thousand dollars a year to keep its servers running. All of that money had to come from donations, and at various times, PayPal suspended processing of the accounts. At one time, a judge suspended the wikileaks domain name. All of this legal wrangling had to be attended to, and it all had to be done *pro bono* by lawyers. WikiLeaks was a labor of love. It had no financial payoff. Its purpose was to help to make the original documents public so the citizens of the world could participate in their own governance. The theory was: if governing is done in secret, it is open to abuses. Public accountability only occurs when the information is available about how the government operates. So Madeleine forgave Olivier for not having any money. He was doing worthy work that served the world. He was starting WikiLeaks.

Olivier couldn't find a trace of Mitchell Davis anywhere. But he did find a lot of information about Bruce Bockenheim, Josh Bockenheim, and Te. He did think that Mitchell's article about Josh Bockenheim and the guns was the reason Mitchell disappeared. In March of 2008, he and Madeleine got Ann on Skype.

"You must know what role your husband plays in this," Madeleine told Ann. "You must tell him what you know and ask him to find Mitchell Davis. You cannot wait any longer to know this."

"Ann," Olivier added. "Are you afraid of Chance?"

"No," Ann answered. "Not at all. Why would you even think that?"

"I'm concerned that you have taken a long time to tell him things. Often that means a person is wary or afraid."

"I don't want to ruin the time we have together, Olivier. He's not home enough, and when he is home, I want things to be happy and light and joyful. When your minutes are precious, why change the atmosphere by adding burdens? Mitchell Davis has been gone a long time. Perhaps he did leave on his own accord."

Olivier waited a moment before he answered. "Perhaps," he said.

Chapter 32: Will

2008
Copper Hollow

By late February, Joey Anhalt clearly understood that all was not well in his work with the police to save his baby boy. He had given no more money to Merkel, and had not agreed to any of Merkel's requests for meetings about drugs. Joey continually called Monk and told Monk the stories which Merkel had told him about murdering people. In fact, Joey began to think maybe he should hire a private investigator to look into both Merkel and Monk.

As Joey drove home from his latest trip to see Monk, where he had once again asked for an update on the police sting, Ralph Merkel's truck pulled into the next lane. Merkel said, "I heard you been talkin' to Monk about me. Jes' leave it alone." Merkel used his thumb and forefinger to make a shooting gesture, pointed at Joey's head. Merkel may have been used to intimidating people, but Joey, because he was Joey, immediately called Monk to tell him what Merkel did.

Joey was not easily intimidated. Monk was always polite to Joey. But he never took any action against Merkel.

Calling the police seemed to be getting Joey nowhere, so he installed motion lights all around his house. He slept with a shotgun next to him. This went on for most of the winter, with Joey dodging Merkel, and Merkel making threats. Joey had to assume that the law didn't want to do anything, because Officer Monk stopped calling him back.

Finally, in early March, Joey marched into Monk's office and issued an ultimatum. "If you don't get moving and work on my case," Joey told Monk, "I'm going to call Ed Brentwood and tell him everything that has just happened."

Now, the citizens of Copper Hollow had been following the Mayor Plotzky case, and they were well aware that there was a federal investigation headed up by Ed Brentwood. It was becoming a town joke, "I'm gonna call Ed Brentwood," whenever one person was unhappy with the actions of another. Joey knew he was making an empty threat. Why would Ed Brentwood even take his call? This had nothing to do with the investigation of the Mayor. But Joey said it, because he thought it would annoy Monk. He thought maybe it would shake Monk up, and make him take an action.

When Joey got home, he saw that a rock had been thrown through his living room window. As he was cleaning up the broken glass, Joey's phone rang. A male voice he didn't recognize said, "You shut up and stay away from Brentwood, or your barn is going to be burned down."

Joey said, "It's insured."

The caller said, "Well, then that nice house you got'll be burned down, too."

Joey called Monk again. "They're threatening to kill me and burn my house down. Merkel threw a rock through my window. And how did they know I was goin' to call Brentwood? I only tol' *you* that."

Monk said, "Come on into the office. We're going to settle this once and for all."

Joey was happy to go into the police station. He wanted a confrontation to get this all out in the open and settled. He couldn't go on living under a threat like this, and he still had no resolution on the problem with his baby boy. He dressed up in a nice suit, so he could look like the rational person in the room, and got into his truck to drive to town. As Joey was driving to the police station, two police cars surrounded his car, forcing him to stop at the side of the road.

He recognized the officers as Scooter Willett and Darrell Monk.

"I'm on my way into the police station, Darrell," he said to Officer Monk. "Like I tol' you."

Darrell loomed over the car door. "Get outta the car, Joey," he said, leaning in the driver's side window.

Joey got out, and Darrell pulled his hands behind his back and handcuffed him. "You're under arrest," he said.

"What am I under arrest for?" Joey asked.

"For solicitation of murder," Officer Darrell Monk answered. He pulled Joey into his police car and settled him into the back seat, handcuffed.

"What are you talking about?" Joey hollered. "Murder who?"

"Jim Thorpe," Darrell answered.

Joey Anhalt, IV, could not be found. Nobody knew what had been done with him or to him, nobody had gotten a phone call from him, and nobody knew where he was. When his brother noticed he was missing and asked the Copper Hollow police where he was, they denied all knowledge. "Joey Anhalt?" Darrell Monk said. "I ain't seen 'im."

When they booked Joey Anhalt into the Copper Hollow jail, and charged him with murder for hire, Jim Thorpe, at least the fake Jim Thorpe who was bald, middle-aged, and crawling on his roof to install Christmas lights, was still very much alive.

Seven days after Joey Anhalt told Officer Darrell Monk that he was "going to call Brentwood," a special grand jury was convened in Copper Hollow. Ralph Merkel, confidential informant, was the sole witness. Merkel testified that Mr. Joey Anhalt, IV, paid him $50 to murder Molly Anhalt, Jim Thorpe, and if necessary, a neighbor who might possibly be a witness. He testified that Joey Anhalt gave him money to distribute drugs. He testified that he does not know Molly Anhalt, that Joey Anhalt coerced him into trying to set her up, and that Anhalt's plan was to have her arrested for drugs and then murdered before trial, as if a drug dealer did it. He described in detail the "other murders" which Anhalt had told him he committed. Faced with frightening testimony about a monstrous criminal on the loose, the Copper Hollow grand jury voted to indict.

Now, the thing about a grand jury is: it's one-sided. The prosecutor gets to say whatever, and the defense isn't even there. No defense is presented. It's supposed to be a preview of what case is going to be presented, so a jury can decide if there's even a basis to take somebody into court. Basically, if the argument doesn't make the jury giggle, the person is indicted. This is where we get the phrase, "A grand jury would indict a ham sandwich." A judge in New York said that, in 1985, and then it started appearing in books and tv shows.

After the grand jury indicted him, Joey Anhalt IV got a lawyer, and his lawyer was not Will Pruitt. He tried to pick a good one, which meant one from the City. Sadly, the lawyer he picked wasn't good enough. Two police officers testified in Joey's bond hearing that they heard the tapes Ralph Merkel made of Joey, and that Joey was a drug dealer. They said the tapes showed Joey offering to pay Ralph the sum of fifty dollars to kill Jim Thorpe. Joey's lawyer argued that this was loose talk. Joey was sitting in a truck with Ralph, and they were discussing a drug dealer who was endangering Joey's child. So Joey said, "I'd like to get a baseball bat and tie that guy to a tree and hit him with the baseball bat and shoot him." That this statement coincided with giving Ralph fifty dollars was coincidental. Joey had given Ralph much more than fifty dollars, but the money was not for killing anybody. It was for participating in a police sting. The man, Joey thought, was feeding drugs to his child's mother, endangering his baby. They were sitting in a truck together, watching the house, waiting for the drug dealer to come out. Who wouldn't be filled with anger and frustration at that thought? But thinking is not doing, and Joey wasn't doing anything except assisting the police, as far as

Joey knew. This is the argument Joey's lawyer made. But when the police officers sit in the courtroom and say "What sting?" it becomes very hard for even the best defense attorney to make his point. Maybe there was no sting. Maybe Joey was delusional. Maybe Joey imagined it all. After all, the tapes that Jeanine Sherwood transcribed said Joey was a drug dealer. Everybody knew that Joey Anhalt was a loose cannon, who would get his teeth in something and hang on like a rabid dog.

Visiting Judge Lowell Mikulski didn't see the need for the tape to be played in court. He didn't see the need for Ralph Merkel to be brought in to testify. The officers' testimony was good enough for him. The defense attorneys pointed out that there was no Jim Thorpe, that the name had been fabricated, to work Joey into a frenzy. But the judge found the phantom nature of the alleged victim to be immaterial. He decreed that Joey Anhalt would stay in jail until his trial. Bail was not granted.

So Joey's lawyer didn't get to explain that this was all a set-up, and that Joey was told his child was in danger, and that Ralph Merkel was a paid police informant, and that Joey was being extorted by Ralph the whole time. Nobody got to hear that. Nobody at all. Because Joey wasn't granted bail, and he couldn't talk to anyone to prepare his defense, and he didn't get a day in court. Joey went to jail without being able to tell his family where he was. Joey Anhalt was lost, missing, disappeared. It was as if he had been sent to Guantanamo Bay. He was there with no bail, and his trial date wasn't set. He was kept from talking to anyone, even a lawyer, for a long time.

Officer Darrell Monk personally represented to the court that Joey Anhalt, IV, was far too dangerous to be allowed out on bail. He must be kept in jail, Monk entreated the court. This man is trying to hire people to kill others. He is a danger to society. The prosecutor charged him with solicitation to commit murder, attempt to distribute drugs, suborning perjury, and drug use. All because the transcripts that Jeanine Sherwood distributed from the tapes said it. The court docket was too crowded, and Copper Hollow was too unimportant, for anybody to actually listen to the tapes themselves. If they had tried, they would have heard tapes too garbled to be transcribed, spoken in the deepest dialect of the mountains. *Holler-Speak.*

Now, the case against Joey Anhalt IV depended entirely on tape transcripts prepared by Jeanine Sherwood, of the testimony given by Mr. Ralph Merkel, confidential informant to the Copper Hollow police force. Merkel was granted immunity from prosecution for perjury before the grand jury. This was something that came to the attention of Mayor Ray Plotzky. He asked Deputy Charlie Wenzel, "How the hell can you give somebody immunity from lying to the grand jury? What sense does that make?"

"We're talkin' 'bout Ralph Merkel, Ray. The way you know if Ralph Merkel is lyin' is, you kin see his lips movin,' How would Merkel even talk to somebody, if he didn't have immunity from lyin'?"

"So Joey's been set up? Why? By who?

"Hey," Charlie said, "You remember when Darrell put those guns in the house because we needed to git Samson Kruger back in jail after he got out on parole?"

"Yeah, but that was a good cause, Charlie. Samson was a danger to his wife and kids, Darrell thought he had to get him out of there in a hurry."

"Well, Darrell says Joey is tryin' to hire somebody to murder Molly."

"I unnerstan', Charlie, but I can't help thinkin' stuff like that don't sit right."

"Okay, I din't do it, Ray. Ask Darrell what's goin' on."

Of course, nobody except his immediate family knew that Joey Anhalt was in jail. Mayor Plotzky found out, and he thought he should look into it, but the details of his own problem made it hard for him to take any action on anybody else's problem. He was trying hard to sell his house, his car, his horses, and his vacation cabin. Anything to pay the lawyers. But his house was his mom and dad's house, too, and his little sister's house. Where were they all going to live?

His own problems were making it very hard to get anything done as mayor. He'd done some research into that thing about Jeanine Sherwood's bank account, that he saw in the Joey Anhalt file, when he was looking for Mitchell Davis. In this town, if you were Ray Plotzky, and you needed information, you would usually just ask for it and folks would give it up. He had a good relationship with the bank teller at Jeanine's bank, so he made a discreet request for a favor. In these times of FBI activity surrounding him, he figured that was one more thing he shouldn't 'a done, but he was feeling pretty desperate for information about what was going on, and he did it anyway. He was starting to put the pieces together. *Jeanine Sherwood started making* big deposits to her account right after Mitchell Davis went missing. That was when she was working for Will. She didn't win the lottery. She didn't have any kin that died. She's Tommy Sherwood's daughter. She's Officer Monk's girlfriend. Officer Monk don't have no money. A mayor is not supposed to be able to look in a person's bank account, but the FBI does it all the time, Ray thinks. So if we start connecting the dots, what do we get?

Jeanine is being paid by somebody to shut up about what she knows about the day Mitchell Davis came to Will Pruitt's office with his article about Josh Bockenheim. That's what we get. And Jeanine is dating Darrell Monk, which means Darrell Monk knows or is involved, because Jeanine is not the girl who would keep a secret from her boyfriend. That makes Darrell Monk the likely person to have done whatever deed had to be done to make Davis disappear. Just like Darrell Monk is involved in this setup of Joey Anhalt. And Darrell Monk hates me, it appears, or he wouldn't 'a done this without tellin' me. The FBI is after me, and when they get to Darrell Monk, they're going to jump for joy and try to pin this on me, too. So this is bad, and it's only the beginning of bad, because it's the tip of the iceberg when we realize we got Josh Bockenheim running guns in toaster pie boxes to Afghanistan, like it said in Mitchell Davis' article.

All this goin' on, and I'm the one in the FBI target sites. I got no proof of anything, just a story that makes sense, but with all the charges against me, there's nobody who even wants to talk to me about anything. I can talk to my lawyer, at $500 an hour. When I call Congressman A and Congressman B, they take a long time to get back to me, and sound nervous on the phone. The person I think is doing this to me *is the prosecutor at the federal level. That's Ed Brentwood. He's the guy who's prosecuting me.*

As a result, Mayor Plotzky lapsed into analysis paralysis. He saw no way out, and no path to follow. He had no trusted friends, as one by one they turned their faces away. Who wouldn't turn away from a man who's being accused of espionage? He was under a RICO indictment. That meant: anybody who talked to him could be followed by the FBI, too. He never got back to Ann Kiernan about his investigation into the disappearance of Mitchell Davis. Ray Plotzky felt skewered. He couldn't turn this way, he couldn't turn that way, he could only slowly sizzle and burn.

Tommy Sherwood told Will Pruitt that Ann was looking for Mitchell, but Will didn't see the wife of Chance Kiernan as a threat. After all, wasn't Chance Kiernan working for Josh Bockenheim, too?

So Joey Anhalt stayed in jail, and Ray Plotzky stayed under indictment, and that made Will Pruitt feel a little more secure, and life went on in Copper Hollow. Flawed people, in a flawed system, with authority on their side.

March 2008
Copper Hollow

In response to Madeleine's insistence, and because she knew it was right, Ann prepared to tell Chance about Mitchell Davis. Things had been going well at home. Chance had been home for nearly a month, and their life had settled into a calm routine. She felt a closeness to him again, and she no longer worried that he was going to leave her. At breakfast on the first day of Spring, after the children left for school and Chance seemed relaxed and unhurried, she pulled out the folded copy of Mitchell Davis' article. She gave Chance the original article, the one that made Josh Bockenheim a hero. Her plan was to introduce the information about the guns in the toaster pies later, after she saw how he reacted. Ann was smitten with Chance Kiernan, but she wasn't in denial about him. She would watch his reactions as she fed him the information slowly.

First, she told him Mitchell wrote this story for the *Mercury*, but it wasn't going to be published. She watched his face. He read the article. Then he folded it up and put it in his pocket, instead of returning it to her. He showed no expression on his face. Indifference.

Second, she told him Mitchell had given the story to Olivier. He tightened his lips and nodded. Annoyance.

Third, she told him about Mitchell's phone call from the girls in Ohio, and their secret information about the guns. His right hand twitched, as if it wanted to do something but his brain was overriding its desire.

"And your friend, Olivier, knows about this, too?" he asked calmly.

"Yes," Ann nodded. "Mitchell e-mailed him about it." She watched his face, then she added, "Olivier is thinking of posting it on his blog, if Mitchell doesn't turn up soon."

Ann thought she saw a flash in Chance's eyes, but maybe it was her imagination.

Finally, she told him Mitchell had decided to take this information to Will Pruitt.

"Okay," Chance said slowly. "That would be appropriate. And what are the publishing plans for this information?" He was completely calm, totally unperturbed, except for the twitching right hand.

"That's the problem," Ann said. "Mitchell never returned from Pruitt's office. He told Olivier he was going there, and then he disappeared. We looked for him, Olivier and I both did. Olivier is holding off on doing anything until we can verify that Mitchell is really missing."

Chance's face stayed completely calm, his voice gentle and quiet. His only "tell" was the twitching right hand. It was a small twitch, one that may not be noticed by anyone but a wife. It was the tell of a man of action who was uncharacteristically using his words.

"Where did you look for Mitchell?" he asked softly.

"Olivier looked online. He said Mitchell's email was cut off and all his public profiles were shut down. He looked at this place called Sunshine Press that publishes information about companies like Josh Bockenheim's. I went to see Mitchell's landlord and Reese Babbitt at the *Mercury*. They both told me they had received emails saying he was going back to school. But they didn't know which school or his new contact information. Of course, his cell phone has been disconnected."

"But you didn't believe them when they said he went back to school," it was not a question. His right hand closed into a fist, but remained resting on the table. It released again, and he pressed it flat, hard, against the tile tabletop surface, until the knuckles turned white.

"No," said Ann. Her voice started to quiver. She knew that Josh Bockenheim had some relationship to Chance. She knew it all along, before she ever got in the middle of this. She never, ever suspected that Chance was actually involved in Bockenheim's activities. But all the same, maybe she should have. She wondered in her own mind why she went so far into this before ever mentioning it to him. Better to say everything now than let it come out later, so she added. "I filed a missing person's report with the police. In January, while you were away."

He used his left hand to grab his right hand, lifted it, massaged it, calmed it down. For a moment, he was silent, rubbing his right arm all the way to the elbow, holding his right hand flat against his chest.

For a flash of a second, Ann's face became Kate's face. In his mind's eye, Chance saw Ann lying in blood on the living room floor. He saw Timmy and Jeff lying there with her, in this deserted farmhouse, in the middle of nowhere, with no one to see. It took all of his self-control to stop himself from leaping to action, battening down hatches, searching for the intruder. It was his fault. He should have told her more. He should have explained what was happening. But how do you explain war to an American woman and two little boys? They never lived in fear in their own homes. They never ran from troops, darted from bullets, ducked from bombs. He should have learned from his mistake with Kate. He should have brought Ann in on what he was doing. He should have insisted to Joe Bridgewell that Ann know more. He should have realized his wife would be vulnerable, and his family was not safe. None of them knew that the war had come home. And this was the problem, as Chance Kiernan saw it. The war was here, on our shores, in our homes, and we didn't know it. Americans didn't know the war was here, and that was why they did not stay alert for it.

With his wife still there at the kitchen table, Chance pulled out his mobile phone and called Colonel Joe Bridgewell. "Joe," he said, purposely so that Ann could hear, "we have damage. We're bleeding the civilians."

Then he got up and left the room, so she could hear nothing more. Ann was smart. She would figure it out.

By the time he returned to the kitchen, Ann was washing the dishes. She had finished crying, but her face was still red.

He touched her back gently. "Ann," he said in a soothing voice, "I will find Mitchell Davis."

She nodded, but her tears would not let her speak.

A short time later, Chance Kiernan got the call from Colonel Bridgewell. "Change of plans," Bridgewell said. "CIA knows who ordered the attack on your convoy. Go with their guys to Indonesia. The guy's name is Abdullah. He's a drug trafficker. CIA's going to lure him to Indonesia with the promise of amnesty. When he gets off the plane, pick him up."

"What is the charge?" Chance asked. *There were many drug traffickers in Afghanistan. How did they know this one ordered the Taliban to kill him? How could they pick up a foreign national and bring him to trial in the U.S., without requesting the Karzai government to extradite him? Was Joe ordering an arrest, or a kidnapping?*

"He's being arrested under the federal narco-terrorism law. *21 USC 960A*. Drug trafficking with intent to support terrorist activities," Joe said. "It lets us pick up suspects anywhere in the world, without asking their governments for permission, as long as we as we allege that they were using drug money to fund terrorism. We're only bringing him to Indonesia to prevent harm to those who attempt to arrest him."

"When did that law pass?" Chance asked.

"Any minute now," Joe answered.

Any minute now. Chance could feel the dirt from the slippery slope sink from under his feet, like the sands pulling back from the ocean tide. Now we lived in a world where we wrote laws around what we wanted to do, preemptively. We no longer waited for someone to break a law and then arrested them. We were tailoring laws to fit our desire to "get" somebody. All we had to do was say that they were using drug money to fund terrorism, and we could send Chance Kiernan to their country to grab them and bring them back to the U.S. Or send a drone to kill them, and everyone standing within a hundred feet of them. We didn't have to prove anything. We didn't have to present a case. All we had to do is say it, and stamp Classified on the evidence. For that matter, we didn't need evidence, just a hunch, or a tip from one of their enemies.

"My wife and children need fulltime protection," Chance said, through gritted teeth.

"We're sending a Blackhawk for them," Joe responded.

And before the sun set, Ann Kiernan and the two Kiernan boys, boarded the helicopter and whisked away.

Present Day
Paris

"Just like Mitchell Davis?" Andrew asked Olivier.

398

Olivier opened his mouth to speak, but Madeleine reached out her hand and held it up flat in a stop sign position.

"The Espionage Act of 1917," Madeleine reminded.

Chapter 33: Andrew

Present Day

Paris

"**B**ad things happen, Andrew," Olivier continued, "when a nation is at war. More horribly, they happen even if the nation does not know it is at war."

"I don't understand," Andrew told him. They were sitting comfortably in Olivier's living room. Their discussions could no longer be conducted in the public setting of a café, so they stayed home. Madeleine offered to bring something from one of the takeout organic stores that dotted Paris. She was rabid about eating organic at home.

"Remember that these events took place in 2008. This was George W. Bush's time. That same year, Barack Obama was elected. Obama promised to end these wars in Iraq and Afghanistan. But how did he do that? He dramatically increased the drone strikes. He also invoked a little known law that had not been used for many years. The Espionage Act of 1917."

Madeleine interrupted. "The Espionage Act of 1917 was intended to allow the U.S. to operate without dissent when it entered World War I. The Act effectively cancelled the right of free speech as it related to criticizing the government's actions during war. After all, the United States was drafting men into war, and asking women to take jobs in factories to build war machines. They were asking manufacturers to change their equipment and build tanks instead of cars. They were also asking the entire nation to sacrifice to get behind the war effort. So it made sense, at the time, to prevent dissent in the streets."

Olivier picked up from there. "This law allowed the United States to punish citizens for saying or doing anything that supposedly undermined the war effort in any way. It meant there could be no protest against the war, or even against the economic policies of the government. Citizens could be jailed for twenty years for speaking up against anything the U.S.A. decided to do in either war policy or economic policy. It was World War I, Andrew. It made all the sense in the world to suspend free speech for the moment in time it took to engage in this global conflict. The nation had to be brought together for this team effort.

"But this was an extraordinary measure, passed to help the nation fight a world war. It effectively cancelled the right of free speech in the U.S. Constitution. It cancelled the right to object to any action of the United States government. Most importantly, it also cancelled the right of the press. Journalists normally are considered exempt from any form of suppression. The norm is that a journalist can publish documents that the journalist receives, even if those documents were stolen or procured through espionage. But this law cancelled that right for journalists, too. It said that even journalists could be jailed for publishing information that criticized the government."

Madeleine brought all of them glasses and set a bottle of pinot noir on the coffee table. "After World War I, that law was set aside and mostly forgotten. It was invoked again, in the wake of the Vietnam War, for the Pentagon Papers. The Pentagon Papers were a study of the history of the Vietnam War, which stirred rising dissent over the moral and legal justification for war. They were released to the New York Times in 1971 by Daniel Ellsberg, who had been one of the authors of the papers. But the U.S. Supreme Court declined to prevent the *New York Times* from publishing the documents. There was no proof that the documents' publication would harm the security of the United States, the Supreme Court said.

"The Espionage Act was invoked a few times in the 1980's, for actual spies. But it wasn't until after 2008 that the Espionage Act began to be applied to whistleblowers. Not spies. Not people who benefited financially from the disclosure of secrets. But people whose conscience could not abide what they were being asked to do. In 2010, the Obama administration began prosecuting whistleblowers for leaking to journalists. The concern became that the journalists also would be prosecuted for publishing the information. This concern arose because of the venomous reaction to the disclosures by Private Bradley Manning to WikiLeaks. Journalists could now be prosecuted as spies. The two most famous cases of its application were the jailing of John Kiriakou and the Bradley Manning case. Kiriakou was an ex-CIA agent who was jailed for leaking the information about waterboarding by the CIA. Bradley Manning, of course, is the famous case of the soldier who uploaded documents to WikiLeaks."

"What?" Andrew said. No wonder the *Copper Hollow Mercury* wouldn't post anything controversial. Copper Hollow was a hotbed of government secrets. "Are you sure? Why haven't I read anything about this in the mainstream news?"

Olivier looked at Andrew with a grimace. "This is what we would ask *you*, Andrew."

2008
Afghanistan

Luke Trout hadn't been feeling well for quite a while. He was thinking maybe it was a stomach virus. It kept him from sleeping, made him vomit his food, and was giving him acne. But he was a Marine, and Marines are not sissies, so he had to man up and work through it. His sergeant, HamHock Hartman, had assigned him and Private Chil-Beans Ramirez to a team that was going to scout out an area that had been reported to have Taliban activity.

"Contrary to public opinon," Chil-Beans said, "these Unmanned Aerial Vehicles require a lot of manpower." UAVs, or drones, needed people on the ground, to scout out whether the target would be able to avoid civilian casualties. The report was that Taliban were hiding in a children's elementary school. The drone wasn't going to attack unless Luke's team could verify that there were no children in the school. They reached the village, and began verifying. As they approached the school, they saw a stooped old man, leaning on a cane. He was accompanied by a boy, his grand-son. The old man told them, through their interpreter, that his name was Rasool. His grandson was Hyat.

"Ask him if the school is being used by children," Luke said to Juma, the interpreter.

"Not now," the old man said, in a voice so distressed by age that it was barely above a whisper. "Because we stopped when we heard the *benghai*. Now we keep the children at home and they do not even have a school for learning."

"What's the *benghai*?" Luke asked Juma.

"It means buzzing flies," Juma said. "But I haven't heard it before. I don't know what he's talking about."

"He means the drones," said the twelve-year-old grand-son, Hyat. Hyat spoke English. The old man grabbed Hyat's arm, cautioned him with a shake of the head, and Hyat stopped talking.

Juma questioned the old man.

"Rasool says they lived in another village before. There were so many *benghai* flying overhead that they had to run away from their homes. It was too dangerous for their child-ren. So they came to live here, where they are all stuffed to-gether in a few houses. They left their homes behind in the old place because they were afraid. When they heard the noise of the *benghai* here, they pulled all the children out of the school. He says everybody stays inside now and only goes out when they have to get food."

"So, the villagers are expecting drone attacks here?" Luke asked Juma.

"They hear them in the sky," Juma answered. "He said you can't see them, but they sound like buzzing flies."

They had to go get HamHock and tell him about this. Would the Taliban still be in the school, if they had already heard the buzzing flies? As they turned to leave, and the old man and boy walked on, the boy turned back. "Go home," the boy yelled in English. "Go home to your own place, and leave us alone."

Present Day
Back in Paris

"If Chance Kiernan were in Afghanistan, and a young boy yelled to him to go home, it would have meant nothing. People are different, and Chance Kiernan would have taken no offense. It would not impact his mind or his psychology," Madeleine said. "But saying that to Luke Trout had a meaning.

"*Home* was an important place for Luke Trout. Home was where his mother lived. It was Copper Hollow. It was comfort. He believed he was fighting in Afghanistan to protect that home. He wanted to believe that the regular Afghan people, whom he saw as very much like the poor families of Copper Hollow, appreciated the help they were getting from the U.S. Marines. It jolted him to hear those words from a young boy. Luke figured that the words that came from the mouths of babes were true and honest. Then a few hours later, something else happened that really hit Luke hard."

Later that same day, Luke and Chil-Beans were looking for HamHock. They wanted to tell him about their encounter with the old man, Rasool, and his grandson, Hyat. Along the way, they passed a local neighborhood market bazaar. To Luke, it was similar to a farmer's market. There were a number of flyers, pasted on the wooden walls of the stalls.

Juma, their interpreter, stopped Luke and showed him one of the flyers. "This says: if you need help, call the Taliban. It gives the phone number for the Taliban."

Luke shook his head. "You mean, we're out here looking for people who are hiding, and they're pasting their phone number up on the bulletin board at the grocery store?"

"Yes," Juma said. He didn't understand why this was a surprise to Luke. "They need people to know where to find them, in case the people need help."

"Help? How do the Taliban help them?"

Juma began to feel impatient. Was this boy a moron? "What do you think the Taliban do?" Juma asked. "Why do you think the villagers hide them and protect them?"

"Hold it, Juma," Luke said. "The Taliban make all the women hide in their houses and wear burkas."

"Nobody cares about that," Juma said. "The Taliban stops crime. Nobody else does."

Luke didn't get it. He felt like he had fallen down the rabbit hole in Alice in Wonderland. His stomach hurt again, and now he was getting a headache. He was going to have to go to sick bay for real when they got back to base. Maybe thinking was his problem. He should follow HamHock's advice. HamHock always said, "You ain't paid to think, Trout."

Present Day, Back in Paris

"How do you know all this stuff?" Andrew asked Madeleine and Olivier.

"The part about Luke Trout, he wrote in letters to his mother, Charlotte. Charlotte showed the letters to Ann Kiernan," Madeleine said.

"Most of the other parts are bits and pieces I have put together through simply reading the history and information that is publicly available on the Internet," said Olivier. "There's nothing secret here. It's all public, but there are no news organizations that are connecting the dots."

"But if everything is so public, what happened to Mitchell Davis? Who would stop him from making his story public? Where is he? And who killed Will Pruitt?"

"Andrew, how can we answer these things, when we still don't know who killed Kate Kiernan, Chance's first wife? And for that matter, who is Chance Kiernan? And why is our friend, Ann, still married to him?" Madeleine had so much more to tell Andrew.

"We would never have found out any of these things, Andrew," Olivier offered, "if it hadn't been for a change of heart that impacted Chance Kiernan himself."

"What made Chance Kiernan change?" Andrew asked.

"We think it was the avalanche," said Madeleine.

BOOK FOUR:

COLLAPSE

Chapter 34:

2008

Jakarta, Indonesia, and Copper Hollow, USA

Cengkareng Airport, on the island of Java, was under construction, as usual. The construction forced Chance Kiernan to park his rental car too far from the international terminal, and this was definitely going to make him late. If he was late, the CIA agents who were assigned to work with him would proceed without him, in their own way. He hated when that happened.

The instruction to the Indonesian government was to deny entry at the point of Customs. Haji Abdullah Khan would be detained when he showed his passport. The CIA agents were to pick him up in the customs office, and question him until Chance arrived. He worried that they might decide they could take him somewhere else, so they could question him more effectively. Chance was to make the arrest and tell the CIA that he would accompany Abdullah to New York.

Chance knew that Abdullah was the person who ordered the assassination of Hanif, and probably also the meeting at the Serena Hotel, where Chance himself was targeted. He didn't want the CIA to take control of Abdullah and leave him out of it. He had further questions, questions he did not want the CIA to hear.

Chance had an excellent capacity to mind his own business. He also was highly skilled at keeping his mouth shut. But the one thing he truly enjoyed, while he travelled all over the world, was a nice hotel room, an upscale rental car, and directions to a bar that was frequented by the locals. Chance Kiernan enjoyed absorbing the local culture, the local music, the local language, and the local customs, whatever they were, wherever he went. Very few people knew that he spoke Farsi, French, German, Italian, Russian, and Mandarin. He was a complex man, with a complicated past, which he never mentioned. The night before, he had found a highly entertaining bar, and he had eavesdropped on a number of conversations, while he was drinking his bourbon. He was not a man who visited strange women. One would have thought he would be, but he wasn't, and this was not the only unusual trait that formed his character.

I was born the son of a military man, Chance thought, and that has marked me throughout my life. My father was Army, and he was often away. My mother raised four children, each only one year older than the other. She dragged us around from military base to military base, packing and moving usually on her own. We changed schools almost every year. My brother and two sisters were my only long term friends. I was ten years old before I ever entered the United

412

States of America. When I did enter, our first assignment was in California, so some would say even that did not count as America. Our assignments were usually overseas. We attended military-base schools and visited military-base doctors. Military life was the only life we knew.

And then when I turned eighteen, I joined the Army myself. I had a high school diploma. It was my first real experience living in the States, and even then, I lived on Army bases. And like sometimes happens, I was a natural for military life. I loved the Army, I enjoyed my job, and I excelled at it. It was actually my calling. Everybody is not suited to be a soldier, but I was. I fit the job description, and I rose in the ranks. I was sent to language schools, and ultimately, I ended up in Delta Force. There was never a second thought about what I would do, never a consideration that I might leave the Army. I moved on from Delta to the Defense Intelligence Agency. I had many missions all over the world. I married Kate. We had the boys. Twins. Everything was wonderful. We had a suburban house in California. Off-base, for a change.

And then one of my missions followed me home. Followed me home, and opened the door to my house and murdered my wife. And that's when I knew that the war was not being fought only on foreign soil. That's when I realized the war had come to America and lived on American soil, in American neighborhoods. I do not know who killed Kate, or how they found me, but I have a list of suspects. I am not actively looking for her killer, but I am actively alert and aware, should I come across a clue. I believe, if belief is any part of my inner being, that the clues will eventually form a pattern and lead me to the answer. I believe that I will someday know who and how it happened.

I don't do politics. I don't care what politicians think, say, or do. I don't care who gets elected. I don't concern myself with whether a war is "just," or "moral," or even "legal." If I started to think like that, I would not be able to do my job. I understand that politics is dirty, shifty, and underhanded, and I stay out of it. I trust in my chain of command. I believe that Joe Bridgewell has a handle on what he's doing. I would have to say I work for Joe Bridgewell, more than I work for the United States government. I trust Bridgewell.

And that's what makes me able to take down Haji Abdullah Khan. That, and the information that he gave the order to kill Hanif.

And so, Chance Kiernan arrived in the back room of the Customs office in Jakarta. There he saw an imposing, six-foot tall, olive-skinned man, with a well-trimmed black beard, dressed in the tailored suit of a New York business man. He spoke English well, with a British cadence. He greeted Kiernan with the air of a man who was there to do business, to seal a deal. He showed no hint of fear or anxiety of what was to come. Perhaps he, too, had killed before. He had the air of a man who did more than give orders.

Chance took charge of the prisoner Haji Khan, a.k.a. Abdullah. The CIA officers filed the paperwork that said Abdullah was turned over to be tried in a New York court. With his hands cuffed behind his back, Kiernan led Abdullah out of the room, and onto the helipad on the roof of the customs building. There, a helicopter waited to take Kiernan and Khan to a safe house. Chance Kiernan had one question: What is Josh Bockenheim doing?

Abdullah never arrived in New York; his paperwork forever after will remain listed as "awaiting trial." If Colonel Joe Bridgewell had thought the order was to bring Haji Khan to trial in an actual court, he would have sent somebody else. The deal was: Joe Bridgewell never had to say what he meant. There could never be a paper trail. And this is why Chance Kiernan could abide the uncertainty surrounding Josh Bockenheim. Because many things could not be written down, and many things could not be said. "Homeland Security" was a term that could be given a wide range of definitions.

Shortly after Chance Kiernan picked up Abdullah in Jakarta, the feds came to arrest Ray Plotzky. Juliette March was there, and Ed Brentwood, and half a dozen other agents, all dressed in their full SWAT gear, like a swarm of ninja robots in black roach shells. Juliette had made a last-ditch effort to change the way this went down. Ray's lawyer had made it clear that Ray would turn himself in, if they ever came to the conclusion that he would really be arrested. Juliette lobbied to at least allow the active mayor of Copper Hollow to turn himself in of his own volition. Hotter minds than Juliette's, however, ruled the day, and so a troop of men accompanied her, all dressed in their Halloween-costume riot suits. Juliette's little Powerpoint presentation to her boss had made no impression. The lure of an opportunity to wear their SWAT gear was too seductive.

When the SWAT team arrived at Ray's house, Ray was out in the woods, hunting. The judge told him he wasn't allowed to carry a gun, as a person under indictment. Ray took this to mean he had to hunt with his bow and arrow.

So Ray was behind his house, in the forest, carrying a quiver full of sharp, pointed sticks, that he had the ability to fling directly into the heart of a fleeing animal. The SWAT team didn't see him there, so they stormed into his house and scared his mom half to death.

Mom Plotzky screeched and dropped her pot full of potato water onto the kitchen floor when the first black-masked Darth Vader impressionist slammed his way into her dining room. This caused the man to pull his hand-gun out, which, when he saw himself pointing a gun at an old mom wearing an apron, made him nervous, which made him embarrassed, which ended up causing him to pull the trigger, which fortunately was pointed at his own foot. The ensuing comedy gave Mom Plotzky enough privacy and breathing room that she managed to get Ray on his cell phone. He circled back around the woods, and met his lawyer on the other side. They drove to the federal courthouse to turn Ray in while the feds were sitting in his living room drinking coffee with Mom and Dad.

Once Ray was arrested, Will Pruitt had second thoughts about Joey Anhalt. Joey was still sitting in jail, awaiting trial. Will thought maybe that was a little dangerous, given the way Joey hammered at things. He didn't want Joey to go to trial, especially now that Ray was locked up. It seemed like an extra complication. Will pushed some buttons and pulled some strings, as the Will Pruitt's of the world tend to do, and in a little while, Joey's attorney received word that the case was going to be dropped, if Joey would plead guilty to a minor felony. Suborning perjury. The perjury was: asking Ralph Merkel to testify that Molly was using drugs. This was so inside out and backwards that Joey wanted to refuse, and stay in jail to wait for his trial, but his lawyer talked him into leaving. "Who knows when your trial will even be scheduled?" his lawyer said. "You've run out of money to pay me, so you'll be turned over to the public defender. Get out while you can."

So Joey was released from jail, with a conviction for suborning perjury.

However, Will Pruitt ran into an unintended consequence. In their hurry to get the case settled, the judge did not agree that Ralph Merkel's perjury before a grand jury could be granted immunity. Merkel went to jail for perjury in Joey Anhalt's case. Oddly, however, this judge did not prevent the prosecutor from entering convictions against Joey. After all, they had made a deal. Justice, as ever, was the missing element in the justice system. Joey got out of jail, but he still couldn't do anything about what had happened to him. And he was still completely broke from paying the lawyer.

Ralph Merkel's grandmother, however, had plenty to say about what happened. She called all the clan into her kitchen. "They done Ralph wrong," she said. "He was workin' for the poe-leese."

A man shouldn't go to jail from workin' fer the poe-lease, the family all agreed. En masse, they showed up at Will Pruitt's office. A Copper Hollow clan, made of Merkels and Ellinghams and even an Anhalt or two. They wanted justice. Get Ralph home. Pruitt tried to get Ralph released, but the judge would not allow it.

"I got my eyes on you," the Merkel grandpappy told Will as they were leaving.

"I'm doing the best I can," Will answered.

The next day, Will's mailbox had been battered in by a baseball bat. The following week, his basement windows were broken. The week after that, his truck stopped running because he had sugar in his gas tank. Clan justice was going to stalk him until he set things right. Will had better learn to hunker down, because this justice was going to follow him until he got Ralph home.

A few days later, Charlotte Trout wept in the living room of Elisa House. She sat on the sofa, while Roberta handed her tissues. Charlotte described her worry about her heroic son, Luke. He had been temporarily transferred to Kabul's Green Zone, where he was doing administrative work. Luke had been acting erratically, and his sergeant sent him out of the field for a while. He couldn't sleep, and the doc gave him some sleeping pills. It wasn't enough, so they added some anti-psychotics. To help with the rages. The Navy psych team was on it, and they were getting ready to send him back stateside. Charlotte worried that they were going to discharge him from the Marines.

"He can't get drummed out of the Marines," Charlotte sobbed.

"No, no, Charlotte," Roberta said soothingly. "It would be a medical discharge. He wouldn't be drummed out. He's done a good job. He's been injured on the battlefield, Charlotte. That's how to understand it."

"It would kill him," Charlotte sniffed. "It's all he ever wanted to do, to be a Marine. It's his *career*."

Roberta put her arms around Charlotte and hugged her. "Luke is a wonderful boy, Charlotte. A fine young man. He's done a great job and he'll come home and be your pride and joy again, like he always was. He'll find his way through this."

Charlotte burst into wailing. She cried so loudly that all the women in the shelter came out of their rooms to see what was going on.

"You don't unnerstan'," she said when she could talk again. "A man can't go be a Marine, and then come home to live in his childhood bunk bed and stock shelves at the Piggly Wiggly."

All the women in the room knew exactly what Charlotte meant. Luke couldn't come home unless Charlotte went back to Jimmy. It would never work to have her son come home and not be with her. Even then, he would need a real job, a man's job, not the jobs that Copper Hollow had to offer.

One woman timidly raised her hand to talk. "What is it, Shirley?" Roberta said. "You don't need permission to talk here."

"I work at the BoxMart," Shirley said. "They got an article in the paper saying they would give jobs to the vets."

"That's great," Roberta said.

"No," Shirley said, "No. It's not great. The jobs are part-time, and they pay minimum wage. It's not right."

All the women nodded. *It's not right*, they agreed. *A man needed to be a man.* Luke Trout was a man right now, but if he returned to Copper Hollow, Copper Hollow would bring him down.

"It's not right," the women repeated. They shook their heads while Charlotte Trout cried.

At Jo-Beans, Al and Buck and Clem and Red didn't have much to say about the unemployment rate in Copper Hollow. Unemployment is always high. More important to them is the *Copper Hollow Mercury* article about Mayor Ray Plotzky's arrest for espionage.

Clem brings up what they are all thinking. "You think Ray'll turn on the Congressman?"

"Nah," says Buck. "He'll keep his mouth shut. They's prob'ly a big job waitin' for him when he gets out." Like they do in the Mafia, they were all thinking. Somebody's picked to take the fall, then they take care of their family and set them up when they get out. That's what happened to Ray, the boys at Jo-Beans believed.

"You know it was Congressman A they were really after," Al adds. "Because he's a Republican."

"Yeah, tha's what Tommy Sherwood said," Red offers.

"What I'd like to see is Will Pruitt get his," Buck inserted. "After what he did to Ralph."

"Yeah, Ralph Merkel got the short end o' the stick that time. His grandma said they tol' 'im what to do, and then they stuck 'im in jail fer it. He had a five-year jail sentence hangin' over his head. They said if he didn't do what they wanted, they'd haul him in and make him serve it. Tha's why he agreed in the firs' place. Then they double-crossed him and stuck him in jail anyway."

"Who did that?" Clem asked. "Will Pruitt?"

"Not Pruitt hisself," Buck answered. "Pruitt's boys."

They didn't know exactly who Pruitt's boys were, but they were sure those boys were out there. They wonder if Ray will turn against Will Pruitt, now that Ray's locked up. They say somebody ought to come to town and do Will Pruitt's job, instead of Pruitt next time. It's better to have a born-here in that job. They say Will Pruitt was a bad man, who should have gone to jail instead of Ray Plotzky. For what he did to Ralph Merkel. They say if Ray Plotzky weren't a convicted felon, he'd be re-elected.

"I hate to see Ray go to jail."

"Even so, Ray'll be back," the patrons say. "Ray'll be back."

Having exhausted the topic, and summed up the situation on Ray Plotzky, they turned to other events of the day. "Hey," said Clem. "You hear Pete Fink got a cougar when he was out huntin' t'other day?"

"They ain't no cougars in these woods nc more," said Red. "They's extink."

"Well, a mountain lion then," Clem responded. "They's still mountain lions."

"Tha's the same thing. Mountain lion, cougar. They ain't any."

"So what's that thing stuffed in Pete Fink's living room then?"

"He prob'ly bought it from Jake's Taxidermy. I bet it's an old one, from when they had 'em." They all laughed at this. Clem slapped his knee.

"Woon't supprize me," Al added. They all nodded. Pete Fink was a blowhard, too, jus' like Tommy Sherwood. Everybody knows thar warn't no mountain lions in these hills no more. But blowhards? Those were abundant.

As soon as Joey Anhalt was released from jail, he showed up at the *Copper Hollow Mercury*. He asked for Mitchell Davis. Joey couldn't tell his story, because his Alford plea had an attachment that said if he ever told anybody what happened to him, he would go back to jail. As Joey understood it, an Alford plea says that you won't fight the conviction, but you don't admit guilt, and you promise never to talk about it. So he had in mind to convince Mitchell to go read the open court records for himself. It was all there in the record, should anyone choose to discover it. One just needed someone to provide a road map and some clues and a few file numbers, for the Freedom of Information Act requests. Joey thought Mitchell Davis might be willing to do that work, and expose this travesty. Everything that had been done was a matter of public record. Joey intended to hammer away at it until somebody paid attention. That's how Joey was.

But Mitchell Davis wasn't there, and the editor of the *Mercury* said he wouldn't be back. The editor wasn't interested in Joey's story, although he listened to it before rejecting it. Feeling dejected, and still shaken by what had happened to him, Joey headed back to his hardware store. He was a convicted felon. He couldn't keep a gun for protection. He couldn't call the police for protection. And he worried very much that Will Pruitt, or Darrell Monk, or Ralph Merkel, would get him. He pictured himself lying in a ditch, hit by a car. He imagined that they only released him so they could kill him and pretend it was a drug deal gone bad. And if they came after him again some day? Well, his bank account was empty. He couldn't even hire another lawyer.

Joey was defeated. He couldn't hammer away at the truth any more.

Juliette March, FBI agent, felt spent. She was distressed about how the arrest of Ray Plotzky was handled. She couldn't believe she actually watched a colleague shoot himself in the foot in Mom Plotzky's dining room. More importantly, who were they to have battered their way into that poor woman's house in the first place? Ray turned himself in, like he said he would. This persecution of Ray Plotzky never felt right to her. This wasn't how she envisioned her career when she was studying at the FBI Academy. There were so many Wall Street criminals, so many drug dealers, so many crooked politicians. She didn't understand how they ended up spending their budget and time on Ray Plotzky. At least, this assignment was nearly over. There was nothing more for her to do now that Ray was in jail. She would get a new assignment soon. The only bad part of that was that she would no longer be working with Chance Kiernan.

Faced with the realization that she would be leaving Copper Hollow, she suddenly realized how much she would miss her time with Chance. Of course, nothing had happened between them. Nothing sexual. No, it wasn't sex, but it was innuendo. It was a sexually charged atmosphere when she was with him. She had never had that with any man before. It was an air, a taste, a scent, a sound of sexuality, without being sex. *Is that how he always was, with every woman? she wondered. Is it my imagination that he is interested in me? Or is he always interested, in every woman?*

COPPER HOLLOW

All her life, Juliette had been a good girl. A little bit nerdy. A little bit jock. But a whole lot goody-two-shoes. She never smoked in high school, neither cigarettes nor anything else. She never took pills or got high. She had no tattoos. She always followed directions and waited her turn. She even waited until she was eighteen to pierce her ears. There was no need for her mother to get her a birth control prescription before she graduated high school. Juliette was simply accommodating to the mores of her parents, her school, her society, and her FBI career. She didn't desire to rebel against anyone or anything. The society had been nice to her, and she was nice back.

She grew up in Albany, New York. A blue collar neighborhood, from blue collar folks. Dad worked in the plastics factory. Mom stayed home and cooked. She was an only child. When she wanted to play the clarinet in fifth grade, Dad bought her a used clarinet. When she made the basketball team in high school, Mom baked healthy snacks for everybody on the team. Where she wanted to go, they drove her. What she wanted to do, they cheered.

She went to Carnegie Mellon University. When she graduated, the FBI Academy was next. She worked because she had always worked, and she wanted to get an A. She'd been with the Agency for only three years when she was sent to Copper Hollow. She was twenty-six years old.

And she thought for the first time that she was in love with Chance Kiernan. But she would get over it. She was sure. Besides, he was way too old for her, and he was married. What was he? Forty-five? Juliette wondered if she needed to go home right now, before she did something stupid.

It worked on her, that she had done this to Ray Plotzky. But after all, he was caught giving classified information to a news reporter. It didn't matter that the news reporter did nothing with the information. It was enough that Ray had leaked it. As Juliette understood it, Ray had gone to Josh Bockenheim's office and stolen classified documents. He had turned those documents over to a reporter. This was espionage, as her bosses defined it. And Juliette was just too young, and too willing to believe in the goodness of her nation and her bosses and her authority structures, to challenge that claim. So she filed this experience as Mission Accomplished, and looked forward to her next assignment. She had only a few more days to stay here in Copper Hollow, a few more hearings to attend, a few more documents to prepare. Then Ray Plotzky would be charged with espionage, and it would be one more terrorist, locked away. The American people could feel safe, with the FBI and Homeland Security on the job.

Chapter 35:
2008
Afghanistan

I'm left again with no one standing behind me, ground pulled from under my feet.
--------Afghan poet

Darya and Naseem knew Abdullah had not abandoned them. They knew he did not leave Asa, with his prosthetic leg still new, and the bill for it unpaid. They knew he did not abandon his business, walk out on his children, or choose to live in another land. This was not who Abdullah was. He would never have done this.

He left one day on a business trip. Naseem knew he was going to meet the American CIA. He never returned. He never called. No one knew what happened to him. His brother and Naseem had seen him off at the airport. They saw him take the Ariana Airlines flight. The flight did not crash. All they could assume was that the CIA had him.

This was very, very bad. Had he been taken to Guantanamo? Or had his own enemies and competitors found him and killed him? There had been no phone call, no message, no gossip, no clue. They could wait for some time, but business had to be conducted, to pay the bills. This was not something the women could do in his place. Abdullah's work was not women's work, and regardless of the intelligence or the knowledge his wives had, they could not fill in for him.

Naseem thought to use her position in the Parliament to make inquiries about Abdullah. Abdullah's brother agreed to assist her with those inquiries, as there were many members she would not be able to speak with unless she was accompanied by a male family member. She made as much noise about it as she could, and then eventually, General Hekmatyar took up the cause.

"Where is Haji Khan?" Hekmatyar, Governor of Helmand Province, and rumored to be one of the main drug lords of Afghanistan, asked. But no one knew. Haji Khan, a.k.a. "Abdullah," believed to be a major drug smuggler, whose wife was a member of the Afghan Parliament, had disappeared. The United States State Department denied any knowledge. No, they said, he was not meeting with the CIA in Jakarta. It didn't happen.

Months passed, and business had to be conducted. The family needed the income, as they lived well and had expenses. Suppliers and buyers wanted answers. Abdullah's brother offered to take care of Naseem and her children, because she lived in the house in Kabul with his family. But Darya and her children had no one. It was decided that Darya should return to her father, in her village.

This was not a good idea, in Darya's mind. She remembered her one visit to her father's village. She left there when she was eleven years old, and had no desire to go back to that style of life, after living like a princess in Abdullah's castle.

"Naseem," Darya said. "Why can't Farzam come and take over Abdullah's business? Just until Abdullah gets back. So it doesn't get taken by his competitors. Between you and me, we know who all his contacts are, and we know his books and his procedures."

Naseem thought about it. "I could discuss this possibility with Abdullah's brother, Mansour. Mansour is not interested in doing it himself, because he has an appointment in the government of Hamid Karzai, but I can see that he would want the business to continue. For the family."

And thus it happened, that Farzam moved into the big house with Darya. He brought his first wife and his son. He was Darya's cousin, thus he was a suitable male relative to escort her. He could take care of Darya and her children, and run the business, until Abdullah returned. Hekmatyar continued to press Karzai to find Abdullah. Not long after that, high level officials in the Afghani government began to pressure the Americans to leave.

During the night, while Luke Trout was in the medical quarters, a member of the Afghan National Army strapped explosives around his chest. Because he was fully authorized to be in the combat area, this man walked into the barracks of the Puma Platoon Marines and blew himself up. The blast killed HamHock Hartman, Chil-Beans Ramirez, Mojo, Blake, and Captain Jenkins. Lucas Trout was not injured, because he was in the medical clinic and not there with his team. Three weeks later, Luke wrote a letter home to his mother, about his feelings, about how he could not sleep, about the antipsychotic drugs the medical clinic prescribed for him, about the man-boobs the drugs were causing him to get, about the time he saw the boy run over by Ham-Hock's car, about the time he shot a father in front of his children. He wrote about the boy who told him to go home, and the Taliban's telephone number posted in the market bazaar. He wrote about losing Captain Jaggers, and Captain Mercer's brain injury. He wrote about how he felt when he survived, and his buddies died. He wrote about how much he loved HamHock and Mojo, and Blake and Chil-Beans. He wrote about how he believed it was his fault, that he couldn't stop it, that he couldn't change it, that he couldn't be a hero. He wrote about the feelings of hatred he felt when he looked at the "ragheads." He wrote about how he hated himself for feeling that way. He wrote about the little girl who died in his arms, whose blood was on his hands. He mailed the letter.

Then he pulled out his 9 mm and shot himself in the right temple. Boom. Fast. So he wouldn't change his mind.

When they sent the body back, Charlotte moved out of Elisa House, and returned to her husband. Jimmy needed her. The *Copper Hollow Mercury* reported Luke Trout as a war hero. Killed in action. All the Trout and the Ellingham clan attended the funeral at the funeral home on Main Street. Traffic was backed up in the town so badly, they had to close the streets and put police out to direct cars around it. Charlotte and Jimmy Trout, the bereaved parents, hugged and cried together. The entire population of Copper Hollow mourned.

Ann Kiernan attended the funeral of Luke Trout. Her husband had just returned from Indonesia. "What is the point of this?" she shrieked at him, her voice wavering between tears and anger. "What are you doing over there? Why does it take ten years to train Afghan troops, when we train our own Marines in ninety days? Why are we so hated that the very troops we are supposedly helping will kill themselves for the honor of killing us?"

And for one rare moment, Chance Kiernan turned to his wife and said, "Why do we send money to build playgrounds, which sit vacant like monuments to our stupidity, when the children in that town have all died from starvation? Why do we send buckets of U.S. taxpayer money, which end up filling the pockets of government officials, and getting sent to their personal Swiss bank accounts?" He put his arm around her, and for a fleeting moment, she remembered why she married him. He held her close, and whispered in her ear, as he kissed her cheek. "I am doing what I can, with what I have, where I am. The world is not black and white."

Then he picked up his car keys and left the house. He, too, wondered why we were fighting a war that killed as many of our military heroes by their own suicide, as by the hand of the enemy. He, too, felt enraged by injustice. But Chance Kiernan knew that the world was full of many shades of gray. He knew that war was hell. He knew that people were complex. He knew that war was meant to be hidden and secret. It was not meant to be exposed, so that civilians could see its horrors. He believed in putting one foot in front of the other and carrying on through adversity. He believed that problems could be solved, but solutions were imperfect. He believed the war was already on our soil. He started the car, and drove directly to the hotel room of FBI Agent Juliette March.

It was a long night in the pub at the Parkside Inn, but neither Chance nor Juliette was drinking. They were scheming about how to get the message through to their respective managements. Until this point, both FBI Agent Juliette March and TDU Agent Chance Kiernan made the decision to look away from the abuses of privacy and prosecution in Copper Hollow. Tonight, as Mayor Plotzky settled into his new home in jail, and Lucas Trout's body lay in a closed-casket for the memorial service at the Copper Hollow Funeral Home, they each decided it had become their business. Chance Kiernan called Colonel Joe Bridgewell, and told him he needed a meeting up the line. Juliette March requested a similar meeting in her own department silo. Together, they put together the threads and the patterns, to explain their case.

"When the laws are written to target a specific person, and local law enforcement is about 'who' instead of 'what,' we've lost our nation," Juliette said. Chance said nothing. He was busy fuming. About Te. About Ann. About the empty playground. About the children in the houses who heard the buzzing flies of the drones and had to stay out of their school.

Fall 2008
Copper Hollow

Meetings up the line for Juliette and Chance had been arranged. They had prepared briefings for their bosses, talked about what they believed happened in Copper Hollow, and collaborated on how to present their case. They were insiders, speaking out about the system, up the line, to their management. They were not whistleblowers, who aired the dirty laundry in the press. They were loyal servants to the nation, fully obedient to their assignments, working the system from inside, expressing their opinions to their bosses.

Their meetings were scheduled to be held in Washington D.C. on September 19, 2008. But on that day, Chance's bosses and Juliette's bosses were too busy to see them. The meetings, which had taken weeks to schedule, were cancelled. On that day, **U.S. President George W. Bush gave this speech:**

THE PRESIDENT: Good morning. I thank Treasury Secretary Hank Paulson, Federal Reserve Chairman Ben Bernanke, and SEC Chairman Chris Cox for joining me today.

This is a pivotal moment for America's economy. Problems that originated in the credit markets -- and first showed up in the area of subprime mortgages -- have spread throughout our financial system. This has led to an erosion of confidence that has frozen many financial transactions, including loans to consumers and to businesses seeking to expand and create jobs. As a result, we must act now to protect our nation's economic health from serious risk.

There will be ample opportunity to debate the origins of this problem. Now is the time to solve it. In our nation's history, there have been moments that require us to come together across party lines to address major challenges. This is such a moment. Last night, Secretary Shaneson and Chairman Bernanke and Chairman Cox met with congressional leaders of both parties -- and they had a very good meeting. I appreciate the willingness of congressional leaders to confront this situation head on.

Our system of free enterprise rests on the conviction that the federal government should interfere in the marketplace only when necessary. Given the precarious state of today's financial markets -- and their vital importance to the daily lives of the American people -- government intervention is not only warranted, it is essential.

President Bush would later give Congress a three-page request for billions of taxpayer dollars to be available to be used at the discretion of Secretary Paulson. No questions asked. Should they refuse to approve it, Congress people report, they were told it may become necessary for the President to invoke martial law.

The short version: the United States of America had run out of money. Not profit, but cash flow. As any small business owner will tell you, it isn't lack of profit that shuts down an organization. It's lack of cash. Cash and profit are two very different things.

At that moment in the history of the world, it appeared that the only liquid cash available to make the wheels of commerce trade again, was drug money. The drug economy flows more than enough cash than it takes to run the world. Words were circulated on the mainstream news about how the mortage loans defaulted and this caused the problem. Perhaps it did. But the problem that was caused was a problem of cash flow, and it was only cash that could solve it.

As a result, the investigation of Bruce Bockenheim for money laundering was cancelled. Instead of being indicted, Bruce was *appointed*. To the President's Task Force for financial recovery. Somebody had to know how to get that drug money flowing through legitimate channels, to straighten this out. Who better than a prominent hedge fund manager? Bruce Bockenheim returned to his Manhattan apartment. The threat of money laundering charges against him was annulled, removed from the record, and erased. Chance and Juliette never did get their meetings up the line. Everyone was too busy.

Chapter 36
2008 - Present Day
Copper Hollow

Although Juliette and Chance could not get their high-level meetings, they worked at telling their story where they could, to their bosses, and to their colleagues, one at a time, over and over, in as many ways as possible. Over time, they kept in touch, and continued the pressure. With the consistent pressure Chance and Juliette applied to their respective internal bosses, eventually the message spread. The Department of Defense boss, the FBI boss, and Congressmen A and B finally became alarmed. The argument Chance and Juliette made was: prosecutorial discretion means "use common sense in how you apply resources." It did not mean "select someone to target and invade their privacy until you find something." This was an important concept, Chance believed. He was a patriot. He needed to remain one. But while the Lessons Learned meetings and the Improvement Quality Checklists began to reflect the concerns brought up by Kiernan and March, these forward-looking concepts had no impact on cases already closed. Nothing that was happening in these internal meetings, these insider debates, and these in-house closed proceedings would go back to impact a case that had already happened. So Ray Plotzky sat in jail.

The espionage charges against Ray Plotzky made everyone look away. Wow, they all thought. Imagine that, the rumors said. The Mayor of little Copper Hollow was a terrorist, selling secrets to Al Qaeda, the gossip claimed. Who'd have thought? Well, it made sense, when you realized how his dad was growing Mary-Wanna on that farm, and they were raising agro-terrorist animals there, the gang at Jo-Beans babbled. Guv-mint had to step in and shut that down. One by one, his friends deserted him. Who wouldn't? They'd been betrayed. *Living next door to a terrorist all this time, and they never knew it, said the group-think in their heads.*

After a few months, Ralph Merkel was released on bail, pending trial. Within a week of his release, at the Elisa House, Mavis Ellingham checked back into a room. Will Pruitt's barn caught fire, and two of his horses died.

Joey Anhalt put his hardware store up for sale. He'd spent all his money on lawyers, and he could no longer carry on.

Juliette March requested a transfer to the New York office, far away from Copper Hollow, where she would not run into Chance Kiernan again. She was rethinking her career, and considering law school. She'd developed a distaste for FBI work, and she couldn't understand why.

Mitchell Davis, like Haji Abdullah Khan, was never found. Chance Kiernan told his wife that Mitchell had gone into the Witness Protection Program. When Ann told Madeleine this, Madeleine said, "Whatever you need to believe, *ma cheré.*"

In Afghanistan, the new Afghan police officers wearing their green uniforms smiled at their graduation and certification ceremony. The American trainers handed over the AK-47s to the new police, and the Afghan police force turned in unison and shot their trainers. The incident was not reported in the mainstream press. No Congressional investigation ensued. Platoon by platoon, the Americans left, among cries of "good riddance."

Naseem remained in the Parliament, growing stronger and more united with her own connections. She worked with the elected Afghan president to get the American occupiers fully removed. Their central government struggled, and toppled, and churned again, but settled into its own position in the landscape of Afghani life. Abdullah's brother provided for Naseem's family. Asa learned to walk on his prosthetic leg. Naseem hoped to send him to law school, and get him involved in government.

Farzam returned to his village. "The arrangements have been made," he reported to his grandfather. "Our transport is secured. We have signed agreements with the warlords in

437

power, for our security." He would handle Abdullah's business. The plan to change out of poppies was dropped. The poppy business thrived. Abdullah's offer to the CIA to transition out of the drug business, and teach others the way, co-incided with Abdullah's indictment under Rule 960A of the narco-terrorism act, passed at the same time he was indicted. He disappeared without explanation, and is to this day listed in the American court system as "awaiting trial."

Darya planned her wedding to Farzam, as soon as the logistics of declaring Abdullah dead could be managed.

Construction for the gas pipeline from the Caspian Sea across Afghanistan began. Chinese banks considered whether they would provide the financing. Security arrangements were secured on the same path for the gas pipeline that was currently in use for the Quetta, Pakistan, drug corridor, from Herat to Quetta, through Kandahar. Why pay for security twice, once for the oil and a second time for the poppies?

As Spring arrived on the mountain, green tufts of scraggly growth exerted the will of survival in the rocky earth, defeating the behemoth of the towering giant, yet again.

Epilogue
Present Day
Paris

The Afghan poet asked: How can wetness leave water?

Over the next weeks, Olivier and Andrew worked together to check their facts. They reported carefully. One thing that bothered Andrew was the role of Josh Bockenheim's companies. Madeleine helped him understand.

"Let me make it simple, Andrew. The world has a cash flow problem," Madeleine explained. "The checking accounts are empty, but the bills are due. Banks are allowed to loan one hundred times more money than they actually have in their vaults. They get 99% of their money from the federal reserve. They count on loan payments to pay back the federal reserve, and its fees. When the loans default, the banks cannot pay their own bills. Then people show up at the window, to take out their cash, and the cash is not there. When this happens, the people panic. They all show up at the window. They all want their cash. And the house of cards collapses. This happened in 2008, because there were too few people paying their mortgage payments. It can happen again, because nothing changed. If too few people pay their student loans, for example, it could happen again.

"Drug money flows in cash. It comes into the banks dirty. It goes out of the banks clean. If the banks didn't have it, the wheels would grind. Drug money is the oil of the financial empire. At that moment in time, in 2008, dirty money saved the system."

"And if the dirty money never went into the banks?" Andrew asked. "If it stayed as cash on the streets, passing through the halawa system of the Middle East?"

"It doesn't stay on the streets, because if it did, there would not be enough riches for it to buy," Madeleine answered. "Of $100 Billion sold in heroin, only $4 Billion of that remains in the producer country, Afghanistan. The farmers who produced it make maybe $1.5 Billion. The rest is distributed to those who allow it to leave the country, through their transportation or their permissions and fees. That leaves the rest of the $96 Billion to fuel the world economy of many countries. Every penny of that money enters the banking system, in cash. And the total is not $100 Billion. It is $2 Trillion or $3 Trillion. Three times what is required to grease the global money supply. It is the world's liquidity. Take it away, and all that is left are electronic promises. When the U.S. entered Afghanistan, the Afghans provided a minority share of the heroin market. By the time the date was set for the troops to leave, Afghanistan owned well over eighty percent.

"How will you trust me if I break my promise?" Madeleine told him. "Money is a concept. If I ever believe that I cannot have it back when I put it in the bank, I will stop putting it in the bank. I will stuff it in my mattress instead.

If the people do that, the banking system will fail. Our entire system of economics depends on the trust of all the people who pick up the hammer to pound the nail. If they decide they will not do it, the house will not be built. Power is at the bottom of the pyramid, Andrew, not the top "

Olivier sat down on the sofa next to Madeleine. "This is what makes it critically important to keep the people from knowing they have this power," Olivier inserted. "The man who picks up the hammer to pound the nail has the final say of whether or not the house will be built. If that man on the bottom refuses, the exploiters have no way to enforce their threats. This is what makes the Internet such a threat to the people in power. This is why it becomes important for governments to prosecute whistleblowers. Because they understand that corruption cannot continue in the face of freely flowing information."

"We can never be sure what part of the myth of Copper Hollow actually happened and what part was legend," Olivier said. "It became like the puma. Lots of people reported seeing it, but nobody ever caught one, and the scientists said it was extinct."

Andrew concluded, "Could it have been Ralph Merkel who killed Will Pruitt? Or Joey Anhalt? Or Josh Bockenheim? Or some agent of the U.S. government?"

"The only thing clear is that no one would be prosecuted for it, because it was listed as suicide," Olivier answered.

Finally, the blog was ready. The blog was launched. Al Jazeera, Current TV, and the Thom Hartmann show reported on it. Russia Today ran feature articles. Twitter followers tweeted links to it. It never appeared in the mainstream U.S.

media. Despite a black-out on mainstream media, independent blog articles catch on, and they can reach people quickly. As more people in the DoD heard what Josh Bockenheim was doing, the internal political disputes required that they shut the operation down. News reports reached individuals, workers in the government systems, and the individuals balked. *People who work for the government are people, like all of us. They have varying opinions. Some saw Bockenheim's operation as an unfortunate consequence of doing the greater good. Some saw it as heinous and evil, a step in the deterioration of our society's integrity.* With the strength of a system that strives to avoid conflict, the committees refused to act. Nobody would continue to do what had always been done. Nobody would take the next step forward. When the operation shut down, the Afghan government no longer owed Josh Bockenheim a favor. It insisted on prosecutions of Te contractors. The DoD stopped sending contracts to Te, and banned it from working in Afghanistan.

But the Department of Homeland Security, the FBI, the CIA, and others had built an extensive infrastructure of surveillance, for the purpose of catching terrorists. There were fewer terrorists than there were government employees looking to catch them, however. This caused the government employees to need to show results for what they did. On the theory that our nation had to be ever-vigilant, massive surveillance structures were built. For the most part, these were built on the newest technologies of data mining and patterning. For lack of real terrorists to use them on, the government employees, desperate to show results on their performance reports, used them on the Occupy movements, the peaceful demonstrators, the vocal bloggers, and the dissenting citizens of the United States. They sent more SWAT teams to persecute family farms, which someone somewhere saw as a threat to U.S. farm exports. They increased surveillance on any dissenters. The Espionage Act of 1917 was used more and more against whistle-blowers, until the Mainstream News Media stopped reporting anything that resembled truth about the actions of the government. The individuals working there felt they had to do it. They became afraid.

Josh Bockenheim's security business in Afghanistan had dried up. He switched his focus to developing the software for data mining and pattern recognition. He changed the name of Te, and moved the company to Switzerland. His world view remained the same, but he channeled his business into surveillance of U.S. citizens. He wanted to help to operate the drones.

If the business Josh Bockenheim ran in Copper Hollow continues today, nobody knows it. If you don't know it is there, you will not see it. Perhaps it is a hydra. Once established, it keeps operating on its own accord. Cut off its head, and another grows back. Maybe there, maybe somewhere down the road, across the street, around the bend. As Ray Plotzky learned, stopping it is like playing a game of Whack-a-mole.

"Individual people, in their own minds, always believe they are the good guys," Madeleine told Andrew. "Josh Bockenheim, Will Pruitt, Joey Anhalt, and Ray Plotzky, each saw their own actions as the actions that were on the side of

Right. When they come to work every day, people respond to their reward systems. They all want to be the good guys. But if there are more terrorist precautions than there are terrorists, the precautions will be used against the citizens whom they were meant to protect. The dissenters and protestors and whistleblowers will be declared to be the terrorists. Homeland Security can't give SWAT gear and drones to a local police department and not expect that the local police will look for an opportunity to use them. People are flawed and fallible. They act in predictable ways, and those ways are seldom rational."

"So who killed Will Pruitt?" Andrew asked.

"Now that you understand," Madeleine answered, "does it even matter? Someone pulled the trigger, but the problem was systemic. If it hadn't been one person, it could easily have been another. Flawed people, in a flawed system, operating in a broken world order."

"And the only way to fix it," Olivier added, "is to tell its story loudly and openly for all to hear. If the story is told, then eventually, the people on the bottom will refuse to pick up the hammer to pound the nail."

"The Juliette March's of the world will refuse to follow orders," Andrew suggested.

"And the Luke Trouts will refuse to enlist in the military. There is a range of behavior that people will agree to do, because it is within their value systems," Olivier said. "Within that range, people will follow orders. If an order is given outside that range of ethical values, however, people will balk. The purpose of revealing information and uncovering truth is to allow people the freedom to decide what is outside that range. The society picks its ethics, and its people act within them. The only reason to hide the behavior of a government agency is precisely because it has acted outside that range of ethics."

"Or because the information gives aid to the enemy," Andrew said.

"Revealing to the world that the United States threatens world governments in the interests of U.S. corporations, and represents corporate interests over public interests, does not give aid to the enemy, Andrew. Unless the enemy is defined as the American voting public," Madeleine said.

Whether Madeleine was right about leaked documents being about government misbehavior rather than military strategy . . . well, the American public would never know, because the Mainstream News didn't report what the documents said. Americans went back to sleep. On the front page of the *Copper Hollow Mercury*, the "come-heres" continued holding their fund-raising events, their plays, and their art shows. The "born-heres" continued announcing their weddings, their births, and their deaths. Life continued as usual, and all appeared, looking in from the outside, to be well. At Jo-Beans, Ray Plotzky became a topic of conversation less and less each day, until finally he was forgotten. If he remains in jail, no one knows, for he never returned. In the next mayor's election, no one ran for the office. The children of the next generation stopped being told of the events of their forefathers' expulsion from the mountain. They moved away from Copper Hollow, to find jobs. In time, the history books rewrote the story, and Copper Hollow no longer existed; it was not in the past, nor the present, nor the future, for the legend died. Its history was re-invented by marketing brochures and tourist pamphlets.

That is why you cannot find it on a map today. Like the mountain lion of the Blue Ridge, Copper Hollow faded into extinction.

After the Blog articles appeared, the men from Headquarters accessed Andrew Meyers' cloud server backup account. There they found the name of Olivier Beauchemin, and traced his wife Madeleine's friendship back to Ann Kiernan. Because of all the activity on websites from Olivier Beauchemin, the DoD Boss sent a Blackhawk to Copper Hollow to pick up Chance Kiernan. He had to go to Headquarters, to convince them his wife was not a danger to national security. After all, she had given secret information to a news reporter, just like Ray Plotzky. The pattern recognition program written into the data mining software spit out her name as a potential terrorist.

Shortly thereafter, Chance Kiernan drove his wife to the airport. They said good bye. Their marriage was over. She would go back to her life in California, resume her old job and her old friendships. She would start over. Perhaps, she told Chance, she would run for Congress. Chance had lost his second wife. His first wife, Kate, was murdered for what she knew, in his earlier missions. Now, he had to remove Ann from the path of harm. It seemed that he would need to remain unmarried, he thought. *Pathetic. Totally pathetic.* As the single engine plane took his wife away, flying over the hills of the Blue Ridge, the sun set behind him. Brilliant streaks of red and orange enveloped the hills, changing their colors and making the mountains pulse. The ospreys dove overhead, and the egrets cawed. Spring freshened the air and infused it with promise. Chance drove his car down the dirt road behind the airport, and parked it on the muddy trailway. He entered the forest on foot and walked the mountain alone.

And in the stillness, deep in his heart, he heard the mountain echo its warning from long ago:

As they approached the Trout homestead, the officers each unconsciously reached for their guns. There could be trouble, as they were too aware. Mountain men could cause a scene. They were well-armed. They had an army of sons and sons-in-law who would help them out. More importantly, they were defending their homes and believed they were right. Mountain men believed the United States of America was a free country. They couldn't imagine that the U.S. government was actually taking their homes. It was inconceivable, completely outside the values they'd been taught. Ray Plotsky was well aware that the mountain men would consider defense of their homes to be the act of patriots.

In the forests of the Blue Ridge, only the mountain lion heard Chance Kiernan cry.

Want more Chance Kiernan?

Copper Hollow is Book Two in the DawnFire Saga. Book One, The Tempest Illusion, prequel to Copper Hollow, is available now. Find it at www.FTMoore.com

Book Three, Virgin of the DawnFire, sequel to Copper Hollow, is coming soon.

Virgin of the DawnFire

In the early dawn, two Haitian men arrive at the airport in Curacao. They are carrying the potion to make a zombie out of the evil and dark Josh Bockenheim. Stopped at the airport, they make a call to their high priestess. The exotic and beautiful Brigitte Arceneaux is both a voodoo priestess and a doctor of biomedicine in Haiti. But the failure to stop Bockenheim's plot sets off a cascade of events which collapse the world's economy. Martial law is declared in America, and the starving citizens line up to ride buses to the FEMA refugee camps. As the citizens of the world respond to the chain of disasters triggered by Bockenheim's plan, it is up to Arceneaux and Chance Kiernan together to renew the world order.

Read on for a Preview of Virgin of the DawnFire

Preview: Virgin of the DawnFire
Prologue
A Time Like Tomorrow, But Brighter

West of Port-de-Paix, Haiti,
in the northern mountain forest

Sweat glistened on his black skin, in the jungle heat, as Francois Saint-Pierre marked the edge of the ritual circle with the blood of a freshly-killed chicken. Streaks of red sky peeked over the green-covered mountaintop, but the light was fading quickly. Francois worked efficiently, despite the distraction of the gnats and mosquitoes that attacked him every few seconds. He swatted, and squatted, and pushed on with his task. He had to mark a fifty-foot diameter circle on the parched dirt in this clearing. *Enough for the dancers to comfortably twist and writhe until they squeezed the energy out of the earth,* he thought.

He heard the startled chirp of a bird, and looked up to see a warbler fleeing from a white-necked crow. The red eyes of the crow peered at him, and he looked away, wiping his eyes with the back of his hairy arm. He dropped the bled-out chicken carcass in its straw basket, and pulled a Bic firelighter out of his burlap sack. The torches stood as sentries around the circle. As he lit each torch, he whispered, "Erzulie, I honor you." He smelled the gas of the torchlight, mixed with the copper-scent of fresh blood. The smell evoked memories of other nights like tonight, other ritual dances, and he felt the tingle in his loins that signified the power of *voudoun*. His ten-year-old son came running up the hill from the village below, scuffing the bloodied edge of the circle as his sneakers slammed in the dirt.

"Take care, Baccary," Francois said. "The dancers need to see the limits of the circle painted on the ground. If you scuff the edge, someone could step outside and break the cone. This would let the evil spirits in."

Baccary came to a stop, so he could look down at his sneakers. There was a blood mark on the bottom of his right foot, and he pushed it in the dirt to clean it off. "Mama wants me to pluck the chicken," he said.

Francois nodded. "It's in the basket." He pointed with his head. The chicken would feed the dancers after the celebration. One chicken for everyone, mixed with black beans and rice in a garlicky tomato sauce. After, of course, the food was offered in sacrifice to Erzulie. They were expecting at least twenty dancers tonight. The mambo said they would need that many to raise enough energy to initiate the potion.

As he watched Baccary lugging the chicken basket down the hill, hanging onto its handle with both hands, Francois smiled. He felt good about his family, and good about the work they would do in this dance ritual tonight. It made him feel empowered. *There is precious little a Haitian man can control in life,* Francois thought, *But the dance of the voudoun? That, by itself, is almost enough to make up for all the rest of life's problems.* It was the one thing in his life that made him feel like a man.

He wanted everything to be ready when the dancers arrived. With all the strength in his muscled arms, he dug away a pile of hematite stones from a hidden pit, and lifted a 3-foot diameter round copper plate from its burial spot. Carefully, he centered the plate onto three stone pillars in the center of the circle. The mambo used copper for her altar, which was one very practical reason that the circle was not set up until the sun set. She said the copper focused the circle's energy and electrified the potion. The mambo was scientific in her instructions. She always wanted things an exact way. She wanted what she wanted when she wanted it, and Francois knew to give her instructions careful heed. She would bring her own ritual tools when she arrived, carrying them in her black medicine bag. Then, when the dancers generated enough energy, she would imbue the potion with the magic necessary to right the wrongs the Demon-Man, Josh Bockenheim, had inflicted on Haiti. It pleased Francois that he could take part in this revenge.

In the distance, he heard the clang of church bells from the village. Father Jean-Baptiste must have heard of the ritual dance. He would be ringing for the villagers, calling the faithful to pray before dancing. Perhaps the Father might harbor some vision that the praying would stop the dancing, but he would be misguided in his thinking. The villagers would pray. They would pray for success in the dance. Then when the success came, they would slink into the church and ask forgiveness: forgiveness after the deed, when forgiveness would be useful.

The smell of the simmering chicken wafted up the hill, mingling with garlic and a hint of mango. The time for the dance neared. He hoped Erzulie would be La Sirene tonight. When the mambo transformed into La Sirene, the power increased a thousand-fold. They needed that much power, if this humble village were to take on the mighty beast Bockenheim. Francois quickly did the sign of the cross over his bloodied circle, and sprinkled the holy water he'd purchased from Father Jean-Baptiste on his altar.

When the first villagers climbed the hill to the torch-lit clearing, the night was already pitch black. Men, women, and children joined the circle, talking and laughing about their day. Guava juice, with a faint trace of an unidentified herbal infusion, passed around the group in clay cups. Tongues loosened as the hour grew late. At last, the mambo arrived.

She was as tall and as black as the Masai, and some said her ancestry was East African, mingled with Malian French. She wore a long, rainbow-colored skirt and a light cotton red tee shirt. Her copper bracelets, earrings, and choker reflected the torch-light, and forced the dancers to look away from her face. Her turban-like headdress matched the colors in her skirt and hid her hair. When she stepped into the circle, the drummers raced to their places in the east, south, west, and north, to set the pace. The rhythm of the drums synchronized the dancers.

The mambo opened her satchel and removed her ritual tools. On the altar, she set salt, water, herbs, and a double-edged knife. In the center, she placed an empty glass vial. One by one, the villagers began to dance. After a while, the mambo sang, a keening chant. The dancers' frenzy increased. Soon the spirits of the ancestors entered the dancers, and they writhed ferociously with the building energy.

When the mambo decided that the dancers' energy had peaked, she broke away from the dancing. Carefully, she poured the exact measurements of her potion into a clay bowl. She held the bowl high to offer it for the loa to enter;

she commanded that the contents of the bowl do the will of Erzulie. Then she poured its blessed contents into the glass vial. Using a twisting and spiral motion of her hands, she pulled the energy from the circle into the vial, and trapped it with a cork. At that exact moment, La Sirene took over the mambo's body and the mambo fell to the ground. She remained lying on the ground, gesturing with her hands that the dancers must now begin the feast. The rum flowed. The next morning, every villager who attended the dance swore that the mambo's skirt turned into a fishtail, and that is the reason she was unable to stand.

The next day, Curacao

Francois dressed in his finest white shirt and black slacks. He inserted the mambo's potion vial into a white cotton bag, which hung from a drawstring around his neck. The bag was kept hidden under his shirt. His brother, Jean, accompanied him on his mission. Their task was clear. The mambo instructed them to inject the contents of the vial into the upper spinal column of Mr. Josh Bockenheim, who was visiting Curacao to monitor his construction project.

The mambo gave Francois a syringe for this purpose. The poison, Francois knew, would paralyze Mr. Bockenheim long enough for him to be declared dead. He would be buried alive, the mambo said. After she thought about it, and consulted the ancestors, she would decide whether to resurrect him as a zombie. Maybe she would and maybe she would not, but that was not for Francois to be concerned.

He had never done this before, but he thought it was an excellent idea. Mr. Josh Bockenheim was the Devil. Francois was certain that Father Jean-Baptiste would approve of killing the devil, so he felt no conflict with his conscience about this act. He had a picture of this Devil, and he had a plan to get in to see him. Jean would distract the Devil, and Francois would come up beside him and jam the needle into the back of his neck.

The plan was proceeding well. They were in Bockenheim's office. It was a construction trailer, actually, in the middle of a field marked off for housing lots. Jean distracted the Devil, as planned. Francois moved behind him, as planned. Francois reached into his briefcase and pulled out the syringe as planned. But at that precise moment, the door slammed open and an older man with a short haircut pushed inside. "Hey, Josh. . ." the guy said.

The short-haircut guy looked up in Josh's direction and saw the syringe moving up toward Bockenheim's neck. He lunged across the room, leaping over the desk. In the process, he knocked the needle onto the floor. As the syringe fell, it nicked short-haircut guy's thigh, releasing the poison intended for Josh Bockenheim into Joe Bridgewell's blood stream.

Francois gasped. He had poisoned the wrong man. *What would Father Jean-Baptiste say now?* Recognizing his opening, Josh Bockenheim ran from the room as Joe Bridgewell fell. Francois and his brother Jean grabbed the syringe and the briefcase, and fled to the airport. It would be minutes before the ambulance arrived to take Joe to the hospital; in the confusion, Josh Bockenheim could not describe his attackers.

Back in Haiti, the mambo's office phone rang. "Dr. Arceneaux," the caller from the Curacao hospital said, "we have a critical emergency. A United States Army officer has been injected with an herbal poison we cannot identify. Can you come immediately?"

"*Bien sur,*" answered doctor of biomedicine, Brigitte Arceneaux. "Of course, I can help." And as the Masai princess, voodoo priestess, and would-be assassin shed her mermaid tail to don a doctor's lab coat, Colonel Joe Bridgewell slipped into a coma.

In Bridgewell's hospital room, a young apprentice held Joe's hand and cried. Timmy Kiernan accompanied Joe Bridgewell on this assignment. Timmy was an apprentice electrician, and Uncle Joe signed him on as a worker. It was Timmy's first real job. Timmy and Joe came here to Curacao to build a housing development. Joe would be the project manager. They worked for one of Josh Bockenheim's companies. It would be extraordinary pay. The pay was so extraordinary that after this project, Uncle Joe was going to retire. Joe wasn't Timmy's real uncle, in the sense that he was not his father's brother; but Timmy had always called him Uncle Joe. He'd been there for Timmy all of Timmy's nineteen years. *This couldn't be happening here and now,* Timmy cried.

And so it was that Timmy Kiernan used his cell phone to call his father, Chance Kiernan, in Washington, D.C. "It's Joe, Dad," Timmy said. "He's been hurt bad. The doctors don't know what it is, but Mr. Bockenheim said Joe was injected with something. There were two men, and they came to kill Mr. Bockenheim, and Joe saved him. They're waiting for a woman to get here from Haiti. They said she's a mambo, and she will know what the poison is."

This is how it happened that Chance Kiernan, former assassin for the United States government, boarded a plane from Baltimore, Maryland, to Curacao, so that he could meet up with a mambo from the Massifs du Nord mountains in Haiti.

As his plane landed at the Curacao Airport, where he would meet his son, Chance Kiernan's thoughts wandered back to that day more than a decade ago in California, when he came home to their suburban house, to find Timmy's mother laying in a pool of blood on their living room floor. He held himself back from investigating, so that he could raise his sons in safety. He controlled his instincts, restrained his anger, and forced himself to let revenge wait. But perhaps now he had waited long enough. His twin sons, Timmy and Jeff, had grown into men now. Timmy took this job as an electrician. Jeff ran their farm in the Blue Ridge mountains. *Was it time now to find out who ordered the hit on his sons' mother? He always suspected it was Bockenheim. Could he prove it? And who ordered the hit on Josh Bockenheim?*

As he offered his passport at the customs window, he searched the faces in this modest-sized airport. *Someone on this island got up the nerve to attack a Bockenheim,* he thought, but none of the faces he saw struck a chord inside him that said: this is the one.

Finishing with customs, he went outside into the bright sunlight. He put on his sun glasses, to protect from the glare reflecting off the yellow stucco of the airport terminal. Palm trees and heated air told him he was far away from the she-nanigans of Washington. He took a deep breath, feeling the moisture and the salty scent of ocean air. Flagging a taxi, he pulled open the back door. As the taxi screeched away from the curb, heading out of the terminal toward the hospital, Chance thought, *Is the enemy of my enemy my friend?*

The taxi arrived at the hospital. He paid the driver, got out, and asked at the reception desk for Joe's room. Dr. Brigitte Arceneaux was leaving Joe's room just as Chance arrived. For an instant, he caught the flash in her eyes, and it so disarmed him that he turned to follow her.

She turned back.

"Your friend is in there, Mr. Kiernan," she said, as she flashed her copper bracelet and pointed.

There are moments in life, when you know something, but you have no rational means to know it. There are moments when the flash of an eye, a furtive glance, a nervous tic, or a misplaced adjective telegraphs the hand of your fellow poker player. You pick up the signal, but you do not know how or why. It can be a white lab coat, under which you see the shadow of the string of an amulet hiding. It can be a copper bracelet, worn on the wrong wrist. It can be a mark in the hair, where a queen's tiara left an impression. Details, in the observation range of deep experience, can be clues that foretell expectations and reveal mindset. Body language, tiny facial movements, missed cues, intonation. These are the tools that transmitted the clues that kept Chance Kiernan alive all those years doing wet work. They became the clues that translated in his subconscious, faster than his conscious mind could process them. Some called them instinct: these feelings of his gut that made him the warrior who stayed alive.

It was always Chance and Joe, always a team through the years. But it was Joe who'd been hurt most often, whose life had been in danger many times. He'd been hospitalized twice for gun shot wounds in the past. Now, it seemed, he was in danger from an assassin's poison dart. Chance knew that he and Joe did not react the same way in dangerous situations. *If I had seen someone about to kill Josh Bockenheim,* Chance thought, *I would have delayed my reaction long enough to let it happen. But Joe is Mr. Good Guy. The hero who goes by the book.*

He focused on Dr. Arceneaux, swishing her hips as she walked down the hallway, away from Joe's room. And then he saw it. She turned and looked back, flashing that bracelet with a flick of her wrist. And in that instant, with the instinct of the assassin, he had his answer. Brigitte Arceneaux was the assassin who ordered the hit on Josh Bockenheim. He could feel it in his gut, and he always trusted his gut. That meant she was also responsible for poisoning Joe. *Friend or foe?* He knew only this: she was a woman who would kill and that made her, in the Book of Kiernan . . .

Useful.

[Sign up to be notified when Virgin of the DawnFire is released]

459

About the Author

F T Moore is a former software developer who worked for multiple defense contractors over thirty years. After writing the DawnFire Saga, Moore is hiding in the hills. Moore is the author of the political satire: *Packing for FEMA Camp* and blogs about life in America

Author of the DawnFire Saga

The U.S. Army trained him as an assassin. His women taught him the dangers of a world painted gray. Now he's our only hope for a new beginning. In a world filled with terror, can freedom be regained? Follow Chance Kiernan, from Delta Force to renegade patriot, in the *DawnFire Saga* by F.T. Moore.

Blog: AuthorFTMoore.wordpress.com

Follow F T Moore on Twitter @FTMoore1

Find more books by F T Moore at:

www.FTMoore.com